All That
Glitters

ALL THAT GLITTERS

GILBERT MORRIS

CROSSWAY BOOKS • WHEATON, ILLINOIS
A DIVISION OF GOOD NEWS PUBLISHERS

All That Glitters

Copyright © 1999 by Gilbert Morris

Published by Crossway Books
        A division of Good News Publishers
        1300 Crescent Street
        Wheaton, Illinois 60187

Cover design: Cindy Kiple

First printing, 1999

Printed in the United States of America

Library of Congress Cataloging-in-Publication Data
Morris, Gilbert.
    All that glitters / Gilbert Morris.
       p.   cm.
    ISBN 1-58134-107-5 (alk. paper)
    I. Title.
  PS3563.08742A78 1999
  813'.54—dc21   99-15297
                                   CIP

15	14	13	12	11	10	09	08	07	06	05	04	03	02	01	00	99
15	14	13	12	11	10	9	8	7	6	5	4	3	2	1		

ONE

◇

AFTON ALWAYS WONDERED what her life would have been like if she had left the empty apartment thirty seconds earlier.

Or if it had been a beautiful spring day instead of a spiteful September dusk that masked the Edinburgh street with a bone-chilling cold.

Or if she hadn't gone back to the flat at all.

Later she told Colin, "I've always felt it was strange. It made me believe in all the Presbyterian sermons I'd heard about predestination. 'What is to be, will be'—that sort of thing. So many things had to happen in order for me to take that call. It just was meant to be, I believe."

Afton Burns had returned to the two-bedroom flat where she'd spent seventeen of her twenty years in much the same way a wounded animal seeks a familiar lair. Since the funeral she had been there only once to gather her clothing and personal items. Colin had seen to selling the furniture and storing the rest of the things she would want when painful memory had lost its keen edge.

All afternoon she'd wandered the streets blindly, and it was with a shock that she looked up to see that her Judas-like feet had brought her "home" again. She stood for a long time in the heavy fog staring up at the window of her bedroom, then remembered something her grandfather had said once. A bereaved relative had insisted they would rather not see the body of a loved one, that it would be better to remember them as they were.

"No! That would not be guid!" Malcolm said sternly, in a burr that could take the edge off steel. "Ye'd best see the truth." Then his stern mouth had gone gentle and he'd added, "Ye see, 'tis the time for sayin' 'Fare weel.' It makes ye know that something is over, and that 'tis time for thinking aboot the part that's yet to come. Ye can't hang on to what has been and gone. So ye look to God for what's yet to be."

Afton swallowed hard and went up the dark stairs to say good-bye to all the life she'd known. As she rummaged through her purse to find the key, she thought how hard it had been to lose her grandfather two years before. Her grandmother had died before Afton was born. But she'd had her mother—

No! Don't do that! she told herself harshly as the memories began to wound her afresh. She blinked her eyes hard, entered the flat quickly, and came to a sudden stop.

She'd known the furniture was gone, but seeing the barren rooms, the naked windows stripped of drapes, and the stark walls without the familiar pictures was like discovering a cold corpse instead of the warmth and personality one expected.

Her steps slow and leaden, she walked toward the window and realized suddenly that she'd walked around an empty space—the spot where her mother's reading chair had sat for as long as she could remember. Some trick of Afton's mind filled her vision with a sharp image of her mother sitting there in the lumpy horsehair armchair, her fine face intent on the old black Bible, caught in the dim light of the brass lamp with the ugly floral shade that sat on a Queen Anne table with one broken claw.

Wrenching her gaze away from the empty room, Afton stared blindly down at the street below. She was a melancholy figure in the late afternoon gloom with her delicate cloud of strawberry blonde hair, her gentle blue eyes, her wistful expression. Even the set of her slight shoulders seemed vulnerable.

A swirling fog lapped at the gray stone of the two-story buildings that lined the streets, then settled heavily into a thick carpet on the pavement. Dead, lifeless sticks thrust out of window boxes, and the pigeons that cheered the landscape with their absurd strutting and boastful chuckling had abandoned the inhospitable evening for their cozy lofts. Afton looked up, but those stars that burned so fiercely light-years away could not cut their way through the Edinburgh fog, so she stood for a long time staring at the murky canopy that masked heaven.

When the streetlights blinked on, Afton roused herself from her reverie, sighing deeply. Casting one last look over the ghost of her world, she left the flat, locking it firmly with a ceremony of conclusion.

The telephone rang.

She hesitated, thinking it must be in the next flat . . . but no, it was shrilly insistent through their—her—apartment's thin door. Puzzled, Afton fumbled with the key, then hurried back inside. The only telephone in the flat was an ancient wall-mounted model by the kitchen door, and as she hurried to it Afton again experienced the unpleasant *deja vu* of going through a familiar ritual in a completely foreign setting.

"He-hello?"

"Hello! I wanna speak to Miss Afton Burns. She there?"

It was a brash American accent that Afton didn't recognize. "This is Afton Burns."

"Oh." A silence built, and then in a much more subdued tone the man said, "I'm—I mean—" There was another uncomfortable pause, then, in a resigned tone, "This is your father, Afton."

Once Afton's tennis partner had accidentally planted a hard backstroke with her tennis racket right to Afton's solar plexus. Kyle Patton's simple words had the same result. Afton couldn't seem to breathe or move. In the dimness of the empty room she leaned back against the wall for support, holding the old telephone receiver in a strangulation grip. She could not seem to make sense out of it: *This is your father, Afton.*

It was as if someone had said, "This is King Henry the Eighth, Afton."

"Uh—you there, Afton?"

"Y-yes," she murmured faintly, "right here."

"Okay, well . . . are you okay? I mean, I just heard about your mother today! Got a letter from those lawyers she worked for. Two months ago it happened? Seems like somebody over there woulda let me know something, you know?"

"I—I'm sorry—" Afton hesitated, realizing she hadn't a glimmer of a clue what to call this man. "It—it happened suddenly . . . her heart, you see . . . and . . . I just assumed someone . . . ."

"'S okay, Afton. It's just that I wish I coulda been a little more help."

She stood there in the semidarkness, numbly thinking how strange it was that she had not heard her father's voice since she was three years old. Well, she had seen him on a talk show on BBC about five years earlier. But that man had not seemed connected to her in any way, no more than this man on the phone was connected to him. All of these men—the man on the telly, the man on the phone . . . her *father* . . . were strangers. People she didn't know.

When Afton had turned eighteen, Jenny Burns gave her daughter a small trust fund. Afton had suspected it was money her father had sent over the years, but Jenny Burns made no explanation, and Afton asked no questions. Afton had recalled getting letters and cards from her father when she was very young, but they had abruptly stopped. She thought that probably her mother had decided to cut off all communication with Kyle Patton then . . . when she was about six years old. That would have been about the time her father had made his first slasher movie, *Heart Seize.*

Jenny Burns, a glowing young girl with bright, laughing blue eyes, lavish red hair, and a wicked wit inherited from her father, had met Kyle Patton when he was producing and directing his first movie, *The Piper*, a stirring drama about the massacre at Culloden. They'd been young, idealistic, and passionate—about *The Piper* and about each other. Against the advice of her family and friends, Jenny Burns married Kyle Patton after a whirlwind romance of two months. Kyle Patton was so wildly devoted to his new wife (and to the romance of Scotland) that he insisted upon following an old Commonwealth tradition of taking his wife's family name, rather than she taking his. *The Piper* was directed and produced by Kyle Patton Burns, and Jenny Burns had been proud of that all her life. It was the last thing Kyle had done that she'd been proud of.

After they finished *The Piper*, Kyle and Jenny returned to

America. Kyle's star rose in Hollywood, while the stars faded from Jenny's eyes. Kyle Patton Burns was declared a genius; *The Piper* was nominated for two Academy Awards. Successful actors and actresses fought to work for him. Jenny Burns fought to keep him. Kyle fought to stay in the realm of the stars. Three years later, as Kyle was in the middle of making *Path of the Prodigal,* Jenny had given birth to Afton, alone at a chic hospital in Beverly Hills.

Two weeks later Jenny returned to the simple, churchgoing life she'd always known in Scotland. It was almost forty-eight hours before the news of his wife's departure had intruded upon Kyle Patton Burns's busy schedule. The movie was completed in the same week that he obtained his divorce. *Path of the Prodigal,* produced and directed by Kyle Patton, was a tremendous success. No one seemed to miss the "Burns."

Jenny Burns's father, Malcolm Burns, was a colonel in the Salvation Army in Edinburgh. Afton devoted herself to the Army, and she came to love her grandfather dearly—who was truly more like a father to her—so much so that she found herself more and more involved with the Salvation Army as she grew up. When she'd finally gone to the University of Edinburgh to study nursing, she still was an active member of the Army.

After Kyle Patton divorced Jenny, he reached the pinnacle of his meteoric career, collecting three nominations and one Academy Award for *Path of the Prodigal.* He also collected two more wives and divorces. He turned from making movies of quality drama to slashers that were ugly but still appeared to be money-makers. Afton had often wondered if her father was as rich as it seemed he must be. But with a mental shrug she had always dismissed such fruitless speculations. For whatever reason, Jenny

Burns didn't choose to depend upon Afton's father for money; her mother worked as a clerk-typist at a modest solicitor's firm until the day she fell ill. Afton Burns had decided to be a nurse, and she and her mother had lived in an idyllic, if quiet, world for so many years . . . until this night. Until this telephone call from this stranger.

"You still there?"

"Yes," she answered quickly. "I'm here."

"Yeah. Like I say, I just found out about your mother. I know I've been a sorry father, but now I want to do something. What can I do? Just name it and it's yours."

"Um, I really . . . just now I can't think—"

He cut in quickly, decisively, as that was the kind of man he was. "Money? How you fixed for cash?"

Afton almost answered, *I have exactly 116 pounds to my name,* but it was difficult to say such things to someone she didn't know. The uncomfortable strangeness washed over her again at the thought. "I have enough," she finally, lamely replied.

"You working? In school? What?" Patton insisted. "I know I'm being pushy, but it's the only way I know, Afton."

Perhaps it was the use of her name that brought her guard down. "I've had two years at nursing school, but I still have my work study to complete."

"Got a job waiting on you?"

"No, not yet, but I—"

"Listen up, Afton. I'm shooting a picture now in Kentucky. Always need lots of people with a film. You could be a big help, and besides, I really want to see you." He paused, perhaps to see if she would respond, then went on hurriedly, "It would give you a chance to get out of Edinburgh for a while. Even if you don't want to work, maybe it'd be good for you to get away. What do you think, kid?"

In spite of his light tone and careless words, Afton could hear a note of pleading in his voice. Though she was not the least bit impulsive, she decided to go. Why not? "I would like that very much, thank you," she said with constrained formality she couldn't hide. "Perhaps it *would* do me good to get away. And I would like to work. To make myself as useful as possible."

"Great!" her father said heartily. "Give me your bank account info, and I'll wire you some money first thing tomorrow. You make your flight arrangements, and call me collect. I'll come pick you up. Fly into Lex. Here's my cell phone number—"

"One—one moment, please," Afton said a little breathlessly. She was far from accustomed to making sophisticated travel arrangements, especially with so little consideration. "You—you said Lex? That is a town in Kentucky?"

He laughed, and it was a good laugh. Afton liked it. He said in a more careful tone, "Okay, kid, first give me your bank account stuff. Then I'll make sure you understand about the flight and con-tacting me."

Afton excavated busily in her bag for paper and pen, and finally they worked out the details. She said, "Good-bye, and thank you so much." Again she sounded too formal, so she added with some confusion, "I'm—I'll look forward to getting to know you."

"Yeah, me too, Afton. Call me tomorrow." He hung up.

She stood in the empty apartment, savoring the feelings his invitation had awakened. Someone was there! Although she had not allowed herself to dwell upon it, the fact that she had no close relative was a dark loneliness always dwelling just on the edge of her thoughts since the loss of her mother. Now there was someone, and Afton said a quick prayer of thanksgiving for the door that had just opened in her life.

Locking the door, she left the key with the couple in the downstairs apartment who had consented to watch over it until Afton decided what she wanted to do with the flat. She walked quickly through her familiar neighborhood, a section of Edinburgh that had decided to give up being residential fifty years ago. There were still many flats, but more often the plain square buildings had been converted to doctor's offices, real estate centres, and small, nondescript shops. She was only three blocks from the large gray, stone building that housed the central Edinburgh offices of the Salvation Army. Her mother had chosen the flat because it was so close.

As she turned into the door crested with the large peeling sign—SALVATION ARMY, CENTRAL HEADQUARTERS, EDINBURGH DISTRICT—she wondered what she would have done after her mother's death if it had not been for the kindness of the people in the Army. Her Grandfather Malcolm had served in this place most of his life, and his memory was still a living presence, even more so than her mother's. Jenny had practically grown up in the fortress-like building, and one of the things that amused her about herself was that she had learned to play a trumpet when she was only twelve and had donned the bonnet and cape of the Army "Lassie" then. Many times she'd played at street meetings.

Smiling, and realizing it was her first light thought for nearly two weeks, she thought of how much she'd come to enjoy both church and street services, though they were worlds apart. In the Presbyterian church she'd attended all her life, she sat on a hard, high-backed pew and listened to Bach's soaring hymns on a great throaty organ and solemn sermons. The street services were a gypsy-like adventure outside the taverns and pubs in the rougher sections of the city, with the Army band singing and playing enthusiastically, if not expertly, laughing and talking with men and women who would curse the door of a church but who loved to see the high-spirited Salvation Army bands play and sing.

They'd especially loved her Grandfather Malcolm, who played the bagpipes so vigorously you could hear the mournful call for blocks. He'd thundered at the people, laughed with them, poked fun at them, let them poke fun at him. They gave him money, and sometimes he gave it back to them, growling at them to buy some ice cream for their children instead of whiskey for their rotten guts. He was never hesitant about putting an arm around a man's shoulders and listening with great attention when he spoke. Malcolm laughed with people, cried with them, and cried over them sometimes. They knew instinctively that he was real and that his love was real. Afton hoped fervently that she could have a love like his, as big as all the world, someday.

Colin McDaniel met her with a worried frown on his clean-cut features. He was a pleasing-enough looking man, with neat, shiny brown hair and expressive brown eyes. He was not quite six feet tall, with a disciplined slimness and careful posture. He always wore subdued suits and dignified ties. His shoes were always mirror-shined, and his pocket handkerchief was always just so. Afton wickedly wondered if he glued the discreetly folded strips of linen in the left breast pocket of his suits.

"We've been waiting for you, Afton," he said in his cool and quiet voice. "I was getting concerned."

"Oh, you shouldn't have waited," Afton said repentantly. "I meant to tell you to go on if I was delayed."

"No matter," he replied, taking her arm and walking with her to the small plain dining room where the Army leaders usually combined the evening meal with talk about the work at hand. There was a table that would seat ten, but only five were dining tonight, including Colin and Afton.

"Good thing you got here, little girl," Major Camberlie boomed. "Colin here would ha' starved us to death waitin' for ye." Rising, he pulled her chair back and patted her arm as she sat down. Major Camberlie had been her grandfather's closest friend, and after Malcolm's death Camberlie had done his best to be a surrogate father and grandfather to her. He was a big man with a big voice and a big heart. "Have a bit o' this fish, and hurry ye up too, afore it's as cold as straight out of the loch. What ye've been aboot, little girl?"

"I was at the flat, just to make certain it was all cleared and cleaned up."

"But you didn't need to do that, Afton," Colin chided. "I saw to it. Thought you'd not like to go back there, with it so empty and sad."

Afton gave a small shrug. Unwrapping the newspaper, she breathed deeply of the fish-and-chips steam. They were still hot and deep-fried greasy. Afton never tired of them.

"What have you decided about your schooling, Afton?" Captain Elaine Hunter asked. Small-boned and over sixty, Captain Hunter's looks were still youthful and delicate-looking and belied a strong will and forceful personality. The glance she had for Afton was one of concern.

"I—I've decided not to go back for a while—"

"No need to," Captain Simmons coaxed. "Best thing for you is to stay out a term, rest, get some color in those sunken cheeks and sparks back in those bonnie blue eyes! You've been working hard, girl. You can help me, Afton. I need a good trumpet these days." He was a roly-poly Cornishman with the jolly spirit and elastic temperament needed for a rough-and-tumble street ministry.

"Lot of rest ye'd be a-givin' her," Major Camberlie pronounced wrathfully. "Ye'd have her blow her lungs out in this fall night air w'in a week!"

Simmons shook his head and began to argue that would be the very thing for Afton. The argument waxed and waned, flowing with comfortable familiarity around Afton as she ate ravenously. The room was dark with old paneling, and the plain Salvation Army uniforms were dark, the ancient scarred wooden table almost black with age; but the air was light with laughter and sharp Celtic wit and the security of a family's easy love. Afton relaxed, contented.

With the air of settling the matter, Colin said with finality, "Perhaps you can find some light work close by and stay here for a while. In a month or two you could refurnish the flat. Make it new, for a new start."

"No," Afton said quietly. "I have something to tell you all. I got a call from America today. From my father."

"Your father?" Major Camberlie's kind horse-face drew into stubborn lines. "I'm surprised he bothered."

"Oh, well, he didn't know about Mother," Afton said quickly. "He only just got a letter today. From the solicitors. Evidently

Mother had left instructions for them to notify him, but they just wrote a letter and posted it at their leisure."

"Aye, well, I suppose he felt obliged," Captain Hunter commented with an alert Yorkshire-terrier glance at Afton's face. "Precious little good he did your poor mother while she was alive."

"He asked me to come to America. To—to—Kentucky." Every face at the table reflected doubt, and she added hastily, "Just for a visit. He's making a new film. He's going to give me a job. They— they pay quite well for . . . in American films, don't they?"

"He's going to give you a job," Colin repeated with disbelief. "Surely you're not thinking of going?"

His clear brow was ridged, and Afton knew that his plan for her had been quite different. Everyone, including her mother, had hoped that she and Colin would make a match of it. Looking at his earnest face and worried eyes, Afton reflected how good Colin had been to her, and how good he was for her. But she suddenly, brutally faced the facts squarely. *I'll never feel the same way about Colin as he does for me. Another reason for going to America.*

"I believe I must go," she answered calmly. "He is my father. He's my only relative."

Colin was frowning in earnest now. "He's certainly shown it, hasn't he now? Has he ever once tried to be a father to you?"

Slowly Afton replied, "I don't know, Colin. I believe there were things—problems—between him and my mother that she never spoke to anyone, especially me, about. I've often wondered if he didn't try to be a bigger part of my life. I think, especially when I was younger, that he did . . . but he just finally gave up."

Major Camberlie cleared his throat with discomfort. "Weel now, there may be something in it, Afton. Malcolm told me more than once that Patton tried to arrange visits and such, and sent money and gifts. But your mother . . ." He shook his head sadly. "She couldna see it. His life, his ways, she wanted no more part of it."

"All the more reason for you to stay here," Colin said stubbornly. "Surely you must know how cinema people are, particularly Americans. Your mother was wise, Afton."

"Yes, she was," Afton agreed quietly. "And I can well understand why she was afraid to love him and his ways." Looking directly into his honest brown eyes, she went on, "But he is my father, Colin. And I have nothing at all to fear."

TWO

◇

FIRST OFFICER RONNIE ADLER felt persecuted. Hauling off his cap with a flamboyant gesture, he ran his hand through his crisp chestnut hair (being careful to leave one strand artlessly falling over his tanned forehead) and grumbled, "I don't think this one should count."

"Oh, no, you don't," Angie Feldman, the tiny, lively flight attendant demurred. "There's that little bird from Britain in first class."

"Gimme a break! You don't call that one a shot?"

"You're the one who made up the bet," Captain A. C. Strickland taunted. He was just barely tall enough to meet airline requirements, and he kept his almost bald head out of sight at all times beneath his billed cap. He was happily married to a former flight attendant— back when they were called "stewardesses"—and they had five great kids. Although he wouldn't have changed places with Ronnie Adler for all the diamonds in Africa, it did him good to see his hustling copilot fall flat on his face. Pushing the needle in a little deeper, he asked with a great show of pity, "Maybe you're right, Ron. Maybe we should give you a break and call off the bet."

The standing wager was that Adler could make a date with the most attractive woman on the flight. The stakes were the cost of dinner at any place the winner chose. So far Captain Strickland had bought Ronnie Adler fourteen very expensive dinners.

The older pilot kept on rubbing it in. "I kinda thought you were a minor leaguer, Ron. C'mon, let's hear you whine some more."

"I'm no welsher," Adler protested. "But look at what I've got to work with! There's only twelve chicks on this flight, and none of 'em are in my class!"

"Mmm-hmm," Angie hummed. "Yes, I have noticed that 'your class' usually wears a D-cup, chews gum with her mouth open, and screeches at the sight of rare prime rib. The last one told me, 'I'm a veterinarian, so I don't eat meat!'"

Captain Strickland laughed, and even Ron Adler chuckled. Angie, too, would be happy to see the handsome copilot strike out. As far as she could tell, she was the only attendant on the line to give him a straight-arm that kept him at a discreet distance. Winking at A. C., she sighed theatrically. "It's kind of the death of a legend, huh, Captain? Like the Duke's death in *The Shootist*, when he lost out to a punk kid."

Ron Adler jolted up straight and maneuvered his large frame until he was clear of the control yoke. His fine face was set, his clear blue eyes determined. "Okay, that's it. You doubters just wait and see whose nest the little bird ends up in tonight!"

"There you go, champ," Angie egged him on. "Elvis hasn't left the building yet!"

"Hey," Captain Strickland called after him, "why don't you do your smoldering Al Pacino imitation?"

"No, no, do the Brad Pitt," Angie teased. "Cry."

With a last disgusted look Adler disappeared through the cockpit doors.

"Whaddya think?" Captain Strickland asked with faint hope.

Angie tilted her head to the side, considering. "She's out in public for the first time, if you get my drift. You know, never been away from home. And it's Scotland, by the way, and not England. She's very nice, beautiful, cool manners. But—" Angie made a little elfin face. ". . . when our Ronnie wants to turn it up full blast—" She shrugged.

The captain of Flight 1201, New York to Lexington, acted very unprofessionally just then. He smacked the yoke of the 707 with his hard fist, and Angie flinched. If they hadn't been on autopilot, the hit would have made the monster plane shudder. "Blast!" he muttered. "Wonder where he'll take her to dinner to soften her up for the kill? Probably rent the Presidential Suite at the Excelsior! And probably that's where I'll have to buy dinner! Aw, you know it's not the money, Angie. Sometime I'd just really like to see him get shot down. Far as I know you're the only woman that's had sense enough to duck."

Angie giggled. "Don't despair, O Captain, my Captain. You're right, I do have a faint remnant of womanly smarts left even after four years on this job. And I think that maybe, just maybe, our snake charmer's about to get bit."

"But I thought you said—"

"Yeah. But she really is different."

"Different how?"

One fine blonde eyebrow tilted upward speculatively. "For one thing, I don't think Golden Boy has ever aimed at a girl that plays first trumpet for the Salvation Army band in the slums of Edinburgh."

"Huh? Joke, right?"

"Nope. Her grandfather was a general or something, and she's been out with them a lot. For their—um, street things. Whatever."

Strickland was taken aback. "Then you mean she—uh, looks like one of those—you know, like—uh, Carrie Nation or something?"

Angie made a little grunting sound. "Not hardly. That's what I mean . . . I just knew she must be putting me on. So I talked to her for about half an hour, tried to catch her in something. I just love to trip up those tippy-toe do-gooders. But she's not like that, not at all. She's—I know it sounds funny—she's warm and kind."

"So she'll probably turn to buttery syrup when Adler does his Al Pacino," Strickland said glumly.

"I don't think so," Angie murmured. "Somehow I got the feeling that our little dove might have eyes like a hawk." She returned to the cabin.

Several minutes later, just ten minutes out of Lexington, the captain was making the announcement for the passengers to fasten their seat belts when Ronnie came back in and parked himself under the yoke without a word. His expression was thunderous, Captain Strickland noticed. Angie hustled in busily and gave Strickland a thumbs-up, her eyes merry.

"Okay, Ron," Captain Strickland said with mock regret. "Guess I'll go back and get confirmation." This was part of the bet; the girl had to admit to one of the crew members that she was going out with Adler.

"Give it up, Captain," Ronnie grumbled. "She's a real loser."

"Why, you don't mean you aren't taking her out?" Strickland asked in mock shock.

"I did just happen to overhear, Ronnie," Angie said sorrowfully.

"So sad. But she did give you such a nice brushoff, didn't she? I mean, I was a little afraid you were going to fall out of the seat, but you didn't after all, hmm?"

"Couldn't have cared less," Adler grunted. "All those English broads are cold."

"Don't think so," Angie speculated. "Not with those green velvet eyes. I'm afraid, Ronnie love, that you were just overmatched and outclassed."

Captain Strickland grunted laughter, and a red-faced Adler said with intense irritation, "You gonna land this bucket or fly on to Florida without bothering to stop?"

"I gotta meet this lady," Strickland told Angie. "Keep her on board until I can get back to give her my congratulations. Ron, you can stay in the cabin and sulk until she's gone."

As soon as the engines stopped, Captain Strickland hurried back to the first class cabin and saw Angie talking to a trim young woman with a glorious halo of curly reddish-blonde hair. When he reached them Angie said, "Captain Strickland, this is Miss Afton Burns. Miss Burns, this is our pilot, Captain A. C. Strickland."

Strickland grinned widely. "I sure am glad to meet you, Miss Burns."

Shaking his hand firmly, she smiled warmly, and her blue eyes were the color of clear summer sky. Captain Strickland, even though he was a very happily married man, felt as if he'd just done a barrel roll in a crop duster. She said in a musical voice, with only a slight Scottish lilt, "It's my pleasure, Captain." Nodding toward the cockpit, she said warmly, "Would you be so good as to tell First Officer Adler that I hope he finds a suitable companion for the evening?"

Strickland and Angie exchanged grins, and Strickland said, "Ma'am, you have no idea how happy I'll be to give my copilot your message. And I'm going to offer him my great sympathy—for missing the pleasure of your company."

Afton had strictly enjoyed the entire incident with the handsome copilot. When she had begun her journey at Glasgow Airport, she had been subdued and confused. Colin had been patient, with perhaps overmuch longsuffering. He'd assured her he would be faithfully waiting for her distress signal from America. Her other friends had been less obvious, but one and all had let it be known they were convinced she was making a mistake.

Only six days had passed since her father's call, and she had spent most of the hours over the Atlantic wondering if she ought to turn around and go back on the next flight. Much of this apprehension, she knew, was the result of her first trip away from home. Or perhaps it was the knowledge that now *home* was a rather nebulous thing. Her existence had been as precise and ordered as the morning services in the grand church she attended, and during the flight she had begun to realize that the rhythm of her life had been irrevocably broken and probably would never again be so safe.

Maybe I've been too safe, she had thought, staring down at the gray wrinkled sheet that was the North Atlantic. It occurred to her that leaving Scotland and coming to America was the first major decision she'd made in her entire life. Except about Colin, of course. But now she began to doubt even her perceptions of him, and her view of the possibilities of their relationship as well.

I've never had to depend on God—not really. The thought that had suddenly intruded into Afton's thoughts came as a shock to her. She knew very well what the Bible had to say about faith, had used the "faith" Scriptures in speaking and witnessing, but now it came to her that she really had never been put to the test.

Shifting uneasily in her seat, Afton had tried to shove the thought out of her mind, but that proved to be impossible. She had picked up the flight magazine and tried to concentrate on a story on how Rolls Royce automobiles were made, but it was meaningless to her. What did million dollar cars have to do with her?

Taking her small Bible out of her purse, she opened it at random. She started to read from the fourteenth chapter of Matthew. Her eyes ran over the verses, but only when she began to read the story of Simon Peter's walk on the water did she suddenly become aware that God had something for her in this particular passage. She read slowly, thinking of each word, and a vivid picture of Peter as he got out of the boat came to her. She had a wonderful ability to visualize literature, and now she seemed to see the turbulent waves and Simon's face as he began to doubt. Her lips moved as she read.

> But when he saw the wind boisterous, he was afraid; and beginning to sink, he cried, Lord, save me. And immediately Jesus stretched forth his hand, and caught him, and said unto him, O thou of little faith, wherefore didst thou doubt?

And at that moment Afton knew that God was speaking to her heart. *O thou of little faith, wherefore didst thou doubt?*

Afton felt a sense of shame, and closing her eyes, she prayed, *Lord, I am a woman of little faith. I'm afraid, just as Peter was afraid— but I know that You can stretch forth Your hand and save me, just as*

You did Simon. She prayed earnestly, and somehow it became clear to her that God was going to make her into a woman of faith.

Sighing, she longed for her Grandfather Malcolm, wishing she could go to him as she had so many times before and let him make her decisions. But then she remembered that he actually would rarely do such a thing. He would listen, then talk, and after a time somehow she would be able to decide for herself. What would he say if he were here now and she could tell him how insecure, how unsettled and unsafe she felt?

Immediately Afton heard plain echoes of his blustery voice. *Safe? Who ever told you, lass, that to be safe is the best thing? Was David safe? Was the Baptist safe? Was even the Lord Jesus safe? I tell ye, the best thing we can do is to get ourselves in a great mess so that only God Himself can get us out of it!*

Ruefully Afton smiled to herself. *And that's aboot wha' I've done, Malcolm!*

As she was reflecting on those things, the tall pilot with the dreamy eyes and impossible eyelashes stopped and bent over her as he was casually strolling toward the business class cabin. He looked down at her and smiled.

Afton Burns had been reared in a Christian home, but it was certainly not a nunnery. She knew that look, very well. She'd never been the object of such a quest by a man who was quite so absurdly good-looking, but the look was the same. With his first words—which were simply "Hello there"—Afton knew exactly what kind of man First Officer Ronnie Adler was. The low, falsely intimate tone of his voice clearly communicated that he thought she was pretty lucky to be the recipient of his attentions.

Mischievously Afton decided to just go along for the ride. She knew very well it wouldn't do much damage to Ron Adler's ego. The question of whether Afton was sharp enough to play such a sophisticated game with such an expert did not occur to her. In truth, Afton Burns was not nearly so insecure and unsure of herself as she sometimes thought.

Ron Adler turned his charm on Afton much as Horatio Nelson turned the guns of the *Victory* on the French at Trafalgar—full-bore and point-blank. She could see that he was a little taken aback when she remained merely polite and didn't run up the flag of surrender at the first broadside.

When his first strategy failed, he switched tactics. Sliding casually into the empty seat beside her, he leaned close, his broad shoulder lightly pressing against hers. Sweetly she asked, "Am I crowding you, Mr. Adler?" He stiffened with surprise, and gracefully Afton moved away from him as if it were merely a polite gesture on her part.

He was speechless for a moment, and his mouth was actually hanging open a little.

Wickedly Afton thought, *He rather looks like a fish, doesn't he? What is it Americans say? Shooting fish in a barrel? I've never done such a thing . . . I wonder if Americans actually do . . . ?*

He was asking her to dinner that evening and appeared to be greatly offended that Afton's mind was wandering.

She gave him a brilliant smile, and he immediately listened expectantly. "Oh, thank you, Mr. Adler! But I am so sorry, I am having dinner with my father tonight. Perhaps you would care to join us?"

"Uh—your father? Can't do it. I'm only in town tonight,

Afton," he responded with great sorrow. "Couldn't you put off your old man until tomorrow night? Just for me?"

Afton's eyes opened wide, her fine eyebrows rose slightly, and she responded, "Give up dinner with my father for—oh, dear, that is, I mean—um—" She appeared to be suitably embarrassed.

First Officer Ron Adler appeared stunned.

Flitting down the aisle, Flight Attendant Angie Feldman appeared greatly amused.

"'Scuse me, gotta go," Adler growled and stampeded back to the cockpit.

Afton caught Angie's laughing blue eyes and nodded innocently.

◇   ◇   ◇

Kyle Patton was standing apart from the other people waiting for the passengers to deplane. His arms crossed, he frowned darkly. Afton stopped uncertainly when she saw him. She knew him immediately, and Kyle Patton knew her instantly too. His face paled.

Dropping his arms, he walked slowly toward her, his eyes riveted upon her face.

She would know him, of course, from the single photo her mother had given her of him and from occasional photos in magazines. He was much heavier than the last time she'd seen him on the telly. Kyle Patton was a handsome man, about five-eleven. But some pouches of flesh bulged over his collar, and the elegant jacket of his Armani suit strained a bit over a bulging stomach. He had been balding, Afton remembered, but now his brown hair looked thick and healthy, and Afton thought with a jolt that he must have had a hair transplant. If so, it had been a very successful one. His strong features were lined, and heavy, with worldliness. But there was an incongruous vulnerability in the lips and a strange innocence in his eyes, which should have been completely jaded after seeing and doing and being so much. Afton saw at once that her father was a man who could hurt—and who could be hurt.

Even now, for all his success and fame, he stood there with an awkwardness that was normally alien to the rich and powerful. He made a jerky move as if to hug her, then quickly changed his mind and stuck out his hand, as if he were postponing a rejection. "Afton—" His voice was hoarse, and he began again. "Don't think I'm crazy. It's just that—it's like seeing a ghost. You are your mother . . . Just like when I first saw her, so many years ago."

Afton's eyes grew misty, and she did something that was most uncharacteristic of her. As a rule she was very reserved and mistrusted embraces between those who did not really know each other. But the unmistakable loneliness and sadness in Kyle Patton's voice and face caught at her. Impulsively she stepped forward, her arms open. He caught her close, whispering, "Afton! My little Afton!" His arms enfolded her, and Afton felt security—and safety.

The intense moment passed, and they stepped back, a little embarrassed. "How are you, Father?" Afton asked hesitantly. After agonizing consideration, she'd decided that she couldn't call him "Kyle," and "Dad" sounded too—well, jocular.

It seemed that she had made a good decision. Kyle responded warmly to her words. "Oh, I'm great, just great. Especially now . . . it's so good to have you here." Turning, he clasped the hand of a tall, elegant woman standing slightly behind him. "Afton, I'd like you to meet Stella Sheridan, my fiancée."

Afton's face went blank. She had thought her father was already married—again. To his fourth wife, she thought.

Patton gave a mirthless chuckle. "Maybe you've lost count, but I've been going through an endless divorce case with Lita. Don't tell me you haven't seen the tabloids? You must be the only one on earth . . . Anyway, if it ever ends, then Stella and I are going to give it a go."

"'Give it a go'? Such a romantic, your father," Stella Sheridan commented to Afton. With a cool smile, she offered Afton her hand. "It's a very great pleasure to finally meet you, Afton. I hope we will be friends."

Stella Sheridan was elegantly coiffed, expensively dressed, expertly manicured, and immaculately composed. Naturally pretty, Stella had taken every pain to maximize her good qualities and make herself a smooth beauty. Her golden blonde hair shone richly. Her small nose had been carefully sculpted by the best plastic surgeon in Hollywood. Her lips had been enhanced by silicone years before anyone else had thought of doing so. She was thin to the point of fashionable emaciation.

Even though Afton had not been consciously paying any attention to the woman beside her father, she had been aware of the ever-present lightning appraisal that women always give to other women. As Stella greeted her, Afton now knew that the older woman had seen no threat and was being as kind and warm as any actress ever was. Afton was to find out that almost all screen stars, major or minor, had that same surface warmth and politeness. They also had a faraway look in their eyes even when they were focused on you and speaking to you. It was as if minor events were touching their skin and occupying the tiniest fraction of their minds, but their real life was much deeper inside, beneath layers and layers of onion-skin personae, where the heart and blood was. Rarely did anyone see their humanity, much less touch their hearts.

"I'm so happy to meet you, Miss Sheridan," Afton responded. "I like, and respect, your work very much. I think my favorite was *Never Too Late*. Quite a memorable job you did with that difficult character."

That got down to the heart and blood. Stella Sheridan's flat dark eyes brightened considerably. "Oh, you are so kind! I must tell you that Mrs. Etheridge was one of my personal favorites. I'm amazed that you recall it—let's see, *Never Too Late* was—several years ago now."

"As I said, it was quite a memorable job, Miss Sheridan," Afton said politely.

"Yes—well, you must call me Stella," she said with a generous air.

"Surely."

Kyle took Afton's arm and waved toward the double glass entrance doors. "C'mon, let's go on to the car. This way."

"But my luggage—" Afton protested.

"Houston's handling all that," Kyle said carelessly.

"My luggage is in Houston?" Afton asked, alarmed.

"No, course not," Kyle grinned. "Houston Rees, my P.A. And don't worry about getting the right ones—he'll pay some skycap to retrieve your luggage . . . Here we are."

Afton was still trying to figure out what a P.A. was and what a skycap was when all thoughts were erased from her mind. Her father was holding open the door to a black Lincoln stretch limousine and impatiently motioning for her to climb in. Stella had already disappeared into the velvet depths.

"My goodness, Father, is this yours?" Afton whispered as she hastily climbed in. It was sinfully luxurious, with a long expanse of facing rear seats, a wet bar on one side and a television, VCR, and stereo unit on the other. Afton slid into the seat facing Stella, and her father sat beside his fiancée.

"Hm? Oh, yes, it belongs to Summit Decipher, my production and distribution company," Kyle said absently. "That cop's looking suspicious . . . hope I don't have to move this blasted thing. Hate to drive it." Kyle touched a button, the darkened window rolled down, and he called out, "Officer? We'll be moving within just a few minutes—"

The young airport security guard bent down to look curiously at the occupants of the outrageously expensive car. Obviously he didn't recognize Kyle or Stella, but he nodded carelessly and mumbled. "All right, sir. No more 'n ten more minutes please."

"No problem," Kyle replied carelessly.

"This is very nice," Afton murmured, gazing around at the splendor of the car. The interior alone was undoubtedly more expensive than a flat in Edinburgh. "And, Father, I suppose I must thank you for purchasing me a first class ticket. That—that really wasn't necessary, but it certainly was nice."

"First class?" Stella repeated, her eyes glinting. "Yes, I hope it was nice." She shot a sidelong glance at Kyle, who shrugged.

"You and I flew first class to and from Moldova," he reminded her. "I'm sure going to do it for Afton."

"Kyle, I am certain that flying first class on Uzbeki Airlines or whatever the devil that piece of junk was—"

"Ukrainian Air," he corrected her, grinning boyishly.

"—was quite different from flying first class on Pan-Global from Glasgow," Stella finished wrathfully.

"Oh dear," Afton murmured. "I'm so sorry, I didn't mean to—"

"Not your fault," Kyle said quickly.

Stella looked wrathful for a few moments longer. Then her expression suddenly changed. "That man was smoking a hookah on the flight out," she grumbled, giving Afton a sly look. "Did you have a hookah smoker?"

"A hookah? You mean like the caterpillar in *Alice in Wonderland?*" Afton couldn't help but ask.

"Well, they still have smoking sections on Uzbeki Airlines," Kyle said mischievously.

Eyes flashing—now with mirth—Stella went on indignantly, "Ukrainian Air. And coming back, that woman had a pig. Did you have a pig?"

Giggling, Afton shook her head.

"See?" Stella said triumphantly to Kyle, who laughed and kissed her lightly on the cheek. She smiled with what seemed to be genuine pleasure. "I apologize, Afton, if I made you uncomfortable. Please understand that it certainly is nothing personal. I'm the Assistant Producer on *Hearth and Home*, which means I'm responsible for the budget."

"You mean you aren't starring in the picture?" Afton asked with surprise. She had thought that an actress of Stella Sheridan's caliber would be in a starring role. Stella had never been a superstar, but she was a highly respected actress who had played mostly minor roles but had throughout a long career only accepted parts in what might be termed "meaningful" movies. She'd always received critical acclaim both for her judgment and her skill.

"Oh, no, of course not," Stella demurred, though she preened slightly at the implied compliment. "It's not right for me at all. Besides, Kyle and I have pretty much decided that we make a good team, so I decided to redirect my career into production and direction."

Kyle started to say something, but at that moment a man tapped on the window and asked, "Are these the right bags, Mr. Patton?"

Kyle gave Afton a questioning look, and she glanced at the three tattered unmatched suitcases, which looked quite forlorn on a huge platform dolly. "Yes, those are mine. And yes, that's all, Father."

Inching the window down he called out, "That's it, Houston. Hurry up. Let's go before we get ticketed or towed."

In a few moments Afton was startled as the long limo smoothly pulled away from the curb. For the first time she noted that the window dividing the occupants of the limousine from the driver was up; the car was so well-insulated she hadn't even heard the driver get in.

"That's Houston," Kyle told her. "You can meet him later. Good man."

"And he is your—P.A., did you say?" Afton asked.

"Yeah. Personal assistant. But actually I just promoted him to Unit Supervisor, so technically he's not just a P.A. anymore," Kyle answered. "But everyone on this movie is doubling up on responsibilities and tripling up on titles. If you know what I mean."

Afton didn't, but she was busy searching the landscape outside. "I see. Where exactly are we? And where are we going?"

The car was effortlessly floating past old, windowless buildings made of tin, many of them enclosed with grim, high barbed-wire fences. Some of the lots were filled with materials such as wire, insulation, scrap steel, crates and boxes, and old trailers. "Ugly, isn't it?" Stella commented, her tiny straight nose wrinkling with distaste.

"Parts of Edinburgh look just about like this," Afton said absently. "I suppose it's difficult to make an industrial area pretty."

"Right," Kyle agreed. "But there are lots of beautiful locations in Kentucky. Most of it, as a matter of fact. This is pretty grim. But where we're shooting, Afton—Ajax, Kentucky—is great."

"If you like the wilderness," Stella said coolly. "Untamed wilderness. Untamed, wild, primitive wilderness."

"It has a Dairy Queen," Kyle teased. Stella made a face at him.

"I won't mind," Afton said confidently. "In fact, I'm looking forward to it. I've lived in the city all my life. I'm ready to see something different."

"That's good," Stella commented. "Ajax is different all right. From the rest of Planet Earth. And you certainly won't feel oppressed by its teeming millions."

"Aw, c'mon, Stella," Kyle said. "It's a lot bigger than, say, its nearest suburb—Blue Tick Bend. At least Ajax has a Holiday Inn. I've had to rough it in worse places. Like when I was shooting *Heart Seize* in the Alaskan tundra. Had to stay in an igloo."

"You didn't," Afton gasped.

"No, I didn't," Kyle admitted and winked at her. Again Afton saw genuine warmth and pleasure in his eyes. She smiled back at him.

The scenery outside changed to hills gently rising and falling, some manicured, some untamed, with oak woods growing unchecked. Most of the fields were muddy shades of brown, but some of them were a fertile emerald bluish-green. "Are those golf courses?" Afton wondered.

"No, horse farms," Kyle told her. "Kentucky has the finest thor- oughbred farms in the United States—no, in the world, I guess. I'd sure like to retire to one here someday. These are some of the most beautiful farms here I ever thought to see," he finished, his voice dropping wistfully.

"You won't," Stella said bitterly. "No way you'll ever get out of L.A. And I'm telling you, Kyle, you'd better hold on to the house in Malibu and not let that fiend Lita get her talons on it."

"Yes, dear," Kyle said sarcastically.

Afton felt a rush of sympathy for him. She felt he truly believed he would be happier on a secluded farm in Kentucky than he was with the life he'd chosen.

That's it . . . she pondered sadly. *After all, he has made his choices, and he makes the same ones every day . . .*

Maybe Stella was right after all.

THREE

◇

THE PRIDE OF AJAX, KENTUCKY, was the ancient Holiday Inn on the outskirts of town, close to Interstate 75. Surrounded by truck stops and convenience stores and shabby six-room mom-and-pop hotels, Afton thought it interesting that all of the businesses seemed to have neon signs—red, green, orange, purple. Until now she hadn't realized that one hardly ever saw neon anymore.

"Neon City, the natives call it," Kyle chuckled. "Got more neon signs than businesses."

Stella yawned prettily. "Neon was so out of vogue. Now it's retro chic."

They pulled into the parking lot, past the lobby, to the back of the hotel. Houston Rees opened the door and gave Afton a hand as she climbed out. He was built like a football player, with a bearish bulk, she thought, and she found out later that he had in fact been a defensive lineman with a pro team for two years. He had guarded blue eyes offset by dark hair and a cinnamon tan. He said nothing, so Afton introduced herself, offering her hand as she did so. "I'm Afton Burns, Mr. Rees. It's a pleasure to meet you."

He looked surprised at her friendliness but quickly recovered to shake her hand. "It's my pleasure, Miss Burns. Your room is 201, upstairs overlooking the pool. I'll bring your luggage up in a few moments."

"Thank you." She turned to Kyle as he and Stella got out. "If you don't mind, I'd like to rest. I feel as if I'm sleepwalking or dreaming or something."

Her father nodded. "Jet lag. Best thing to do is take a nap—but not too long a one. The crew usually meets about 8:30 for drinks in the lounge before dinner. How about if I come get you then? You can meet everyone."

"I'd like that," Afton agreed. "To meet everyone, that is. I don't drink."

"Figured you didn't." He took her hands and smiled. "I know you're a good Christian girl like your mother. Listen, Afton, these are all . . . um, Hollywood people, you know? I mean, we can be pretty rough. But I want you to know I wouldn't want to do any-thing in the world to change you."

He turned to leave, and Afton called after him softly, "I'm very glad to be here, Father. I'll see you at 8:30."

She was ready when Kyle came to get her. After a much-needed two-hour nap, she had taken a long, luxurious hot shower and dressed simply in khaki pants and a cozy wool sweater of creamy white. Her single accessory was a heavy, ornate gold brooch inset with a spray of pearls, the only bit of jewelry that had belonged to her grandmother Lan, Malcolm's wife. Afton wore light makeup, skillfully applied. Her mother had, somewhat uncharacteristically it seemed, taught Afton how to use it as it was intended—to enhance natural beauty, not to form a mask. She nonchalantly pulled the crown of her hair back and fastened it with a gold barrette, secretly glad that the careless, tousled look was fashionable. It was difficult to fix her thick, curly hair in a smooth, sophisticated manner.

When she opened the door, Kyle stared at her, a faint smile on his lips. "You look so pretty, Afton. You *are* so pretty. Just like your mother." He lightly took her arm and led her downstairs. "I really loved her, you know," he murmured, staring into the far distance. "Haven't said that to anyone in a long time . . . Haven't felt that in a long time. Jenny was the most perfect thing I ever had. My biggest mistake in my life was letting her go." He sighed deeply. "Or running her off, I guess I should say."

Afton didn't know what to say, so in silence they went inside the lobby, down a hall, to a door marked LOUNGE.

It was a fairly large room, about thirty feet wide and forty feet long. A massive oak bar ran along one wall, with shaded fluorescents backlighting it. The only other lights in the room were imitation kerosene lamps on the tables and spaced along the walls. The light bulbs were a muted amber color, which cast a dim orange glow over the room. The color scheme was indiscernible, though Afton thought it was tomato red and pine green, and she smiled when she noticed that the wallpaper above oak wainscoting was a tartan plaid. Indifferent prints of horses were hung underneath each kerosene lamp.

Cigarette smoke hazed the air, and an incongruously bright neon-ridden jukebox blared. The lounge was full of people, and they were all shouting to be heard over the man who was singing about how sad some lady's eyes were as he walked away in the rain. The din was terrific.

Kyle guided her to a round table in one corner, where Stella was seated with Houston Rees and three other men who called out raucously to Kyle, "That's your daughter, Kyle? What a looker! You'd better get a bodyguard for her!"

"You bums show a little class for a change, will ya?" Kyle grumbled. "This is my daughter Afton. Stay away from her. As a matter of fact, don't even look at her."

The men laughed uproariously, which immediately told Afton that they'd had a couple of drinks already. Smiling, she nodded as Kyle made introductions. "Afton, this is Dave Steiner, best cameraman in the business. That's Harlan Freeman, the best electrician and sound man in the business. That's Charlie Terrill. Guess what he is."

Charlie Terrill was a burly, craggy man of about forty with an enormous barrel chest, great hairy arms, and hands like buckets. "The best blacksmith in the business?" Afton guessed, her eyes twinkling.

This brought a shout of laughter from the table, and Terrill took Afton's proffered hand, caressing it carefully as if he were afraid he'd crush it—which he likely could very easily. "I'm the makeup artist, Miss Burns. Blacksmithing on the side."

Afton shook hands all around and said polite pleasantries. Harlan Freeman, the sound man, was a slender black man with two gold hoop earrings and a shaved head. Even in the murkiness of the lounge he wore sunglasses. Dave Steiner, the cameraman, was a rather nondescript man except for a shock of blazing white hair and the most piercing eyes Afton had ever seen light on her. "Welcome to America, Afton," he said courteously in a high-pitched tenor voice. "I am most happy to see that you must take after your mother and not your father. One of Kyle Patton is enough."

"All right, Dave, you can say nice things about me later. There's Messalina and Tru." He waved toward the man and woman who had just entered the lounge as they blinked with confusion in the semidarkness. Catching sight of him, the man pointed, and the two made their way through the crowd of people to the table.

Afton was startled when she recognized them. The woman was Messalina Dancy, a high-profile actress. She was about thirty years old (though Afton, already observing certain characteristics of Hollywood people, thought that Miss Dancy would never admit to being a minute over twenty-six) and very striking, though not beautiful in the conventional sense. Only five-six, she radiated an assertiveness and strong personal magnetism that immediately drew one's eyes toward her—both in person and especially on the screen. Her hair was a fine tawny blonde, long and wispy, and her dark blue eyes positively sparked. Disdaining fashionable skinniness, she was defiantly curvy.

Messalina Dancy had had a soaring career for the last six years, capped by the enormous success of her last film, *Entrapment*. Afton knew that Miss Dancy had done nude scenes in her last two films; she'd heard much about it because up until last year, Messalina Dancy had stubbornly refused any part that required any stage of undress.

When she finally consented to do the movie *Blindness and Light*, the movie magazines and talk shows had made much of the fact that she'd consented to do a partial nude scene and had in fact stubbornly refused to use a body double. She'd been quoted as saying, "How stupid body doubles are. If the part requires a character who dresses in rags, that means I am dressed in rags. If the part requires a character who dresses in Chanel suits, that means I wear

Chanel suits. If the part requires a character who is nude, then I am nude. Who is this person who stands in as my body—which means stands in as my character? Not for me, oh no."

In some peculiar way Afton had admired her determination, though not the reason for it. Now she wondered a little at the wisdom of choosing Messalina Dancy for the starring role in a family-oriented movie such as *Hearth and Home*, but with an inner shrug she decided that such things were her father's area of expertise and it was not her place to question it.

Truman "Tru" Kirk, however, was a logical, sure-money choice for Kyle's movie. Thirty-five years old, he was an immensely popular television star, but *Hearth and Home* was his first movie. Afton was a little surprised at the gentleness in his eyes and handshake. He actually looked a little uncomfortable when she told him she recognized him from his famous television series *True Blue*, which was syndicated to the BBC. He played a cop, a simple man who was merely trying to do his job, but he kept finding himself in the position of being a do-gooder. The series had struck a chord with the American people, and Tru-Blue Kirk was one of their heroes.

He wasn't a heartbreakingly handsome man, though he was attractive, with a proud posture and clean-cut blond hair and a benign expression. He had an aura of gentle charm that was so tangible, it must be genuine. Truman Kirk reminded Afton a little of Gary Cooper when he was older, and Jimmy Stewart when he was younger, and she couldn't imagine anyone better suited to play the part of a hardworking, honest farmer.

Everyone shifted around, and the men fetched more chairs until all eight were crowded elbow-to-elbow around the table. A general conversation was almost impossible with the deafening music, so the talk tended to be to the people sitting on either side of one. Afton turned to Charlie Terrill on her right and asked, "If you don't mind my curiosity, however did you get to be a makeup artist, Mr. Terrill?"

He laughed, a generous booming sound. "Four sisters!" Holding up his meat-hook hands, he stared at them as if they belonged to someone else. "Hard for even me to believe that I used these hams to make people like Messalina pretty. If I weren't getting rich at it, I'd get out and make an honest living."

"That's show biz, Afton." On her other side, Dave Steiner smiled at her through the choking blue haze. "A blacksmith to trace the delicate lashes of a beautiful woman, and a true artist like myself to waste his talent filming forgettable trash! Most of it anyway. Here, let me get you something to drink."

"Just a soft drink will be fine, thank you."

Steiner winked. "Soft drink? You mean one of those pastel drinks with a little umbrella?"

Afton returned the wink. "A Coca-Cola with an umbrella will do, thanks."

Steiner went to the bartender and yelled in his ear for what seemed a long time just to order a drink. With an abashed air the young man hurried around the bar to squat and reach behind the noisy jukebox. The mournful music simmered down a few decibels. Hurrying back around the bar, he quickly fixed Dave a tall glass of Coke with a jaunty paper umbrella in it.

Kyle smiled wryly at Afton's drink. "That's what I ought to have."

"True. Especially in the South," Dave Steiner commented.

Messalina asked, "What's being in the South got to do with drinking Cokes?"

"Why, Coca-Cola is the brainchild of a son of the South, ma'am," Dave answered with an exaggerated Georgia accent. "Matter of fact, it was invented by a Confederate cavalry officer, Captain John Pemberton. He served under General Joe Wheeler."

Harlan Freeman snorted. "Sounds like some more white folks' bragging to me."

"It's true," Steiner insisted. "He was a sort of medicine show operator, I understand. Made something called Triplex Liver Pills and Globe of Flower Cough Syrup. Then he patented something called French Wine Coca, Ideal Nerve and Tonic Stimulant. So maybe Afton's drink's got more of a wallop than ours."

"I don't believe any of this," Tru Kirk grumbled. "But at least your lies are interesting, Dave."

"Why, you illiterate *actor*, I'm not lying." Dave leaned forward and continued in a scholarly manner, "It was in 1886 when Pemberton unveiled a syrup he called Coca-Cola, a new variation of his French Wine Coca. Same year that Sherlock Holmes was unveiled by Arthur Conan Doyle."

"Uh, yeah, that makes it true for sure," Charlie Terrill taunted him. "Everybody knows that year. Good one."

Pointedly ignoring him, Dave continued in his bookish manner, "Pemberton took out the wine, added extract of kola nuts and a few oils, and blended the stuff in a three-legged pot in his back-yard. And you know what it was used for? Hangover! It seems that most druggists just put a spoonful in plain water for a dosage. Then one day a lazy clerk didn't want to walk to the freshwater tap, so he mixed the syrup with fizzy soda water. And that, boys and girls, is the way we got Coca-Cola." Steiner sat back in his chair and crossed his arms with satisfaction.

Kyle watched Steiner, then commented, "Dave, you know more stuff that's not worth any money than any man I ever met."

"That's a terrible character flaw you've got there, Kyle," Dave told him. "You're still throwing out everything that doesn't have a cash value."

"I haven't noticed you tearing your check up, Steiner," Kyle snapped, taking a hard swallow of his drink. His face was florid, and Afton couldn't tell if the remark had truly stung him or if the liquor was simply making him ill-tempered.

Stella put in coolly, "We're all quick to grab at a dollar, Dave. But you've got to admit, Kyle has gone against high tide for too long now to be classed as purely mercenary."

"True," Dave agreed easily, "and I talk too much. Sorry, Kyle. No offense intended." His tone was light, but his sharp blue eyes scanned Kyle's face relentlessly.

Kyle shrugged and took another drink.

Afton wondered at the sudden tension caused by the remark Dave Steiner had so obviously made in jest. Her father was not— by reputation at least—a tightwad or greedy; quite the opposite, in fact. He was known in the business as a generous man who believed in paying everyone a fair wage, from the stars of his movies down to the last freight handler.

Of course, Afton admitted to herself, Kyle Patton's career had changed radically since those long-ago days in Scotland when he made The Piper and then the next year Path of the Prodigal, two movies of high integrity and artistic merit. They had made Kyle Patton one of the most successful producers and directors in America. They had also made the star he had discovered at the University of Edinburgh, Alastair Cowan, one of the highest-paid actors ever.

But neither *The Piper* nor *Path of the Prodigal* had made Kyle fabulously wealthy, for though they had been critically acclaimed movies and had been popular, they had not been blockbusters. Kyle then did a wrenching suspense movie, *Heart Seize*, also starring Alastair Cowan. It had made millions. After that Kyle made *Under Death Bridge*, which had a lot less suspense and a lot more gore, and Alastair Cowan had regretfully refused the part and had gone on to do other films of unfailing high quality.

Then Kyle had done *The Rack*, *Eyes Shaded*, and finally *Run, Jane, Run*. These had been nothing but slash-burn-bleed movies. Kyle had made money on all three horror movies, but he had known that Alastair Cowan had taken the high road, and he, Kyle Patton, had taken the low road.

Now although his reputation for slash-and-gore was well established, Kyle had stubbornly decided to return to movies with quality, with integrity, with a moral content and message. Though he and his production company, Summit Decipher, were nearly broke, he was determined to produce *Hearth and Home*. Alastair Cowan, who was still Kyle's close friend, actually called Kyle and asked if he could be in the movie, after he heard through the grapevine about the movie's high content. But Kyle had already made an agreement—a loose verbal agreement, yes, but still Kyle had given his word—with Truman Kirk. With gratitude but bitter regret, he was obliged by honor to refuse Alastair Cowan. Alastair, knowing full well Kyle's circumstances and the reason why he had to refuse him, made certain that he kept in close touch with Kyle after that. Cowan had been quoted as saying that whatever their creative differences, Kyle Patton was a man of the highest integrity and one of the most honest men he'd ever had the pleasure to work with, and that he counted Kyle as one of his closest friends.

Afton didn't find out about the extent of Kyle's friendship with Alastair Cowan until much later, when Kyle told her that he felt Alastair's loyalty and friendship were worth a million times whatever he'd gotten from Alastair's roles in his films.

But at the moment Afton was lost in thought about her father's career, as most of what she knew came from reading American magazines and tabloids she had always hidden from her mother. When she mentally shook herself to rejoin the conversation, Dave Steiner was saying soothingly, " . . . good movie, good cast, good crew, Kyle. We'll make it a hit."

"If we're not hit by going hungry first," Stella said idly.

Kyle frowned and took a long pull of his straight whiskey, then tossed back a drink of water. "Been rich four times, Stella. And I'll be rich again. That's what we're here for."

Afton watched her father as he drank steadily, way too much. His hands were clumsy, and he lost his easy air of authority and his ease of speech, slipping into a broken and argumentative style. This continued all through dinner, and at about eleven o'clock the tired hostess politely inquired if they were quite finished.

Ignoring her, Kyle said too loudly, "We gotta get that train scene right tomorrow, all of it! So ever'body get to bed and let's hit it early!"

Harlan Freeman shrugged and said in a Morgan Freeman voice as if to Miss Daisy, "Yassuh, Mistuh Boss Man, suh. Early fo' me."

Harlan, Messalina, Truman, and Charlie all rose and wandered and weaved to the door, with Kyle following them blustering loudly about the train scene. Dave, Stella, and Afton remained seated, watching them—mostly Kyle.

Stella's enigmatic dark gaze fixed on Afton's face. "You must be exhausted, Afton."

"Yes, I am tired."

Silence fell on the three. Stella and Dave were staring hard at Afton, as if trying to make a decision about something.

Finally Afton asked quietly, "Is something wrong?"

Dave and Stella glanced at each other—some sort of signal. Then with an air of decision Stella said in a precise, calculating voice, "Afton, did you know that your father is one of the most talented and gifted producers and directors alive today?"

"Mm . . . I suppose not," Afton replied carefully. "I know he's successful, of course. He gets a lot of publicity, even in Europe. And his movies do well in Great Britain and the Continent, and also in Japan, I understand."

"Yes," Stella agreed. "But did you know he is also one of the poorest?"

"So you keep implying, but I thought—" Afton stopped, controlled her voice, and went on evenly, "I thought he was very well off."

"In a way, he is, but it's not in ready cash. He has—tremendous assets, I suppose you'd say." Frowning slightly, she chewed on her shapely lower lip and went on, "You see, he owns—or rather, Summit Decipher, which is owned by Kyle Patton—owns exclusive rights to all of his films. Now, Kyle has never re-released *The Piper* or *Path of the Prodigal* or *Heart Seize*. He's never even sold syndication rights to TV or for home video. So those two movies are a potential gold mine that—" She frowned fleetingly. "—that for some reason Kyle refuses to cash in on. Anyway, the last four movies have been a bust. Summit Decipher, and Kyle himself, are horribly cash poor."

Afton was confused. "But I thought Father's last movies were box office successes. And wasn't *Heart Seize* a smash?"

Dave snorted. "That money's long gone. Kyle spent an outrageous sum for special effects and sets for those four slashers. True, they got a good box office for horror movies, but they hardly paid for the kind of production money spent on them. But can you tell Kyle that you don't need to spend money on gallons of real blood imported from Kenya, every drop of which has to be tested for everything from AIDS to bubonic plague, instead of using Karo syrup and food coloring like everyone else? No. Can you explain to him that F/X people can make plastic guts instead of insisting on pig intestines that cost—oh, sorry, Afton. Anyway, you get the point. You can have a successful movie, but if you paid too much to produce it, it's still a loser."

"I understand," Afton replied with only a hint of discomfort. "So how is *Hearth and Home* getting financed?"

"Well," Dave flashed her a brilliant smile, "your father has convinced me and several other talented idiots who still believe in the Tooth Fairy that this picture is going to save the world, so we're all working for scale plus a contingency bonus. Kyle thinks *Hearth and Home* will rescue his finances, his production company, Messalina's reputation, even Tru's denseness. Tru actually thinks that starring in *Hearth and Home* will automatically make him smarter."

"What?" Afton asked in confusion.

"Never mind, Afton," Stella said, her eyes pointing daggers at Dave. "It's just that Truman Kirk is considered to be a rather . . .

um, naive man in the business. Anyway, Dave, *Hearth and Home* may very well do all of that. And I must remind you that if it does succeed, Truman Kirk will have obviously made a very intelligent decision. And I think *Hearth and Home* has the potential."

"I know, I know, that's why I'm here. That's why you're here," Dave shrugged. "But can we finish it?"

Suddenly Stella looked haggard, even under the kind glow of the muted lighting. "I don't know, Dave. We've scraped the bottom this time. Summit Decipher is financed to the max—twice. We even got a quick-and-dirty refinance on the condos in Aspen. There's nothing left to sell or borrow on."

"But we *are* almost finished," Dave said thoughtfully. "All of the city scenes in Moldova are done. Most of the stuff in the woods can't cost all that much, can it? And we are down to a skeleton crew."

Afton sat quietly for a few moments, listening to Dave and Stella discuss the problems of finishing the film. Abruptly she asked, "What happens if the film isn't finished on time? Will that affect the creditors?"

Stella grimaced. "Sweetie, did you say it! Everything will go to Monarch Cinema, which has bought up all of Summit Decipher's paper—they've assumed the loans and are the sole mortgagor. The head of Monarch Cinema is a lovely man named Santorini Santangeli."

"He was thrown out of the Mafia for unethical behavior." Dave scowled. "He's been after Kyle's scalp—and Summit Decipher—for years."

Stella started to say something else, but Kyle slouched back into the deserted dining room. "Let's not bother Kyle with it right now. And, Afton—"

"Yes?"

"Kyle's really very happy to have you with him. Please don't judge him too harshly. He's a good man."

Afton replied, "I know. I'm glad that you see that too, Stella."

After a long, uncomfortable silence, Stella added, "And I'm glad you're here too, Afton. I hope we'll be friends."

"I'd like that," Afton said graciously.

"Lovely," Dave grumbled. "We can all be friends. Starve together. Live in the sound trailer. With our friend Harlan. Charlie can dress us for our coffins when we die from hunger and exposure."

"Nobody's going to die," Stella said calmly, "except maybe you when I finally get tired of your nonsense and murder you."

"You're a witness, Afton," Dave said as he stifled a yawn.

Afton smiled warmly. "I hope so, Dave. I certainly hope so."

FOUR

◇

As AFTON STOOD TAPPING at Kyle's door before dawn the next morning, she could hear him talking loudly to someone. So she waited in the darkness until there was silence in the room, then knocked again.

"Door's open," he called out. Stepping inside, Kyle waved to her from the king-sized bed where he was sitting cross-legged and dialing on the ancient beige telephone. "Have a seat, kid. They're sending up breakfast. We all need to eat and get on location by daylight."

He listened intently to the telephone, then began talking in a bluff, hearty voice completely unlike his own. "Hey, Rini! How ya doin', baby? Good, good. Yeah, we're cookin' right along. No, no problems, everything's smooth as silver. Yeah, Rini, that's why I called, to baby-sit you a little bit. Just calm down. We're gonna wind it up right on schedule. What? What? Oh, no. Huh-uh, I can't do that, Rini, and you can't do it to me. I've told you a million times, and I'm telling you again, when we get this picture at the post it's gonna make us all rich and famous. Handsome, too. Listen, Rini, I'm running on a real tight budget here, how about fronting me—"

At this point Kyle abruptly cut off his words, and Afton could hear a tinny but loud voice coming from the receiver. She was embarrassed and was relieved when a tentative knock sounded on the door. Afton hurried to open it, and a black waitress pushed in a cart covered with white linen. Delicious smells roamed up from it.

"Will you need anything else, ma'am?" the waitress asked.

"No, I'm sure this will be fine." Afton smiled. Kyle, even though his face was growing red and his brows beetled, pulled a ten dollar bill out of his pocket and practically threw it at the waitress, who managed to snatch it without seeming to do so, smiled broadly, and left.

As Kyle continued an ever-louder and angrier conversation, with interest Afton investigated what must be a typical American breakfast. She was astounded at the sheer quantity. A large urn of steaming, strong coffee almost burned her when she carelessly brushed her fingers against it. On a platter under a large silver cover was a mountain of bright yellow scrambled eggs. Under another steam-clouded silver cover were bacon, ham, and sausage. In a basket covered with a white towel was a pile of homemade biscuits, while on a plate was toast, and in still another basket were pastries and bagels. Salt, pepper, jams, jellies, butter, and cream packets littered the tray. Afton almost laughed—she'd heard Americans ate ketchup on everything, and for sure and certain, there it was. What did one put ketchup on at breakfast?

Afton fixed a cup of coffee for her father, then realized with a hint of wistfulness that she had no idea how he liked it. Just to be sure, she set the cup and saucer on a plate and added cream packets and sugar and a spoon. Without looking up, Kyle grabbed the cup and emptied half the contents in one gulp between sentences.

At that moment Stella came out of the bathroom, obviously freshly showered and made up. Afton was startled, then embarrassed, and then frustrated at her naiveté. Ducking her head, she buttered a biscuit, slathered blueberry jam on it, and grabbed a piece of greasy bacon.

"Good morning, Afton," Stella said pleasantly with no hint of discomfort.

"Good morning," Afton mumbled, then took a large bite of biscuit so that she might have a few moments to recover.

Ignoring the food, Stella drew a cup of coffee from the urn, threw herself down in the chair by the small desk, lit a cigarette, and listened intently to Kyle.

The conversation had turned really ugly. Kyle's voice rose harshly, and his face was drawn into tense lines. "Oh, you think so, Rini? Let me tell you, do you think I don't know how you sleazed around and picked up all my paper at a premium, just for a chance to get dug into Summit? You think I'm too dumb to understand your little consolidation agreement? And now you're moaning and groaning over advancing me a few measly bucks? What? No, you listen to me, Rini! Rini! You—!" Slamming the receiver down, Kyle stared at it as if he'd like to heave it through the window.

"Nice going, Kyle," Stella muttered. "You sure don't have to worry about asking for his stinking old money anymore."

"Stella, shut up!" Kyle savagely jumped off the bed, scattering coffee and dishes everywhere. "I don't need Mr. Santorini Santangeli! Who does he think he is, the Godfather? I was making hit movies when he was still herding goats in Sicily!"

Afton quietly moved to clean up the mess by Kyle's bed. He stared at her as if only now recalling her presence. With an obvious effort he calmed himself down, then bent down to help her. "Don't pay any attention to me, Doll. It's just artistic temperament. Nothing to worry about. Right, Stella?"

Stella didn't answer. She just watched Kyle with narrowed eyes, blowing a thin string of smoke from exquisite crimson lips.

Someone banged on the door twice, then opened it. Houston Rees stuck his head in. "Kyle?" he asked uncertainly. Afton thought he'd probably been outside waiting until the angry voices died down.

"Morning, Houston. Ready to go?" Kyle asked with false brightness.

"Kyle, you should eat," Stella said darkly. "It's going to be a long day."

Without answering her Kyle picked up a biscuit and rushed out the door, waving it in punctuation to the rapid-fire orders he was giving Houston Rees. Afton and Stella could hear him banging on doors, yelling at everyone to get up and out and to work.

Slowly Afton put the broken dishes into a small plastic wastebasket by the desk. "Is he always like this?"

Stella shrugged carelessly, then went to pour herself another cup of coffee. "Pretty much, when he's in the middle of a picture. But he's been really testy on this one. We need more money, and we need more time, and Rini won't give Kyle either of them."

"I'd—I'd truly like to help," Afton said quietly. "I don't want to just stand around looking foolish. I like to work. Do you think I could do something? Anything. I'll . . . um, clean or run errands or—"

Speculatively Stella looked Afton up and down. Afton was a slight girl, with a slender, delicate frame and huge, vulnerable eyes. "You don't know what you're asking for, Afton. Long hours, mostly outside now, in the weather. And pressure. Tension and pressure."

"But I'm used to hard work. I've been in nursing school for two years," Afton spiritedly protested. "Nursing is hard work."

"Yes, I would think so. Hmm . . . maybe that's just what you should do, for now at least," Stella said, rising and smoothing the crease in her immaculate navy pants. With an artificial smile, she went on, "Just try to take care of your father. I mean, make him take better care of himself. If you can."

"I can try," Afton said sturdily. "And I may not look it, but I can be quite firm when need be."

"I'm sure," Stella said absently, gathering up a briefcase, cigarettes, and purse. Without another word or glimpse behind her, she left the room, leaving the door open. With a rueful glance at the mounds of wasted food, Afton followed her.

The first weak dawn lighting was just breaking in the east. Afton was surprised to see so many people scurrying around, and so many vehicles—perhaps a dozen Jeep Cherokees, two immense travel trailers, four eighteen-wheelers, and two smaller vans. She followed Stella, who immediately left her to rush to one of the vans to talk to the driver. Dave Steiner joined Afton, smiling at her bemused expression.

"Quite a circus, hm?"

"I had no idea the crew was this large."

Dave shook his head. "This is just a bare-bones crew, skinned down to practically nothing. We took a crew with lots of fat to Moldova, and Kyle started running out of money. We had to cut down to bare essentials."

"These are bare essentials? But what do all these people do?" Afton asked.

"Well, Houston Rees is the Unit Manager. We did have one Moldova Unit Manager, and Houston was the Kentucky Unit Manager, and then we had two Location Managers. Now Houston's it. Stella's the Assistant Producer, but she's also working as Production Coordinator and Script Supervisor. Charlie Terrill's not only the Chief Makeup Artist, he's also the Wardrobe Consultant, Assistant to the Designer, the Seam—Seamstress? No, Seamster, I guess."

"Ah, of course," Afton agreed gravely.

"And Harlan Freeman, bless his black heart. He's supposed to be the Electrical Best Boy." Dave grinned mischievously.

Afton looked puzzled.

"You know, best—never mind. His title is Chief Electrician. But he's also the Generator Operator and Sound Chief."

"What about you, Mr. Steiner?"

"Dave, please. Oh, my title is Chief Cameraman. But I've also got an impressive list of aliases such as Digital Transfer, Digital Film Recorder, Camera Systems Op, Camera Loader, Still Photographer. I do have four assistants. See those idiots running around like the Keystone Kops? They're mine," he sighed.

"I feel so useless," Afton murmured. "I wish I wasn't so ignorant, so I could help."

"Don't say that too loudly," Dave said in a dire warning whisper. "Because somebody will sure put you to work if you go on like that."

After a great deal of shouting and cursing and loading, unloading, and reloading an enormous number of odd items, everyone finally got into the Cherokees and vans and headed for the nearby town of Grand, Kentucky.

"It's the largest suburb of Ajax, though not the nearest. That would be Blue Tick Bend," Dave announced to Afton with the grandeur of a tour guide. Forgotten by Stella and her father, she had asked to ride with Dave in his van. Callously he'd made his four assistants ride in the back with the cargo. "After all, the population of Ajax is over 500," he continued in a snooty-sounding voice, "while Grand's population is a mere 300."

The sunrise lit the sprawling fields, and in the ten miles from Ajax to Grand, Afton noticed that she didn't see a single house. "The land is much like Scotland," she mused, "but I suppose we're much more packed in. It's difficult to comprehend the *hugeness* of America."

"Kentucky's a good location state," Dave commented. "Cheap. And how Kyle found this town I'll never know. Just about every building is pre-1900. And this country—hills, farmland, pasture, rivers, lakes, old highways, back roads—is perfect for *Hearth and Home*. Just like that little village in Moldova, and how the devil did Kyle find that place? Perfect, untouched little nineteenth-century houses with every room crammed full of period furniture, even linens and beeswax candles and books . . . Guess they were some apparatchik's dacha or something."

Dave talked all the way, and Afton listened closely to all his musings. She found this moviemaking business extremely interesting.

They arrived in the small forgotten town about an hour after dawn. Grand, Kentucky, wasn't much. A railroad track divided the town into segments. Half of the businesses were on the west side, including a feed store, a brick one-room bank, a dusty department store, a lawyer's office, and a small, dark grocery store. Across the tracks were a brick church almost swallowed by ivy, the smallest fire station Afton had ever seen, a police station that also housed City Hall, and a pleasant green square with ancient oak trees and stone-paved walks.

"Uh-oh," Dave muttered darkly. "Look at that." At the end of what was evidently Main Street, just on the other side of the small grocery store, was a Dairy Queen, its red and yellow plastic frontage garishly cheerful. Out on the street, a portable electric sign with removable letters announced with splendid disregard for both spelling and irony: *BANANA SPITS, ONLY $1.29.*

"What's wrong?" Afton asked.

"Barely dawn yet, and Rees has already blown it," Dave sighed. "Rees was supposed to have everything gone or covered up that doesn't fit 1901. Pretty sure they didn't have Dairy Queens then. Or banana splits either. Kyle's gonna go postal."

He was right. The caravan came to a halt, and Kyle spilled out of the lead car screaming for Houston Rees, who came hurrying out of the second car. Kyle was profane, insulting, and cruel.

Dave watched the ugly scene with a deliberate expression.

Afton bit her lip. "I wish he wouldn't do that. Especially to Mr. Rees. He seems quite eager to please."

"Yeah, he is, and believe me, it's tough to find someone like that in this business," Dave told her. "Most everyone, from the stars on down to the freight handlers, are nothing but hungry sharks. Everybody's a wanna-be, you know? They all want to be stars. Bright, shining stars. Even Houston Rees. He tried, but he couldn't make it. Got some work as a double, and then he wrecked both his knees in a motorcycle stunt. Kyle made him his driver, then his personal assistant, and then decided to give him the chance to move into a more stable career as a Unit Manager." As Dave watched Kyle and Houston Rees, his sharp blue eyes narrowed. "Houston really isn't very good at management. It's hard on Kyle."

"Hard on Kyle?" Afton repeated with a metal edge to her voice. "Looks much harder on Mr. Rees to me." Kyle ranted on, barely stopping to draw breath. Houston Rees faced him squarely, his face beet-red, not saying a word.

Dave shrugged. "Don't mind your father's temper too much, Afton. It could be me next, or even you. Doesn't mean anything."

"No, not me. Not ever." Afton shook her head firmly.

Dave was about to get out of the cab, but he turned to look at her quizzically. "That so? Funny. I got the impression you're—uh, religious."

She laughed. "Oh, I am. And proud of it."

"But then what about that turning the other cheek thing?" Dave asked curiously.

"I deserve a certain amount of respect, just as I always treat people with respect. I don't honor God by being a doormat. I can't even honor my father by condoning such awful behavior. And if he needs someone to politely tell him he's behaving like a moron, I'll do it." Afton's shapely mouth was set in an unmistakably firm line.

Dave stared at her, his bushy silver eyebrows raised high. His lean, lined face struggled against the amusement that lay just beneath the surface. Finally amusement won. He grinned broadly, his eyes sparkling. "Well, well! I see you've got something of your father in you after all! You know, I'm looking forward to seeing the immovable object Afton Burns meeting the irresistible force of Kyle Patton. Okay, let's go break up the fight."

Afton followed Dave through the crowd, as most everyone in the crew had gotten out of the vehicles and were standing close—but not too close—to Kyle and Houston. By the time Afton and Dave reached them, however, Kyle had discovered something much worse than a Dairy Queen and banana splits. He stopped his shouting to look at the steel-gray ribbons of the railroad tracks, and his face became almost ludicrously blank. Then, his eyes burning, he turned to ask Houston in an ominously quiet tone, "Where's the train?"

"It's not here yet, Kyle," Houston answered. His face was now pale, and beads of sweat covered his brow, despite the cold morning breeze. "It'll be here, Kyle. Relax, it'll be here."

"It's not here . . . It's not here!" Kyle's voice rose on the last word, and his cheeks grew livid. Afton stepped beside him and put her hand gently on his arm. She didn't say a word, and she didn't look up at her father. She smiled encouragingly at Houston Rees, who watched her blankly.

The touch seemed to take Kyle off guard. He stared down at her, the outrage plain on his face for a moment. He seemed paralyzed. Then he snapped his mouth shut and tightened his jaw, and his shoulders seemed to loosen.

Afton felt the tension in his arm ease and then smiled up sweetly at him. "I wish you wouldn't get so angry, Father. I've seen so many men in hospital with heart attacks over stress. I don't want to lose you now that I've just found you, do I?"

She led him away, talking softly, and Kyle followed her with a slightly dazed expression. Stella stepped up to Dave's side and muttered, "I don't believe it. Have you ever seen anyone sweet-talk Kyle out of a towering rage?"

"No, I haven't, but I certainly hope I see it again," Dave replied.

The opportunity came in less than ten minutes. Houston Rees had slipped away to talk frantically to Southern Pacific Railroad on his cellular phone. Stella and Dave joined Afton and Kyle when he rejoined them. "Kyle, I have some . . . uh, there's a small glitch," he said throatily, then swallowed hard. "The train won't be here until tomorrow."

Afton saw that Kyle's temper flared like a torch, but with a single small, guilty glance at her he clenched his jaw, then said tightly, "Houston, it was your responsibility to have that train here at dawn today. What are we going to do with all these people?"

He jabbed his forefinger toward a crowd of people milling around in the closed-off street and the sidewalks. Almost everyone in the town of Grand, Kentucky, had turned out to be extras for the movie. Charlie Terrill had come the night before and met with the locals who had volunteered. He had brought the wardrobe and makeup trailer and had managed to supply period costumes for each of them, even the very old men and small children. Afton saw with amusement that some little boys were trying out a stick-and-hoop.

"I—I don't know, Kyle, I just don't know," Houston said helplessly.

"That's also your job, Houston. To know what to do with the crew and stars and extras," Kyle said ominously.

"But I—could we—what about the Fourth of July scene?" Houston asked, almost pleaded. "The pavilion's ready."

"That's a good idea, Kyle," Dave agreed. "Light's good this morning."

Kyle frowned and stared down at the ground, kicking a pebble in the street crossly. "Fourth of July—where's Tru?" He came alive and started striding down the line of Jeeps. "Tru! Get out here!"

Truman Kirk lazily unfolded from one of the vans. "Here, Kyle."

Kyle stopped, propped his hands on his hips, and said almost accusingly, "Tru, can you do the Fourth of July scene today? I know, I know, it was supposed to be next week, and it's going to take some real acting to get it right."

"I dunno, Kyle," Tru said, bewildered. "I—uh, need a little bit of time to—uh, double-check the lines in that scene."

Stella stepped up and said smoothly, "I'll assist Tru with the scene while all the rest of you are setting up. You can do it, Tru. The scene's a red-blooded American making a patriotic speech. You look it, you breathe it. It'll be a first take, I promise you, after we work on it for a half-hour or so."

Truman Kirk's honest blue eyes lit up, while Kyle almost smiled at Stella's deft handling of the man. As abrupt as a summer storm, Kyle stepped back and yelled deafeningly, "All right, people! Get this show over there by the park! Set up Tru's trailer first!" He turned to Houston Rees, who looked vastly relieved. "Houston, you herd the locals over there and give them the setup speech. Harlan and Dave can get the equipment ready. Charlie, you grab some warm bodies and get the scenery, okay? I'm going down to the cabin to check it. Afton, you come with me."

He looked down at her, his young-old face almost wistful. "How was that?"

"Nice," she answered. "Very nice."

"You're a good influence on me, do you think?"

"I hope so." They all broke up into what seemed an impossible confusion, people shouting and pushing, getting into and out of vehicles. But as Kyle and Afton got into the lead car and sped away, she saw that the caravan was inching toward the park, and the extras were excitedly hurrying behind them like camp followers.

They turned off the main highway onto a farm road that was paved but obviously ancient. The woods, bright with autumn, crowded close on either side. Here and there the warm greenish blue of evergreens glimmered through the thick burnt reddish brown tangle of undergrowth and the fortress-like hardwoods.

Kyle grew lost in thought. At length he growled, as if to himself, "That train should have been there. It's been like this every step of the way, ever since we got here. The rest of the footage has been so smooth, even the scenes in Moldova. But it's been like I've been cursed ever since we set foot in Kentucky."

"Well, you handled the problem very well, Father," Afton said quietly.

He gave her a sidelong glance. "Mostly your doing. I know I'm a big ugly beast when things go wrong. But so much is riding on this picture, Afton. My whole life, in fact."

"I know it's important, Father. But it's not as important as you are."

Kyle twisted nervously behind the wheel, mulling that over. "What does that mean? You think this film is me, in a way?"

"Not at all. It's a movie, and it may be good or bad, meaningful or not, successful or not. But you're different. You'll be around when that film is just dust."

"Oh." Kyle chewed on his lower lip. "I see. Your mother used to say things like that. And her dad, your Grandfather Malcolm. I liked him. I liked him a lot. As a matter of fact, it was almost as bad to lose him as it was to lose your mother. Well, no, that's a big lie. Nothing hurt as bad as losing Jenny. But anyway, Malcolm was quite a man."

"Yes, he was. He was a lot like you."

Kyle nearly went off the road. "Like me!"

Afton was amused. "Oh, you may not agree, but I think the two of you are very much alike. Both strong men, both men who can get others to do what they want, both leaders, determined to succeed. Of course, your goals weren't the same. But he was just as determined to do well for God as you are to make good movies."

"I never thought of it that way," Kyle said slowly.

"You and Grandfather both craved immortality," Afton said. "He looked for it in the things of Jesus Christ. You want to gain it by making great pictures."

The remark silenced her father, so she took in the unending countryside. Soon Kyle took a turn off the highway onto a narrow country gravel road bordered by towering oaks that scored the azure fall sky with a kaleidoscope of colored leaves. The land rose and fell in gentle slopes, rising at times to a crest that allowed her to see for miles. The colors were so garish they almost hurt her eyes. Leaning back, she breathed deeply; she cracked a window slightly. She could smell wood smoke and road dust.

The skinny gravel road dipped down into a narrow valley, almost a gully. A creek crossed the road, and the sturdy Jeep bumped hard across it, then wound through a stand of pines and into a clearing. A small square dirt foundation had been formed, and to the side was an enormous pile of logs stripped of branches but with the bark still on them. They were notched at either end, and some of them were pointed like a giant's stakes. Also in the clearing was a confusion of pickup trucks, backhoes, tractors, and about twenty men, all dressed in dirty jeans or overalls and flannel shirts. The men were all milling aimlessly around.

Kyle braked to a quick stop and jumped out as soon as the vehicle stopped. Breathlessly Afton followed him. A short, squatty individual with a full black beard that covered the top buttons of his green plaid flannel shirt came hurrying to meet them. He had the nervous eyes of a squirrel, darting this way and that but helplessly coming back to Patton.

Kyle opened his mouth, but Afton firmly stepped forward, her hand outstretched. Her father never introduced people, it seemed, and Afton thought it a lamentable lack of manners. "I'm Afton Burns. Good morning."

"Mornin', ma'am," the man said, snatching off a dirty cap that said *John Deere* and barely touching her hand. "I'm Jimmy Dean."

Kyle impatiently, and needlessly if it was for Afton's benefit—she'd never heard of Jimmy Dean—explained, "I've hired Jimmy Dean. Toomey. Not sausage."

"Jimmy Dean Toomey," the man added proudly. "Third Production Assistant, Kentucky Unit. That's what Miss Stella said."

"Where are the oxen?" Kyle demanded, niceties over.

"Uh, well, Mr. Patton, they got here last night, but—" Jimmy Dean Toomey's square dirty hand cut the air in a jerky slicing motion. "But they ain't exactly here now."

Kyle took a deep, ragged breath, and Afton tensed. "What does that mean, Jimmy Dean?"

"Hah! That rhymes!" the nervous man said, his eyes rolling wildly. Kyle wasn't amused, and he gulped, "Well, it ain't exactly easy, Mr. Patton. We got 'em unloaded, finally, and they did stomp all over us, but ain't nobody got anything broke." He made his funny slicing signal again and went on vehemently, "All these guys been around stock of all kinds—horses, brahmer bulls, longhorns, sheep, goats, big ornery hogs—but none of us had never seen an ox!"

"Where are they?" Kyle demanded, glancing impatiently around the clearing. "Don't tell me you lost them! Not eight one-ton oxen!"

"Oh no, sir, no sir, they ain't lost," Jimmy said hurriedly. "They're right over there, just on the other side of that line of trees. Somebody's hay field. They're eating it."

Kyle relaxed. "Well, that's a relief. So many things have gone wrong, I was afraid maybe rustlers had stolen them or something."

"Nothing like that, Mr. Patton." Jimmy Dean wasn't amused. His nervous, squinty eyes ran around in a circle, and he cut the air into several thin slices. "But there is a problem."

"Gee, what a surprise," Kyle grunted. "What?"

"Well, them oxen, ain't a one of us who can do a bloomin' thing with 'em! You can't lead 'em. They don't care. And you can't push 'em either. Bob Sanders tried a cattle prod, and if that hoof woulda connected he woulda got kicked to New Jersey. Them varmints decided they wanted to go over to that field and eat it, and so they just went on over there and commenced to eatin' it. So if you want to use them crazy critters for work, you better have somebody who's crazy enough to work 'em!" Jimmy Dean's indignation gave him the strength to finish on a sure note.

Kyle's brow furrowed as he listened to Jimmy Dean, and Afton watched him carefully. Amazingly, however, Kyle seemed not to be nearly as angry at this indignant farmer—or whatever countrified kind of gentleman he was—as he'd been at Houston Rees. Then it occurred to Afton that Jimmy Dean Toomey had at least tried to do his job. It seemed that Houston Rees had simply been negligent.

Kyle said thoughtfully, "That does sound like a problem, and I don't have an answer right now. I sure can't see any of my team knowing how to handle a team of oxen." He studied the group of men milling about behind Jimmy Dean, close enough to listen but far enough away to look innocent. "Have you asked your men if there is anyone around here that could help? Anywhere in the county? Maybe someone who comes in big at ag fairs, something like that?"

Jimmy Dean turned and called, "Hey, Wilton! C'mere, wouldja?"

A goosey-looking young man with wispy-thin blond hair came strolling over, hands stuck in his jean pockets. He was wearing a black T-shirt that declared BLUE GRASS IS BEST. "What's up, Jimmy Dean?"

"You've worked for everybody and their daddy 'round here," Jimmy Dean said. "You know anybody who'd know the first thing about handling them oxen?"

Wilton sucked his lips, his watery blue eyes wandering around the sky. "Mr. Frame. He'd know. He owns everything and everybody around here. He's an old geezer too. Bound to know someone."

Jimmy Dean snapped his fingers, then cut another slice of air for good measure. "Course! Mr. Joel Frame. Shoulda thought of him my own self."

"I can take you to his house and introduce you, Mr. Patton," Wilton said. "I know him pretty good. He calls me, and I come help out when his dogs are whelping."

"Okay, then let's get going. We're wasting daylight. And this cabin—you people gonna get it built or not? Then do it, Jimmy Dean. Now." Kyle climbed back into the Cherokee. Afton hurried to get in, with a lazy wink at Jimmy Dean, who looked unhappy at his exalted position of Third Production Assistant, Kentucky Unit being threatened.

Wilton sat up and laid his arms across the back of the front seat to give Kyle directions. Afton couldn't help but notice that Wilton hadn't been introduced to the wonders of mouthwash and deodorant. His pungent savor filled the cab of the Jeep.

"What's up with the cabin, Wilton?" Kyle demanded.

"Ain't been doin' too much, Mr. Patton," Wilton answered desultorily. He spoke, Afton thought, as if he had a mouthful of mush. She found out later that it was Copenhagen chewing tobacco, but even without a lipful of snuff, the local citizens spoke almost as thickly as certain dwellers of Scotland.

"Why not?" Kyle growled. "It came with instructions, didn't it? There is someone on the crew who can read, I hope."

"Oh, sure, most of us can, Mr. Patton," Wilton affably replied. "We got the instructions, all right. We're workin' on it."

Kyle let out an exasperated breath and then explained to Afton, "We got a log cabin kit from Tennessee. All the logs are pre-cut, and it just goes together like a big jigsaw puzzle. That crew is a housing construction crew. Can't see why there's a problem. Besides, I would have thought there'd be a lot of log cabins in Kentucky."

"Well, not since the war, Mr. Patton," Wilton said idly.

"World War II?" Afton asked, puzzled.

Wilton stared at her with pale blue eyes. "No, ma'am. The big war. With the Yankees."

"Oh," Kyle murmured. "That war." He suddenly realized that for these people, lost in these hills and woods and in time too, the Rebellion was still far from settled—and had never been lost.

FIVE

◇

"HOW MUCH LONGER before we get to this man's place?"
Wilton had been ogling Afton, trying to engage her in what she
supposed was an American attempt at flirtation, but he swiveled
his head around and looked at Kyle with surprise. "We been on Mr.
Joel Frame's place for the last twenty minutes."

"But this is a state highway, isn't it?" Kyle argued.

"Naw, this is Mr. Frame's private drive. Goes right to his house.
'Member where this here white fence started way back yonder?
That's where his land starts. He owns everything you can see in all
directions, and then some. He used to own most of this part of
Kentucky, you know. But the govamint wanted 60,000 acres to add
to Dan'l Boone National Forest. Was Mr. Frame's land, for timber,
he told 'em, and said it was worth a lot of money, which I reckon
it was. He sold it to 'em years back for eight."

"Eight thousand?" Kyle asked idly.

Wilton stared at him, and a touch of a smile filtered through
his stained lips. "Naw. Million."

Kyle almost drove off the neatly manicured road. "Million? This
man's a millionaire and you think he knows about working oxen?"

"Sure," Wilton answered carelessly. "He worked this land afore he was rich. And he's still got who knows how much land he still works, but not with his own two hands, o' course. Miles and miles, Mr. Frame still owns."

On the left was a gate with an ornate arched entrance. The wrought-iron gates stood cordially open, and the road still looked like a new and well-maintained highway, with acres of emerald grass covering the gentle hills as far as could be seen on either side. "That's the drive up to the house," Wilton said, jabbing his head.

Half a mile down the beautifully tended drive through an arching tunnel of red maples they drove onto a circular drive that topped a slight rise. The crown was a great house that looked a good deal like the mythical Tara—three stories high, painted a clean blinding white, with enormous Grecian columns on the main house and two graceful one-story wings extending out on both sides. In front of the house was a diamond-bright silver Rolls Royce, an Airstream mobile home the size of a Greyhound bus, and two red four-wheelers covered with mud.

Kyle slowly got out of the Jeep and looked the place over carefully. "Maybe I ought to give up movies and become whatever Mr. Joel Frame is."

Wilton spat. "He's just a timberman and farmer, like his daddy and granddaddy on back was. Thing is, they was all smart farmers. He probably won't be in the big house. Most times he's out back messin' with the dawgs or down to the stables."

Wilton led them around the brick walk that encircled the house. In the back was an enormous garden, which the walk skirted. Directly behind the gardens, the walk forked. Slightly below on the left was a neat row of dog runs, each with a sizable A-frame doghouse with a nameplate over each door, and each with its own miniature white picket fence enclosing house and run. To the right the walk led down to two low buildings, obviously stables. Wilton took off his cap and scratched his head, then thumbed to the left. "That's him down there with the dawgs." He led Kyle and Afton to the neat canine village.

The man was standing by the side of one of the dog runs, talking, but the entity he appeared to be speaking to was not in sight. When they drew close, the man turned, and Afton was struck by the thought that the man might be smart and a bazillionaire, but he did look like a mere mortal. Fairly tall and thin, shoulders work-stooped, he had a thatch of silver hair that stuck out in a rooster-tail through the back vent of a raggedy striped train engineer's cap. His clothing was modest—jeans and a denim shirt—but Kyle noted his cowboy boots, which were stingray-skin. Those, Kyle knew, had likely set Mr. Joel Frame back a couple of thousand dollars. Frame studied them with eyes sharper and younger than the rest of him.

"Mr. Frame, this here's them picture folks," Wilton remarked, which he apparently considered introduction enough.

"I'm Kyle Patton, and this is my daughter, Afton Burns. It's a pleasure to meet you, Mr. Frame, and I hope we aren't disturbing you." Kyle thrust out his hand and was sorry at once, for Joel Frame had a grip like an alligator's.

"My pleasure, and the only thing you're disturbing is me making a fool of myself trying to get Princess to bring—there she is. She's too curious not to come see about you herself." Mr. Frame's voice was deep and steady, and his entire weathered and tanned face lit up like a candle as he turned to see the dogs. Princess was evidently a mother, for she had come out of her roomy doghouse with four pups. She was an indifferent-looking dog to Afton, with a pretty face and expressive brown eyes but an average build, her coat a mottled red and gray. The puppies were red, round, and jolly, with alert, upright, pointed ears.

"Nice place you have here, Mr. Frame. And nice dogs."

The last statement sharply attracted the man's attention. "You know hounds?"

Kyle was tempted to bluff but decided this sharp-eyed old man was too clever. "No, no, not really." He decided not to tell Mr. Frame that his second wife had had a yappy, fussy little poodle that Kyle despised.

"Red Heelers, these are. Can herd cattle, tree coons, run down squirrels." He bent down to rub Princess's ears, and Kyle reflected that he'd never seen a dog like that except grubbing in trash cans. "Princess's my good girl," Frame was murmuring. "She's my best dog. Last time I'm going to breed her, I think, even though I can get fifteen for the pups."

Kyle looked at Princess, who was trying to scratch with her hind leg but was missing every other try. "Well," he remarked judicially, "you ought to find lots of buyers who'd pay fifteen dollars for fine pups like that!"

Wilton choked as if he'd just gulped down his Copenhagen, and Mr. Joel Frame idly stood back up and watched a blue jay jauntily sail overhead. He looked back at Kyle and Afton without a trace of expression on his nutmeg-brown face. "I mean fifteen hundred, Mr. Patton."

Afton giggled uncontrollably, and Kyle had to laugh. "Okay, I give up! I'd say anyone who'd give that for a dog would have to be pretty well up on his Red Heelers."

"Yep," Mr. Frame dryly agreed. "Most everyone around here uses 'em to help train and control their thoroughbreds. Darndest thing you ever saw. Blamed dogs love thoroughbreds. Act like they think they're big toys or something. Follow 'em, boss 'em, herd 'em, sleep with 'em. You folks care to sit down over there in that gazebo thing? My wife's idea . . . I thought it looked like some fancy woman's birdcage, but I hafta admit I do sit in it sometimes, just watch the dogs and think . . ." He led them to a lacy white octagonal-shaped gazebo with comfortable white wicker furniture inside.

Mr. Frame insisted Afton take a chaise lounge, and he and Kyle sat in great rockers with overstuffed cushions. As they talked, Mr. Frame rocked slowly, the straw creak of the chair making a soothing background sound in the quiet.

"Wilton here was kind enough to bring us to ask you a favor, Mr. Frame," Kyle said after some small talk. "I need some help with my movie. Or maybe information would be more accurate."

"What's the trouble?" Frame asked, eyeing Kyle curiously.

"My film takes place in the early part of the century," Kyle earnestly explained. "It's about a young couple who leave their home in the city to make a new start with a little timberland. They stay with it throughout the first war and then struggle through the Depression. Point of it is, they nearly sell out, but they finally decide that it's better to stay with the land than to go back to the city. I know it sounds kind of corny, but that's it."

Mr. Frame speared them with his black eyes, then smiled gently. "Sounds like a movie about my life. 'Cept I never did start out in the city . . . just almost went a time or two. Finally me and Molly decided to stay here on the land. I did build her that big house," he said, waving nonchalantly at the mansion looming up on the hill. "But I still don't think I'll ever feel as much at home there as I did in that cabin me and my dad built with our own hands."

"You and your father built a cabin?" Kyle exclaimed. "It sure would be a big help to me if you'd come over on location and give my crew some pointers. They told me they can build houses, but it seems like log cabins are way too complicated for them."

Joel Frame pursed his thin leathery lips to consider. At length he nodded. "Be proud to."

"I'd really appreciate that, Mr. Frame," Kyle said gratefully. "Now I'm kinda embarrassed to ask you for another favor, but I understand you're likely the only man around here that might know how to help me out. See, I know in the early days most of the lumber men used oxen to work in the woods."

"Sure did."

"Well, I got the oxen all right, but turns out they're smarter than my crew," Kyle grumbled. "They moved right in, go wherever they want to; they're eating up the countryside, and nobody can do a cursed thing with them. Could you maybe give me a name? Somebody that I could hire to work the team? I'd be willing to pay a good wage to someone who could handle those beasts."

Frame took off his cap, smoothed down the spikes of paper-white hair, and then settled it securely back on his head. "I could do it, but I guess Molly'd have conniptions. I am getting kinda old to be ramrodding a yoke. That's the problem. I know some men, but they're like me, too old. Let me think on it a minute."

He stood up and walked to the door of the gazebo, staring out across the miles and miles of green expanse that belonged to him. Finally he came back, settled himself down deliberately in the rocking chair, and nodded slowly. "What exactly is it you're need-ing out of these oxen, Mr. Patton? You want somebody just to keep 'em from wandering off, to feed 'em, stuff like that?"

"No, sir, no." Kyle shook his head stubbornly. "I've got to have shots of them pulling the timber, just like back then."

"That's a real trick, Mr. Patton," Frame said dryly. "I know some men who could just keep 'em from killin' themselves or someone else, but there's only one man I know that can really work them. But I just don't know if he'll be interested in the job."

"Who is he? Where is he?" Kyle demanded excitedly. "If I can just talk to him, I know I can persuade him. Every man's got a price."

Frame eyed Kyle and made a skeptical grunt. "Well, I dunno about that. But I guess there's no harm in seeing about it. I'll take you to meet him. He just happens to be working for me right now."

"What's his name?" Kyle asked, eagerly jumping up out of the cushy rocker.

It seemed to take Joel Frame a long time to consider this, as if he weren't sure whether to trust Kyle with the mysterious oxen-worker's name. Finally, he slowly said, "Peregrine. Everybody just calls him Peregrine."

◇ ◇ ◇

As it turned out, Joel Frame insisted they would have to ride the four-wheelers to find the elusive Peregrine. Wilton wandered down to the stables to tell lies with the hands, and Frame and Kyle mounted the squatty vehicles easily. Kyle patted the seat behind him, and Afton reluctantly climbed on. The things looked like dangerous little boys' toys to her.

Her instinct pretty much proved to be right. Kyle and even Joel Frame rode through the green pastures, disdaining the neat dirt roads and bridle paths, toward a far expanse of deep woods. They drove much too fast, it seemed to Afton, and she was horribly frightened, but Kyle was actually whooping with excitement. Resignedly she shut her eyes tight, clasped her father in a death-grip around his waist, and bent her head. Over and over again she was thrown off the seat and felt that at any moment she might go cartwheeling into the empty air.

They finally came to a halt, and slowly Afton opened her eyes and looked around. They were surrounded by enormous pine trees, so thickly grown together that one could barely see the sky. Immediately in front of them was a barbed-wire fence. "He's in there somewhere, I got a good idea about where," Frame said, neatly stepping through the two strands of barbed wire. "I'll be back in a while. You two just rest a bit."

It was about twenty minutes actually before two men appeared out of the thick woods so suddenly that Kyle and Afton, in deep conversation about the movie, were almost startled out of their wits. They hadn't heard a sound; it was as if Mr. Frame and the man with him had suddenly risen out of the earth.

"This is Mr. Kyle Patton, the producer and director of the movie," Mr. Frame announced politely to the man. "This is his daughter, Miss Afton Burns."

Afton's first thought was, *He looks like a wolf*. He wasn't a big man, perhaps five foot ten, in his mid-twenties. His body was wiry, taut-muscled, like a swimmer's or long distance runner's. Afton was struck by the contrast of his loose-jointed, apparently relaxed stance and the vigilance of his eyes and the tautness of his mouth.

He had the most unusual eyes Afton had ever seen, and she reflected that they gave him his wolflike appearance; they were almost almond-shaped, uptilted a little, and of an odd color that was hard to determine. At first they seemed light brown, but as they shifted beneath narrowed lids, they glinted with golden or amber light. His hair was dark, shiny black, long and uncombed, and he had a day or two's rough growth of beard. The lupine look was heightened by his wedge-shaped face, slanting down from sharply defined cheekbones to a tapered chin. His mouth was well-shaped but was pressed together in a hard, suspicious line.

He took his time, studying first Kyle, then Afton with the same guarded expression.

"This is Peregrine," Frame said dryly. "You know. Got one name, like Falstaff or Hamlet."

"Or Cher or Madonna," Kyle said brightly, but Joel Frame looked blank. "Pleased to meet you, Peregrine." Kyle held out his hand.

Peregrine looked at it for a few seconds, then grasped it, gave it an up-and-down once, and snatched his own hand back. Afton went through the same treatment. His hand was rough, callused, and warm. He met her gaze as disinterestedly as if she were a mannequin. Still he said nothing.

With bluff good humor Kyle said, "Well, Peregrine, Mr. Frame tells me you can help me out of a big mess I've got on my hands."

Peregrine waited, watching Kyle.

With exasperation now showing, Kyle went on, "Oxen. You can work oxen?"

Peregrine nodded slowly. When he spoke, Kyle and Afton almost jumped from the shock. "Yes, sir," he said quietly. His voice was soft, though not feminine. He spoke very slowly, not with the country drawl that the other locals had, but with great deliberation. Afton wondered if he might be slightly retarded, though somehow his eyes had a sharp, comprehending expression, while many mentally handicapped people had a rather dull gaze. She had to admit, however, that the man's lack of expression did tend to make him look blank.

Kyle was blustering on, " . . . so if you'd be interested in helping me out, I'd be glad to pay you—uh, ten dollars an hour?"

Peregrine merely watched him as if he were a sleepy beetle lumbering across a rock.

Desperately Kyle said, "No, no, I meant twelve dollars an hour?"

A sign. Peregrine's mouth twitched ever so slightly.

"Fifteen," Kyle groaned. "Fifteen dollars an hour."

Peregrine nodded, a sharp downward jerk of his head. Then he turned back and disappeared as suddenly and silently as he had come.

Peregrine disappeared so quickly into the shadows of the pines that Kyle didn't have time to call after him. Dumbfounded, he turned to Joel Frame, who seemed much amused. "What does that mean?" Kyle demanded irritably. "Did that twitch mean yes, he'd come to work for me? For fifteen dollars an hour? Or did I just imagine the whole thing?"

Frame grinned sunnily. "You just go on back to your location, Mr. Patton. I think you'll find by the time you get there that Peregrine will have those oxen fed and bedded down in the barn for the night."

"But—he—" Helplessly Kyle pointed to the woods. "But it's miles from here! He went the wrong way!"

"Yep, he does that," Frame said mysteriously, mounting his four-wheeler again and gunning it with vigor. "But then sometimes I think maybe Peregrine's going the right way, and the rest of the world went wrong."

SIX

◇

JOEL FRAME STUCK OUT HIS HAND at their farewells, and Kyle, wincing with dread, took it. "I sure would like to take you up on your kindly offer and come take a look at the scenes at the cabin, Mr. Patton."

"We'll be looking forward to seeing you, Mr. Frame," Kyle replied, but added anxiously, "But what about my oxen? And that Peregrine guy? How am I supposed to get in touch with him?"

"He'll be around," Frame replied. "You're meaning to stable them in that barn just over the rise from the cabin site, right? Like I told you, Peregrine's probably already got 'em bedded down for the night."

"But—I didn't think—how do you know where the site is?" Kyle asked. The cabin site was in the middle of miles of unmarked woods. Actually, it was just on the edge of Daniel Boone National Forest. It had taken Kyle and a high-powered law firm two months to get permission to use the site, which was in reality a place where an old cabin had been built around 1850.

Frame smiled pleasantly. "'Cause that's my great-great-great-grandfather's old place. And just so's you'll know, the barn still belongs to me. And so does that hay field—and all that hay that your oxen's been eating, Mr. Patton. So you might say I have a vested interest in your movie—and in seeing that you get a good man like Peregrine to watch out for your critters. A good day to you, Miss Afton."

They collected Wilton Simms, then returned to the cabin site, where Jimmy Dean Toomey and his construction crew were still milling around looking busy, though the bare square of foundation dirt was still without a single laid log. As was his custom, Kyle jumped out of the Jeep while it was still shuddering to a stop. "Jimmy Dean!" he yelled at the top of his lungs. "Get over here!"

Unhappily the squat little man waddled over to Kyle. "Now, Mr. Patton, afore you get all het up lemme tell you that one of them two-ton varmints came wanderin' up here to the cabin site, and it took the whole crew of us all day just to head it back to the hay field."

Kyle gave a greatly exaggerated sigh. "I don't suppose it occurred to you to try to head it back to the barn? Inside the fence? No, didn't think so. Anyway, I'm supposed to have a man coming to take care of the beasts."

"Mr. Frame, he knew somebody?"

"Guess he knows the man, but I couldn't say the same for me." Kyle suddenly was irritated with himself, for he was talking about Peregrine in riddles just as Joel Frame had. "Man who works for him. Name's Peregrine."

Jimmy Dean's squinty eyes opened almost to normal size, and he began his signaling; he vehemently sliced off a good-sized chunk of air. "That half-wit hermit? With the dog and who knows what all else critters?"

Afton bristled for some unfathomable reason. "Mr. Joel Frame doesn't seem to be the type of man to recommend a crazy man for such a difficult job. After all, it does appear that none of you have the tools—mental or physical—to do it."

Both Kyle and Jimmy Dean stared at her, Kyle with a tinge of amusement, Jimmy Dean with a hint of shame. Then Kyle shrugged impatiently and said, "I am tired of doing this donkey work. I've got a movie to make, and I've spent all day dealing with morons and crazy mountain men and dumb beasts. I'm going to go see about those animals, and if I have to bring in artillery, I'm going to get them into that barn!"

With that he stalked toward the line of hackberry trees behind the cabin clearing, heading for the hay field that was about half an acre beyond it. Afton, Jimmy Dean, and Wilton Simms scurried after Kyle.

When Kyle stepped out of the woods at the edge of the hay field, he stopped so abruptly that his three followers almost barreled into him. With a soft whistle Kyle murmured, "Will you look at that!"

Right down the middle of the field, Peregrine was sauntering along with a small stick in his hand, idly swatting at the tops of the tall grass. Beside him, ambling along, was the monstrous form of a massive ox. Peregrine had his left hand resting against the beast's ridged neck, and he had to reach up to do it. Once when the ox started wandering off to the left, Peregrine whistled sharply, a single commanding note between his teeth, and hurried around to the ox's other side. "Hup," he muttered and lightly slapped the ox's rump with the stick. Docilely the animal made a course correction, so that he was headed straight for the barn just in sight on top of a rise to their left.

The little huddled group at the edge of the woods was silent, mostly awestruck. Behind Peregrine and his pet, in a straggly line, three of the other oxen moseyed along, stopping occasionally to lower their barrel heads and snack, sometimes wandering a little this way or that, sometimes stopping and raising their heads to look around with dull curiosity. But as the four watched, dumbstruck, they could clearly see that the three were docilely following Peregrine into the fenced acre that housed the barn.

"Well," Kyle commented dryly, "that takes care of one problem. So there's only about 10,000 more." Absently pushing through the three behind him, he hurried back toward the cabin site. Wilton and Jimmy Dean followed him, but Afton stayed to watch the pied piper leading the four oxen until they all disappeared into the barn.

◇ ◇ ◇

For the next two days Kyle sent Houston Rees to the cabin site to supervise construction, and he took over the scenes shot in the town setting. Afton went to the set with her father, but after about half a day she found herself longing to be back at the cabin in the woods with the animals . . . and perhaps finding out more about the mysterious Peregrine, though she didn't exactly fully form the thought in her mind.

By the end of the second day of shooting the town scenes, she had decided that moviemaking was a deadly dull business, once one got past being starstruck at such famous people and being breathless about making a film that perhaps millions of people would see. It was hard, repetitive work. It took three times as long to set up the scenes—or even a single shot—than it did to actually film it. The stars and extras spent hours simply standing still, getting placed, while the crew adjusted the lighting and went over and over the camera angles. Stella insisted on coaching every one of the hundred-plus extras, telling each one exactly where to stand, where to walk to, their expressions, what they must do with their hands.

Afton found herself helping Truman Kirk with his lines, for Kyle had not yet been satisfied with the takes of the scene of Tru making an impassioned speech at the little turn-of-the-century town's Fourth of July picnic. To her surprise and pleasure, she found Truman Kirk to be exactly as gentle and unassuming a man as he appeared to be. This was unusual, she already knew. Most Hollywood people, whether they were stars or lowly gaffers, were never what they seemed to be. They were something else altogether, mostly people who were looking for an edge, an advantage, and whose main life occupation and preoccupation was to be famous and rich, which to them meant they would be adored by millions.

Messalina Dancy grandly ignored Afton. Whenever Afton would accidentally cross her line of vision, she would nod coolly toward her, as a queen would to her lowly subjects. Afton always smiled politely and thought that Messalina Dancy, for all her beauty and fame and riches, appeared to be unhappy most of the time.

After the second day of accompanying Kyle to Grand for the town scenes, Afton had had more than enough. She decided she would ask her father if she could go with Houston Rees to the cabin site. Secretly she thought it would be more fun to hammer nails or slather mud or whatever it took to put a log cabin together than to stand around all day watching Kyle yell and Stella fuss and actors obediently stand around like cattle. With a guilty smile Afton thought it would be much more absorbing to watch Peregrine's oxen eat all day than it was to watch a movie being filmed.

Pre-dawn was raw, gray, and chilly. Afton dressed warmly, deciding to wear her black slacks made of a thick, nubby tweed and an Oxford shirt beneath her warmest wool sweater. She reflected that though she had a scant wardrobe, she did have the nicest woolen items, nicer even than Stella's and Messalina's. *That's certainly one good thing about home*, she thought with satisfaction. *You can get the softest, warmest, best-quality woolens and tweeds for practically nothing. They certainly make the expensive American things look chintzy. I suppose they're made in Taiwan or Nepal or somewhere . . .*

Knocking on Kyle's door, Afton sternly arranged her face into neutral lines. She still found it slightly embarrassing to walk into the hotel room her father shared with a woman who was not his wife; in fact, Kyle was still legally married to Lita, his fourth wife. Neither Kyle nor Stella seemed at all uncomfortable with the situation, which Afton thought was odd, as her father did seem to be sensitive to her Christian sensibilities in some areas. Kyle definitely curbed his raw language and stubbornly insisted that the others— even Stella—do the same. Once he had even muttered a half-apology for his drinking and had mentioned, Afton supposed as a sort of cushion against sudden shock, that she needed to stay away from the crew members who constantly used, abused, and talked and laughed about drugs. "Can't get away from it," Kyle had muttered with furtive embarrassment. "It's sort of a mark of the nineties movie scene, I guess. Everyone has their drug of choice. Some use drugs just at New Year's Eve parties, some use it 'recreationally,' some use them all the time."

"Do you?" Afton had demanded sharply.

He had cast his ashamed gaze downward. "No. Not anymore." Afton hadn't pushed him further.

Stella answered Afton's soft knock, in sharp contrast to Kyle's peremptory "It's open!" Stella was dressed immaculately and expensively, as usual, in a hunter green pantsuit with a Hermes scarf. "Good morning, Afton," she said in her voice of chilly reserve. "Please come in and have some breakfast." The usual regimental feast had arrived.

"I'll just have a scone, thank you," Afton said, helping herself. Stella did pour her a cup of coffee, which Afton reflected was a definite sign of a thaw; usually Stella asked Afton to fix *her* coffee.

This morning Stella even smiled, a mild twist of her full lips. "'Scones,'" she repeated liltingly.

Afton chuckled. "Oh, I know you call them 'biscuits.' But it's so difficult, you see, because what we call 'biscuits' are what you call 'cookies.'"

"Then what does 'cookies' mean in Scottish?" Stella teased.

Her blue eyes gleaming, Afton said solemnly, "'Cookies' mean nothing in the Queen's English."

"What kind of existential conversation is this?" Kyle demanded as he hung up the phone. He was always on the phone first thing in the morning.

"We were just discussing the futility of life," Stella explained gravely, "using the metaphor of the total meaninglessness of cookies."

"Oh," Kyle said absently, grabbing his usual breakfast—a biscuit and a cup of coffee. Then he banged out the door, leaving it open to the hostile morning, ordering back over his shoulder, "Time to go to work, ladies. We're wasting daylight!"

"The sun's not even up yet," Afton groaned, cramming the last bit of her own scone in her mouth and gulping her thickly sugared-and-creamed coffee. Grimacing, she hurried after her father. She still didn't like coffee and thought wistfully of piping hot and strong Earl Grey tea.

By almost running she managed to catch up with Kyle. "Father, would you mind if today I went out to the cabin site with Mr. Rees instead of—"

He wasn't listening, and he interrupted her as he stepped along, frowning at the movie cavalcade as the tailpipes hazed the chilly air. "I'm going to go out to the cabin site first thing this morning," he said as if he were dictating his schedule to a secretary. "Last night Houston said they were still having problems. By Monday we'll be through with the town shots, if Tru can keep his lines straight for an hour or so at a time. That cabin's got to be finished by then!" He glanced sideways at his companion, who was almost jogging to keep up with his fierce pace. "Oh, do you want to come out to the cabin with me, Afton?"

"Yes, please," she answered breathlessly.

"Were you saying something?" Kyle asked with an attempt at politeness.

"No, nothing at all." Afton was growing accustomed to her father's singlemindedness when he was working. She had seen him yell "Cut!" at the top of his lungs right in the middle of a scene it had taken hours to set up because some extra's nose was shiny or some leaf had blown the wrong way or some key grip sneezed.

As it turned out, Houston Rees was long gone; he had left before dawn so he would get to the cabin right at sunrise. He'd told Afton that nobody could accuse the locals of laziness because the construction and logging crews were always bright and cheery at the most horrendous early hours. It was getting them to do one iota of work that was the problem.

Practically dragging Afton, Kyle jumped into a Cherokee that was warmed up and took off as if they were the pace car in the Indianapolis 500. *He always drives this way,* Afton sighed to herself. *I think my driving lesson was safer, even if I was on the wrong side of the road.*

They skidded onto the dirt road that led to the cabin site. At least the loggers had been working, Afton saw. Enormous trenches scarred the narrow road, and the fields on the left as well. Kyle had gotten permission from Joel Frame to clear a few trees and for the skidders to make a rude road to a site near the cabin but out of camera sight. They would need quite a bit of room for the trailers and vans.

Two walls of the cabin were up, Afton saw as they hurtled into the clearing, but on one side was a helter-skelter scramble of logs that looked like a giant had spilled his toothpicks. A third wall was halfway up, but no one was working on it, though there seemed to be a full crew there. Afton's heart sank. It seemed impossible that this shambles would be a completed log cabin within two days.

Kyle leaped out of the Jeep, his face tight. "What the devil is going on here!" he shouted. His face set like flint, he surveyed the men milling around. The nearest man was sitting in the bucket of a bulldozer, smoking and watching Kyle—and especially Afton—with narrowed eyes.

"Where's Houston Rees? And where's Jimmy Dean? And who the devil are you?" Kyle demanded belligerently.

Slowly the man flicked his cigarette to the dirt, ground it out with a steel-toed boot, then stood up. He was tall, powerfully built, handsome in a kind of jaded and overdone way. His stance was arrogant, and his long, slow perusal of Afton was insolent. "I'm Roy Dale Puckett, and I guess you're Mr. Kyle Patton himself. Pleased to meet you, boss." His tone just bordered on sarcasm.

"My pleasure," Kyle said curtly. "You're one of my loggers, I take it?"

"I'm a logger."

Ignoring the rebellious tone, Kyle demanded, "Then why aren't you logging? And is there anyone here who has the faintest idea of who's in charge of the construction crew? What's happening here, besides nothing?"

The man's steely blue eyes narrowed, but he simmered down his tone to bare civility. "What's happened, Mr. Patton, is there's been an accident." He crossed his massive arms as he looked down at Kyle. Roy Dale Puckett was quite an intimidating man; he must have been six-four and was huge.

Kyle wasn't intimidated, however. He glared up at Puckett. "What kind of accident? Someone hurt?"

"Yep. We were using the log winch to hoist up the cabin logs, and the winch busted. Dropped the load, busted that feller's leg, and scattered the good little pigs' neat little woodpile to tarnation." Roy Dale's stony blue eyes glinted with amusement.

"Who . . . ? Who was it?" Kyle almost screamed.

"Jimmy Dean's leg got busted up pretty bad," Roy Dale

answered in a bored tone. "Your Mr. Rees took him to the hospital, along with my crew boss."

Kyle paced furiously, his expression thunderous. Finally he looked up and shouted, "Does anybody here have the faintest idea how to get this cabin built?"

Nobody answered. Nobody even looked at Kyle.

After a long pause Kyle wheeled and stomped over to where Afton stood quietly. "Afton, you go to town—no, no, I guess I'd better go, blast it. You stay here in case I miss Houston." He was in the Jeep without waiting for her answer, shouting out the window as he left. "If Houston shows up, make him stay right here! Tell him to put these clowns back to work, and I don't care if it's counting dirt clods! I'm going to go see Jimmy Dean and find out about another crew boss—one who can get the job done!"

Afton watched the truck disappear; then when she looked around and saw the men staring at her, she felt a little frightened. They were all rough-looking, although some of them—most of them, she noted once her powers of perception cleared—didn't seem threatening at all, merely curious. It was, however, the bold stares of Roy Dale Puckett and another young man who had sidled up to him that disturbed her most. She had been among the slum dwellers and hostile youth gangs in Edinburgh—but never alone.

Now the silence closed in about her, and she felt the pressure of Puckett's slow perusal and his friend's sly grin. For a brief moment she felt resentful of her father, then sensibly realized that he was accustomed to having people around who could handle themselves.

And so I can, she told herself firmly, *and so I shall.*

"I should think if you're not going to work on the cabin, you could get that mess cleaned up," she said crisply, waving at the scat-tered tools and tangled logs. "I don't think my father is going to pay you if you aren't working. Didn't that appear to be his mood, do you think?"

Roy Dale winked down at his buddy. Then both men stepped closer to her. The other man resembled Roy Dale, although he wasn't as muscular. He was better-looking in a way, as he was younger and not so hard-looking; in fact, his expression was one of intense absorption, like a child's when he doesn't quite understand the conversation. "Well, well, Bobby, we got a new boss, looks like. Lot finer-looking than Jimmy Dean Toomey, huh?" Roy Dale grunted. Both men laughed uproariously. "What's your name, darlin'?"

"I'm Afton Burns," she answered levelly, standing her ground. "Mr. Patton is my father."

"Is he?" Roy Dale's eyes glinted. "You got a different last name, though, huh? Does that mean you don't know who the mother is?" Again he and his would-be twin laughed loudly, though Afton noticed through her disgust that the younger man seemed quite blank at the joke, only laughing when Roy Dale did.

Noting Afton's dark glance, Roy Dale sobered and said bel-ligerently, "This here's my brother Bobby. And we got the same last names and all, case you're wondering."

"I wasn't," Afton said quietly. "I wouldn't be so rude. You'll excuse me, I'm sure." Whirling, she walked in the direction of the barn, her head held high. Pausing, she turned and with deliberation added to the general company, "If any of you want to work, get to it, and I'll see to it that you're paid. If not, then you might as well be on your way."

As she left she heard Roy Dale murmur something that made a few of the men laugh, but she noticed that most of them kept their eyes averted and were already at work cleaning up and getting the stack of logs back in an orderly pile. Making her way through the woods, she caught a glimpse of the barn and drew a sigh of relief in the solitude. Somehow she felt she might have done something more to assert herself. But she had little experience with such things, and she finally decided she'd done the best she could, and as well as could be expected under the circumstances.

All eight of the oxen were out of the barn and were dotted over the generous pasture enclosed by the barbed-wire fence. She paused, admiring the massive proportions of the beasts. Moving along the fence to her right, she made her way to where one of them, a male with a wide white blaze on his face, was leaning against a fence post. He seemed impervious to the barbs, for he was leaning hard, and the post sagged precariously with his enormous weight.

Timidly reaching through the strands of wire, she waggled her fingers in front of his face. He rolled a gentle brown eye in her direction. She started rubbing the stiff white bristles of fur between his sweeping horns, and he gave a plaintive sigh that made her laugh. "You like that, do you?" She scratched and rubbed his head for a long while as he continued to melodramatically sigh and roll his eyes. "Oh, you! You're just a fraud, like so many patients I've seen! Healthy as an ox, but moaning for sympathy."

She left him leaning against the post, his eyes almost shut. The morning sun was warm and was making Afton a little sleepy too.

She walked idly along the fence line, occasionally stooping to pick a wildflower that looked like a miniature buttercup or to watch some bug scuttle busily along. The fence enclosed about an acre, she supposed, with the barn up against the far corner. Afton decided to walk around the enclosure and maybe go poke around in the old barn a bit. She thought Joel Frame probably wouldn't mind.

Slowly she walked, enjoying what was turning into a fine, crisp fall morning. The leaves were radiant; the sky was a fine robin's-egg blue with wispy clouds. She had almost reached the barn and was searching to find a gate in the fence when something heavy settled on her shoulder. Gasping, she wheeled, thrashing out frantically.

"Here, here . . . it's just me, Miss. Sorry, I sure didn't mean to scare you." Roy Dale Puckett stared down at her, evidently repentant, and backed away a step.

Afton relaxed, but not much. "You think laying your hand on a person's shoulder when they think they're alone in the woods won't scare them? By heaven and the saints! You frightened me out of my scarce wits!" Afton's Scottish brogue, which was normally very faint, became much more thick when she was startled.

He blinked once, twice, then had the grace to look sheepish. "Really, I am sorry, Miss. I thought about hollerin' at you, but that didn't seem quite right either. I mean, standin' off in the woods hootin' at you like some fool loony bird or somethin'."

After a few tense moments Afton smiled, albeit reluctantly. "Yes, I suppose I can see your point. So, Mr. Puckett, now that you have found me—?"

"Yes, ma'am. Well, it's like this." His voice was low and uncertain.

"Uh—I guess I came to apologize. I didn't act much like a gentleman back there. I was just showin' off, I guess. Men do that, you know."

"No, boys do that, Mr. Puckett," Afton retorted succinctly. "But I accept your apology."

He flashed a quick, charming smile at her. "Well, if you do, then maybe you'll call me Roy Dale."

Afton took a few moments to consider this. She knew that her habit of calling mere acquaintances by their titles and last names was considered quaint—even odd—by Americans. Still, her mother and grandfather and all of the people who were important to her had trained her that to use a person's Christian name was a mark of respect and that it was uncouth to use a person's given name without permission. However, she had noticed that Americans simply didn't address each other by their Christian names, not even in acknowledging introductions, and now she wondered if people might not think her custom was rude or snobbish. Finally she murmured, "All right—Roy Dale. And please call me Afton."

Gravely he searched her face. Afton watched him carefully for signs of his previous unwelcome boldness, but he seemed genuinely polite. "Good, that makes me feel a little better. I'd like to be friends, Afton."

Afton was uneasy with the situation and couldn't seem to judge where this was going. Hesitantly she answered, "Well, yes, of course. I'm sure we can be friends."

"I'm sure too." With a flourish he offered her a huge, slightly grimy hand.

Politely Afton slid her hand into his.

He shook it, then tightened his grip just a bit. Still smiling in a placating manner, he stepped close to her and lowered his face to hers, lightly sliding his hands up her arms to her shoulders.

For a few paralyzing seconds Afton couldn't move, but then she came alive, shuddering and struggling backwards, and whipping her face back and forth to try and escape his kiss.

He laughed with what appeared to be genuine amusement. "Aw, c'mon, Afton! You want it—I saw you looking at me, checkin' me out! Give me a break—I won't tell Daddy you're playin' around with the help!"

"Stop it! Get away from me!" Afton wriggled out of his meaty grip and backed away, wiping her mouth with a shaking hand. Though she was frightened, her mild blue eyes blazed. "Don't you ever touch me again!"

His heavy features hardened. "Just calm down, little girl! It's not that big a deal! I wasn't trying to rape you, you know, just a little kiss between friends."

He stepped toward her again. Desperately Afton stumbled back but felt the sudden sharp pain of the barbed-wire fence pricking her back. With a little cry of pain, she tried to sidle to her left, but Puckett compensated and slid to the side, so that she literally rammed into him. He grabbed her, muttering, "Just who do you think you are anyway? Better 'n everybody else? Too good for me? I don't hardly think so, little girl, I don't care who your daddy is."

As she struggled to free herself from Puckett's iron grasp, the Scripture she'd read on the plane leaped into her mind: *O thou of little faith, wherefore didst thou doubt?* Afton stopped struggling and prayed, *Lord, stretch forth Your hand and save me now. . .*

Suddenly Puckett's stormy eyes focused on a point just behind

Afton's left shoulder, then narrowed to knife slits. Confused, Afton turned to see what had distracted him.

Nonchalantly Peregrine sauntered up to the fence, laid one brown hand on the top wire, and magically sailed over to stand close on Afton's other side. So smoothly that it seemed as if he was moving in a kind of dreamy slow motion. He reached over with one hand, plucked Puckett's grimy hand off Afton's right arm, then swatted Puckett's other paw away from her waist. "Howdy," he said in a rather foolish-sounding, careless tone.

"Howdy," Afton echoed numbly.

"Wha—whaddya think you're doing, half-wit!" Puckett snarled, stung because of Peregrine's sudden appearance out of nowhere, and because of his own hesitation at the surprise. "You better take a walk, fool. This is none of your business!"

Peregrine shrugged and studied Afton's face. The color in her cheeks was high and hectic, and her eyes were pleading. "You all right?" he asked, as if he were asking her the time.

"Y-yes, but—yes, but would you please walk me back to the cabin, Peregrine?" she responded, valiantly attempting to regain her composure.

"Sure." He shrugged.

"Oh, no, you don't," Puckett growled. "Me and Afton ain't finished with our business yet." Again he grabbed Afton's hand and yanked hard. She whimpered a little, and Peregrine stepped up, quick and mean. His strange wolf-eyes blazed with a turgid amber. He had to look up into Roy Dale Puckett's face, and the bigger man sneered, "Whatcha gonna do, fool? Whip me?"

In an instant, but with an effort of sheer willpower that was plain to see, Peregrine relaxed. He almost smiled. "Naw," he drawled. "But he is." He nodded to a point behind Puckett's back.

"Oh, yeah, right—" Puckett began, disdainful of an old trick that invited a sucker punch.

Then he heard a wet, throaty growl right behind him, right at about the level of the meaty part of his thighs. Slowly Puckett's big bear-head swiveled around.

With dreadful fascination Afton saw the monster behind Puckett.

It's a dog, she thought, but the realization gave her no relief. It was still a monster and still fearsome. A muscular male German shepherd, he was clearly an attack dog straining to do just that. But this dog was even more frightening because it was so battle-scarred. His left eye was missing, his left ear was shredded, and lurid red patches of scarring on his left side clearly announced that this dog, at some time and in some horrible place, had faced death and had beaten it.

Peregrine casually reached over and with exaggerated patience pried Puckett's hand loose from Afton's arm again. "Let go. Or Stonewall ain't gonna like it."

Roy Dale's fingers went lax, his head still turned, his now-wide eyes unblinking, watching the dog behind him.

"Sit," Peregrine said conversationally.

Afton thought for a ludicrous moment that Roy Dale Puckett was going to obediently sit down; his knees jerked, but he seemed to catch himself when the dog sat down instead.

"Watch him, boy," Peregrine said.

With a final warning growl, the dog stared balefully at Roy Dale Puckett.

Peregrine, in the same careless tone, said, "Now, you better go."
Puckett went.

Afton felt stunned, and the thought came to her, *I called on God, and He reached out His hand and saved me—just as He pulled Simon Peter out of the waves!* Something came to her spirit then, and she knew she had taken a step of faith. And she knew somehow that it was just the first step, that in the days to come she'd be required to take other plunges by faith.

SEVEN

◇

FTON BURNS was definitely agitated and addled. Peregrine, in contrast, seemed calm and relaxed. Leaning against a fence post, he squinted up at the sun as if noticing it for the first time, then studied the woods, the barn, the oxen—the air. Afton realized that he was giving her time to collect herself, and she was grateful, but she simply couldn't seem to regain a calm enough frame of mind to carry on a meaningful conversation. Awkwardly she pushed back her hair, rubbed her cheeks and temples, jammed tense fists into her jeans pockets. After taking two ragged breaths, she tried to speak in a light tone of voice. "I think perhaps I might have overreacted to Mr.—I mean—er—him. His—um—his—um—"

With frustration she realized that Peregrine wasn't going to make any of those soothing it's-okay noises to help her get over this terrible discomfort. She stopped blathering and watched him with something very close to resentment, for he appeared to barely be paying attention to her. Then she wondered if perhaps he truly was a little slow. But then she reminded herself that regardless of what the reality of the situation was with Mr. Roy Dale Puckett, Peregrine had rescued her from his unwelcome attentions, at the very least.

Or rather, the dog had.

Afton stared at the dog uncertainly. He still obediently sat, watching her with a curious but not unfriendly expression. Afton studied the dog for a long time, and the dog calmly returned the careful perusal. Finally she asked, "Did you say his name is Stonewall?" The dog's one and a half ears pricked up.

"Uh-huh."

Afton cleared her throat. "I'm—indebted to you. And to Stonewall. I thank you for—for—helping me."

Peregrine's golden eyes touched her lightly, then rose again toward the high sky. "You're welcome."

"Embarrassing," Afton muttered, almost to herself.

"It is?" Peregrine asked idly. But again she saw an intense coppery glint as he darted a glance at her face.

"Yes, quite," Afton replied uncomfortably. "I don't know if I'm embarrassed because I was mistaken in what was just a—a—perhaps a friendly—um, American—thing that I'm not familiar with—"

"Nope," Peregrine grunted. "It ain't that."

"Oh," Afton said uncertainly. "Then perhaps I'm embarrassed because—um, well . . . I don't know why I'm embarrassed."

"Me neither," Peregrine said sturdily.

"Mr. Roy Dale Puckett is the one who should be embarrassed," Afton said with sudden belligerence.

"Yep."

"I certainly didn't want him to paw me like that," Afton asserted. "And I certainly didn't 'check him up.'"

"Check him out," Peregrine corrected her.

"That either," Afton ranted on. "And how dare he ask *me* who I think *I* am! Who does he think *he* is?"

"I dunno," Peregrine said, mystified.

"As if I would allow some—some—strange man to just kiss me because he decided I would like it!"

"Yeah," Peregrine said uncertainly, then amended, "I mean no."

"Well, I certainly am glad that you and I had this talk." Afton stamped toward the woods, tossing her head defiantly, then turned and looked back over her shoulder. "Well? You promised to walk me back to the cabin site, Peregrine. Aren't you coming?"

One corner of Peregrine's mouth twitched almost impercepti- bly. He snapped his fingers, and Stonewall stood up, his tail wag- ging. "Yeah," Peregrine replied.

◇ ◇ ◇

When Peregrine first saw the forlorn, two-sided piece of a cabin, his mouth twitched again. Afton, watching him avidly, noted that both sides twitched in unison, and it might have become a smile if he hadn't immediately pressed his lips together so stubbornly. Then his finely arched brows joined, and with deliberation he crossed one arm across his chest, propped the other on it, and placed a contemplative forefinger on his mouth. "Lincoln logs," he pronounced carefully.

"I beg your pardon?" Afton said blankly. "I don't think I heard you correctly."

"Prob'ly not," Peregrine said affably. "Noisy here."

It was too. Behind them the men were standing in a ragged semicircle, and Kyle Patton was striding back and forth in front of them, talking to them. It was one of his stock pep talks to the grunt crews—delivered at the top of his lungs. The two main points were what dummies they were and how broke he was, having to pay such dummies to do nothing but be dummies.

Afton watched her father sadly. He was making a fool of himself, he was only harming himself, and he was only punishing himself. Normally, if he had suffered such a loss of self-control in a more private setting, she might have quietly moved to his side, laid her hand on his arm, and spoken softly and soothingly to him. But as this was practically a spectacle in an amphitheater, she didn't feel it would be right for her to interfere.

Finally Kyle's voice lowered somewhat, and he stalked over to Afton and Peregrine. "Look at it," Kyle muttered scathingly. "It looks like a six-year-old boy put it together."

"Huh," Peregrine grunted. "Boys do Lincoln logs better 'n that."

"You said that before," Afton said curiously. "What are Lincoln logs?"

Kyle stopped his restless pacing and stared at Peregrine. Peregrine met his glance evenly but then gave him a vacant grin. Kyle continued to look at Peregrine in disbelief, then stared at the cabin, then back at Peregrine. "Lincoln logs," he repeated in a shocked tone of voice. "You said Lincoln logs."

"Yep. I said that."

"What are Lincoln logs?" Afton repeated impatiently.

Ignoring her, Kyle said very slowly, his eyes pinned to Peregrine's face, "You're saying that this cabin was supposed to have been put together like Lincoln logs?"

Peregrine shrugged.

"Blast it to kingdom come!" Kyle shouted, back in full voice.

"By all the clans! What are blasted Lincoln logs!" Afton demanded in a tone uncannily similar to her father's.

Kyle turned to her and spoke very rapidly, exhaling loudly with exasperation. "They're toys. Little logs named after Abe Lincoln. They fit together just so."

"Aye," Afton said impatiently, propping her hands on her hips. "And?"

"And this cabin isn't put together like Lincoln logs!" Kyle turned and shouted accusingly to the group cowering behind him. "Didn't any of you people play with toys?"

Some said no; some said yes. Kyle wasn't listening anyway.

He turned back to Peregrine, his expression now shrewd. "You know how to put this—this—" His eyes cut to Afton, then he spluttered helplessly, ". . . this *accursed* thing together, don't you?"

Peregrine considered this for so long that Afton grew afraid he'd forgotten the question. But at long last he did answer. "Just thought it looked like Lincoln logs. Ain't seen the how-to book," he said lazily.

"Can you read?" Kyle demanded. Afton winced.

Peregrine blinked. "Finished third grade. Twicet."

Afton almost giggled, but Kyle plowed on, unfazed. "You're hired," Kyle said.

One of Peregrine's eyebrows lifted, and he looked at Kyle as if he were a foreign curio. Kyle sighed. "I'll pay you twenty dollars an hour."

"For baby-sittin' eight oxen and buildin' one cabin," Peregrine said carefully, as if he were merely double-checking his duties.

Kyle knew better. Sighing, he said, "I'll double your pay. Thirty bucks an hour. So will you supervise this crew and get this cabin put up?"

Peregrine studied the men behind them. "That crew?"

"You want another one?" Kyle said desperately. "If you can find 'em, I'll hire 'em."

"No. They'll do for me. Question is if I'll do for them." Afton listened in rapt surprise. Three sentences in a row was the longest speech she'd yet heard the man string together.

"You'll do fine for them," Kyle said darkly. "And for me."

To Afton's surprise, Peregrine turned to look at her, and there was a clear, intelligent question in his expression. A nervous lump rose in her throat, and almost before she knew it the thought jumped up in her mind: *You'll do for me too, Peregrine. You'll do just fine.*

Even though Afton had said nothing—she merely stared at Peregrine with wide, startled eyes—he appeared to be satisfied. He nodded to Kyle. "Reckon I'm your man."

◊ ◊ ◊

"So the Lincoln Log Principle was clearly violated," Afton said gravely.

"Clearly," Kyle said dryly. "I do swear, a six-year-old boy would have known how to lay those logs. Guess that's why Peregrine knew."

"I don't get it," Dave Steiner said, frowning. "I guess I'm just a schlemiel, but I don't get it."

"It's like this," Kyle said, intertwining his fingers at right angles. "The logs in this kit came pre-notched, so they'll fit together real snug. Right?"

Dave nodded.

"Okay. Here comes these geniuses, and oh, yeah, they get the part about the interlocking corners. But what do they do? The idiots start laying two sides! What are they gonna do at the other two ends, do you think? Shove those logs in with a crowbar? Or just hang laundry from the notches?"

Dave roared. "Well, hey, Kyle! You're gonna have two walls twenty feet high! What else could you want?"

"They couldn't even do that," Kyle grumbled. "That's why one part of one wall fell. They hadn't sunk the foundation poles in the corners. Imbeciles just laid two logs down on the ground and started stacking them up like they were playing Jenga or something!"

Afton sighed. "Poor Mr. Toomey. He was seriously injured, Father."

"I know, and I'm sorry about that," Kyle said belligerently. "Don't fret so much, Afton; he's covered by my insurance, and I'm going to give him some severance pay to help out. But give me a break! The man's the foreman of a construction crew—you'd think he'd know better than to play pick-up sticks with 500-pound logs! You can't place logs just so with a log winch. Even I could see that! It's like trying to shoot pool with a baseball bat!"

"Yeah, he ought to have known better," Dave agreed, his blazing blue eyes trained steadily on Kyle. "Houston tells me you hired a half-wit to finish the cabin."

Kyle shrugged. "He does stand erect, on two legs," he replied caustically. "He's usually clothed and in his right mind. With that crew, he qualifies as the sharpest one around."

"I don't think Peregrine is a half-wit," Afton said much more vehemently than she had intended.

"You don't?" Kyle asked slowly. Stella's eyes narrowed as she suddenly turned her full attention to Afton. Dave regarded the Scottish maiden with surprise.

"No," Afton muttered, then stuttered, "I m-mean, y-yes. Yes, I do think so. I mean, no. No, I don't think Peregrine is a half-wit. I think he's much smarter than he is."

Stella smiled tightly, and even Kyle grinned. "It's all right, dar-lin'. I think you're much smarter than you are too."

"I meant smarter than he *seems*."

Dave sighed theatrically. "It's just too bad," he said with a deeply tragic air, "that I seem to be the only one here who's actu-ally smarter than I am."

◊ ◊ ◊

Three days later Peregrine and Joel Frame stood in the darkening twilight and studied the finished cabin. Joel Frame sucked his lower lip, making a sarcastic wheezing sound, while Peregrine's mouth was twisted in what might have been wry amusement.

"That's it, is it?" Frame asked.

"Yes, sir, that's it," Peregrine answered agreeably.

"How'd you raise it?"

"Four men to a log."

Frame nodded. "Fireplace?"

"Kinda."

"Them fake rocks?"

"Yes, sir."

"Never could figure out why a person would want to make fake rocks," Frame murmured in wonder. "Looks like a man would feel like a plain fool, working in a place that manufactured rocks."

"Or using 'em to build fireplaces," Peregrine added dryly.

Frame nodded sympathetically. "You know what?"

Peregrine knew a rhetorical question when he heard one, so he waited.

Frame answered himself, resuming his perusal of the cabin. "Looks like Lincoln logs."

EIGHT

◇

A FTON HAD NOT BEEN INTRODUCED to the girl and didn't know
her title. She was very young, perhaps only seventeen or eighteen, with the face of a mischievous pixie contrasted by her luxu-
riant ebony, waist-length hair. She was an aspiring actress, of
course. But on the way to stardom she was marking time doing
what Afton had dubbed "the scene-shouter."

"Snap beans and sky, take 9," she yelled, snapped the clapboard
importantly to the camera, and scurried out of the shot.

Messalina Dancy appeared in the doorway of the cabin and
looked up at the early morning sky, smiling. Her clothes were
shapeless and colorless—a long gray skirt, black button shoes, a
plain gray buttoned blouse, and a simple white apron. In her hands
she held a wide shallow earthenware bowl full of green beans. After
pausing for a moment, staring heavenward, she settled herself into
the cane-bottomed chair that was placed to one side of the cabin
door and began to snap beans.

"Cut!" Kyle yelled. "Messalina, love! What are you doing?"

As if a black cloud suddenly covered the summer sun,
Messalina's beatific expression darkened to rage. She lunged out of
the chair, the bowl fell, cracking neatly in two, and the verdant

green beans scattered like dandelion seeds on the wind. "I'm acting, Kyle! For the millionth time, what do you want?"

Kyle jumped out of his director's chair, scowling, and stamped
over to Messalina. "Yes, Lina, you're acting, and you are doing it
superbly. But it's still acting! You've got to *be* Anna Kay! *Be* her!
Be her! How many different women have I seen you *be*? I don't
know! Many! And it's never been that nonsense about 'you made
the part yours.' You, Messalina Dancy, actually became that
woman. You became Gabrielle in *Slow Dancing*. You became
Diane Robb in *Dwindling Fast*. You became Lady Macbeth. It
wasn't that Messalina Dancy did a superb job acting like Diane
Robb. You *were* Diane Robb! And now I want you to *be* Anna
Kay Wingfield."

Messalina listened to Kyle, to every word, but the lines of stub-
bornness in her mouth and brow grew more and more pronounced.
"Save the garbage, Kyle. You know me. You know that stupid flattery doesn't do a thing for me, doesn't work for me."

"It's not flattery, Lina," Kyle said, and suddenly his voice was
soft and kind. He reached out and took her hand and stroked it,
much as a father would an upset child. "It's the simple truth about
you, about the depth of your talent. Now, what's wrong? Can't you
just tell me?"

Messalina calmed down somewhat, but as she sat back down
in the chair, she still flounced temperamentally. Frowning, she
stared intently into the far distance and chewed on her bottom lip.
Kyle, standing by, crossed his arms and waited, his expression
patient and kind.

Afton sat in another of the collapsible canvas chairs, slightly
behind her father's and Stella's. Watching him deal with the tem-

peramental actress, she thought with a sudden revelation of respect that here was Kyle Patton's element. Here was his gift. Here was his depth of talent. Afton looked around and once again tried to make sense of the scene—the cabin, the strong, attractive woman in her poignantly patched old clothes, the trees, the rich black dirt surrounding it . . . and the snarl of electrical cables, the tangle of equipment, the gigantic lights, the crowd of people dressed in jeans. To Afton it was jarring, a meaningless vision of things whose meaning she could never adequately sort out.

Kyle Patton saw a poignant story to tell, and he knew exactly how to move each piece, each person, each moment in order to tell that story in the most compelling manner.

Afton's attention was drawn back to Messalina when she finally spoke. Although Afton was seated at least thirty feet away, she could hear Messalina clearly. Everyone was silent. Afton reflected that she would have been terribly self-conscious to have everyone listen to her so avidly, but then she remembered that was exactly what Messalina Dancy was there for. It was her life to make people watch and listen to her.

"Kyle, I admit I'm not in Anna Kay's skin," Messalina finally said with frustration. "I know, somehow, I can feel a click or something when I take over a character . . . or she takes over me. And I know I haven't reached that, haven't been able to achieve that here. And I know why. I just don't know how to fix it."

"Tell me," Kyle said quietly. "I can fix it."

Messalina gave him a shrewd look that slowly settled into trusting lines. "Okay. I got her in Moldova, you know? I was there. I had a good life, my husband was wonderful, we were young and strong and adventurous and yearning to make ourselves be important to each other, to make a life that was important to both of us. That I clicked into."

"Yes, you did."

"But now—here—" Messalina dramatically swept one hand across the whole world in front of her. "It just doesn't work, Kyle! What is Anna Kay Wingfield doing here? Snapping beans? That's the message of this movie, and the true meaning of life?"

"Yes," Kyle said calmly.

Messalina gave him a look that would have felled one of the oxen.

Kyle went down on one knee and picked up a green bean. Slowly he snapped off the top, pulled the pith-string down, and pried open the leathery outer skin. Reaching inside, he took one of the tender young beans out and held it up between his finger and thumb. Staring directly into Messalina's eyes, he spoke so softly that Afton almost couldn't catch the words. But they drifted to her as gently as dandelion fluff on a lazy spring breeze. "Do you see this? This one little sprout? Can't you see her, see Anna Kay? Last year, and the year before that, and the year before that she found the best little green beans, the ones that were perfectly shaped, the ones that were the prettiest green, the ones that had the best vegetable-wholesome smell. Anna Kay every year would mark those plants that gave her and her husband the finest green beans, and she spent days and weeks babying the dying plants so they would go to seed . . . and she hoarded those seeds, because they were one of her treasures. Hers. Anna Kay's and her family's."

He stood up slowly and turned his face up toward the sun. Messalina watched him, her entire posture of single-minded absorption, her face strained with concentration. Kyle lifted his hand and slowly traced a long, lazy arc. "Do you see that? That sky? That square of sky and those three clouds? That sun?" He looked down at Messalina. "Those all belong to Anna Kay Wingfield. They are hers. No one sullies them, no one can lay claim to them, no one can keep them from her, or her from them. And do you know why?"

"Why . . . why?" Messalina whispered as if she were in a trance.

Kyle knelt again and thrust his hand into the soft, black dirt at her feet. Grabbing a fistful of the rich earth, he thrust it under Messalina's patrician nose. "This. Because this belongs to her. This earth. If even one little piece of this earth belongs to you, you also own the sun and the sky and the moon and even the air!"

Messalina leaned back in the chair, relaxed her shoulders, laid her head back to catch the sun, and closed her eyes. Kyle stood up, brushed his hands smartly against his jeans, and said, "Let's take a break, everyone. Half an hour." He left Messalina sitting there in her cane-bottomed chair.

But Afton thought that somehow, miraculously, Messalina Dancy had disappeared. Anna Kay Wingfield was resting outside her cabin in her own little piece of sun.

◇ ◇ ◇

"Well, now, that was something else altogether, Mr. Patton," Joel Frame asserted. He and Peregrine were leaning against one of the prop trailers. It had a fold-down side, and Kyle had ingeniously converted it into kind of a refreshment stand, installing two coffee urns, an ancient Coke box that actually held soft drinks in slushy ice, and mounds and mounds of doughnuts and pastries and bagels. After dealing with Messalina, Kyle decided he'd celebrate with a big gooey Boston cream. He knew that he'd gotten through to the actress, and he was certain that "snap beans and sky, take ten" would be the last take.

"Good morning, Mr. Frame, good to see you again," Kyle said with genuine pleasure. "Good morning, Peregrine. Is there any-body in the—where the devil's somebody who's got sense enough to pour coffee and—"

Afton laid her hand on his arm and smiled up at him, cutting off the growl that threatened to rise into a full-blown shout. "Sorry, Father. I volunteered to help out, but I got so interested in that scene I sort of wandered off."

Kyle grinned as Afton hurried up the two steps into the trailer and inquired crisply, "And what may I serve you fine gentlemen on this fine morning? Hot coffee perhaps? A sweetie?"

"I'll have the sweetie," Peregrine immediately volunteered, staring pointedly at Afton.

"That's a generic Scottish name for a pastry, Peregrine," Kyle grunted, eyeing him suspiciously.

"Oh," Peregrine said blankly. "Still want one. The best one. Please."

Blushing furiously, Afton gave him a doughnut, making sure it was the plumpest and freshest-looking one, and then poured him a Styrofoam cup of coffee. Still eyeing Peregrine suspiciously, Kyle asked for a fat Boston cream with his coffee. Joel Frame was con-tent with just coffee.

"So what do you think, Mr. Frame?" Kyle asked heartily. "Ever seen a movie shoot before?"

"Sure haven't. Looks like a banshee convention for an hour,

and then five or ten minutes of dead still," Frame commented. "Guess it makes sense to you. Sure don't to me. 'Cept about what you said to that lady." His eyes slid to Kyle with calculation. "You believe that, what you were saying to her? All that about the earth?"

Kyle nodded vigorously, and his heavy features grew animated. "Yes, sir, you bet I did. I do. Would never have wanted to make this movie if I didn't. It's based on *The Good Earth*, you know. Novel by Pearl S. Buck." Kyle was going to elaborate but stopped when he saw Joel Frame nodding sagely.

"Thought so."

"You did?" Kyle couldn't hide all of his surprise.

"Mr. Frame, now, he can read real good," Peregrine declared. Kyle shot him a sharp look, but Peregrine's voice was a meaningless monotone, his expression one of barest interest.

"Yep, sure can," Frame said, the sun-and-smile creases around his eyes crosshatching. "I'll never forget that book. *The Good Earth* by Pearl S. Buck. Volunteered to read it in high school. Thought it was a handbook for the Future Farmers of America, about agriculture. I was a real hotshot in FFA."

After cautiously checking Frame's face, Kyle laughed. Even Peregrine looked amused, though Afton wasn't quite sure how it was that he did. He wasn't smiling, and his eyes didn't light up. It was just something that surrounded him . . . was given off by him . . . some hidden signals or primeval scent or minute changes in posture that she sensed on some deep, visceral level.

"Bet by about Chapter 3 you were surprised," Kyle rumbled.

"Naw. I was lost about the third sentence of Chapter 1. All about a Chinese woman and her big feet." Frame shook his head, and his eyes gleamed like onyx. "But by Chapter 3 I'd kinda figured out what she was getting at."

"Not surprised," Kyle said shrewdly. "Seems like you and her are a lot alike."

"Yep," Frame said with satisfaction.

Peregrine, to Afton's vast amusement, made a big production out of staring at Frame's feet with an air of great mystery. Kyle and Joel Frame ignored him.

"Anyway, what did you think, Mr. Frame?" Kyle asked again, growing earnest. "About the set? The props? Have you seen inside the cabin?"

Frame shifted his weight, took a cautious sip of his coffee, and sucked his bottom lip. "Yep. Peregrine showed it to me yesterday after all you people had left. Got a lot of fine things. Amazing to me that you could rake up all that old stuff that looks pretty new."

Kyle's eyes narrowed. "Mr. Frame, I paid a prissy man with a ponytail and eyeliner—name of Terry Bellingville III—a big bunch of money to figure out what was right for the scenes in this movie. He had to decide on and find and buy and ship every single thing you see. Every jar. Every piece of crockery. Every piece of paper. Every kitchen rag."

"Reckon that's your basic Production and Set Designer's job, is it?" Frame mused. "They make a lot of money, do they?"

"He did," Kyle said. "Did he earn it?"

"Let's just say he bought an awful lot of old stuff that's in real good shape, Mr. Patton," Frame hedged, exchanging a glance with Peregrine.

Kyle sighed. "Okay, give it to me. I can take it. And I really want to know. I really care."

Frame shrugged his work-stooped shoulders. "Them bottles you got, twinkling in the window. They're fine bottles. Look just as good as when they were made . . . in 1920."

Kyle blinked, then frowned ferociously.

Frame went on, "They're made from a two-piece mold. Kind you ought to have is a bottle that was made in a three-piece mold."

"What else?"

"Saw some marbles in there," Frame said cheerfully. "Nice blood alleys."

"They had marbles back then," Kyle said defensively.

"Sure they did, Mr. Patton. Clay marbles. Glass marbles weren't made until 1930."

Kyle groaned, and Frame now looked repentant. Quickly Kyle took a deep breath and said, "Just go ahead. Tell me all of it."

"Awright, son." Frame shrugged. "You got the wrong kind of lamps, you got your manufactured joints in the bedroom furniture, that lady's wearing shoes that won't be around for another twenty-five years, that Browning rifle's maybe twenty years ahead of its time."

"Anything else?" Kyle demanded.

Peregrine, who had been looking around vaguely and humming tunelessly, muttered under his breath, "Oxen."

Kyle rounded on him with frustration. "Peregrine, even you know that oxen were in existence back then."

"Yes, sir," he readily agreed.

Frame looked at Peregrine curiously. "What about the oxen?"

Peregrine looked up at the morning sun, that same sun that had received so much movie-star attention this morning. "Eight of 'em."

Frame's eyes grew as round as the blood alley marbles he'd just been talking about. He looked at Kyle, dumbfounded, and Kyle stared back at him, mystified. Frame sputtered, "Did he say eight? Mr. Patton, your Mr. Ponytail bought you *eight oxen?*"

"That's right," Kyle said, completely confused.

Frame's face worked strangely; either he was about to sneeze, or he was desperately attempting to arrange it into the expression he intended. "Eight?" he repeated.

"Yep," Peregrine answered in a bored tone. "Gotta pull a log, you know."

This was much too much for Joel Frame. He burst into raucous laughter that came from deep down in his belly.

Afton, who was quite as mystified as her father, was watching Peregrine. When Joel Frame dissolved into helpless laughter, the corners of Peregrine's mouth turned up—he actually smiled!

Afton smiled too. Then she found that she was laughing like an idiot, even though she still didn't get the joke.

"What's so funny!" Kyle demanded darkly.

"I—I don't know," Afton stammered, desperately trying to stifle her giggles.

"Whatcha gonna do with them eight oxen, Mr. Patton?" Frame asked, wiping his eyes. "Drag Kentucky to New Jersey?"

Kyle stared at him, his hazel eyes sparking dangerously. Afton grew anxious, watching him, as it appeared that an explosion was imminent. But then his jaw worked, his eyes crinkled, and he began to laugh. "I think I'm beginning to see your point. Eight oxen—little overdone, huh?"

"Little," Frame agreed.

Kyle shook his head with a mingling of exasperation and

amusement. "Can't wait to tell Stella the good news and the bad news. Bad news is that we got a whole caravan full of useless props and a cabin that looks like a city kid's playhouse."

Frame couldn't resist. "And the good news?"

"Good news is," Kyle answered with a wry grin, "that we got enough oxen to haul the whole pile back to California."

NINE

◇

AFTER THE BREAK, the crew started setting up the "snap beans and sky" shot again. Charlie Terrill primped and patted and brushed Messalina and Tru. Harlan Freeman was everywhere at once, pointing and giving orders to assistants who scurried frantically to do incomprehensible things to inexplicable electrical tangles. Dave Steiner ran back and forth around the four cameras, peering through the lens and yelling about the lights. Houston Rees was all over the set, checking and rechecking props and even policing the place for unscripted sticks and rocks and dirt clods.

Afton was watching, settling into her chair for another long session of staying out of everyone's way, when she saw Peregrine. He was just disappearing into the woods in the direction of the barn.

Before she thought about it too much, Afton jumped up and slipped through the frantic crew activities unnoticed and followed him. By the time she'd reached the edge of the woods he had already disappeared. With a little tinge of disgust, she reflected that she must feel exactly as Roy Dale Puckett had said he did; she just couldn't bring herself to stand in the woods and halloo for Peregrine like some crazy lost woman. So she forged ahead to the barn, and when she came out into the clearing she saw him.

At first she thought he was doing something absurd, as the child-man Peregrine seemed wont to do. He was posed right in the middle of the open pasture by the barn on a small mound. His leonine head was thrown back. His left arm was thrust straight up toward the sky.

Afton was motionless, silent. Even though his posture seemed odd, she was still drawn to him with an urgency that bewildered her. He was compelling, so dramatic . . . primitive, mysterious, simple, unreachable, unknowable.

Not true, Afton argued with her thoughts with a vehemence that startled her. *I know him . . . I know some of him. I know that stupid, illiterate dirt farmer act is his joke upon the world; he plays it absurd, he plays it silly, he plays it broadly, he plays it thinly . . . but it's still just theatrics.*

Afton sighed deeply, unable to take her eyes off Peregrine's statue-still figure. *So, Afton lass, where does that get you? Knowing no more than yesterday, 'twould seem so . . .*

Why does he put on the Peregrine mask?

Who is he?

The heavy silence was rent by a wild scream from the sky. Afton shivered; she knew that cry, and she'd always thought that it was so wild, so primeval, it could have been the first sound heard in God's world.

Throwing her head back, she searched the brightness until she found it. High, star-high, wheeling and circling, gliding and dancing, the hawk drew an invisible vortex in the air with Peregrine at the center. With a suddenness that took Afton's breath, the hawk turned itself into a bullet that disappeared until it refashioned itself on Peregrine's gauntleted arm.

"Ohh . . ." she murmured, enchanted.

Peregrine heard her. Snapping his head around, he saw her instantly, and his face lit up; then quickly his alert, intense expression was replaced by a dull, polite greeting. "Howdy, Miss Afton," he called. "You wanna come see my bird?"

"Yes, I'd like that," Afton answered and made her way to the fence. Peregrine fiddled with his heavy leather glove for a moment, and the bird adjusted itself, batting its wings with ill humor. Then he made his way to the fence line to meet Afton. She noticed that Peregrine kept his elbow bent and close to his side, with his fist outermost. With his right forefinger he smoothed the fussily ruffled feathers of the bird's breast.

"He's breathtaking," Afton breathed without preamble.

"She," Peregrine mumbled. "She is somethin', ain't she?"

Afton was disappointed; she had hoped Peregrine might drop his simpleton act if they were in private. Still, she determined to act naturally with him and hope that he might learn to trust her enough to let her see the real man—whoever or whatever he was. "What's her name?" Afton asked.

"Boadicea," he mumbled.

Afton was startled, and her eyes widened. "Boadicea? After Boadicea of the Iceni?"

"Yep, that's it," he said, nodding vigorously. "That's her whole name. But I usually just call her Boo."

Afton narrowed her eyes to knowing slits. "You even pronounce it correctly." The queen's name was pronounced "Boo-di-kuh." Afton had heard it pronounced a variety of interesting ways, even by Englishmen.

Peregrine merely shrugged helplessly, as if it weren't his fault he'd accidentally said it right.

"You know a lot about Roman and Celtic history, do you?" Afton asked sardonically. "Did you learn it the first time you were in third grade or the second?"

Golden bits of amusement flashed in Peregrine's eyes, and he turned to look at the bird. "Boadicea . . ." he murmured softly, and Afton thought he was speaking to the hawk, but then in a distant voice he went on, "She fought Roman legions to defend her daughters' virtue and for the honor of her tribe. She was magnificent and terrible . . . and she almost defeated them . . . she almost won."

Afton drew in a sharp breath, and her mind reeled. Peregrine was speaking passionately, eloquently—to her.

The too-brief moments passed, and Peregrine, with the abrupt movements of a child whose attention has wandered, turned to Afton. His otherworld eyes were steady on her, however, watching her as intently as if she were an insubstantial vision. She began to babble. "I—I was growing bored with the—the—scene they were shooting, and I saw you coming this way and thought perhaps I might come—um, see if Stonewall is here. I like dogs. And look— here's a very great surprise! A hawk!"

Reaching out her hand, she started to pet the bird's satiny head, but with serpent quickness Peregrine snatched her fingers away. "No, no—sorry, Miss Afton, but don't do it that way. She doesn't like anything touching her where she can't see it coming and isn't sure what it is."

Though Afton was startled, she still shot back, "Yes, I suppose you'd understand that sentiment very well."

Peregrine's wolf-eyes flickered. Then he gently brushed Afton's fingers down the bird's breast. Boo seemed resigned to it. Slowly, his hand holding hers as gently as if it too were a small wild bird,

Peregrine and Afton petted the hawk. With each stroke Peregrine moved further and further up the bird's chest, until their fingers were brushing right under the cruel beak.

Afton seemed to be hypnotized or paralyzed or both; she had the most peculiar sensation that she was in a dream, a dream that would go on and on forever, just her and Peregrine, stroking and calming the wildly beautiful hawk.

Abruptly Peregrine dropped Afton's fingers and busily adjusted the jesses that encircled the bird's claws. "She's a falcon, you know. All falcons is hawks. But not all hawks is falcons."

Afton, feeling as if she'd been rudely wrenched awake, nevertheless recovered from her dissociative condition. "Yes, I know. Falcons are the nobles in a society of aristocrats. She's a peregrine, isn't she?" Afton asked with mild interest.

Now it was Peregrine's turn to stare at Afton, nonplussed. "You know falcons?"

"Not much." Afton stroked the bird again, now confident. "A little. I know she's a peregrine because even though hawking hasn't been fashionable since the eighteenth century in England, in Scotland they've always used peregrines for hunting grouse. They still do. They are quite distinctive, even among hawks, aren't they? Especially their eyes. I always thought that peregrines had human eyes, only a thousand times better."

Boadicea was a spectacularly handsome hawk. Compact and athletic, she sat quietly enough, seemingly content with the company and the attention. But even in that stillness, sitting relaxed upon Peregrine's fist, her breast feathers now loose and sheened, she had an aura of fierce strength, of innocent cruelty, of compact power. The feathers on her slate-blue back were as tightly laid and seemed as impervious as a coat of mail. Her wings were so long, the dark primaries crossed nearly at the end of her white-tipped tail. Afton touched her breast again; it was a lovely shade of pearl gray striped laterally with delicate black lines except over her crop, which was a soft salmon pink. The base of her beak was butter yellow, but the iron curve of it was a polished onyx black.

And her eyes, indeed, were not at all like other hawks' eyes. All birds of prey, except the peregrine, had small, round eyes of hard glass. Boadicea's eyes were large, a liquid black, expressive. At her first contact with Afton, the bird had assessed her with a hungry hunter's eye and had found her unsuitable; now she looked upon Afton with a tolerance that was akin to politeness. Afton could swear that the bird's lustrous eyes perceptibly softened when she looked at Peregrine.

"How did you find her?" Afton asked.

"I shot her," Peregrine answered, and the raw depths of a grievous pain was clear in those three hard words. "It was an accident, of course. Peregrines are the fastest animal on the entire earth, did you know that? They can fly more than 200 miles an hour! That's almost twice as fast as an arrow on the fly. So I ask you, how the devil could I have possibly shot her? How, unless God thought it was some kind of sick way to—" He drew himself erect so jarringly that Afton heard a bone crack in his spine. "Uh, anyways," he continued in a thick, dull voice, "there she was, with an arrow stuck in her side. I took care of her and then set her a-loose. But she came back."

"And she keeps coming back to you?" Afton asked in a calm, safe tone.

"Uh-huh."

"Yes, well, I can certainly see why," she said crisply, ignoring

Peregrine's restless and somehow sad gesture of pushing her, or her words, away. "She loves you, Peregrine. She wants to be with you. She forgives you for what was simply a cruel accident. So you'd best forgive yourself."

He stared at her, and defiantly she lifted her chin. His chameleon's face shifted from rebellion to resentment and finally to a reluctant respect and admiration. "Miss Afton," he intoned, "you ever shot a longbow?"

◊ ◊ ◊

It wasn't until Afton and Peregrine actually walked onto the set that she realized exactly how odd they must look. Peregrine slouching along, vacant vagabond grin intact, fiddling with one glove, Boadicea's leather gauntlet. Behind him the gargoyle dog padded silently. Afton walked beside him, laughing because Peregrine was again making sly dumb-shrewd jokes about the great surplus of oxen "General Patton" owned. Peregrine kept calling him that and then pretended to be flustered at making the mistake.

As soon as Afton stepped into the clearing by the cabin, she was tremendously self-conscious. Here she was tripping along through the woods with some wild man, laughing flirtatiously. She pressed one hand to her cheek; it was warm, and she knew that her color was heightened and she looked overanimated, as women so often do when they're in the first stages of attracting a man's attention. Severely she told herself to calm down and tone down, but it was completely unnecessary. No one gave them a second look; in fact, Afton wasn't certain anyone had even given them a first look. Every single person on the set was immensely absorbed in the current scene, even though it wasn't being shot and wasn't actually in the movie.

Messalina Dancy had Kyle, Stella, Charlie Terrill, Dave Steiner, and even Joel Frame, Afton was aghast to see, lined up in a ragged row. She was striding up and down, an angry drill sergeant dressing down the knobs.

"I'm telling you, Kyle, that I look much too beautiful! And so does Tru! It doesn't do one whit of good for me to act my head off if I look like the prom queen wearing her mother's old clothes in the school play! And Tru looks exactly like True Blue Dawkins, only without the cop's uniform! And what does Charlie do? He boofs me and puffs me and twitches my hair and brushes and combs and straightens me! It's wrong, wrong, wrong!"

"But, Messalina—" Charlie said helplessly. It was incongruous to see the big man so cowed, and also to picture him "boofing and poofing" anyone.

"Shut up, Charlie!" Messalina thundered. "Can't you see I'm trying to make a point here? Here I am, after years of work, hard work, grinding, desolate work—and that's just to grow good snap beans! And what do I look like? I look like I've never seen a piece of dirt or a minute's work in my life! So what are you going to do about it?"

"But, Messalina—" Charlie said again.

"Am I right, Kyle?" Messalina asked belligerently, then continued on with magnificent disregard for the fact that Kyle had opened his mouth to answer. "You know exactly what I'm talking about, don't you, Stella? Of course you do, you're an actress, you know! And you, Mr. Frame! I'll bet your mother or grandmother or whoever sure didn't look like me at the end of the day!"

"Nope, neither one of 'em ever did, Miss Dancy," Frame solemnly promised.

Peregrine whispered, "Looks like Miss Dancy's found her motivation. 'Bout two tons of it."

Afton nodded agreement.

Messalina stopped pacing up and down like an angry tiger and stood, her fine head cocked to the side, her hands stuck on her hips indignantly. "Don't you see what this scene is about? This is an important scene, people! Here I am—I'm tired, I'm beat down, and I'm looking at a lifetime of more work. . . and there's my husband—" She pointed accusingly at Tru, who looked greatly alarmed. ". . . who's being ground down too, and it grieves me! But yet there's something drawing me, something that I can't quite grasp yet . . . but I'm just beginning to get the first glimmer of true understanding." She jabbed her finger toward the cabin. "That is my home, and I'm just now realizing how precious it is, how wonderful it is to earn something, because then you truly do own it, forever. So look at me! What do I look like?"

"Mad?" Joel Frame was the only one with guts enough to attempt an answer.

Messalina grandly ignored him. "I look fresh and cute!"

Peregrine grunted loudly, but Afton poked him in the ribs, and he grew quiet.

Messalina suddenly became peaceful, her shoulders rounded, her hands fallen at her sides. Afton could only see her face in profile, but it magically transformed into an older woman's face, a tired face, but a good face with lines and creases of wisdom honestly earned. "I don't look weary," Messalina said with a tinge of sadness. "I need to look weary . . . but triumphant. Because I'm just beginning to understand about self-sacrifice and commitment and the price to be paid and the rewards to be earned . . ."

The longest, heaviest silence Afton had ever been a party to fell upon the frozen group in the clearing.

Then, slowly, Peregrine began to clap.

Over 100 faces turned toward them in shock. Peregrine's expression was so still and blank that once again he'd successfully immersed himself in a well of idiocy. Still he beat his hands together slowly.

Then as one the whole assembly began to applaud.

Messalina looked around, stunned for a moment. Then, smiling beatifically, she made a graceful curtsey.

The applause stopped, the crew eventually went back to their beehive buzzes, and still Messalina stood with her "troops." "Too bad I didn't film that," Dave sighed. "That might have been the scene of your life, Miss Dancy."

"No," she said imperturbably, "that achievement is going to be in this movie. If someone can figure out how to help me—help me—"

"Get uglified?" Frame offered with a flash of boyish mischief. He shook his head. "That ain't gonna be easy, Miss Dancy, 'cause you are one magnificent woman."

"Thank you," she said calmly.

Kyle, almost in a daze, turned to Joel Frame. "Can you help me?" he asked, almost pleaded. Afton's heart swelled, for her father could, at the most peculiar times, show such an endearing and childlike trust and innocence. "I'll kill myself if I lose—lose Anna Kay Wingfield because I don't know how to help her."

"Ain't no need for suicides," Frame said dryly. He squinted his eyes, his features intent. "Lemme think on it a minute." With the deliberate motions of a man who's concentrating on solving a complex problem, Frame walked to the cane-bottomed chair, pulled it out a bit, sat himself down, and then leaned it back against the cabin wall. Crossing his arms, he stared off into darkening woods.

Charlie, now relaxed, walked in circles around Messalina, studying her as if she were a particularly interesting display in a store. The actress stood patiently, quietly, her hands loose and relaxed at her sides. "Your hair, Miss Dancy," Charlie said quietly. "It is too finely done. We were going for a severe look—" He reached up one meat-hook hand to touch it, perhaps to "boof" it, Afton reflected with amusement. "But instead it just looks sophisticated and elegant. I think I could still pull it back, you know—would you let me trim it a little? Then I could get some loose tendrils around your face and neck, but not so you look like—uh—"

"A French aristocrat's whore?" Messalina offered slyly. "That's what I looked like in my last movie, even though I played a schoolteacher."

"Well . . ." Charlie stalled cautiously.

"Yes, you can cut it, Charlie," Messalina said graciously. "Whatever I scream at you, you know I trust you."

"I know," he said, a little abashed. "I won't butcher it, Lina. I can cut it to where it'll still look pretty." He caressed her satin-fine blonde hair for a moment. "You have such good hair," he said clinically. "You're lucky—you can mistreat it and abuse it and you still look great."

"You're so sweet," Messalina said absently. "Well, Stella? What do you think?"

One corner of Stella's lips turned up sardonically. "I think I

now know why I was never, and never could be, an actress of your
caliber, Messalina. You really are magical. You have such a great
gift. I hope you appreciate it."

Messalina shrugged, then hurried off, suddenly noticing that
Dave Steiner was doing something she evidently didn't like with
one of the cameras.

Kyle and Stella started talking about changing the actress's costumes, about possibilities for lighting changes to make Messalina
look more harsh, about the various backgrounds that would affect
her coloring. With a relieved air, Tru Kirk evidently felt he was dismissed, and he ambled over to where Peregrine and Afton still
stood, watching and listening.

"She's something, isn't she?" Tru said admiringly. "I'll never be
anything like that. I'll never come across with that heat, even if I
was set on fire."

"No, you're quite different, Mr. Kirk," Afton solidly maintained. "And frankly, I think that you trying to emote such unre-
strained passions would be quite ludicrous and untrue."

His brow furrowed, and his mild blue eyes were hesitant. "You
think so, Miss Burns?"

"I know so. You—you're calm, you're serene, you're like a
slow-moving river, like a weathered boulder that's stood for cen-
turies—" Afton broke off, embarrassed at her effusiveness. She
knew that Truman Kirk was a heartthrob and that women acted
like mooncalves around him. She certainly didn't want to come
across like some adolescent groupie.

But Truman Kirk was a simple man who enjoyed simple plea-
sures and had an unquestioning belief in people's sincerity that
reflected his own uncomplicated honesty. "Why, thank you so

much, Miss Burns," he said with obvious pleasure. "That makes me
feel a little better. I know I'm not the star of this movie—Messalina
is. But I don't want to just be a mumbler in the corner either 'cause
John Allen Wingfield isn't."

"No, he isn't," Afton confirmed.

"What is he?" Peregrine guilelessly asked Tru.

"Why, he's strong, he loves his wife, he loves God," Tru
answered without thinking. "He's a simple man, but not stupid.
He's just quiet, just takes time to think about things. Needs his pri-
vacy to make decisions, and then he works real hard to make the
right ones."

"Uh-huh, thought so," Peregrine remarked idly. "You seem like
that kinda man."

Comprehension of Peregrine's tactics slowly dawned on the big
man's gentle face. "Yeah? I've done that, you think?"

"Mr. Kirk, you *are* that," Afton answered. "So you hardly need
to worry about any acting lessons."

Turning, he watched Messalina as she animatedly moved
around, joking with this one, frowning at that one, bossing the
other one. He smiled. "Maybe not. Thanks, Miss Burns. Thanks,
Peregrine."

"Please call me Afton," she insisted.

"Okay, if you'll just call me Tru. It's my real name, you know,"
he added with a tinge of embarrassment. "Not a stage name, I
mean. Truman Kirk is my real name, but everybody just calls me
Tru."

"Thank you, Tru," Afton said.

"Well," Peregrine drawled, "I reckon you can call me
Peregrine."

"Uh—thanks, Peregrine," Tru said quickly.

"Peregrine, perhaps you should get a stage name," Afton said mischievously. "Since no one around here uses their real name. Except for Mr. Kirk—I mean Tru."

"I'll study about it," Peregrine said with a thoughtful air. "Miss Burns. Miss Afton Burns." Then in a singsong voice he recited, almost sang, like a child's nursery rhyme:

"Flow gently, sweet Afton! among thy green braes,

Flow gently, I'll sing thee a song in thy praise . . ."

"That's a poem, isn't it?" Tru asked, frowning.

"It sure is," Afton said, casting a jaundiced eye upon Peregrine's doltish expression. "By Robert Burns."

"'Sweet Afton' . . . by Robert Burns . . ." Truman worked it out with difficulty. "Afton Burns?"

"That's exactly right," Afton declared, still staring suspiciously at Peregrine. "But most people don't put it together. Most people don't know about Robert Burns, a rather obscure poet worldwide, but generally considered to be Scotland's voice. And certainly most people don't know the poem 'Sweet Afton.'"

"They don't?" Peregrine said innocently.

"But I just have one question," Truman said.

"Hmm?" Afton said absently, still staring at Peregrine, who was watching her with an unreadable expression.

"What's your real name?" Truman asked.

"Sweet Afton, that's it," Peregrine answered quietly. "Sweet Afton, for sure."

TEN

◇

WASHING."

Joel Frame stood up and pronounced the single word with the reverent air of a philosopher revealing the secret of the mystery of life.

People were scattered around and looked at him curiously. Kyle was standing nearby, arguing about something with Stella and Houston, but he looked up alertly when Joel spoke. "I beg your pardon, Mr. Frame?"

"Washing." Frame repeated the word impatiently. "Where's Miss Dancy?"

Still obviously puzzled, but eager to work with the shrewd old man, Kyle ordered a nearby crew member, "Go to Miss Dancy's trailer and ask her to come out here please. And somebody go find—oh, there's Tru." He signaled, and Truman hurried over, followed by Afton and Peregrine.

Messalina joined them, and Joel Frame stared at her with a clearly assessing eye. "Miss Dancy, you got a washer and dryer?"

Although the actress was as mystified as everyone else, she answered Joel Frame respectfully, as people were inclined to do. "Yes, I do, Mr. Frame."

"Do your own laundry?"

"Well, no. Not anymore. I have a maid."

"Uh-huh," he nodded knowingly. "What about ironing? Folding? Putting the stuff away? Thought not. Hard work, isn't it? Time-consuming."

"Yes, it is," Messalina agreed.

Frame nodded. Still in a deep reverie, he walked over to where a gaggle of canvas chairs were huddled together, with Kyle's director's chair in the middle. Followed by the little group, they all moved the chairs around until they were in a loose circle, then seated themselves. Except for Peregrine, who resumed his stance leaning against the refreshment trailer nearby. Stonewall sat alertly beside him.

"Lemme tell you a story," Frame said. "About my grandmother. I used to watch her when I was real little, too little to help. Then when I got bigger, I was out with my daddy and granddaddy haulin' timber. But my granny, see, she used to do the washing once a week. But it'd take two days.

"First she'd lay a good fire in a little pit, and she'd drag out a great big black kettle. She'd pour a little cool water in it before the fire got going real good, to keep from cracking it, you see. Then she'd haul out two more kettles, for rinse water, and she'd set up a battlin' bench my daddy had made her out of a hard old chestnut tree."

"What's a battlin' bench?" Messalina asked with interest.

"Oh, it's just a long piece of wood, stood on legs so it'd be about waist high," Frame answered, his eyes warm with memory. "About a foot wide, maybe four feet long. We called it that 'cause you'd take the clothes or sheet or whatever out of the hot water, one at a time, and work on it with paddles. Squish it around, like, to make the lye soap work through and through, and then you'd 'battle' it out with a paddle. Then she'd rinse it and battle it again and scrub out any heavy stains. Then she'd dump the whole lot back into the hot water and boil them so the soap would work its way into the creases.

"After about twenty minutes of boiling them, they had to be lifted out, steaming, and carried over to the other tub and rinsed. My mama rinsed everything twice, in two kettles. After that, she shook 'em out and hung 'em up to dry."

Kyle, Afton, Messalina, Dave, and Charlie all looked completely absorbed, thinking about and visualizing the brutal work of the simple chore that Joel Frame had described. Stella looked slightly bored and lit a cigarette each time she finished the last puff of one.

After a long time of quiet reverie, Kyle murmured, "That might be it . . . that could . . . be . . ."

Messalina said quickly and firmly, "That is it, Kyle. And I want to do it. All of it. I don't care if it takes two days. You can just shoot the whole thing if you want and edit out whatever. But I'm going to do it. Mr. Frame, could you explain to the crew or some of those cabin persons how to make a—a—battlin' bench? And where do you suppose we could find three big kettles? One of them black, did you say? . . . Oh, yes, blackened from the fire, of course. And paddles? What kind of paddles? How big?"

Joel Frame held up one gnarled hand. "Just rein in your team there, Miss Dancy. I thought of this 'cause I kinda had an idea about helpin' Mr. Patton out with props and things. See, there's the Bowie County Heritage Museum just a few miles from my place. I think they might have everything you need to furnish this cabin. I know they got an old battlin' bench and bottles and chairs and even beds and quilts and such. I think I could persuade the museum board to let you use the stuff."

"Oh?" Kyle said eagerly. "That would be just great, Mr. Frame. Just great! Do you think they would? I mean, a museum's exhibits and all . . ."

"Since they're all Mr. Frame's stuff," Peregrine piped up, "I 'magine he can talk them into letting you borrow it."

Frame smiled. "You know, it would be kind of a thrill for me to see my mama's and daddy's and grandparents' stuff in a movie."

Messalina, still Anna Kay Wingfield, clamored, "But what about soap? What kind of soap did you say they used?"

"Lye soap, Miss Dancy," Frame replied.

"I want you to get me some lye soap, Kyle," she announced firmly.

"But, Lina, I don't think you can buy that stuff anymore," Kyle said helplessly.

Frame grunted. "You didn't buy the stuff, Mr. Patton. You made it. Leached it out of wood ashes."

"Then where can we buy some wood ashes? And some leach?" Messalina demanded.

"Buy some—" Frame stopped his helpless exclamation and shook his head. "Miss Dancy, I gotta tell you, you're a great actress. Even an old ignorant lumberjack like me can see that. But why don't you just let me worry about the washing. I'll make sure it's right. And, ma'am, I think you're going to find that it's gonna weary you real good, just like you're wantin'."

"That's good," Messalina murmured with satisfaction. "That's very, very good."

Frame sighed. "Yes, ma'am. If you say so."

◊ ◊ ◊

The company at dinner was relaxed, even jolly. Houston Rees seemed at ease for the first time since Afton had been with them. Messalina, who was normally easily offended and caustic, was rapturous at the thought of her washing chores the next day. Truman was a little subdued, for Kyle had broken the news to him that he would start working with Peregrine and the oxen in the morning. He was game, however.

Stella, in contrast to the rest of the company, looked tired and was irritable. After the first course—she'd picked at a rather indifferent-looking shrimp cocktail—she pleaded a headache and excused herself to go to bed.

Afton stayed until her father was ready to retire, which was after he'd talked long and animatedly with Charlie, Dave, Harlan, and Houston about the change in plans. She watched and listened with quiet joy, for her father was not now the morose and half-drunk man who usually finished his dinner at eleven o'clock. He ate and drank sparingly and was as excited and cheerful as a sixteen-year-old boy with a new car.

The two walked to their rooms together, and Afton savored the time. She rarely got to be alone with her father. "It looks like the tide has turned," he told her, grinning. "It was just one disaster after another crisis after another calamity when we got here. But now things are really shaping up. I've kind of . . . regained my vision." He looked at her stealthily. "Thanks to Mr. Joel Frame—and you."

"Me?" Afton was genuinely surprised. "Not me! I've done nothing except get in the way, it seems. I'm no help at all."

"Not in making movies," Kyle admitted, and went on with some difficulty, "but you've helped me, Afton. You've helped me more than you'll ever know."

"But how?"

Kyle shrugged and looked down at his feet. He walked so slowly that he and Afton were barely moving. "I thought I'd never forget anything about your mother," he said in a low, strained voice. "But it turns out I'd forgotten everything about her. Everything important, that is." Finally he looked at Afton. "I'd forgotten that there are people who are truly good and honest. People who are real all the time, every day, and who are proud to be exactly what they are without trying to be more, to be better, to be—other."

"Thank you, Father," Afton said with quiet dignity. "I'm proud that my mother was like that, and I'm so happy that she instilled it in me."

"Yes, she did, Afton," Kyle said, his eyes roaming over her face, her hair. "But there are things about women that can't be taught to them or assumed by them. Virtue. Purity. Innocence. It was so difficult for me to believe that's what Jenny was. And now I'm seeing it all over again, miraculously . . . in you."

Afton was a little embarrassed and averted his gaze.

"I'm so proud of you," Kyle said, "and that is exactly what's helped me. I'm proud of you, and I want you to be proud of me. Afton, it's a great thing to have the respect and admiration of a person like you. And that's what I want."

Afton took her father's arm and entwined her own. "I already have a great respect for you, Father, and there are many qualities about you that I do admire."

Kyle grinned down at her, patting her cold fingers. "I said you were honest. That was a qualified statement, but tactfully and cleverly disguised."

Afton teased, "You have enough flatterers and camp followers, General Patton. You'll just have to take it straight from me."

"Glad to," he said affably. They'd reached Afton's door, and Kyle stopped her before she went inside. "Afton, this will sound odd, but it's true—you and I don't know each other very well yet. But I want you to know that because you're my daughter, I love you. I would love you even if you weren't such a wonderful girl. I've been a lousy father, I know, but I'm finding out that I am a father, and I have a father's feelings. I just wanted to tell you that."

He slipped away before Afton could say a word.

She was exhausted and fell asleep immediately after a quick shower.

Until she was interrupted by voices, loud and urgent. And insistent knocking on her door.

Afton's eyes flew open, and she bolted upright in bed. "Coming!"

She threw on a flannel robe and clutched it around her in the cold room, then wrenched open the door.

Her father stood there, his face ashen, his eyes wild. "Afton, Afton, what are we going to do?"

"What . . . what is it?" Afton asked with dread.

"The cabin," Kyle grated in a hoarse voice. "There was a fire. It's gone. Everything's gone!"

◊ ◊ ◊

Afton thought her father was exaggerating the tragedy, and said so. "It's not such a great loss, Father. After all, you had decided not to use any of the props. And all anyone has ever said about that cabin was that it wasn't right anyway. And you're insured against such losses, aren't you?"

"Of course," he said bleakly. "But you don't understand, Afton. It takes time to realize an insurance settlement on a loss. And this movie was running on the thinnest sliver of a shoestring you ever saw. I just don't have the money to replace everything—and to pay everyone for the downtime. And besides, we've already shot a week's worth of footage featuring that cabin! Time, Afton, time and not the loss of money or property is what's going to ruin me. I've got a deadline hanging over me on this movie, with not an inch of wiggling room. It's hopeless."

Accusingly he jabbed his forefinger at the black, smoking square of earth. The cabin and everything in it had been reduced to a pile of dirty ashes. Pieces of colored bottles sparkled, out of place in the ruins, and chunks of fired earthenware stuck out of the blackness. The crockery wouldn't have burned, of course, and probably the fire wouldn't have been hot enough to even blister it. But it had all been broken, falling when the wooden shelves holding it had burned to nothing.

"Oh, I'm so sorry, Father. I didn't understand," Afton murmured.

They stood together, looking at the devastation, without saying anything more. Afton slid closer to her father. With a deep sigh, his hand brushed against hers; she clasped it and held it.

A pickup truck drove up. Peregrine and Joel Frame were still climbing out when two of the company Jeeps wheeled in behind them. Peregrine and Joel Frame came to stand by Afton and Kyle. "Sure sorry about this, Mr. Patton," Frame said quietly. "Gotta put a crinkle in your movie."

"Yeah, you could say that," Kyle agreed without emotion. He was a tired and defeated man. Joel Frame glanced sharply at him, and Peregrine too searched his face. Then he looked questioningly at Afton, and she shrugged helplessly.

Several sets of footsteps sounded behind them, but Kyle seemed too apathetic to even turn around. Finally Stella said in a disapproving voice, "Kyle, Rini's here."

"What?" That brought Kyle out of his blue funk all right. The four turned to see Stella, Houston Rees, Charlie Terrill, Dave Steiner, and another man in a phalanx behind them.

Stella made introductions in a smooth manner, and Afton studied Santorini Santangeli, the CEO and major shareholder of Monarch Cinema.

Afton supposed she had been rather expecting Marlon Brando from *The Godfather*, and Santorini Santangeli was nothing at all like that, or any other Italian stereotype. Tall, dark-haired with distinguished gray at the temples, he was an elegantly slim man with an aura of sophistication. His gray, pin-striped suit was exclusive, with that intangible quality that immensely expensive clothing always has. His eyes, dark, heavy-lashed, and heavy-lidded, were piercing and predatory, and his jawline was unyielding. His voice, however, was pleasing, with an intimate quality. To Afton's surprise, he stepped forward and embraced her father and then kissed him on both cheeks. When Stella introduced Afton and she offered him her hand, he bent over it as if to kiss it, but he actually just barely brushed his firm lips against her skin.

Stella perfunctorily introduced Joel Frame and Peregrine as if they were characters from some squeaky-clean sitcom rerun—perhaps *The Beverly Hillbillies*—and Frame shook Rini's hand in a distant manner. Peregrine threw up his hands and said, "You ain't gonna kiss me, are you, mister?"

Only Frame laughed, and he did it without uneasiness at the great tension of the scene. Santangeli's eyes flickered for an instant, but then he turned back to Kyle, effectively dismissing the two men.

"Kyle, I can't tell you how very sorry I am for the great difficulties you've been having on this film," Santangeli said with an air of tragedy. "And now this." He motioned to the desolate cabin site.

"Thanks, Rini, I appreciate the sentiment," Kyle said slowly. "But—you'll excuse me, I know you understand I'm still a little frayed around the edges—but what are you doing here? And how did you get here so quickly? The cabin just burned last night, or rather early this morning."

"No, no, my friend, I didn't come here because the cabin burned," Santangeli protested. He made a quick, very Italian gesture with his well-manicured hands. Afton noticed an enormous ruby pinky ring that sparkled like dark blood in the weak light. "I came because you seemed to be having so many troubles, little difficulties, frustrations. And now with this—" He gestured eloquently toward the smoking ruin. ". . . I'm glad I did. I have a proposition for you, and I can see now that I can really help you out, Kyle."

Peregrine, Joel Frame, and Afton drifted off discreetly, to distance themselves from what was obviously a private business matter between Kyle and Santangeli. Afton muttered under her breath, "Marvelous. Mr. Santangeli is going to make my father an offer he can't refuse."

To Afton's surprise, both Joel Frame and Peregrine chuckled at this reference to the most famous line in *The Godfather*. Wearily she realized that it wasn't very funny—because it was probably the truth.

They walked back to Frame's truck. Afton leaned against the front bumper, grateful for the still-warm engine. The morning was bleak and raw and cold. Winter was waiting in the wings, preparing to burst onto center stage. Afton tried to make desultory conversation about the weather, but all three of them were very conscious of the knot of people nearby. Kyle's voice was high with tension, and Rini Santangeli's was clear and carried easily. So Afton, Joel, and Peregrine could not help but overhear most of the conversation.

". . . advance you some more, Kyle, all you need to finish this film in style," Rini was saying persuasively.

"What about the deadline?" Kyle asked wearily.

"Well, if you go ahead and let me refinance Summit Decipher now and put it under the Monarch Cinema umbrella, the deadline won't matter," Rini answered quickly. "The paper wouldn't be on Summit then—it would be included in Monarch's conglomerate, with access to Monarch's assets. It would be foolish for me to call a loan on my own company for a missed deadline."

Kyle was frowning with concentration, but his shoulders were rounded with weariness, and his whole demeanor was that of a man in despair. "How much would Monarch be willing to advance me?"

Rini smiled, and Afton thought it looked much like a shark's visage. "Kyle, you know that Monarch is a large and very successful company. It has assets and cash flow that I simply don't have personally, which is why I can't help you out by myself. Join

Monarch. We can sit down and work out a new budget, and a new deadline, and I'm pretty sure I could persuade the board to go along with whatever you need."

"I need two million," Kyle said in a dead voice.

"Done," Rini said instantly.

The lump of dread was a raw burn in Afton's throat.

Stella took Kyle's arm and patted it reassuringly. "It's the right thing to do, Kyle. It's the only thing to do."

"Yeah, I know," Kyle said listlessly. "Okay, Rini. You gonna go on back to L.A. and get the papers done?"

"Actually, Kyle, I've already taken care of that," Rini said ever so smoothly. "I was so optimistic about being able to help you out that I brought the numbers men and a first draft. Why don't we go on back to that fleabag hotel right now and get it done, so you and your people can get back to work? And by the way, of course I want you to allow plenty of room to pay everyone for their downtime . . ." He took Kyle's arm, leading him to one of the Jeeps. Stella followed them.

Charlie, Dave, and Houston stopped to speak to Afton and the two men. They looked as if they were going to a funeral. "Afton, why don't you and Dave take the Jeep Kyle brought out. Charlie and I'll take the other one," Houston said, still organizing people.

Joel Frame said lightly, "I've suddenly got a hankering for one of them Holiday Inn cinnamon buns they make special. Would you like to ride with me and Peregrine, Miss Afton?"

"I don't want to go to town," Peregrine said almost petulantly.

"Yes, you do," Joel Frame said firmly. "You like them cinnamon buns too."

"Good gracious, Peregrine, it's not Piccadilly Circus, you know," Afton said with unusual sharpness. "Thank you, Mr.

Rees, but I'm going to ride with Mr. Frame. Come along, Peregrine."

As they climbed into Frame's enormous Dodge Ram pickup, Peregrine muttered darkly, "Y' know, I never did insult Boo by trainin' her to a lure."

"No?" Afton retorted tartly. "Then perhaps you might consider that all along she was training you."

"That's what I'm afraid of," Peregrine grumbled.

"You are not," Afton argued. "I don't know what it is you're afraid of, Mister Peregrine, but it's not that some woman's going to housebreak you. And besides," she added with splendid disregard for the *non sequitur*, "none of this will get you out of my archery lesson this afternoon. We have a date."

"Like I said," Peregrine mumbled in his dummy monotone, "that's 'zactly what I'm afraid of."

Joel Frame obviously wasn't listening to Afton's and Peregrine's nonsense. He drove fast, keeping up with the Jeep in front that held Kyle and Rini, with Stella driving. They could see Rini, turned all the way around in the front seat, talking and gesturing to Kyle, who sat motionless in the backseat, staring straight ahead. Joel stared at them, his eyes narrowed, sucking on his lips.

Abruptly interrupting Afton as she was asking Peregrine about Stonewall and Boadicea, Joel asked, "That Mr. Santangeli, he's worth a lotta money, is he?"

"Lotta money," Afton repeated dully.

"Powerful man in Hollywood, it looks like."

"Powerful man," Afton agreed, sighing.

"Holding Kyle's paper on his production company, is he?" Frame asked.

"All his paper," Afton affirmed.

Frame shot an amused glance at Afton, who was staring blankly ahead. "You're startin' to talk like Peregrine," Frame teased. "Better watch the company you keep."

"Thanks," Peregrine muttered.

Ignoring him, Frame said, "I know it's not my business, Miss Afton. But I'm an old man with nothin' better to do than poke my nose where it don't belong—"

Peregrine made a funny grunting sound in his throat.

"—but I'm just real curious about this whole deal," Frame went on. "Lemme see if I got this straight, if you'll indulge me, Miss Afton. I can promise you I'll keep it confidential-like. Peregrine will too."

"I don't unnerstan' what anybody's talkin' about anyways," Peregrine said cheerfully.

"Yes, I'm so sure," Afton said sarcastically. "Mr. Frame, I'll be happy to tell you anything you want to know. In fact, it would be a great comfort to me to be able to talk to you about it because I know very well that you're not just a nosy old man, any more than he's a half-wit." She jabbed Peregrine sharply in the side with her elbow, and he mumbled, "Ouch," but Afton ignored him. "In fact, I would take it as a personal favor if you would—um, offer to counsel my father on this matter. He, too, has a great deal of confidence in you and respects you."

"Glad to hear you say that, ma'am," Frame said quietly. "'Cause I would kinda like to talk to your dad before he goes to makin' deals with the devil. But I'd like to know what I'm talking about before I start talking, if you get my meaning. Not like some other people."

"I know what I'm talking about," Peregrine said in an offended tone. "It's just that nobody else does."

"Good," Frame said, fashioning his own *non sequitur*. "'Cause I got an idea, boy, and you're gonna know what I'm talking about."

"Excuse me, but what do you mean?" Afton said, bewildered.

Peregrine's face mirrored Afton's puzzlement; he stared at Joel Frame, who seemed exceedingly pleased with himself. Sudden comprehension dawned on Peregrine's sculptured features, and he told her grimly, "It means, Miss Afton, that Mr. Joel Frame's gonna make me an offer I can't refuse."

ELEVEN

◇

WHEN THEY REACHED THE HOTEL, Afton insisted that she needed to go freshen up, for when her father had knocked on her door at 4:30 that morning to tell her about the fire, she had simply thrown on a pair of jeans and a heavy sweater and had left hurriedly. Now she was very self-conscious that she wasn't wearing makeup, though that wasn't the only reason she wanted a few minutes in private.

Mr. Frame courteously let her out at the breezeway that housed the stairs, and Afton almost ran to her room.

When the door closed securely behind her, she immediately fell down on her knees by the bed and prayed aloud. "Father, please don't let that man take over my father's business! Please, dear Lord . . . I feel so bad—something is wrong, very wrong."

For a long while Afton prayed in an earnest and heartfelt manner. As always, she felt very comfortable and secure in her prayers. Even when she was praying aloud she never felt self-conscious. Since she had been very young, Afton spoke with the Lord as other children spoke to their real fathers. Her mother had told her once that as a small child Afton couldn't understand why people—mostly well-meaning but ignorant adults—made com-

ments about "how sad it was about her father!" Afton had a
Father, the most wonderful Father anyone could ever hope for—
God Himself. In her mind she felt that people were a little silly
to wish she had another father, some strange man she could
hardly remember. And besides, she had her Grandfather
Malcolm.

Though Afton's notions of earthly fathers had slowly
changed, she never lost the complete, childlike trust that as a tiny
girl she had placed in the Holy Trinity. For Afton had also, apparently from the time she learned that words represent something,
understood the deep spiritual concept of the Three Persons in
One. As a little girl she often thought of and spoke to her Jesus,
was fully aware of her Holy Ghost's presence, and knew she could
always talk to her Father.

In that notion Afton had never changed. Now she spoke to her
heavenly Father about her earthly father in the most natural
manner.

Slowly, however, the urgency in her pleas changed, and her
voice became less strident. After a while she stopped speaking altogether. Afton wasn't truly aware of this—not in the nagging little
computer-piece of her mind that never shut up, even in the most
reverent of moments—but she just knew, somewhere in her heart,
that it was time for her to be silent.

As in any other conversations between people who loved each
other, now it was God's turn to talk, and Afton's to listen.

For some time Afton simply rested her spirit, and finally words
of Scripture came to her. "But without faith it is impossible to
please him: for he that cometh to God must believe that he is, and
that he is a rewarder of them that diligently seek him." For a long

time she simply let the words flow over her spirit, and then the Scripture that had never left her since her flight from Scotland nudged at her—"Oh thou of little faith, wherefore didst thou doubt?"

Afton felt a gentle rebuke and whispered, *Lord, I believe, help thou mine unbelief!*

She was quiet for a long time, her face utterly absorbed, her eyes closed. Then she sighed, a breath from deep in her soul. "Yes, I see, Lord. You're right, of course. Thank You so much, Father, and I'll do everything I can for him."

She stood up and began to apply her makeup and brush her hair. But as was the norm for Afton's walk with the Lord, she kept up the conversation with Him, much as two people might do who have an intense face-to-face conversation, come to resolve a problem, and then keep talking to each other in passing.

Of course, I should have known, Afton admitted to herself and to the Lord. *It's just so difficult, Father, to see someone you love slowly, slowly sinking . . . But now I see that it doesn't really matter whether he loses Summit Decipher or not. His work, his entire life, is meaningless unless You bless it and make him satisfied and content . . . But of course You can't do that if he won't let You.*

Your will be done.

Eagerly now Afton finished her makeup, checked her hair, changed into a soft turtleneck sweater with a houndstooth wool jacket, and hurried back down to the restaurant.

Joel and Peregrine sat at one of the four-seater tables. They were the only people in the restaurant except for a bored hostess and a waitress who was busy refilling salt and pepper shakers and sugar packets in little wire holders. When Afton came to the table, both Joel Frame and Peregrine hastily rose, and Peregrine held out Afton's chair to help her get seated.

"That's so nice, thank you, gentlemen," she said, smiling at the two men. "And so rare these days."

"My mama woulda whipped me good if I didn't stand for ladies arrivin' or leavin'," Joel Frame grumbled. "Young idiots nowadays wonder where you're goin' when you stand up to respect a lady."

"And you, Peregrine?" Afton asked with innocent politeness. "Was it your mother who taught you such lovely manners?"

The instant withdrawal that darted over Peregrine's features made Afton sorry that she'd baited him. Before he could answer, she trilled on a little desperately, "So, have either of you seen my father? Do we know where Mr. Santangeli has him cornered now?"

"In there," Joel answered, jabbing his thumb toward a door at the back of the dining room. "That's a little spare room they call a 'conference room.' Mostly the waitresses and cooks have their conferences back there, I think. But it does have a twelve-seater table."

Even before Frame finished speaking, the door was wrenched open rather rudely, and Kyle Patton stalked out, talking over his shoulder. He was closely followed by Stella, and Rini wasn't far behind. "Rini, I know you're a busy man. We're all busy. But I can't see that the world's going to come to an end if you give me an hour or so to check over this agreement."

"But my flight back is early this evening," Rini complained.

Kyle came to a mid-stride halt, turned, and crossed his arms. Afton, Joel, and Peregrine couldn't see his face, but his voice was heavy with resentment.

"Rini, are you telling me you flew commercial?" Kyle demanded. "I know that's a bald-faced lie. You haven't set foot on a commercial flight for twenty years."

"No—no, we're in the Lear," Rini said with hasty smoothness. "But I do have to go back to L.A. soon. I have another pressing meeting this evening. C'mon, Kyle, I just want to wind this up so everyone can go back to work."

"Yeah, you want to wind it up all right," Kyle said with open hostility. "Real quick. This whole thing is going down real quick."

Rini's elegant features very subtly loosened. His brow smoothed, and somehow a certain indefinable aggressiveness in his jawline, in his hands, in the set of his shoulders lessened and then disappeared. He smiled and spoke in a conciliatory tone, with just the right touch of regret. "I apologize, Kyle. You know me, I'm a man who's always in a hurry. Of course, you go ahead and look at the contracts; it's just that I thought you had a good understanding of them after we went over each clause. Anyway, I guess I'll go have a drink with my colleagues—that was a lounge down the hall, right? And I'll see you at—" He glanced at his Rolex. ". . . 11:15."

Confidently Rini marched past Kyle and Stella, followed by his "colleagues." Afton, in spite of the gravity of the situation, was amused. If Santorini Santangeli wasn't a stereotype, his "advisers" certainly were. Scuttling directly behind Rini was a small man with a wrinkled suit, reddish hair, and wobbly glasses, clutching a fine leather briefcase so enormous it looked like a suitcase. Behind the little lawyer were two young men, so alike as to be twins, with unremarkable brown hair and ultra-fashionable horn-rimmed glasses. Both were dressed in dark conservative suits, white button-down shirts, dull ties, and brightly shined shoes and had manicured hands, neat hair, and clear complexions. They carried identical briefcases, slim and elegant.

Behind them were two men whom Afton immediately dubbed "The Thumbwrench Brothers." Heavy and massive, with blue-black hair so shiny it was almost greasy, they were dressed in dark suits, black shirts, light-colored ties, and fine dress boots. One had a heavy gold earring in one ear; the other had two enormous gold chains roped beneath his tie. Both wore rings. Earring had four, Necklace had six. Both of them were wearing dark glasses and kept their heads facing straight ahead. Afton reflected wryly that perhaps the massiveness of their necks kept them from being able to turn their heads.

The entourage passed the table where Afton and the two men sat, and not a single one of the men glanced at them. Still standing a few feet away, Stella turned to Kyle and grabbed his arm with desperation. "Kyle, don't be a fool!" she whispered, but her voice was so charged that the hoarse words carried easily to Afton's table. "You made him mad, Kyle! And you know that's not a very bright thing to do!"

"Stella, I said I wanted some time to look over these papers," Kyle told her in a voice tight with strain. "And that means I don't need you shrieking in my ear."

With a tremendous effort Stella took a deep breath, pressed her eyelids together for a moment, and looked up at Kyle beseechingly. Rini and all the men had disappeared down the hall, so she spoke in a more natural tone. "I'm sorry, Kyle. I don't mean to be irritating. But I've got a tremendous stake in this movie too, and I'd appreciate it if you'd just hear me out."

But Kyle apparently could not be conciliated. "Hear you out? Stella, do you think I'm deaf or simply stupid? You've made it clear that you want me to go ahead and sign the agreement. I think I can grasp your point of view. And I'm already half in agreement. I just want to read it before I sign it, like any sane person would do—if there are any sane people who get into contracts with Santorini Santangeli and his mob."

"Shh!" Stella hissed, glancing at the hallway. "Why don't you act like a sane person then, Kyle? Think about it! Rini's made you a very generous offer, especially considering the fact that you're in such a vulnerable position! In fact, you're in a totally hopeless position! And you're going to fiddle around here, badmouthing him and keeping him sitting on his hands in that crummy lounge? *Rini Santangeli?*"

"That I am," Kyle said, clenching his jaw, his face growing flushed. "The great Rini Santangeli himself and his mouthpieces and his goons. Right there in that lounge, the crummy one. Now, why don't you run along and do your job, Stella? Go cuddle up with Rini, make him happy while the crazy man's off tearing out his hair and howling at the moon."

Afton thought that if her father—or anyone, for that matter—had spoken to her in that manner, she might have slapped him. She just knew that Stella Sheridan—confident, tough, smart Stella—would certainly deck Kyle.

But she didn't. In fact, she cooled down to a hostile freeze. "Yes, Kyle, I intend to go have a drink with Rini. And yes, I intend to be courteous to him. Because like it or not, you're going to have to sign that agreement, and Rini's going to own not just you, but me too, and Lina and Tru and every member of this crew. And I think it's only prudent, and discerning, to treat him with a modicum of respect." She walked out of the restaurant, her head held high.

Without ceremony Kyle threw himself down in the empty chair at the table where the three sat, trying to look as if they hadn't noticed the drama. But Kyle was too tired to play little social games or to make small talk. He threw a rumpled sheaf of papers down on the table and slumped down wearily. "The really sicken-ing thing is, she's right," he growled. "She's exactly right."

"Is she, now?" Frame responded politely. "About everything?"

Kyle looked at him with the merest hint of interest. "What do you mean, Mr. Frame?"

He shrugged carelessly. "Seemed like Miss Sheridan don't believe you have a choice. You believe that, do you?"

Kyle listened with growing attention and took a long time to answer. Frame sipped his coffee, apparently unconcerned, but his dark eyes were flashing, and his mouth was set in stubborn lines. Peregrine had half-turned and was staring out the line of floor-to-ceiling windows that overlooked the small bare pool. His face was set in loose, dreamy lines, but Afton saw that his eyes were dark, introspective, a murky mud color.

Finally Kyle replied slowly, "Well, no, Mr. Frame, as a matter of fact, I've lived enough to know that people always have choices. Always. It's just that sometimes the choices are extremely difficult and therefore don't appear to be very good choices to make."

"Uh-huh." Frame's phrase was as dry as the Sahara. "So what you're sayin' is, most times you got an easy choice and a hard choice. And it's the only smart thing to do to take the easy way out."

Kyle's hazel eyes flickered smartly. "That's not what I thought I was saying, no."

"Sounded to me like that's what you said, General Patton," Peregrine drawled rather absently.

Kyle gave him a shrewd once-over. "Sounded like it to me too, now. Don't like it much."

"Me neither," Peregrine mumbled.

Joel Frame set his coffee cup down with a sharp bang. "Watch it there, Mr. Peregrine," he said sternly. "I don't hardly think you're in a position to be preachin' to anybody about running down the easiest road at top speed. But that's not what we're talking about right now. We're talking about Mr. Patton here and his friends from L.A. that's making him this great deal."

"Great deal," Kyle repeated. "Yeah, it is. It's a great deal, Mr. Frame. That man in there already holds a mortgage on everything I've got, except three condos in Aspen and a couple of cars. And he's financed this movie already, to the tune of four million dollars, and that money's long gone, and the movie is bogged down to nothing but a black smoking square of dirt out there in the Kentucky woods." He shrugged, a jerky, jutting gesture of tension. "All he's done is come down here and offer to give me all the money and all the time I need to finish this movie in a first-class way. But I'm mad, good and mad, because I'm in this stupid position. 'Course, that's not Rini's fault. Or Stella's either."

"Mind if I ask you a coupla questions 'bout your personal business?" Frame said idly.

"Not at all."

"The financing—the note's due when?"

"Repayment of the money is guaranteed by a percentage of the movie's gross," Kyle readily answered.

"Then it's not a demand note," Frame said thoughtfully.

"No, sir. The only insurance Rini's got is the default clause."
Kyle made a helpless gesture with one hand. "Customary in this
kind of financing. If the movie goes over budget by a certain
amount, or if it goes past a deadline, then Rini can call in the paper,
which means he'll own a lot of my property."

"There's no buyout provision?" Frame asked sharply.

"Sure. But that provision doesn't go into effect until after the
deadline hour's been breached. Then I'd have twenty-four hours to
pay it off. But the provision is for half again as much as the financed
amount. So, for example, if I wanted to buy out the note now, I'd
have to pay the man six million dollars."

Frame shook his head. "Now lemme get this straight. This
man's got a note on you—at 50 percent interest, which, I hate to
tell you this, Mr. Patton, is illegal, and there's no way he can collect that from you. But anyway, he's given you four million dollars,
and you've given him rights to the movie earnings. Right?"

"Right."

"But now all of a sudden he wants to come down here and refinance that note, incorporate your company, which you say is up
the crick anyway, and then give you a bunch more money and
loosen up on your deadline. Right?"

"Right."

Frame said, "Last question. Why?"

Kyle looked confused. "What do you mean?"

With a hint of exasperation, Frame said very slowly and clearly,
"I mean, why? Why would he want to do this right now? What's
the hurry? If you'll pardon the pun—where's the fire?"

Kyle looked as if Frame had hit him with a baseball bat. Afton,
too, looked stunned. Peregrine only sighed deeply.

"I—I don't know," Kyle said, thoroughly bewildered. "Santorini Santangeli's not much into charitable causes."

"Naw, really? Who woulda thought?" Frame couldn't curb his sarcasm, but then slowly a patient grin lit his craggy face. "Anyways, Mr. Patton, I got a suggestion for you, might be applicable to this situation." He pronounced it "uh-PLIK-able."

"Huh? I mean, I beg your pardon?" Kyle was still a little combat-wearied.

"A suggestion," Frame repeated.

"Oh," Kyle mumbled. "Yes, of course. What is it?"

Now Frame's entire face lit up with childish glee. "Let's go for a ride. Us four. Mr. Rindi Serangeli ain't invited. That's another thing I think Miss Sheridan mighta been mistaken about, Mr. Patton."

"What's that?" Kyle asked, resigned to this bizarre conversation on this surreal day.

"I don't think it's gonna make much difference to that feller whether or not you're rude to him," Frame muttered blackly. "Either way, be nice or not, be courteous or not, be professional or not, you don't want him to own your soul; and I think a good place to start is if you don't worry about whether you get back to him at 11:13 and four seconds like he commanded. C'mon, let's go."

◊ ◊ ◊

Kyle had the keys to one of the Jeeps, so Peregrine drove, and Afton sat in the front, while Kyle and Frame sat in the back. Joel Frame steadfastly refused to answer any of Kyle's insistent questions, while keeping up a steady flow of information about the county, his family, other prominent families in the area, their history. It was small things, earthy, plain things, and it was soothing.

Peregrine drove on the state highway to the east for about half an hour. They met little traffic, and the road became twisting and hilly. Once Kyle remarked, "No billboards, that's it. Couldn't figure out why it looked so funny. Kinda nice."

"Yeah, kinda," Frame agreed caustically.

Finally Peregrine slowed down and took a turn to the right. At first Afton thought he was heading through the woods, but just as they turned she could see a dirt road so narrow it was little more than a path. Two massive pines stood as sentinels on either side of the almost-hidden entrance, and even the Jeep threaded the gap with little room to spare. The stands of oak, maple, pecan, elm, and sweet gum crowded so closely on each side of the lane that whenever it veered even in the slightest, one couldn't see ahead at all.

The timber was magnificent, Afton thought. She had, of course, seen forests before. But this was so different from Great Britain. There even untouched, undeveloped lands were on a smaller, more modest scale, more manicured and more reserved somehow. *America*, she thought dreamily. *It sprawls, it's wild, it's not truly tamed . . . such a young country. My country was like this once . . . but I suppose we're in our twilight, while America is still young and boisterous, rebellious, generous, boldly cutting a broad swath in history . . . Funny. Am I coming to love this country already?*

It seemed that Peregrine drove a long time through pathless woods. He didn't speak to Afton, but once he touched her hand lightly, which made her jump a little and feel foolish. But he merely pointed to the side of the road where a doe and twin fawns lifted alert heads; but as soon as the Jeep passed, they began grazing again.

Another time he pointed, and Afton looked just in time to see a sly, tawny shape disappear into some thick underbrush. "What was that?" she asked.

"Coyote," Peregrine answered. "There's lots of 'em. At night they sing sad songs."

It didn't sound at all peculiar to Afton. She was so in tune with Peregrine now, she reflected, and the thought comforted her.

He drove for almost an hour on the primitive, single-path lane. Then he said quietly, "There it is."

Kyle and Joel quickly cut off their conversation. Kyle sat up eagerly, and Afton leaned forward in anticipation too.

A valley opened up before them. Afton realized that they must have been climbing steadily for the last hour because they were on quite a height that crested the sweeping valley. The little valley had been cleared, obviously a long time ago, but massive trees, all oak, still dotted it. A group of log cabins lay in the center of the bowl-shaped depression.

"Ohh," Afton breathed. "Peregrine, it's lovely!" She stole a glance at her father. He was devouring the scene before him hungrily. But he said nothing.

Without speaking, Peregrine put the Jeep in four-wheel drive to negotiate the steep incline. The side of the hill and the grounds surrounding the dwellings below were covered with prairie grass, tall thin golden reeds that grew as thick as carpet pile. Peregrine made it to the valley and stopped the Jeep before driving onto the grounds. In a loose circle outlining the depression, winter grass had been planted, so the grounds were a cheerful green. Foothills, the stepstools of the Cumberland Mountains to the east, surrounded the valley on three sides.

Without speaking the four got out of the Jeep. Kyle first stood, his keen glance sweeping this way and that, studying the assortment of buildings. The log cabins were of varying sizes. The largest was in the top center of the valley, a rectangular cabin three times longer than it was wide, with windows in dignified spaces down the sides and on either side of the wooden double doors. It had a square bell tower with a simple wooden cross mounted on it.

"What is this place?" he murmured quietly.

Peregrine answered in a quiet tone, with no discernible slur of an accent or of slowness, "This used to be a Methodist camp meeting grounds. My grandfather built it. Now it's mine."

Kyle glanced sharply at him but asked no more questions. He stood for a long time, looking at the pastoral scene. Then he shielded his eyes from the sun, which was a cheery lemon yellow floating directly overhead. Afton squinted to see what he was looking at and then took a tentative step forward and shaded her eyes too. Close behind her she heard Peregrine sigh with resignation.

They could just barely see it. Directly across from them, a ridge like a long finger probed out of the forest into the valley, almost touching with its tip the cabins and the chapel. Set back upon the ridge, right at a discernible line where the oldest and most massive trees began, was a small log cabin. A high stone chimney was outlined against the darkness of hardwood trunks. They couldn't see the cabin very well, as it was quite a distance away; but they could plainly make out the lines of it because of the white horizontal lines of chinking between the logs.

"Would you like to go see it?" Peregrine asked politely.

"Sure would," Kyle said. His voice almost trembled with excitement. Peregrine led the way toward the ridge, and Kyle

walked with Joel Frame. "Mr. Frame, did you and Peregrine bring
me out here for any reason? Or are you just taking me on a pleasant outing?"

Frame answered quietly, "Truth to tell, we weren't really sure
ourselves. I ain't got the foggiest notion what it takes to make a
movie. Only thing I know of is that this place looks exactly like
what you were trying to shoot for with that little toy cabin in that
pitiful acre. Just thought it might be of interest to you."

"Oh, it's of interest to me all right," Kyle said, his tone growing lighter with each syllable. Afton, walking a little behind
Peregrine, glanced back at him. Kyle's eyes were alight and alert,
sweeping this way and that. The heavy liquor-lines of his face were
tightened up. Afton could see that her father's mind was racing at
a terrific speed.

There was a tiny, almost invisible path up the ridge to the cabin's front door. It was a lovely little cottage. The logs were white
oak, roughly squared and dovetailed and weathered to a soft, pleasing dove-gray. The chinking was expertly done but was obviously
also hand-done, without the artificial perfection of grouting guns.
A small shed roof overhang with a rough cedar floor made a charming front porch. The roof was cedar shakes, and the chimney was
cunningly fitted native stone.

"This was my great-grandfather's first home," Peregrine said
with unmistakable pride. "He didn't build it—it's much older than
his time. No one knows who built this place." Without ceremony
he opened the front door, which was a heavy oak cross-buck. The
cabin was empty but clean. At one end was the kitchen, which
consisted of a wooden counter, a sink with a pump, and simple
wooden shelves on either side of the single window. The front and

back walls had two four-paned windows each, symmetrically spaced. The far wall was a mammoth fireplace, with an iron arm mounted on each side for hanging cooking pots and then swinging them over the fire. Just to one side of the fireplace was a steep ladder leading to an open loft that was about half the size of the cabin.

Kyle looked at everything for a long, long time. Then he turned to Peregrine, who for perhaps the first time met his gaze directly. "Would you consider allowing me to lease this place for about a month?" Kyle said bluntly.

"Yes," Peregrine answered without hesitation. "Yes, sir, I would."

TWELVE

◇

K YLE LEFT THE CABIN almost at a dead run, promising to return in an hour or so. Joel Frame trudged patiently along behind him, then stopped and turned to ask about Peregrine and Afton. Kyle had evidently forgotten about them. "You two comin'?"

Peregrine shrugged. "Why should I wanna go back to town? Done been there, seen it. That'll last me for a coupla months."

"I'm staying here," Afton announced. Peregrine looked surprised, and she added, "If that's all right with you, Peregrine. I'd like to look around some more."

He shrugged carelessly, and Joel Frame hurried to catch up with Kyle.

Afton sat down on the top porch step, propped her head in her hands, and searched the panorama of forest, earth, and sky, her eyes alight. "This place is wonderful," she sighed. "No wonder you don't want to go to town. Any town or city would look dirty and ugly and jumbled when you live in a place like this."

Behind her, the wooden porch creaked, but Peregrine's footsteps made no sound. He slipped down the steps and stood directly in front of Afton, crossing his arms and frowning. "How'd you know I'm living here?"

She pointed down into the valley, smiling. "That cabin, the medium-sized one, has a neat stack of firewood, a rocker on the front porch, and most telling of all, the hawk stand under the tree."

Peregrine nodded, looked around restlessly, then looked down and kicked aimlessly at a dirt clod.

Afton decided to try something unusual in a budding man-woman relationship—honesty and candor. "I'm very curious about you, Peregrine. I know that you don't like to talk about yourself, but I'd really appreciate it if you'd tell me about this place."

Turning his head to look down at the cabins, he answered automatically. "Methodist camp. My grandpa built it."

Afton admired his strong profile but sighed at his desultory answer. She was determined, however, and went on, "So, your grandfather, was he a Methodist minister?"

"Yes, ma'am."

"My grandfather was a minister," Afton said wistfully. "My grandfather Malcolm."

Peregrine turned back to look at her appraisingly. "You're sad 'cause he's dead."

"Yes, for two years now."

"I never knew my grandparents," Peregrine said, his gaze roaming over the valley. Then, as if that was entirely too much information to share in one session, he lapsed back into his mysterious mountain man persona. He studied Afton with blank eyes, then asked in a child's polite monotone, "You wanna have your archery lesson now?"

Afton rose, dusted off the seat of her jeans, and replied, "Why, yes, Peregrine, I'd like that very much."

They went back down into the valley, and Peregrine disappeared into what was obviously his cabin without a word to Afton. She waited outside, looking around with an appraising eye.

There were eighteen cabins in all, of varying sizes. All of them were at least two bedrooms, she judged. None of them were as small as the little jewel up on top of the ridge. They looked newer too, much more recent. There were no power lines visible in the valley, but she saw a transformer just out of sight in the tree line at the base of the hill that had the single road leading in; so she judged that the camp must have buried electrical lines. At the far end of the valley, on the other side of the ridge, was a generous barn that was in some disrepair but was still standing and still had a roof. The scene was lovely, pastoral, with a peacefulness that was most unworldly.

Peregrine came back out onto the porch holding a longbow and a leather shoulder pouch, the feathery arrows jutting out of it.

Afton turned to him and asked, "Peregrine, why are you helping my father?"

Undismayed at her abruptness, he smoothly replied, "Main reason is because Mr. Frame asked me to, because he thinks it's something I ought to do. I believe in Joel Frame, and I trust him. Man couldn't have a better friend."

"That's the main reason? What other reasons?" Afton demanded.

Peregrine came down the steps and moved to stand directly in front of Afton so he could look down into her face. They stared at each other, measured each other, tried to fathom each other for long moments. Then Peregrine answered her question in a low voice. "I have other reasons, yes. But I'm not going to talk about them right now."

He turned and walked around the side of the house, and after collecting herself Afton followed, muttering, "I swear, getting that man to open his mouth and say three sentences in a row is the hardest work I've ever done! By all the clans! You'd think words were diamonds and sentences were gold!"

"Ain't they?" Peregrine tossed over his shoulder.

He led her to the back of the cabin, and when she caught up with him he said in a businesslike tone, "I'm going to do this once and show you. Then you."

"But that's hardly a lesson!" Afton argued.

Shrugging, he said, "Free though."

With some ceremony, he pulled out what looked like a deformed glove. Without speaking, but with showy flourishes, he pulled it on his left hand, then adjusted it so it was snug. Once it was in place, he held up his arm for Afton to see. It was a glove, but the fingers were cut out at the knuckle. Reaching up almost to the elbow, it had a sturdy rectangular leather patch sewn on to fit the inside forearm.

"Shield gauntlet?" Afton guessed.

"Good enough. You don't wanna twang this bowstring against your arm. It'd flay the skin off."

Afton shivered but watched carefully.

Peregrine slung the leather pouch so that the long strap crossed his chest and the arrows were at his back. He adjusted it until it was comfortable, then picked up the bow and twanged the string lightly. Nonchalantly he reached up, whipped out an arrow, fitted it to the string, and pulled back so the feathers were almost resting against his cheek. Hesitating for only a second, he released the string, and the twangy hum split the air. The arrow cleanly buried itself in a scarred post about twenty feet away.

In a businesslike manner Peregrine peeled off the gauntlet and handed it to Afton. "It'll be too big, but I'll tighten the ties that hold on the shield." Afton looked at it blankly.

Peregrine slipped off the shoulder pouch and in a smooth motion stepped behind Afton, so close he was almost touching her, but not quite. He lowered the strap over her head, and she could feel him adjusting the weight of the pouch, pulling lightly on the strap, settling it comfortably on her shoulder, and pulling on the buckle to adjust the length.

"How does that feel?" His voice was even, but he was so close that Afton could feel his warm breath stir her hair.

"Um—uh—f-fine, just fine," she stammered, catching her breath.

Gravely he handed the bow to her. "Then shoot, fair lady."

She did exactly as Peregrine did—she thought. She reached up behind her shoulder, pulled out an arrow with only a little fumbling, then tried to fit it to the bow. But it wasn't anywhere near as easy as Peregrine had made it look, and it took her some time to fit the slender notch on the string. Then she curled her forefinger and second finger around the arrow, pressed her thumb against it, and raised it to her cheek.

The arrow fell down.

Afton looked down at it in surprise and a little embarrassment. Peregrine was nonchalant, however, as he bent and picked it up. "Don't worry about it. Just try again."

This time she at least got the arrow to leave the bow. It limped all of three feet and then blooped to the ground.

Afton was getting impatient with herself, but she was the type of woman who just got more determined and more steely. She shot again, then again, and once more. The arrows wandered out there, all right, but all of them fell very short of the post, and none of them would have even come close to hitting it, as they were all way off the mark to her left.

"You're sticking your tongue out," Peregrine remarked conversationally.

"I am not!"

"Sure you are. That's what's putting off your aim."

"Can hardly help it, can I?" Afton muttered. "Have to hold everything on your body just so."

She shot twice more, making sure her tongue stayed tucked behind tightly closed lips. One arrow fell about four feet in front of the target. The other buried itself in the ground about six feet short, the feathered end sticking up jauntily to the sky.

"Better," Peregrine said as he collected the spent arrows.

"Better than what?" Afton grumbled. "And why don't you have a compound bow? I can hardly pull this!"

"What's the point?" Peregrine responded carelessly, but he was watching her reaction closely.

She started, then laughed at herself. "Oh, yes. This is what most people would call 'fun,' isn't it? Not work. After all, it's not like I must kill a buffalo for supper, hmm?"

"I'm having fun," Peregrine said seriously.

"Well—well, me too," Afton said, a little flustered. "But won't you please help me just a bit? It would be much more fun for me if I was at least able to get close to that blooming post."

"Okay." He moved so close to her he was almost touching her. Afton looked up at him, startled, but with a mischievous glint in his sunset eyes he said in a low, intimate voice, "Now, you hold the bow like this." His hands on both of hers, he pulled the bow up, the string lax, the arrow resting on both of their hands. "Sight the target now. Don't wait until you've pulled, and don't look at the string or the arrow. Just at the target. Good. Now pull back . . . smooth and easy. Relax your fingers." He took his hands away but still was standing so close he was brushing against her. "Now shoot."

The bowstring twanged, and the arrow flew like a bullet— straight up over the trees and disappeared.

"That's real good," he whispered. She dropped the bow, but neither of them noticed.

His hands slid down to her waist, and he moved around her with the graceful economy of a dancer until he was facing her. She looked up at him, her eyes round and glittering, her lips slightly parted. Very slowly he lowered his head and kissed her gently. She moved closer to him, responding to him, breathing deeply the crisp outdoorsy scent of him and relishing the feel of his muscular back and shoulders. His hands tightened on her waist, and then he encircled her with his arms and pulled her even closer.

The kiss and the caress ended naturally, with mutual consent. Afton stepped back a little, and Peregrine steadied her with his hands for a brief moment. Each searched the other's face with a hint of anxiety, and with a hope of seeing pleasure. Both seemed satisfied with what they saw. Peregrine smiled, and Afton's smile lit her face like a candle. "I just have one more question," she said, her voice light.

"I knew it," he groaned. But his eyes were still smiling.

"Do you think we could include this in all of my archery lessons?" she asked with wide-eyed innocence.

"Reckon that could be arranged, Miss Afton," he said, though without the dullness in his normal country boy's voice. "Good thing for me that you're about as sorry an archer as I ever did set eyes on. Gonna take lots and lots of archery lessons for you, ma'am."

◇ ◇ ◇

"Hey, Mr. Patton, we gonna open with a prayer?"

"Yeah, you need it, Jo-Jo!"

"Miss Dancy, you wanna come sit with us? Please?"

"On your lap, I suppose you mean."

"Aww . . ."

"Huh? Well, sure, sure, Mr. Kirk, gosh, you can sit here! I mean, you're a big star. You could make all of us sit on the floor so you'd have all these bench things to yourself if you wanted . . ."

The crew in the chapel at the Methodist camp was in high spirits for some reason. Kyle had gone back to the Holiday Inn, loaded them up into the twelve Jeeps without a word of explanation, and trucked them back to the camp. Film crews, accustomed to the vagaries of the high-strung people who created the phenomenons called movies, rarely questioned inexplicable orders. They usually just sighed, muttered to themselves, and did their work. In spite of the fact that the regular grunts on crews—the grips, the handlers, the assistants to the assistants, etc.—were not particularly well-paid, there was a never-ending supply of men and women who would kill for their jobs. Any job on a movie set, from being a star's slave to cleaning the toilets, was highly desirable. There you were, right where the film was being made, with the stars and the fabulously rich and powerful producers and the directors and casting executives, any one of whom might "discover" you, the newest, youngest, brightest star on the horizon.

Eventually the fifty or so people got seated. The chapel was plain and simple. Two rows of wooden pews so ancient they were black lined a wide center aisle in the pegged floor. The nave was merely a six-inch platform at one end, with two polished oak boards for an altar rail. Through the small four-paned but evenly-spaced windows the early afternoon sun shone cheerily, making fairy-dust motes dance in the beams.

Peregrine unobtrusively stood to the side of the platform, leaning against the wall, his arms crossed, his face unreadable. Afton and Messalina sat in a front pew. Afton had seen with an unwelcome tinge of discomfort that Messalina had slipped up to Peregrine and spoken to him privately before seating herself at the end of the pew closest to him. Afton valiantly fought down a wave of jealousy, though Messalina had actually made Peregrine laugh quietly at some private joke. Afton hadn't yet been able to do that.

After the crew finally settled down somewhat, though they were still talking and laughing, Kyle jumped up onto the empty platform. Afton wondered if there had ever been a pulpit and what had happened to it.

"Okay, people, settle down!" Kyle called, and the silence was instant.

"You know I'm not one for giving pep talks," Kyle said casually. "But I'm in a situation right now where I've got to. So just give me a break here for about half an hour or so, okay?"

"We gettin' paid?" someone called, and a wave of chuckles widened through the crowd.

"You betcha, Jo-Jo," Kyle answered, grinning. "After all, that's what I do—pay people to listen to me, like it or not."

Laughter and catcalls greeted this sally. Jo-Jo, a high-spirited would-be comedian, was an eighteen-year-old boy with riotous red hair, freckles, and a chipped front tooth. He was one of Dave Steiner's assistants, and Dave had told Afton that he didn't know squat about cameras and photography, but he good-naturedly worked like a bought-and-paid-for slave.

Kyle joked with Jo-Jo and the other hecklers for a few minutes. Afton's respect for her father grew during this time. In spite of his occasional outbursts of temper, when he spoke so harshly to anyone and everyone around, most of the time Kyle was relaxed and comfortable with this rowdy bunch. He generated a warmth that was genuine and personal. Afton had noticed before that he knew every single crew member's name, right down to the last freight handler.

"All right, let's get down to it," Kyle said when the crew had quieted down a little. "Here's the deal. I know crew gossip; I know you people probably know more about my problems on this film than I do. Monarch Cinema's made me an offer. Mr. Santangeli's promised to invest more money, enough to finish this film in style, and to extend our deadline indefinitely so we can take our sweet time about it. And he's also promised raises for everyone."

Kyle waited, his sharp and roving eyes watching for the crew's reaction. Afton, too, turned to look at the assembly. Some of the crew members, mostly the youngest ones, let out a half-hearted cheer, then looked around self-consciously at the old hands like Charlie Terrill and Dave Steiner. They looked grim. Charlie Terrill looked as mean as the Bad Guy Gunslinger in an old cowboy B-movie.

It got very quiet in the chapel.

Dave Steiner called, "We're waiting for the other shoe to drop, Kyle."

Kyle licked his lips, the only sign of nervousness he had shown yet. "I think you already know why you're here. We can finish this movie right here, and personally I think this location is better than anything I've dreamed of."

A gentle hubbub that sounded like agreement rippled through the crowd, but Kyle quickly held up his hand, and everyone returned their attention to him. "Now, just like every decision we make has an upside and a downside, so does this, and I'm going to give it to you straight. But before I do, I want to ask you all a question." He waited, partly for effect and partly to make sure everyone was giving him full attention. It seemed as though his eyes bored into every person's face in the room in turn. Finally he asked quietly, "What is *Hearth and Home* about?"

No one answered; several people dropped their heads to avert their eyes from Kyle's shrewd gaze. He waited for long, tense moments. Gently he prodded them, "C'mon, people, it's not a trick question. Most of you have worked with me before. You know I don't gather up the crew for a weekly meeting to have a pep rally. You know what I do. I give every single person that touches my films in any way a copy of the script and ask them to read it. I have enough faith in you to believe that then you'll understand exactly what we're working for."

He waited.

To Afton's great surprise, the black sound man and electrician, Harlan Freeman, shifted lazily, propped his arms against the back of the pew, and spoke in a low, throaty voice. "That's right, Mr.

Patton, and I always liked that about you. That's why I work for you every time you ask me. Because you give me enough credit to know that I want to make something, to create something, something that I have a right to be proud of."

"Because you worked for it, right?" Kyle said easily. "That's it, people. That's what this movie's about, that's what this meeting is about, that's what life is about. Most of you, I know, are from L.A. Harlan there is from Watts. He, and most of you, could be out stealing cars and VCRs and selling dope to make money; all of you pretty ladies could be selling yourselves for a lot of quick money. But you don't; you're here working like fools for scale. Why is that? Well, I know, even if you don't. It's because it's worth it, and like Harlan said, if you've worked for it, you've got a right to be proud of it."

Again a silence fell on the room, and each face was thoughtful, introspective. Even Jo-Jo looked somber.

Kyle gave them a few minutes, then made a sweeping gesture with his hand. "This place, like I said, is the perfect location for *Hearth and Home*. The problem is, we'd be living the movie, and the movie's all about hard, backbreaking, long hours of work. And we'd have to work, people, work like you won't believe. Because if we decide to go for it, we've got a deadline in four weeks or Monarch Cinema takes over anyway, and I think you know enough about the business to see that their movie won't be anything like the movie that Summit Decipher is creating. I'm not even sure they'd do the film. Monarch could take a loss of a few million just so they wouldn't have to bother with a film that they really don't believe in anyway.

"The other problem is money," Kyle said bluntly, facing them squarely. "I don't have any left. Not much anyway. Not enough to pay you for the month."

"Aw, Kyle, c'mon . . ."

"So we're supposed to be this noble for free?"

"No money? Work our tails off for nothing?"

"What kinda fool would do that?"

Kyle allowed the steam to escape, then said quietly, "What I will do is pay this crew—just you people here, not the Moldova crew or the L.A. editors and all them—a percentage of the gross movie earnings. I'll pay you 8 percent of gross earnings, before any deductions. Straight off the top. Tru and Messalina have gross contingency percentages that are supposed to be paid before any deductions, but they've consented to let me net out this percentage before their cuts. Eight percent, to be split between you—the ones who are in. Anyone can leave right now with no hard feelings. I'm paying everyone scale until the end of the week, and of course I'll fly you back to L.A."

A profound stillness, a loaded silence, made the atmosphere of the room as heavy as the air before a thunderstorm. The dust motes crazily flying in the sun was the only movement. The odd shush of fifty-plus people breathing was the only sound.

Then it broke loose like an explosion.

Deep voices of men, high giggles and calls of young girls, insistent questions from the assistants to their crew chiefs, some grumbling, some eager, some persuasive. Afton heard the pretty young scene-shouter with the glorious black hair say over and over again shrilly, "What's it mean, Dave? Is that a lot of money? Huh? Is it, Dave?"

Dave was frowning, and his mouth was moving; obviously he

was doing some quick arithmetic in his head. When he spoke, he spoke clearly and loudly, and everyone immediately shut up to listen. "If the movie grosses thirty million dollars, and if everyone stays, we'll all clear forty-eight thousand dollars."

Two seconds of quiet, then pandemonium again.

Staring straight ahead, Dave said again for emphasis, "If *Hearth and Home* grosses thirty million dollars, our cut will be two million four hundred thousand dollars. Split between fifty people, that's forty-eight thousand dollars."

Stunned, everyone looked up at Kyle, their expressions ranging from shock to disbelief.

Calmly he said, "That's if the movie grosses that much. It could bomb. It's not your typical film, you know; it's clean, it's about virtues that aren't too popular these days, it's profound, but the story's told in a simple and unadorned manner. It's at the opposite end of the spectrum from blockbusters."

"Still, Dave's math isn't counting on a blockbuster amount," Charlie put in stoutly. "Kyle, you could make a movie about Messalina Dancy and Truman Kirk doing their *laundry* that would gross thirty million easy."

"Yeah, well, that is going to be a big scene in *Hearth and Home*, you know," Kyle grinned. "Which illustrates what I'm saying. Faith, commitment, self-sacrifice . . . not real popular themes nowadays."

"That's not exactly true," Dave added, shrugging. "They're the themes of all the classics, old and new. *Chariots of Fire. Braveheart. Rocky.*"

"*Twelve O'clock High.*"

"*True Grit.*"

"*The Hunt for Red October.*"

"Yeah?" Jo-Jo called, his hair standing on end. "How about *The Piper*? How about *Path of the Prodigal*?"

Every head swiveled toward Kyle. He smiled.

Cheers broke out so loudly that the old rafters seemed to shake.

THIRTEEN

◇

I T WAS 5:30 and getting dark before Kyle and his crew returned to the Holiday Inn. Afton rode in with Kyle, Messalina, and Tru. Peregrine had stayed at the camp. She stayed close by her father, though he hadn't exactly asked her to. She just sensed that he wanted her support and wanted her to be with him.

As the caravan pulled up to the motel, Kyle went around and collected Charlie Terrill, Dave Steiner, and Harlan Freeman. "Come with me. I want you men to be in on this."

Freeman said caustically, "Yeah, that gangstah-wannabe got his bangers. Now you got yours, Mr. Patton."

Afton blurted out, "Sausages? He's got sausages?"

The three men burst into laughter, and Afton didn't mind too much because it seemed to lessen the tangible aura of anger surrounding all three men. "Bangers, that's what we call sausages," Afton added sheepishly.

Kyle, still chuckling, said, "I know, darlin'. No, Mr. Freeman here was referring to 'gang-bangers.' That's—they're—"

"Ah, yes," Afton said, nodding. "Soldiers. In a gang. The frontline fighters."

"Er—yes," Kyle stammered.

Afton gave him a dazzling smile. "You forget, I was a soldier on the other side. The Army."

"Why, of course!" Kyle smiled at her, then turned back to the black man. "So thanks for the offer, Harlan, but I've got the only soldier I need right here." He winked at Afton, then addressed the men again. "Anyway, that's not why I want you to come. No, I know Rini, and I know he's going to sneak around and offer all of you a job. He'll make it good too. So I want you to just go ahead and deal with it right now." As the four men and Afton went into the lobby, Kyle said to the men gravely, "I meant what I said at the camp. If any of you want to leave, there's no hard feelings at all. You're still the best men in this business, and I intend to call you on every movie I make. If I make any more, that is," he added dryly.

Dave and Charlie made disrespectful noises, protesting that they wouldn't work for Rini if he offered them various valuables, among them the island of Sicily, a lifetime's supply of pasta, the Vatican, and the moon and stars. Harlan, whose face was always unreadable because of the ever-present sunglasses, grunted, "Yeah, I know that whitebread slick's gonna offer me a job. Cleanin' his toilets maybe. Mr. Santorini Santangeli ain't exactly ee-namored of black folks, if you catch my meaning."

"He'll try to steal you, Harlan," Kyle said calmly. "And he'll pay you good too. I don't know what for—maybe nothing. But I just want the three of you to have your minds made up. My offer to stay in on this film expires tomorrow at 6 A.M., which is when I'm planning to kidnap the whole lot of you into the wilderness."

Mr. Santorini Santangeli was still in the lounge, waiting and boiling. He was not a man who was accustomed to being kept waiting, especially for over six hours. He had nursed three martinis, which made him just loose enough to be reckless and just careless enough to show his temper.

When Kyle and his companions walked into the lounge, he stalked over to Kyle immediately, and for a frightening moment Afton thought that Rini was actually going to strike her father. Santangeli's elegant face was tightened to the look of skin stretched over a skull, and his hands, down straight at his sides like pistons, kept making fists and loosening, making fists and loosening. Like automatons, Santangeli's two brutes appeared behind him. Cockily Harlan Freeman stepped forward, and the three sunglassed men had a face-off.

"Patton, I told you to come back here at 11:15," he muttered ominously. "You are late, and you are way, way out of line."

"Let me buy you a drink, Rini," Kyle said with frozen politeness. "One for the road. Because you can go, you know. Actually, you could have gone back to L.A. this morning. But that's beside the point. Thanks for the offer, but I must respectfully decline."

Rini's face sagged so suddenly and so completely that Afton, feeling slightly hysterical from tension, almost giggled. But Rini was not at all amused.

"You fool! You can't turn me down!" he thundered, sliding forward another inch. Behind him his goons slid forward, and at Kyle's side Harlan Freeman stepped forward too. It was a ludicrous dance but frightening. Afton's hands and lips were trembling.

"Sure I can, Rini," Kyle said quietly.

"No, Patton, you can't! You idiot! You don't think I'm going to let you get away with this, do you?" Santangeli blustered.

"Get away with what?" Kyle retorted. "I'm just going to go ahead and make my movie, like I've always planned."

Santangeli's eyes flickered dangerously. Drawing himself upright, he stood as still and as tense as a panther in a crouch. "You're going to regret this, Kyle. That's all I've got to say to you—except that I'll be back on November 2, at one minute after midnight, for my money."

"Nope," Kyle said firmly. "But I'll arrange for a showing of the finished film if you like."

Santangeli made an inarticulate snarling sound, then shifted his burning gaze to Charlie, Dave, and finally Harlan. "You three men . . . Charlie, I'll put you to work tomorrow on *Dead to Rights*. Double whatever Kyle's paying you. Same for you, Dave, supervising the camera crew, no actual filming for you. Mr. Freeman, I can always find a place for a good sound man."

"Like out on the street dancin' for dimes?" Harlan muttered.

The rage in Santangeli masked his elegant features again, but his voice was tightly controlled. "I'll double whatever Kyle's paying you, Mr. Freeman, if you'll come back to L.A. with me right now. My Lear's waiting at Lex Airport."

Harlan never looked at Rini or even appeared to glance his way. He and Rini's two goons were still playing their odd stare-down game, though it was rather surreal as they were all wearing dark glasses and the room itself was so dark. Afton was sure that none of the three could possibly actually see each other or anything else and had to gulp down hysterical giggles again.

Finally Harlan growled, "No, thanks, dude. I just wouldn't feel at home. I don't think your baby boys here like me. Think they're probably jealous of you an' me bein' so tight—Rini."

The two goons never moved, and Harlan actually looked disappointed. Rini looked as if he were about to explode. After endless heavy moments he held up one hand shoulder-high, snapped his fingers, and marched out of the room. His "baby boys" followed in step, and then his white-faced lawyers scurried after him, nervously giving Harlan Freeman a wide berth.

Houston Rees, who had sat on a bar stool, motionless and silent during the entire confrontation, stood and walked up to Kyle. His face was pale, and he looked shame-faced. Averting his gaze, he murmured in an almost inaudible voice, "Kyle, I—I gotta go."

Kyle clapped his left hand on the big man's shoulder. "It's okay, Houston. Monarch Cinema is a great company, and I know you'll do well there. No hard feelings." He offered the younger man his right hand.

Still without looking up, he took Kyle's hand and shook it in a cursory manner. Then he slipped out the door.

Stella was next in line. She planted her slim, stiff figure foursquare in front of Kyle, savagely jammed tight fists onto her nonexistent hips, stared up at him angrily, and exclaimed, "Have you lost your mind? Have you lost every bit of sense you've ever had? What's the matter with you, Kyle? This is insane!"

"Miss Sheridan, would you mind if we came in and sat down?" Afton said frostily. "We've all had a very long day, and I know my father is tired."

Kyle looked surprised, and pleased, at Afton's vehemence, but he quickly began to placate Stella. "She's right, Stella, and I know you're tired too . . . and I know you don't know what's going on. Sorry I couldn't take you with us, but it did seem like the right thing to do to leave you with Rini. He likes you. I'm surprised he didn't try to steal you too." Taking her arm, he gently led her to a table—just for two. Sighing, Afton turned to leave, and Dave, Charlie, and Harlan tactfully followed.

"I'll walk you to your room if you like, Miss Afton," Charlie said politely. He was like a great teddy bear.

Afton, in a deep reverie, murmured, "Hmm? Oh. Oh, yes. Thank you." She brightened and went on lightly, "As a matter of fact, I think this Hollywood custom of having big, scary bodyguards is quite nice. Perhaps all three of you gentlemen will walk me? That way," she added with a dark mischievousness completely unlike her usual sweet persona, "I'll be protected in case Mr. Santangeli and his thugs show up with violin cases."

Harlan Freeman laughed gleefully. "Didn't think of that. Betcha Mr. Rini coulda taken a few tips from me on how to do a drive-by. Maybe that's what he wanted to hire me for."

"Probably would have paid you triple for that," Dave muttered.

"Don't matter," Freeman shrugged. "Never thought I'd hear myself say this, but I don't even think white folks oughta be in that man's debt. He's wicked. And I don't mean that as no compliment."

"My father is in his debt," Afton murmured tremulously. "And you're right, Mr. Freeman. That is a frightening place to be."

"You don't worry about Rini," Charlie said comfortingly. "He's hot stuff in L.A., but all that mafioso stuff is just hype. Those two thugs? They're his cousins, and the reason they never talk is because they're so dumb they can't learn English."

"Oh? Are they immigrants from Sicily?" Afton asked curiously.

"Nope. They're Americans," Charlie said, his mild blue eyes sparkling. "They just can't speak English. Too tough for them. Good thing they're Eye-talians. They can talk with their hands, you know."

"Mr. Terrill, I think you're putting me up!" Afton complained.

"Huh?" he said blankly.

"Puttin' you *on*, Charlie," Freeman translated. "Pay attention."

The three men did walk Afton to her door and waited until she had unlocked the old, cantankerous lock and pushed the heavy metal door open. Turning, she said softly, her eyes as bright as twilight stars, "I want to thank you, all three of you gentlemen, for standing by my father. I've prayed for him so much to know that he has friends, people who believe in him, people he can depend on, because like most of us, he's a lonely man. You are the answers to my prayers, and tonight I'm going to say special prayers of thanks for each of you."

The three men were so bemused and touched by this simple declaration of faith that none of them, not even the articulate David Steiner, could say a word.

Afton purposefully gave each man an angelic smile and then closed her door.

Charlie Terrill sighed deeply, Harlan Freeman—even with the dark glasses—looked stunned, but Dave Steiner finally found something to say. "Well, that did it. I'm in love. You?"

"Yeah," Charlie answered him wistfully. "You?"

"For a white girl," Harlan finally grunted in reply, "she gots some class."

◇ ◇ ◇

The next morning Afton felt more than her usual uneasiness at going to her father's room for breakfast. After all, when she'd left him last night, he and Stella were gearing up for what looked like

a long and bitter battle, and Afton had no idea what the atmosphere would be this morning.

Afton didn't dislike Stella exactly. But she didn't like her very
much either. But it wasn't so much an active emotion as it was a pas-
sive reaction to Stella's personality. She was so cool, so distant, so
carefully collected that Afton couldn't get over feeling distinctly put
off. It wasn't that Stella was ever rude to her; quite the contrary, she
was unfailingly polite to Afton. It was just that Stella Sheridan never
at any time seemed to be a real person, a real woman with emotions
and hurts and insecurities and joys. Even when she showed anger, it
was like an accessory she put on, like a very good rendering of a scene
where the actress's part required showing that emotion.

It's like talking to a—a—what's that thing on Star Trek? *A holo-
gram, that's it. She looks, moves, talks like a human being, but she's not
real. She's insubstantial, made of something other than flesh and blood
and bone and sinew* . . .

Impatiently dismissing her own insecurities, Afton went to the
door of her father's room and knocked on it twice.

"It's open!"

Her father sounded his usual distracted, busy self. Afton went
into the room and quickly assessed the scene. Her father sat cross-
legged on the bed as usual, but he wasn't on the phone. He was
actually eating a piece of toast, some scrambled eggs, and some
bacon from a plate he balanced expertly in his left hand. Stella,
already groomed and dressed in a stunning gold Chanel suit with
big chunky accessories, was seated at the small desk, smoking a cigarette and drinking her usual cup of black coffee.

"Have some breakfast, Afton," Kyle prodded, his mouth partly
full. "But hurry up. Daylight's wasting."

"It's not daylight yet, Father," Afton teased, helping herself to a cup of coffee. This little opening gambit had become something of a ritual with her and her father.

"Then pre-dawn's wasting," Kyle shot back. "Eat something, Afton. You're too skinny."

"Don't be ridiculous, Kyle. She's lucky. She's anorexic," Stella responded, winking at Afton.

"Not funny. Blamed women nowadays. Look like starving little boys. Hate it. All men do," Kyle grumbled.

"Miss Dancy doesn't," Afton argued. "She's quite curvy."

"That's why I hired her," Kyle maintained solidly. "She's the only person in Hollywood that looks like she's got an ounce of strength. Even the men look like eels."

Afton giggled, and Stella smiled. "Well, Afton, I'm off to Aspen. I know you'll take good care of Kyle while I'm gone."

"Oh?" Afton said politely. "Are you going on business?"

"Of course. Someone's got to act like a sane businessperson around here. Since your father has evidently gone mad, and the rest of the crew is merrily following him on the way to Bedlam— along with me, I might add—I'm going to try to keep this thing glued together with the only glue that'll patch up this mess. That's money, sweetie. Money."

"Oh," Afton said helplessly.

Kyle quickly said, "Aw, Afton, she growls, but she's really just a kitten. She's going to Aspen to sell my condos. I own three, and I always meant to transfer them to Summit Decipher because I let investors and stars use them for perks. Anyway, those condos are the only things that Stella really wanted us to be sure and keep, 'cause she likes Aspen and is a great skier. But she's offered to go sell them, get some quick cash for *Hearth and Home*."

"Oh, really? That's nice." Afton tried to sound genuine, but her tone was hesitant. It didn't seem to her that it was such a noble thing for Stella to go sell Afton's father's property. If she was such an expert producer and if her father's reputation for making money was as widespread as it seemed to be, why didn't Stella go find another backer? Or at least try?

Stella was watching her, clearly reading her thoughts, and she looked faintly hostile, as if warning her not to let her father see her doubts. Afton immediately did her best to look politely interested. But it didn't matter anyway. Her father had already dismissed that topic and moved on.

"So we'll have some money at least. Enough to get the cabins outfitted and to buy food and pay the locals."

"The cooks are the only paid help; you've lost your Production Manager, and you've hired a drooling half-wit as Location Manager," Stella recited tartly with a caustic smile. "It's good to know things are in perfect order before I leave."

Afton was angry, partly because she hated it when Stella spoke to her father in that horribly patronizing tone. But mostly, she honestly admitted to herself, she despised Stella for calling Peregrine a "drooling half-wit." But sternly she told herself that the problems between her father and this woman were none of her business; indeed, Afton had sensed the Lord's disapproval for the way she rebuked Stella last night in the lounge and had repented of her hastiness. So now she pressed her lips together and tried to look busy buttering a slice of toast.

"Yes, I know, Stella," he said quietly. "But you're standing by me anyway, and I appreciate it. I think it's very generous of you to support me even though you can't agree with my decisions."

To Afton's surprise, Stella instantly and visibly softened at Kyle's words. "Kyle, you've been good to me, and you've stuck with me. We stick together, and that's the way it's going to be. We've got to." With an uncharacteristically jerky movement, she glanced at her watch and stood up. "I must be leaving in just a few minutes." She politely but pointedly glanced at Afton, who hurriedly excused herself and almost ran out the door.

Afton went back to her room to brush her teeth and get her jacket. She was wearing a heavy knit wool sweater with a velvety-soft cotton turtleneck underneath. But she was still chilled. The first orange rays of the rising sun bleakly lightened the landscape, revealing a brittle frost. Afton shivered, thinking that it was going to be a depressing and difficult day, for she thought that her father might be frantic trying to rearrange months of planning for his film.

But she was wrong. Of all the hectic, exciting days of those first two months she spent with her father, Afton later recalled this day as the most exciting, the most wonderful, the most satisfying of them all.

She was still trying to make up her mind between her red canvas fleece-lined jacket—which was very sporty—and her long khaki trench coat—which was very trendy—when Kyle banged on her door and called in a big-bad-wolf voice, "Come out, little girl! No use hiding! I'm putting you to work along with the rest of us grunts!"

Afton flew to the door, her eyes sparkling. She threw it open to see her father, leaning casually against the doorjamb, his arms crossed, laughing. She thought she'd never seen him look so handsome. He'd lost some liquor-fat, she noticed for the first time, and his features weren't so puffy and pasty. The youthful good looks of a high-flying, big-dreaming Kyle Patton Burns were very close to blooming out.

"Work? Do you mean it? Something really hard, really challenging, really useful?" Afton cried.

Kyle, still grinning, shook his head with warning. "Be careful what you ask for, little girl. You might get it."

"I'd like a job please," Afton insisted. "Any job. As long as it's a real one."

"Okay, you're on lookout. First—" Kyle fished in his coat pocket and came out with two small toys. "Here's a pager and a cell phone. They were Houston's. Your first assignment is to find out how the devil he kept up with everything—including everyone's pager and cell phone numbers 'cause I don't know anybody's, including my own. I would imagine he had a notebook of some kind. Somewhere."

"I can do that," Afton said eagerly. "I'll figure it out."

"I know. Then I want you to get a couple of legal-sized notepads and some kind of briefcase from somewhere."

"Right. Then what?"

"Then, little girl, you'll start your real work. You come find me, and follow me around wherever I roam. Got that?"

"Oh, yes, wonderful! You mean I get to be your assistant? And follow you around and take down your orders and things?"

"Yep." He gave her a sharp look and asked quietly, "Would you mind? I'd really appreciate the help, and I—uh, would really like for it to be you, Afton. My assistant, I mean. Work closely together and all that . . ." He finished uncomfortably.

Afton didn't say a word but just threw her arms around his shoulders and hugged him hard.

◇ ◇ ◇

That first day, when the entire crew and all twelve Jeep Cherokees, two travel trailers, four eighteen-wheelers, and four small vans invaded the Methodist Camp outside Ajax, Kentucky, was nothing short of a twelve-hour spectacle.

Afton had successfully completed her first tasks, with Dave Steiner's help. Dave had figured Houston Rees had left all of his working papers and notes at the front desk, and indeed he had. In fact, he had even left his briefcase. "Least he could do," Dave grunted with ill humor. "Kyle gave it to him for his birthday last year. Traitor."

"Now, Dave, my father's not at all angry with Mr. Rees or any of the others," Afton responded spiritedly. "And that's a miracle, wouldn't you say? So you shouldn't be either."

Eight members of the crew, with profuse apologies, had told Kyle the previous night that they weren't able to continue to work on the film. Kyle had, with goodwill as he had promised, booked them on a flight to L.A. the next afternoon. That morning four of them appeared regretful, and one of them actually sidled back up to Kyle and asked if he could rejoin the crew. In the most kindly manner, Kyle had said that he didn't believe it would be good for either of them, but he would be sure and call him on the next film.

The boy, who had been a freight handler, almost cried. But Kyle remained adamant.

"He's a good kid," Kyle had mused to Afton. "But if he didn't believe in *Hearth and Home* last night, there'll come another day when he'll lose faith again."

But Kyle had never gotten angry.

After everything was loaded, Kyle unexpectedly ordered Afton to drive the lead car, as she was probably the only person in the whole crew who had sense enough to find their way around the world if it wasn't a movie set. Afton thought this was odd, as she still had a tendency, if she didn't concentrate very hard, to drift over and drive on the left-hand side of the road. Also, she tended to try to reach for the gearshift with her left hand, which resulted in an odd delayed shifting process, to say nothing of her continually banging her knuckles on the driver's door. But gamely she climbed into the lead Jeep and took off with Harlan Freeman, two young boys who were members of his crew, Jo-Jo, and a rather silly young girl who assisted in Wardrobe.

They didn't get to leave at the crack of dawn as Kyle wanted to. The day before, Peregrine had told Kyle that he would get the loggers out to widen the road so they could get the big trucks up to the camp. The loggers supposedly would be finished by about eleven o'clock. Kyle waited, fidgeting and impatient, driving everyone nuts, until about 10:30. Then he ordered the wagon train to move out. Afton volunteered to go out to the camp just to make certain the work was done, so the trucks and vans wouldn't be stranded on the side of the highway. But Kyle would have none of it. Daylight was wasting.

Afton was happy to see that the stately sentinel pines had been left intact. The loggers had simply carved out a wide spot in the woods close by to serve as a road, passed up the two pine trees, and rejoined the old road just on the other side. They'd only had to cut down three old trees, Afton saw with pleasure, although they'd had to cut back about a dozen saplings here and there that had sprung up right at the road's edge. They'd also had to do a good bit of overhead trimming to allow for the height of the vans. But Afton was relieved that Peregrine didn't have to lose too many trees. She thought again of what an extraordinary sacrifice this was for an obviously withdrawn man like Peregrine to make, and for the thousandth time she wondered why he was doing it.

As soon as they got there, Afton parked the Jeep on the far side of the perimeter around the campgrounds, assuming that all of the other vehicles would line up, roughly following the outline where the grassy yard began. But that assumption was wrong, for the first thing that happened on that boisterous day was that one of the men driving one of the vans just barreled right onto the campground.

Like a freed tiger, Kyle was out of a Jeep, running right up to the moving vehicle, and banging on the back door. "Stop, you ninny! Where do you think you're going? West Virginia?"

The rest of the day was much akin to that scene. Kyle was everywhere, talking—or shouting—continuously. Afton hovered close to his elbow, taking care to keep her distance, for she came to see that when her father was in this high-powered organizational mode, he had a dangerous tendency to wheel about suddenly and barrel on like a bulldozer, knocking whatever or whoever was innocently behind him a-flying.

"First, we gotta see about some furnishings for these cabins,"

Kyle said, striding toward the first one in the loose semicircle of buildings.

Peregrine, appearing from nowhere at Afton's elbow, whispered to her, "Don't worry about that. Mr. Frame's got that taken care of." Gratefully Afton crossed that item off her yellow legal pad.

"Number these cabins—one, two, three, and so on," Kyle went on, pointing, pointing, pointing. "Don't count the meeting hall. I'm going to look at them and assign them."

"Hold on there, General Patton, sir. One of those is mine." Peregrine gulped. "Why don't you let me and Afton assign quarters?"

"Okay, then." Kyle abruptly stopped his march into the first cabin, did an about-face, and yelled, "Hey dummy! No, not you, dummy, the other dummy! Yeah, you, Paulie! Whatcha doing?"

The accused young man, who answered just as readily to "dummy" as to his name, cheerfully called out, "Just unloading these electric cords, Mr. Patton."

"Yeah?" Kyle yelled, already changing directions and heading for another group of girls who were inexplicably running in and out of the Wardrobe trailer with bundles of clothing. "Whatcha gonna plug in? Guess it'd be too much to hope for that it'd be your brain. Put them back, son."

Without turning Kyle dictated, "Peregrine, go herd these little lambs together right now before they wreck your place and my equipment. Get 'em to scrubbing the bathrooms. That'll calm 'em down. Afton, we've got to get the loggers to fill in the ruts that genius made driving the van. Check on some sod too if we can match this winter grass. Can't have big truck ruts in my movie. Hey, Jo-Jo! Uh-uh, don't you duck around that trailer. You get over there and pay attention! That's right, that nice Mr. Peregrine's going to tell all you little children a story! Get over there right now, and bring all your little friends too!"

And so the day went. Afton was delighted and sometimes overcome with laughter at her father's banter. She could readily see, as the entire crew could, that though he was sarcastic, it was merely his way of communicating with his crew. They all had heard Kyle call himself a blooming idiot and a lazy, worthless, good-for-nothing and much worse, so they never took it personally when he called them such awful things, as long as he was smiling.

And that was the best part of it, Afton later reflected. Never, not once during this helter-skelter, mumbo-jumbo of a day did Kyle Patton lose his temper. He laughed and smiled more than Afton had ever seen him do.

Forty-nine people scurried and hustled, worked and argued, listened to orders and gave them, had quick meetings, worked some more, argued some more, and, miraculously, accomplished a great deal of work.

The kitchen in the meeting hall was cleaned, all the ancient dishes washed and stored, all the cobwebby kettles and cast-iron pans and enormous pots cleaned and hung from hooks over an old worktable that was fully eight feet long. The table itself was scrubbed with bleach, then cleaned with steel wool, even the legs. Four twelve-foot folding tables were cleaned and set up, and fifty folding chairs were placed around them. A crew even cleaned the chapel of the meeting hall, mopping the floors and dusting the pews.

One girl found a small wooden cask that held tableware. After taking it out the cleaning crew discovered that it was very old silverware—mismatched, but 200 odd knives, forks, and spoons, all real silver. They were excited by the discovery—until they figured out that silver had to be polished. That took one script consultant and a film assistant all day long.

The trucks were painstakingly parked end-first so as to give optimum access to the equipment and supplies inside, as they were going to have to serve as warehousing too. The handlers groaned when they realized that every single day, every single piece of equipment—every camera, every microphone, every electrical cord—was going to have to be hand-carried up to the cabin site, then hauled back down and reloaded into the trucks.

"So what you want? A nice little highway running through the movie's front yard? Besides, I am not going to allow any more damage done to Mr. Peregrine's place here than is absolutely necessary," Kyle firmly told the freight handlers. "You people are handlers, isn't that right? Then handle!"

But still they remained as cheerful as the rest of the crew. Everyone was buoyed up, eager, diligent. Afton reflected that the possibility of collecting such a large sum of money for the work might be quite an incentive. But upon reflection she decided that wasn't all of it. Getting paid a lot of money was an incentive certainly, but only to do the work efficiently enough to collect your pay. Having such a wonderful attitude about your work couldn't be purchased. It was something else, something more.

These people, they're like a clan, she decided. *You might not like all of your kin, you might not get along with them, you might despise them. But they're a part of you. You belong to them, and they belong to you. You share goals, you share dreams, you share interests . . . So you work together, no matter the goal, no matter the cost . . .*

She was coming to see this was indeed a community—a com-munity of people who also shared and deeply felt loss.

The sun had set, though it was not yet full night. All of the buildings had electricity, and one of Afton's chores that day had been to get a crew to go around with light bulbs and supply each cabin. Squares of yellow light burned onto the shadowed grounds, and there were still about a dozen people out completing last-minute chores and two or three still running from cabin to cabin on their assigned business. Kyle was striding around, yelling, "People, get it done! Time to load up! Let's go, let's go!"

Harlan Freeman was sitting in one Jeep, warming it up and yelling out the window at his crew to get in because he was "tired as a weasely little white man, so it's back to the crib!" Suddenly his strident voice cut off in the middle of a word. Afton, still shadow-ing Kyle, was vaguely aware that he turned his car radio up so they could hear an announcer's deep murmur.

In a few moments the black man loomed in front of Kyle. He put out his hands and rested them on Kyle's shoulders, effectively putting a stop to his relentless jog-and-order. Then, to Afton's astonishment, Harlan reached up and took off his sunglasses. "Kyle—Kyle—" he muttered, his voice rough.

"What is it?" Kyle asked with a tinge of dread.

"It's Alastair, Kyle," Harlan almost whispered, and there was no shuck-and-jive in his deep voice.

"Alastair? Alastair Cowan?" Kyle demanded.

"Yeah. He's dead, Kyle. Accident on the set of *Dead to Rights*."

"No . . ." Kyle whispered numbly.

"They said a stunt went wrong, a car crash scene. The car

caught fire. Alastair was trying to get his double out. The car exploded, killed both of them."

"This—this can't be true," Kyle said in disbelief. "It can't be true!"

Harlan took a deep breath, stuck his sunglasses in his shirt pocket, and put his hands back on Kyle's shoulders. "It's true, man. He's gone."

Kyle wrenched away from him and almost ran to the middle of the grounds, with his back turned to the cabins and crew. This time Afton didn't follow him, though she watched him sorrowfully. She knew that Alastair Cowan had been Kyle's discovery and that the two movies Alastair had starred in had been the triumph of Kyle's career, and maybe of his life. But more than that, Afton knew, Alastair Cowan had been Kyle's friend, perhaps his closest friend. Though Alastair refused to star in Kyle's other movies because he found them objectionable, Kyle still had loved the man, and evidently Alastair had loved Kyle. They saw each other often when they were both in L.A. When they weren't, they still kept in close touch. Afton knew that they even wrote to each other, a most unusual thing for men to do, especially in this day and age of personal assistants and pagers and cell phones and E-mail.

Harlan slipped away, and the news spread quickly among the entire crew. Then Harlan went and stood close to Kyle, though he didn't touch him or speak to him, but merely looked up at the sky, as was Kyle. The moon was rising, a clear, gleaming full moon, and then the companion evening star made her appearance close by. Dave and Charlie went to stand and watch the sky; the other members of the crew slowly filtered over there, until they were assembled in a loose crowd, not speaking, just looking up. Messalina stood close by Kyle, and Tru shuffled up. Tears were rolling down his face. Alastair Cowan, it seemed, had been beloved by millions indeed, and not all of them a faceless public. Almost everyone on Kyle's crew had worked with Alastair at one time or another, but even the ones who hadn't met him were struck by the tragedy.

After all, he was one of them. He belonged to them.

Afton slipped up and stood to the side, because she knew that she didn't belong in this crowd, not at this time.

She looked up. The night was brightening from the sunset, and stars were beginning to unveil themselves. Dreamily she thought that if they turned all of the lights out, she would see more stars than she had ever seen before, even in the clear, high air of Scotland.

Kyle asked in a choked voice, "Lina, would you sing for me?"

Without hesitation Messalina Dancy started singing "Amazing Grace" in the clearest, sweetest soprano Afton had ever heard.

Tears rolled down Afton's face. Not for Alastair Cowan; though she felt the sting of tragedy, she did not know the man, and she was no hypocrite. She cried for her own loss, for her mother, whose absence was still a raw scar on her mind every day, and for Malcolm, who was forever in her thoughts, but so horribly absent from her eyes.

As she cried, she cried for them all. Not just for the ones who had died, but for all of them there, all of them saddened, all of them touched by loss. It was a bond. It made them all the same. Even the man who stood at her side—Peregrine, who must have known terrible loss, for his golden eyes, turned up to the same moon, glinted with unshed tears.

But even as she wept, Afton was conscious of a still, small

voice—one that no one on Planet Earth could hear, for it was inaudible except to her own heart.

You are going to have to have faith for others, daughter. No one but you believes in Me, but your faith will be enough. Be not filled with doubt, but believe that what I have promised, I will do.

And at that moment Afton Burns knew that she was not alone. She felt the small seed of faith that had been planted in her for so many years putting down roots, and she knew that one day she would see the fruit of that faith.

FOURTEEN

◇

Y OUR DADDY NOW OWNS the entire stock and inventory of Mammy Murdock's Antiquities Barn," Peregrine said, sidling up to Afton as a purple-and-silver, long-nosed Peterbilt truck sidled cautiously down the hill to the camp. The trailer was unmarked, but the cab of the eighteen-wheeler was marked "WJ Truckin'."

"He does?" Afton smiled. "Well, I'm certain that he'll be proud to own such valuable antiques."

"Not sure they're antiques, and I'm real sure they aren't valuable," Peregrine responded dryly, "but you can sleep on them and eat on them and sit in them. It looks like by the end of the day most of these people might regard 'em as pretty valuable after all."

Joel Frame had dealt with Mammy Murdock to buy all of her "antiquities" to furnish the cabins, as the shrewd but stubbornly back-hills little old woman was wary of "outlanders." He'd gotten a good deal for Kyle, talking Mammy Murdock into selling both the contents of her "Antiquities Barn" and another unnamed barn that was full of old, ugly, but sturdy furniture as one lot. There were not only plenty of beds, but she also had hundreds of mattresses and box springs, creaky end tables, lamps old and new of all imaginable colors and shapes, scarred desks, dozens of unmatched chairs of all possible uses, cabinets, pie safes, cupboards, old rugs, kindling boxes, and forty-four unmarked boxes of no one knew what.

At any rate, all of the cabins were now not only furnished but stuffed. The crew resolutely refused to throw out anything, and they stashed the boxes in the chapel.

About a dozen of the younger members of the crew formed a sort of club. At night, after the long day was done, they would open a box—only one at a time—and explore the contents, laughing and sometimes wondering what in the world an unrecognizable item was. The boxes contained old squashed hats, cigar boxes, ancient wire-rimmed spectacles (some with thick cobalt-blue frames), rusty skeleton keys, incomprehensible kitchen tools, old jars and bottles, dusty old books, yellowed pieces of hand-embroidered linens, and many, many other wondrous things. Kyle generously told them they could have anything they wanted, and to them it was like a treasure hunt. They did take some of the things to be their own, but they were very discriminating.

They got in the habit of arranging the quirky items along one wall of the makeshift cafeteria, using two mismatched round dining tables that had no chairs to go with them and no cabins to go around them. Everyone looked forward to viewing the collage in the mornings at breakfast, noting the changes, picking out their favorite vignettes. Dave even took black-and-white photographs of many of the most interesting groupings of items. Six months later everyone in the crew would receive an album with fun snapshots of everyone on the Kentucky crew at work, but the photos of the collage were poetic and a little sad.

Joel Frame showed up on the day the crew actually moved into the camp, the day after Alastair Cowan's death. Afton, yellow legal pad in hand, was conferring with Peregrine and her father as they tried to figure out how to feed everyone. Kyle had arranged for the Holiday Inn to cater and deliver three meals a day for three days, but such service was of course prohibitively expensive.

They looked up when Frame's Dodge Ram rumbled down to nose between a Jeep and the electronics truck. It made Afton glad to see her father's face light up when he saw Frame's truck, as Kyle had been subdued and morose all day, often staring vacantly into space. Afton, too, liked Joel Frame immensely and thought he was a sturdy man, a wise man, with a personal warmth that readily showed through his country shrewdness. He was a very comfortable, and comforting, sort of man.

Joel climbed out of the truck and hurried over to open the passenger door. A lady climbed out—Mr. Frame solicitously helped her—and then Frame gallantly tucked her arm through his. "Here we are," he announced. "This here is Molly. My present wife."

"First and only, and likely to stay that way too, Frame. What other woman would put up with the likes of you?" She put out her hand and shook hands sturdily, like a man, with Kyle. Then she stepped up and gave Peregrine a hug that would have thrown a horse. "Hello, John. You been too busy to come see a lonesome old woman? Ah, maybe you have been at that." She turned to Afton, took her proffered hand and held it, then with her other hand put a thick forefinger under her chin to tilt Afton's face upward. "Why, you really are a little angel thing, aren't you? Pretty—and sweet too."

Molly Frame was a tall woman, as tall as her husband. She was sturdily built, obviously a woman who had spent most of her life outdoors. Her cheekbones were wide and angular, her jawline too pronounced for prettiness; but she had an apple-cheeked, wholesome smile. Shiny dark hair blended with glimmering streaks of silver; she had pulled it back loosely and anchored it with a heavy tortoiseshell and gold comb. Her eyes, almost identical to Joel Frame's, were dark, almost black, shining with robust health, gleaming with cleverness. She wore a thick black turtleneck sweater that reached her thighs, faded jeans, and knee-high black rubber boots.

Molly studied Afton's face, and Afton somehow didn't mind the assessment. She stood quietly, steadily meeting the woman's gaze.

"Yes, I can see why my husband's so taken with you, child," Molly murmured, clasping Afton's hand now in both of her rough, outdoorsy ones. Glancing slyly at Peregrine standing nearby, Molly added knowingly to Afton, "Can see why lots of men might be taken with you. So, John, you got, what, forty, fifty people staying with you?" she went on mischievously, taking her husband's arm again with an obviously old habit of affection. "That's good. Good for you."

"Glad you approve, Molly," Peregrine responded dryly.

Afton looked up at him to ask guilelessly, "John? John—"

"Doe," he muttered, then turned away. "Think I better go see about Miss Dancy's fireplace. She said it's smokin' somethin' awful."

"Can't have that, can we?" Afton murmured sardonically. It appeared that Peregrine and Messalina Dancy had been working together quite closely on a number of things, none of which Afton knew about. Neither Peregrine nor Messalina had bothered to report to her, which bothered her much, much more than was warranted, which in turn made her a little snippy.

Joel studied her for a moment, a strange little smile on his face, then turned to Kyle. "Mr. Patton, mebbe you might better get this bunch together in unloadin' teams because you're gonna get a whole wagon train full of stuff here in about an hour or so."

"I am? Oh, by the way, thank you so much, Mr. Frame, for making the arrangements for the furnishings," Kyle said gratefully. "That's been a lifesaver."

"Well, you got a roof over your head and something to sit on," Frame replied, "and now you got two fridges, two freezers, a truckload of food, and a cook on the way. After that you got eight timber men coming to get in some firewood for everybody." He grimaced at the low gray sky. "This here's a summer camp, you know. None of these cabins is really built for winter living. Good thing they at least have fireplaces."

"Yes, and they're great," Kyle said enthusiastically. "Native stone, I believe. Big hearths. Good tall chimneys for a good draw."

"Yeah, and big open caves for all the heat to disappear into," Joel pronounced pessimistically.

"Oh, Frame, how many times we gonna fight about that?" Molly grinned at Afton and Kyle. "Mountain men. Think open fireplaces don't give off any heat. Always griping about it all going up the chimney. I love 'em, and I hate those little shut-up black ovens you men always want to have."

"She loves 'em all right," Frame said sorrowfully. "Got a fireplace in every room in that big ol' house."

"Yes, with that many fireplaces blowing all the heat up into the sky, it looks like it'd snow in the house, doesn't it?" Molly said mischievously. "Mr. Patton, my husband, he's good at buyin' stuff and figurin' out what other folks need to do and going all over the country minding people's business. But I'm the only one who ever gets any work out of anybody, so let me give you a little piece of advice about these people around here. They'll work like dogs for you, but they'll try to get it over on you first. Don't let 'em. You just be firm with them from the beginning, and after they settle down you'll be all right."

"Yes, ma'am," Kyle replied, a little nonplussed.

"After you get them worthless loggers to haul the firewood," she continued in her rapid-fire manner, "you make 'em split it and stack it or they'll just be barreling down through the camp, chunking great big logs down off the trucks."

"Yes, ma'am."

"And I don't know much about moviemaking," Molly said, sniffing, "but I know them loggers. After they finish hauling your wood, you put 'em right to work on building that cabin or they'll be lazing all over your kitchen with their big muddy boots and eating up all the food on the place."

"Yes, ma'am." Kyle shook his head to clear it. "I mean—wait a minute . . . building the cabin?"

"Of course." Molly gave her husband a questioning look, and he shrugged helplessly. "Frame says you need pictures or shots or whatever you call it of a log cabin being built."

"Well—I—uh, wished for it because I had some footage of my star fiddling around with some of the logs from the cabin that burned. But we've lost so much time, and now that footage wouldn't match the little log cabin up on the rise we're going to use. So I gave up on getting footage of building the cabin."

Molly shrugged carelessly. "Looks to me like the building of one is kinda what you're trying to show in your movie, am I right?"

"Yes, ma'am," Kyle said resignedly.

She rounded on Peregrine. "You did mark them trees, like Frame told you, didn't you?"

"Yes, ma'am," Peregrine said resignedly.

"And how much time you got left before that rude Eye-talian comes and repos you?" she asked Kyle sharply.

"One month. Actually, thirty-four more days."

"Well, then." Molly's firm words were an obvious period to the ending of a declarative sentence.

Kyle looked thoroughly mystified.

With sympathy Joel explained, "People worked together, you see. No one man could finish a cabin on his own, not the roof especially. But a man's neighbors generally helped him from the first. That's what Molly's thinking, that with help you could get a cabin built in a day or two. That the crew could, like, kind of be the men who'd be there for your Mr. Kirk or whatever his name is. They'd be there."

"Oh," Kyle murmured, his eyes suddenly going glassy with his introspective stare. "Ohh," he said again, this time with dawning revelation. "Would you excuse me?" He dashed off yelling, "Dave! Charlie! Get over here right now, I need you!"

Afton smiled apologetically at the Frames. "You'll please excuse my father. He doesn't mean to be rude. Well, that's not exactly true, sometimes he does mean to be exactly that. But not this time. Not to you."

Molly and Joel laughed. "He's an energetic sort of feller, ain't he?" Joel remarked. "But he's got a lot to think about."

"I want to give you my most sincere thanks for all the help you've given us," Afton said gratefully. "I appreciate it more than you know, and so does my father. He'll get around to thanking you properly and making arrangements to reimburse you when he has a few thousand less things to do."

"Looks like you're giving him some help with that," Molly said approvingly, nodding at Afton's scribbled and dog-eared pad. "You're a good girl, helping your father out like this. And listen, there's something special I want you to do for me. I know a woman'll pay attention—these men try to look like they're listening, but they don't fool me. They're studying about their dogs and their pickup trucks and their new rifles."

She poked Joel sharply in the ribs with her elbow, and he had the grace—or the smarts—to look repentant. He wasn't sure what about, for he hadn't actually been listening too closely; he'd been thinking about his new rifle.

Molly shot him a knowing look, then continued gravely to Afton, "It's about all the stuff for the new cabin." She continued, now gravely, "It's coming this afternoon from the museum. I know your father is a responsible man, but there's a lot of kids running around, whooping it up, and they can be careless with things when they don't understand how valuable they are."

"Yes, ma'am," Afton said obediently. "I'll personally attend to the unloading. And I know where some padlocks are stashed. I'll ask Peregrine to put a lock and hasp on the door and keep the cabin locked up when we're not using it."

"Thank you, Afton," Molly said, satisfied. "Those things belonged to Frame's family and my family, the Coopers. Some of them are 200 years old, and I'm proud of them. I'd hate to see anything happen to them. All the kids in this county go to the museum and learn firsthand about their history and their heritage. It's important."

"Yes, ma'am," Afton agreed. "It is. I promise I'll take good care of your things."

"Then I won't stew about it any more." She patted her husband's arm. "C'mon, Frame, I've got things to do."

He sighed deeply. "I know. Got to go tend to the llamas."

"Ll-llamas?" Afton repeated uncertainly.

"Yep. Little lost things from Alabama," Frame said with a tragic air. "Rancher gave up on 'em, and they were being neglected. Molly here will likely be feeding 'em in the dining room by next month. Not to mention the eemahs."

"Eemahs?" Afton repeated blankly. Peregrine had finally come out of Messalina's cabin, wiping his hands on a red bandanna. Afton was having difficulty concentrating.

"Yep. My bird dogs are gonna love them. Likely give Princess a stroke," Frame grouched.

Peregrine was heading this way. "Oh?" Afton said with blank politeness. "That's too bad . . . Here's Peregrine. Hello. We were just talking about Mrs. Frame's eemahs."

Peregrine's severe stone features creased into a delighted grin. "Her eemahs? Sure. Big birds, long eyelashes. Don't fly. Run, though, like the dickens. You keep hangin' out with the natives, Miss Afton, and you'll not only learn to speak English, but you'll speak it like a native Kentuckian."

Afton, who was now very distracted by how compelling Peregrine was when he genuinely smiled, had not the faintest idea what he was talking about. "That's nice," she said lamely, blushing a little. She'd been staring at him, and he knew it.

He winked broadly at Molly Frame, who was sternly trying not to smile, then moved down and whispered softly in Afton's ear. "Afton . . ."

She jerked, then blurted, "Yes?"

Softly, caressingly, he whispered, "It's 'emus.'"

◇ ◇ ◇

Afton, growing a little bored watching her father and Dave Steiner work like madmen to set up the cameras to film their very first location scene—a shot of the cabin with a breathtaking sunset behind it—thought about the man everyone knew as Peregrine.

She decided there were really three men. One she named Peregrine, the second she named John-John, the third she named John Doe.

Peregrine was a passenger in life's fast stream and yet a pilgrim wayfaring on his own, wishing the company of no man. He was a caricature, deliberately drawn by a clever man indulging his slyest and most childish tendencies. The slushy drawl, the inarticulation, the vacant stare, the doltish grin—that was Peregrine, but not all of him. Occasionally, if one was watching carefully, the man peeked out from behind the dummy's mask and laughed at his practical joke upon the world.

Then there was John-John, the half-man, half-boy who grew weary of Peregrine's tiresome vacancies but stubbornly wouldn't let go of all of Peregrine's performance. John-John was impatient, weary, and spoke with a cloak of ignorant hillbillyisms but said intelligent things. When Peregrine slipped, John-John took over.

And then there was John Doe. The real man—but the one that

Afton knew and understood the least. She'd seen him that afternoon when he was teasing her about the emus. That was John Doe,
the man who fascinated her, bewitched her, the man she couldn't
stop thinking and wondering about.

She believed John Doe was the man who had kissed her so
affectionately, so warmly, so gladly that day.

But she wondered who exactly was the man Messalina Dancy
was getting to know so well.

◇ ◇ ◇

Twenty feet behind where Afton sat, watching the crew at work on
a night scene, Peregrine and Joel Frame sat in two old wooden
chairs, courtesy of Mammy Murdock's Antiquities Barn. Squeezed
between the chairs was Stonewall's bulk. He was lying very still and
quiet, as Peregrine had had to speak to him sternly over and over
that day as he got somewhat overwrought with all the strangers and
activity. Stonewall, contrary to Afton's first impression, was not a
trained attack dog. He was, however, very loyal to Peregrine and
very protective of him. He would never attack anyone unless
Peregrine clearly told him to, but he was a sensitive dog and had a
tendency to get overtired, as he felt it was his solemn duty to inves-
tigate everything and every activity that had to do with Peregrine.
On this night he was exhausted, and he had barely moved for the
last hour.

Peregrine had dug out a shallow round hole and had lined it
with big boulders retrieved from the hills. Kyle had fussed about
digging up the grass in his "woodland clearing" location, but
Peregrine had ignored him. It was, after all, not exactly Kyle's

grass—it belonged to Peregrine. And Peregrine couldn't see any reason for a man living in 1898 not to have a place for a nice camp-fire outside, especially for crisp, clean October nights like this, and he told Kyle so. Kyle had gracefully retreated, agreeing that it prob-ably would make a good shot for the movie.

"Heard Mr. Patton had a shock last night," Frame said con-versationally, staring into the comfort of the big ruddy flames from the fire Peregrine had built.

"Yes. All of these people were grieved at that actor's death," Peregrine agreed quietly. "Most knew him, but even the ones who didn't were almost in shock."

Frame nodded sagely. "He was one of them. Molly and I saw *The Piper* and *Path of the Prodigal*. Great movies. And that Alastair Cowan is a real man's man. Course, that ain't all he is, judging from how much in love Molly is—was—with him. She kept up with everything about him. Said he was a Christian, a real godly man, and said that made him pretty special. Like the rich man in the Bible getting into the kingdom of heaven. Probably ain't been but two, three of 'em in the history of this old world that's made it."

"You will," Peregrine remarked idly. "So that makes at least four, counting David and Solomon and Alastair Cowan."

Frame grunted with amusement, then shifted uneasily in his hard chair. "You got any idea exactly how Mr. Cowan was con-nected with Mr. Patton's business?"

Peregrine's eyes flickered strangely in the scarlet flames. He glanced at Afton's frail figure sitting cross-legged on a quilt on the ground about twenty feet away. "She told me that her father still owns those two movies, and the other one Mr. Cowan starred in,

Heart Seize, and Mr. Patton's been as stubborn as a donkey about re-releasing them. They only ran in the theaters once, you know. And he's refused to run them again or to sell subsidiary rights to television or to put them on home video. Evidently Mr. Cowan has—had—royalty rights, but he backed up Mr. Patton's decision a hundred percent."

"Uh-huh," Frame mulled. "Thought so. Molly showed me an article where they were interviewing Mr. Cowan—mostly baiting him, because they kept talking about how he and Mr. Patton would make millions for releasing the movies again. But Mr. Cowan said that Mr. Patton might consider a ten-year anniversary release, but nothing else, and he thought that was a real good idee. Said to have 'em showing on the idiot box at 2:00 A.M. every Friday night and in B-theaters as a lead-in to shoot-em-up Jap movies every week-end or collecting dust in people's 400-video collection would be like using the *Mona Lisa* to cover up a hole in your bathroom wall."

Peregrine smiled without humor. "Interesting viewpoint. He must have been a courageous man."

"Yup."

The two men sat in an easy silence for a while, watching the fire. Peregrine rose and collected some small sticks and one big log and carefully arranged them on the already-roaring blaze. Yellow sparks as thick as Roman candles gleefully shot up dozens of feet in the night sky, popping and crackling like faraway artillery.

"Pine's nice for an outside fire," Frame ruminated.

"Yup," Peregrine agreed, dusting his hands on his jeans and reclaiming his seat.

"So Mr. Patton's company still owns them three movies, huh," Frame said idly.

"Guess so."

"And those movies . . . it's a shame, but it's the way of the world that they're going to be worth a lot more now that that Mr. Cowan's dead."

"Yes, sir, I'd think so."

"And that Mr. San Angelee just happened to show up, sur-prising-like, day 'fore yesterday with his papers and his buckets o' money," Frame ruminated.

"Yes, he did," Peregrine answered, now with peculiar emphasis.

"And Mr. Patton came this close to selling out to him." Frame held up a thick thumb and gnarled forefinger.

"That's right, Joel." Peregrine's voice now was filled with con-cern. "Because the cabin had burned . . ."

"Anybody ever ask you or anybody a-tall why that cabin burned down?" Frame demanded plaintively. He obviously didn't expect an answer because he went on, "No. Seems like that little detail just flew out of everybody's head as soon as the fire died out. Didn't matter that any fool would know that fire was set. Had to have been."

Peregrine looked around ruefully at the so-busy crew, scuttling, calling out, adjusting lights, hauling equipment like drone ants, and at Kyle, who was yelling at Dave at the top of his lungs about the camera having night dew on it, and at Afton who sat so still and so quietly, listening and watching. He murmured, "And they call me a half-wit."

Then, repentantly, he added, "But Mr. Patton did take special care to tell me he was leaving all the equipment out here last night, and would I mind watching out for it. Course, I could be a hundred miles away and Stonewall would put a stop to any cute business like that. But I told Mr. Patton I'd watch it. He didn't say anything else, just thanked me . . . But maybe he does realize something's up. He just can't do much about it."

Joel Frame felt that this astute observation required no response, so he grew quiet and thoughtful. His seamed, timeworn face was troubled. Peregrine, too, was staring into the cheerful bonfire, and he seemed wary, watchful, like a wild animal who scents a nearby predator.

About ten minutes later Truman Kirk came out of one of the trailers and headed straight for Afton's chair. He stopped, hesitating, and paced back and forth, obviously troubled. Then, with an air of decision, he went up to her and touched her shoulder. She looked up and smiled, and he went down on one knee to talk to her. He talked for just a few short moments, but Afton's face grew utterly absorbed, and she didn't interrupt. Tru appeared to ask her something, cocking his head with concern, and she nodded. After patting her shoulder awkwardly, he left.

Afton turned back around, her back stiff. Peregrine had watched the exchange curiously. Frame watched first Peregrine, and then Afton, and then Peregrine. He opened his mouth to say something, but at that moment Afton bounded out of her chair and stalked over to the campfire.

"Peregrine, I need your help," she said without preamble.

"Sure," he said. Both he and Frame jumped out of their chairs and offered them to her. She chose Peregrine's and sat stiffly, her back not touching the wooden slats. Frame slid back into his chair, and Peregrine knelt by her exactly as Truman Kirk had only a few moments before. Unconsciously, as she spoke she stroked

Stonewall's big scarred head. The dog sighed contentedly and finally fell fast asleep.

"Harlan called the sound man on Alastair Cowan's movie, *Dead to Rights*," Afton said in a dull voice. "He wanted to find out all about the accident."

"That was bad," Peregrine said with rough sympathy, "but it sounds like the man was a hero."

"He was," Afton agreed. "Anyway, the sound man on the movie said it had happened just like the radio said . . . only it happened on Friday, not Saturday."

Peregrine's smooth forehead wrinkled, and he looked at Joel Frame, mystified. But the old man was nodding, as if he had anticipated this and understood it very well. "Guess *Dead to Rights* was a Monarch Cinema production by that Mr. Santa Angie," Joel said gravely.

Afton nodded, her eyes wide and unseeing, her face distorted with lines of pain.

"And I guess Mr. Santa Angie locked up everybody until he could get his slimy self down here," Frame went on.

"Yes, sir. Locked them up right on the set. Said it was so the insurance people could do an investigation and the police could question everyone," Afton said quietly. "Harlan said his friend said something about suing for—for—something—"

"False imprisonment," Peregrine prompted her.

"Yes, that's it. But . . . Mr. Santorini Santangeli just smiled and said, 'Go ahead, sue me. It'll only take you a few years and a few million bucks to fight my lawyers.' Even the unions didn't raise a fuss. He owns them too, I think."

"Well, he doesn't own your father," Frame growled. "And he didn't get his grubby hands on his movies neither."

"I know, but it may only be a matter of time," Afton said faintly. "Thirty-four days, to be exact. If this movie isn't finished by then—" She shrugged helplessly.

"I think it'll be finished," Peregrine offered. "I think your father can do it."

Afton looked up at him, and her fine, delicate features looked tortured in the inconstant red firelight. "I think so too . . . if nothing else bad happens. I think he can finish it, if no cabins burn down, or no actors quit and go to work for Monarch. It would seem we have plenty of time—if no key crew members disappear into thin air or get their legs broken—or if lightning doesn't strike us all, or if we don't get sick from—from bubonic plague or something!"

"Cheerful, ain't you," Peregrine rumbled. "Try to simmer down, will you?"

"It's not funny!" Afton was almost hysterical. "Don't you see what that man did—what he is? So many things can happen to delay making a movie, and many of them don't have to be sabotage! It could be anything, like the wrong weather or—or—"

"I know, I know, bubonic plague," Peregrine said soothingly. "Listen, Afton, you don't have to worry. There won't be any sabotage here. No bad things will happen here. No one will hurt anyone here, or anything that belongs here, in this place. I promise you that."

Frame sucked his teeth. "I got a coupla good men," he said. "I think I'll put 'em to kinda patrollin' your road, Peregrine."

"Thank you, sir," Peregrine said. "Better?" he asked Afton solicitously.

She smiled tremulously at him and then at Mr. Frame. "Yes. Yes. I'm so glad to . . . talk to someone, for someone to help me. Thank you both."

Peregrine stood, stretched, and crossed his arms. "Nothing bad will happen here, Afton. I promise you."

But unfortunately Peregrine didn't keep his promise.

FIFTEEN

◇

I T WAS MONDAY, OCTOBER 2. Twenty-nine more days until Mr. Santorini Santangeli returned for his money.

Or to watch a movie.

That Monday was cold, with a blustery breeze that swept through the valley of the camp in temperamental fits and gusts. The sky was tinted a dreary shade of gray, and the sun was merely a lighter patch of gray that wearily traced from east to west.

Afton, Peregrine, and Messalina, whose cabins were in a row, came out at the same time and paused on the porches, sipping their first cup of coffee. Messalina called out cheerily to Peregrine, "Come join me. I wanted to talk to you about that quilting box."

"Quilting frame," he corrected her as he obediently went to her porch.

Messalina called out to Afton, "Good morning, Afton! It's a wonderful day, isn't it?"

"Oh, yes, wonderful," Afton called, her voice flat. Moodily she watched the two as they laughed and talked and companionably sipped coffee together. But Afton did reluctantly admit to herself that Messalina had changed since they'd come to the camp.

Ever since she had discovered her Anna Kay Wingfield persona, she had wafted and waned in and out of the character. When the crew had arrived at the camp, Messalina had put on a long black skirt, old men's boots that were two sizes too large for her, and a plain cotton blouse and had set about smartly to clean her own cabin herself, shooing away her personal assistants with disdain. She had scrubbed and swept and dusted and scrubbed more, and had also thoroughly washed and then polished each stick of furniture that had been supplied for the cabin. Messalina had even shooed out spiders, batted away cobwebs, and swept the front porch. Then she had asked Peregrine to teach her how to build a fire. He did so, and the next chore was to gather small sticks for kindling. By herself she scrounged up a small wooden box and gathered enough kindling for about a week.

Watching in amazement, Afton said to her father, "She's truly dedicated, isn't she? Going through all that just to get into character!"

"Yes, she is," Kyle answered, then added craftily, "It might have had something to do with Daniel Day-Lewis."

"Hm?" Afton knew of the actor; many of the stars that movie people talked incessantly about were unfamiliar to her.

"Uh-huh. I mighta mentioned something about him to Lina. He spent two months on Hog Island living in a cabin and—uh, eating roots and berries, I guess, before filming *The Crucible.*"

Afton said severely, "You might have mentioned it to her? Do you really think that's fair?"

Kyle looked injured. "It's what I call giving an actor motivation. It's a director's thing."

"Yes, I'm sure," Afton replied. "A director's thing. You—you're incorrigible!"

"I know," Kyle said regretfully. "It's appalling."

Messalina searched out Kyle as soon as he came into sight that morning and without even a "Good morning" announced, "Today I'm going to do the washing."

"No, Lina, today we're going to shoot the scenes with the other two ladies—"

"No. Today I'm going to do the washing," Lina repeated stubbornly. "Just like Mr. Frame said. It's the only way to make this new start for these scenes."

"Well, maybe for an hour or so—" Kyle hedged.

"No. As long as it takes."

Kyle knew a brick wall when he saw one. "All right, Lina. Please, though, just wait until we get the cameras and sound team in place up at the cabin, so we can film it all. No sense wasting the scene; there's no telling how much of it we might be able to use."

Messalina considered, then reluctantly said, "All right, I'll wait. I'm not in makeup yet anyway. But it won't be too long, will it?"

"No, darling, only about an hour. We'll probably be ready before Charlie gets you ready," Kyle said soothingly.

"Good." Messalina hurried over to the makeup trailer.

Before Kyle could get restarted, Tru Kirk came striding up, grinning. "Mr. Patton, I think I better go ahead and start working with those oxen today. Peregrine said he'd help me get started, but he said they'd need a little time to get used to me. The oxen, that is."

"But, Tru, I've got the first camera crew tied up with Lina, and I wanted to get plenty of footage of you with the oxen," Kyle argued. "So today I wanted to get the panorama scene of you and the loggers working on the cabin."

Truman Kirk's face fell like a disappointed eight-year-old's. He

turned and shuffled away. Afton looked up at her father reproach-
fully. With a grimace and a roll of his eyes, Kyle yelled, "Aw man!
C'mere, Tru! Blast it! You people seem to think this is summer
camp or something! Go ahead and go play with your fool cows!
I'll—I'll tack together another crew, and maybe put Lindo onto it.
We'll probably have miles of footage of dirt and tree trunks and ox
behinds and who knows what, but—"

Tru had turned, listening with childish delight, and ran up to
interrupt Kyle's griping. "Thanks, Mr. Patton, thank you," he
beamed, pumping Kyle's hand vigorously. Then he, too, ran for the
makeup trailer.

"Good grief," Kyle muttered. "Surrounded by morons. Thought
Peregrine was the only one, but turns out he's the only one with
any sense."

"I have sense, and you have sense," Afton said sturdily. "It's just
that you also have heart."

"Great. Guess I better donate my organs," Kyle scoffed, "'cause
that's the only way my heart's going to make anybody any money."

Mr. Joel Frame, cheerfully admitting that he was fascinated
with the movie and didn't have anything better to do, showed up
at dawn. Kyle welcomed him gladly and asked him to advise
Messalina on her washing scenes.

Messalina had her battling board, with four sturdy logs for legs.
She had her washing kettle, duly blackened, with a tripod and a
hook to hang it over the fire. She had her two rinsing kettles, duly
not blackened. She had her bucket for hauling water. She had her
stream nearby to haul the water from. She had a pile of clothes—
white and blue shirts, denim breeches, two white cotton sheets,
and a quilt, all dirty. She seemed very happy.

She asked Peregrine to make her a little fire-hollow, and he did so quickly, lining it with rocks and building a nice little fire. "If you'll use pine, it makes a hot, quick fire, Miss Dancy," he advised her. "Your water will boil faster. But it pops real bad," he warned her. "You don't want to set that long skirt on fire."

Messalina looked down at her ankle-length blue skirt, faded and patched realistically. "What did the women do back then?" she asked.

"They were real careful," Joel Frame answered. "And they made allowances. See, nowadays women swing along any old how, because you've got comfortable clothes. But back then the women always had to be aware of how they walked, how they moved. They were always in danger of setting their skirts on fire, 'cause that's all folks had, you know, for heat and for cooking. And besides that, they couldn't go wheeling about hurdy-gurdy or they'd be knocking things over. Lots of things back then were breakable 'cause they didn't have no plastic." He made an ugly face, as if plastic were as offensive as dung. "And most folks couldn't replace something they had broken. Nobody had enough money. So the ladies, see, they walked real slow, taking their time, real graceful, gliding along. Not like now . . ." His voice was wistful.

"Well, for—Kyle! Kyle, I'm walking all wrong!" Messalina shouted. "Rosalind never told me a thing about this! She's useless!"

"Who's Rosalind?" Peregrine asked curiously as he was stacking small pine logs he had cut just to fit Lina's washing fire.

"My joke of an acting coach. Never mind." Messalina turned on Joel Frame with the determination of a mother tiger and said, "You could teach me, Mr. Frame. Please? It wouldn't take long, I assure you. If you could just show me for a few minutes I'd pick it up. I'm very quick."

The indignation of Joel Frame was a sight to behold. He pulled himself up very slowly and said in a tight voice, "Now lemme get this straight. You want me to prance about like a lady? S'pose you want me to put on one of them skirts, just so's it'll look like the real thing!"

"Believe me, in L.A. many men do just that nowadays," Lina said acidly. Joel Frame began to look outraged.

"Wait, wait, please, Lina," Kyle said hurriedly, repressing a smile. "Look, we're ready to shoot here. And your fire's there, and there's your paddles and dirty clothes and things. You don't want to put this off another day, do you? We can work on this walking thing later."

Lina considered this and finally nodded. "All right, yes, I want to spend this whole day washing, and—hey you! What's your name? Never mind, I don't care! Where are you going with my best quilt? Come back here!"

With relief Kyle went back to Dave Steiner's side, and Joel Frame almost skittered along behind him. "Tell you something," Frame muttered, "my Molly was right about one thing—I can't hardly stay outa trouble without her. Mebbe from now on I better bring her down with me to help ya'll out."

Repressing a smile, Kyle said courteously, "Mr. Frame, we'd be honored if you and Mrs. Frame could come every day. Your assistance on this film is invaluable, and I'm certainly going to credit you. You'll be credited as our Chief Technical Advisor, Kentucky and Mrs. Frame will be the Assistant Technical Advisor."

"Really?" His eyes shone. "You mean, our names and them fancy titles will be on that long list at the end while some music's playing? Nobody ever reads them, I guess, but that would be some fun!"

"Oh, sure, Mr. Frame, people read them," Dave insisted, grinning. "Every person whose name is in the credits. And their mommas and daddies and families."

Kyle was staring at Mr. Frame in a speculative manner. "Yes, that's true," he said absently. "But I've got an idea . . . it should work. Then everyone will read the credits . . . Uh-oh, here she goes, Dave. Guess we all just better stand back and stay out of the way. It's Mrs. Anna Kay Wingfield's washing day."

Peregrine skipped out of camera range just in time, for Lina began her washing with a vengeance. Afton saw that the uncanny stillness and quietness that pervades the atmosphere during filming had prevailed, and her father was completely engrossed in Messalina. So Afton decided that no one would miss her if she went to watch Peregrine and Tru working with the oxen.

She caught up to Peregrine as he was making his way down the rise toward the barn. "Hello," she said breathlessly. She was almost running to keep up with his long, confident stride. "Would you mind very much if I came to watch you working with Tru?"

"Not at all," he replied. "In fact, looks like we've drawn quite a crowd."

A six-man camera crew was busily setting up, reeling out electrical cords, arranging one fixed camera and one on a boom. About two dozen people, including Mr. Frame's six loggers, were propped up on the fence posts lining the barbed-wire fence that enclosed the animals. Afton sighed. Somehow she had vaguely thought she might get a chance to talk with Peregrine, to be with him, to do something together in a cozy atmosphere.

We're making a movie, she reminded herself dryly. *Everything is filmed, none of it is real. It can't be like the day Peregrine and I visited at the barn and I met Boadicea . . .*

"I haven't seen Boadicea since we were here," Afton said. "Doesn't she stay close to you?"

"Not at all," he answered. "She comes and goes as she pleases. Sometimes I don't see her for days. Sometimes I see her two or three times in one day. Sometimes she stays for a day or two." He made a graceful waving gesture. "One day I expect she'll fly away and never come back. It's the way of things, isn't it?"

"Not at all," she answered, unconsciously echoing his words and his staunchness. "Hawks mate for life, don't they? So she may leave you, yes, because you're not her God-given companion. But when she finds her mate, she'll never leave him. That is the natural way of the Lord's world. It's humans who have distorted it."

"You're a very dedicated Christian, aren't you?" he asked with genuine curiosity.

"I strive to be. Sometimes I shine, and sometimes I fall. What about you?"

"Huh?"

"Are you a Christian?"

He thought for a long time before answering. They had almost reached the barn when he said with difficulty, "Only God knows. Here we are. Want to ride an ox?" He looked at her with the vacant Peregrine grin.

"No thanks," she replied gaily. "I'll get my shilling's worth just watching."

She picked out a spot on the fence line, a little ways away from the rowdy, cat-calling, and whistling timbermen. With a start she noticed that Roy Dale Puckett and his brother Bobby were evidently on the logging crew. Neither of them, however, looked her way. With relief she ignored them, determined to enjoy herself. After all, in this situation she could watch Peregrine all she wanted, without anyone thinking anything of it.

Tru was standing at the gate, which was merely a loose post with the ends of the fencing wire looped around it so the post could be moved back and forth to allow someone to enter or leave the enclosure. He didn't look nearly as happy as he had before with Kyle. In fact, he didn't look at all happy. He looked pale, and he looked frightened, though he was trying very hard not to.

Afton immediately went to him and leaned against the nearest fence post. "I wanted to come watch," she said brightly. "Peregrine treats these oxen like they're puppies."

"They don't look like puppies," Tru gulped. "Especially when you get close. I went in the barn. By myself. Thought I'd just—uh, pet them or something before Peregrine got here. They're huge."

"I'm sure they're much more imposing in a closed-in place," Afton replied lamely.

"No. They're *huge*."

"Tru, listen to me," Afton said firmly, trying another tack.

"I'm listening."

"Tru, look at me," Afton insisted.

With great effort Tru pulled his gaze down to Afton's face. He'd been watching the big double doors of the barn as if at any moment the Mongol army was coming through it to massacre and pillage.

"Tru, these animals won't hurt you," she said with great authority. She even stepped close and put her hands on his arms. "There is simply no way that my father would allow you to get into a dangerous position. Aside from the fact that he likes you and wouldn't want to see you hurt, it's only good business. You're one of the stars of this film. You don't allow your stars to get into a position where they may be injured."

"You sound just like him," Tru said, his voice a little firmer.

"Thank you," Afton replied, smiling.

His gaze shifted behind her, and she turned. The great double doors of the barn opened, and the oxen came lumbering out. The noise of them sounded like a whole herd of buffalo, moving very slowly. Behind them Peregrine walked casually, holding a small switch. He whistled sharp and clean, then in a clear, commanding voice called out, "Gee!" The oxen stepped up the pace a bit, and then all of them veered right. Peregrine followed them, then called more commands as they reached the far end of the grassy field. They lowered their massive heads and began to graze.

Peregrine came back. When he drew near to the group, he called out in a silly, singsong voice, "There you go, Mr. Kirk. They's your props!"

Afton realized that Peregrine was back for the crowds and gave him a look that would have sizzled sausage. He flinched, then looked closely at Truman Kirk's white face. One of the loggers— Afton was sure it was Roy Dale—shouted, "Hey, half-wit! You got those oxen outsmarted, do you? You sure?"

Raucous laughter sounded from the timbermen, but most of the crew members standing around looked disgusted and wandered away. Afton frowned at Roy Dale, but he winked insolently and she looked away.

Ignoring them, Peregrine was talking quietly to Tru. ". . . thought it'd be good for you to go pick out the two you wanted to work with, but maybe not. Guess being in the middle of eight of 'em would be kinda overwhelmin'."

"You guessed right," Tru retorted grimly.

"Okay, don't worry. I'll go get Tango and Cha-Cha, get 'em over here at this end, away from the others. They're a team, they're used to each other, and they're both real good-natured. We'll take it real slow from there."

"Okay," Tru agreed, but he sounded doubtful.

Peregrine walked down toward the oxen, swiping his switch in the air idly and whistling. Afton, watching, noticed that the oxen had separated into two groups of four, one group at the far end close to the fence, the other close up by the barn. Within those groups, it seemed as if the oxen paired off and wandered around grazing in couples. Afton wondered if she were just assigning sympathetic attributes to the animals and decided to ask Peregrine about it.

Tango and Cha-Cha were grazing together right by the barn wall. Peregrine got behind them, tapping their haunches lightly to get their attention. They raised their heads in unison and looked behind at the same time, as if they were choreographed. "Haw, let's go. Haw!" Peregrine tapped them again, lightly, on the left haunches. The animals turned to their right, still in unison, and ambled directly toward where Tru stood outside the fence. Unknowingly, his face twisted with dread, he backed up a step. Afton, seeing it, moved directly in front of him, leaning close against the fence. Then with a sudden flash of inspiration she called out, "Peregrine, can I come to you?"

"Surely, Miss Afton," he called, shrugging.

The loggers rumbled and laughed, but Afton didn't care.

"No—" she heard Tru mutter, but she yanked open the makeshift gate and nimbly stepped inside the field. Without looking back, swinging her arms carelessly, she walked toward the big beasts.

"Don't face them off. They'll just stop in their tracks," Peregrine said, grinning. "You'll scare 'em."

"Oh. Beg your pardon," Afton said, veering around them quickly. She reached Peregrine's side and said rather breathlessly, "Tru's really scared, Peregrine. And it's not like just being nervous. It's more like a phobia or something."

"I know. I saw." He thought for a minute, then shrugged. "Can't do much but try to show him these animals are just like real easygoing cows, only I think they're really sweeter-tempered than cows." He gave her a quick, sidelong glance. "You sure aren't scared."

"I'm not?" she said casually.

"You're not showing it."

"Then perhaps I should ask my father for an acting job," she said nervously, "because those are the hugest things I've ever seen!"

"I saw you that day petting Ricardo."

"Ricardo? Oh—the one leaning on the fence. Yes. But that's a very different viewpoint, depending upon which side of the fence you're on," Afton declared.

"Ain't it always? Here, Tango, Cha-Cha, ho! Ho-up! Whoa!" Together the animals stopped at the fence. Suddenly Afton realized that if Peregrine hadn't signaled them, they probably would have plodded right through the barbed wire without a second look.

He walked between them, and at the haunches both were about four inches higher than the top of his head. Grinning reassuringly at Tru, he threw his arms around the two oxen's massive necks. "This is Tango," he said, nodding left, "and this is Cha-Cha."

"Uh-huh," Tru said, obviously not impressed.

"They're real good animals, Tru," Peregrine said quietly, rub-

bing the oxen's necks with almost a caress. "I've never known an
ox to have a mean bone in his body."

Tru still looked doubtful. "Peregrine, I guess it hasn't occurred
to you, but those brutes could do you some serious damage just by
accident and still be sweet things."

"Not possible," Peregrine argued. "Watch." He moved in front
of Tango, knelt, and tapped his right leg. Obediently the ox raised
his massive foot. Then Peregrine did something that made all of
them flinch, and the timbermen let out long, low murmurs and
whistles. He lay down on the ground and maneuvered until his face
was right beneath Tango's hoof. He spoke softly to the ox. "C'mon,
Tango, it's just me, showin' you off. C'mon, boy . . ." The ox looked
supremely bored, but as Peregrine pulled insistently on his foot,
Tango slowly, by tiny increments, lowered it. The huge round hoof
rested right on Peregrine's forehead. Afton noted, somewhere
intermingled with her horror, that the ox's hoof was actually larger
than Peregrine's head.

"See?" Peregrine said casually. Then he tapped Tango's leg
again, and the ox obediently lifted it. Peregrine slid out from under
him and jumped up. "These animals will hurt themselves, trying to
stop, before they'll step on anything, especially a human being.
From the time they're born—even the playful little calves—they
pick their way very carefully. They never step on small animals who
get in the way. They're gentle, harmless creatures, Tru, who work
unbelievably hard, with never a sign of discontent, just because we
ask them to. They'll do anything for the man who takes the time
to make friends with them. Anything."

Tru, who was a talented actor with mobile and expressive features, managed to look amazed, frightened, admiring, and sud-

denly determined all at the same time. "Okay, Peregrine. What do I do?"

"You don't have to do anything except come in here and get to know 'em," Peregrine said. "Just pet 'em. Talk to 'em. And look right in their eyes. They'll pay attention to you if you look right at 'em."

"Talk to them, look right in their eyes," Tru repeated nervously, pulling open the gate and stepping through it. He took a deep breath. "Okay. Okay. Hello, Tango. Hello, Cha-Cha. She a girl?" Tru asked, worried. "'Cause maybe I'd do better with a girl . . ."

The timbermen guffawed, slapping their thighs and pointing at Tru. A bewildered, hurt look passed over Tru's face, and Afton saw Peregrine's eyes and face take on that bizarre hungry-wolf look that happened when he was angry. But no other sign of anger showed itself in his movements or his voice.

Moseying, ambling, slouching, Peregrine made his way to the group of loggers, who punched each other and chuckled like silly schoolboys. "Hey!" Peregrine called with evident good cheer. "Y'all know where you at?"

The men looked uncertain, and then Roy Dale grunted, "Why don't you get on back to your oxes there, half-wit? The boy and the girl!" Roy Dale burst into gales of guffaws again, but this time he wasn't joined so readily by the others except for his brother Bobby. Some of the men had done a double-take at Tru's obvious embarrassment and had lost much of their enthusiasm. Two of them shamefacedly wandered off.

Peregrine, so quickly that no one saw it coming, suddenly was in front of Roy Dale Puckett, reached up, and flicked the end of his nose. Roy Dale's eyes watered, and his reaction was as slow as a sloth's. When he finally gathered his wits, he opened his eyes wide with outrage, but Peregrine was blathering, "Fly, there, Roy Dale. Fly. Oh, by the way, you're on my land. I mean, Stonewall's land. You don't want a run-in with him again, do you?"

The man looked around fearfully, then turned back to Peregrine to say in a bluff of boldness, "You—you flicked my nose! And I ain't scared of that beat-up mongrel of yours!"

"You sure?" Peregrine asked. Then, without waiting for Roy Dale's answer, he lifted two fingers to his lips, the clearly recognizable prelude to a loud whistle.

"Hey—hey—" Roy Dale stammered, putting up a hand in a halt signal.

"Thought so." Peregrine nodded. He turned, then as if in an afterthought turned back around to say with great sincerity, "Y'all be quiet, won't you? You get too noisy, Stonewall's gonna come see about it."

The loggers, particularly Roy Dale Puckett, were deafeningly quiet the rest of the session.

Peregrine returned to Tru, who had moved perhaps one inch closer to Cha-Cha. When Peregrine returned, Tru said sorrowfully, "Guess Cha-Cha's a boy, huh?"

"Yes. All teams are either two males or two females. The size difference is too much to team them together," Peregrine answered in a matter-of-fact voice. "And most of the time working oxen are neutered bulls. The females are just kept for breeding. All eight of these oxen are neutered bulls."

Tru nodded, then took a deep breath and touched Cha-Cha's head between his ears. "Uh—this right?"

Peregrine laughed. "Tru, they're not made of glass. Just have fun with 'em. Watch."

"Peregrine, do not do that foot thing again," Tru ordered, standing very still and moving his mouth funny. "I don't want you to do anything to make them nervous."

"Tru, I hate to tell you this, buddy, but you're the only one that's nervous." Peregrine walked to Afton, grabbed her around the waist, and heaved her up onto Cha-Cha's back, stomach-down. The ox never moved; the only thing that moved on Afton was her jaw dropping.

Still grinning, Peregrine walked over to Tango and jumped up onto his back, stomach—down. His face was only inches from Afton's. Bending his elbows and propping his face in his hands, he said, "Good morning, Lady Afton. Fancy meeting you here."

"I'm going to kill you," Afton gritted between painfully clenched teeth.

"Relax. See, Cha-Cha doesn't even know you're there."

"That's insane."

"No. I mean it. Lighter than a yoke, you know."

"What do you mean?" In spite of herself, Afton was interested and wiggled a little, experimentally, into a more comfortable position.

"Most men can't lift a double ox yoke by themselves. Too heavy. But the oxen barely notice it. To them, a yoke is just something to help them work together. If the oxbow isn't heavy and strong enough, the oxen will snap it like matchsticks the first time they look in opposite directions," he finished airily.

Slowly, Afton propped her own face in her hands and rested her elbows on Cha-Cha's back. The only thing that gave away that she wasn't lying on a stone slab was the warmth and the feeling of the short, coarse hair. "So you're saying I don't weigh as much as an ox yoke."

"Probably not," Peregrine said generously. "At least, I don't think so. They probably weigh a couple of hundred pounds."

"Thanks, kind sir," Afton retorted. "What are we doing up here anyway?"

"Shh." Peregrine jabbed his chin toward Tru, who had quit watching the two of them and was talking quietly to the oxen. He was rubbing them more confidently now and had inched a little closer. "I don't care if he is an actor, used to a million people watching his every move," Peregrine whispered. "No man likes to have an audience when he's scared, and no man likes to have people laugh at him. Now everybody's watching us, and besides that, we've shown him that Tango and Cha-Cha are good-tempered enough not to mind us lounging all over them like they're bearskin rugs."

"You're smart. Did you know that?" Afton whispered.

Peregrine looked a little embarrassed, then looked down and started tracing invisible patterns in Tango's hair with one finger. "Tango and Cha-Cha, they've been teamed together a long time. I can tell."

"You can? I was going to ask you—it seemed that the oxen were paired off, in a way."

"Yes, they are. They do that. Four of them were a team evidently, and they stick together. Tango and Cha-Cha and Sham and Jam are paired." He looked up at her. "After a team's worked together for a long time, they can't be separated. It's almost impossible to team them with another animal. And if one of them dies, the other will grieve himself to death if he isn't taken care of properly."

"Oh, my," Afton said, gently stroking Cha-Cha's broad back. "I had no idea . . ."

Peregrine nodded. "They're tied together forever. All their lives, and even in death."

Afton stared at him, and he was watching her, his eyelids sleepy. But his golden eyes glowed strangely, and he made a jerky movement to reach and touch her hand. But he pulled back, tightening his firm lips until they were a straight line. "Guess I better go back to work with Tru." He slid off and hurried around to grab Afton's waist. "Don't worry, it's easy as falling off an ox," he said, and the entire assembly laughed, even Tru.

"Hey, Peregrine," Tru said, his eyes now sparkling. "Think I could try that?"

SIXTEEN

◇

"YOU CALLED FOR ME, SIRE?" Afton teased her father. He had paged her, and she had hurried to him instead of calling him on her cell phone. She was still having fun playing with Tru and Peregrine and Tango and Cha-Cha, but it was her duty to stay close to her father.

He didn't take his eyes off the scene being filmed as he muttered absently, "Uh—I did? Oh. It's—is it lunchtime?"

"It's almost two o'clock," Afton whispered. "Shouldn't you come down and have some lunch?" Glancing with concern at Messalina, she added, "And Miss Dancy really does look exhausted. She should stop for a while."

"She won't," Kyle whispered back. "And I'm not sure I want her to. This is turning out to be some very compelling footage, Afton. Just watch."

Messalina Dancy had disappeared, completely submerged and overwhelmed by Anna Kay Wingfield. The woman washing had a strong face, lined and given character by an unwavering determination. She appeared to be completely oblivious to the crowd surrounding her, watching her every step, her every expression, her every gesture. As Afton watched, Lina lifted the paddle out of the kettle of bubbling water, the cords in her neck straining. The quilt was looped around the end of the paddle, steaming and dripping. Struggling, staggering, Lina lifted it enough to let it fall onto the battling board. With movements slowed and fumbling from weariness, she untangled the paddle and set it into a bucket that, with obvious impatience and disgust, she'd had to go and find after laying the paddle on the ground, then stick it back in her wash water, dirtying it. Lina had never said a word to the camera crew; she had just scrubbed the dirt and grass out of the paddle and disappeared into the cabin. A mobile camera had followed her, and she never appeared to even see it. She came out with the bucket and had been careful to use it since. But she'd had to empty out the wash water, fill it up again, and wait for it to boil. Her face had taken on the cast of a woman who sees no end in sight to her toil but was determined to do it or die.

Her hair, which had been so carefully arranged in a prim little knot at her neck, was straggly and steam-flattened. Her fine complexion was strain-white except for her cheeks, which were two streaks of chafed red. As she picked up a misshapen bar of soap and began to scrub the quilt, Afton noticed her nails. They had broken raggedly, and the sharp breeze and constant scrubbing with the strong soap had turned them painfully red and raw.

Almost an hour passed. Afton, defeated, had sat cross-legged on the ground just behind and to the side of Dave Steiner's camera boom. He and Kyle "rode" it, and a grip was standing at the base, watching the two and maneuvering the controls to move it up or down or to either side, according to hand signals from Kyle.

Watching Lina, Afton could now see why they called it "battling." The big water-heavy quilt took a long, long time to soap, and then Lina had to beat it with the paddle, as that was the only way to get the soap through and through.

Peregrine appeared at Afton's side and sat down beside her. "You look cold," he commented.

"I'm freezing and paralyzed," she whispered. "But look at poor Miss Dancy. Peregrine, this is not good. She's pale, and she's obviously so exhausted she can hardly lift her arms. It's cold, and she's wet."

Peregrine looked at Messalina Dancy, watching her gravely. "She's not cut out for this. It's too much. Women back then, they were accustomed to this backbreaking work, did it from the time they were little girls. Her doing this all at once is like people who decide to exercise by weight lifting and start out lifting 200 pounds for a couple of hours. Cripples 'em for weeks."

Afton's concern grew, and when her father glanced down, she signaled to him furiously. Obediently he scrambled down from the boom. "It's great, isn't it! Isn't she something!"

"She's crazy," Peregrine whispered furiously. "And you're crazy for letting her do it."

"No, she's not, and I'm not. Peregrine, you may know about oxen and building bonfires and making jerky, but you know zip about making movies. And I want quiet on this set, both of you." Kyle stiffly jerked back upright to watch Lina.

Afton gave Peregrine a little helpless shrug, but he wasn't watching her. He was looking at Messalina Dancy, and his face was dark with concern. This confused Afton, for though she too was concerned about the actress, Peregrine's sympathy irritated her.

He wasn't nearly so concerned when I was—was—so—courageously facing the oxen, she thought huffily.

But Afton's common sense and natural sweet disposition prevailed. *Oh, yes, big courageous lassie . . . facing certain death . . . if Cha-Cha had smothered me, with kisses, that is . . .* The oxen had a tendency to give long, wet slurps with their tongues. Right to the face, if they could get away with it.

Afton was smiling a little shamefacedly to herself, but suddenly Peregrine stiffened, and his face grew grim. Afton looked up at Messalina.

The actress, standing at her battling board, had abruptly stopped working the sopping quilt and was staring down at the end of the paddle she held. Very slowly, as people move when they are about to faint, she laid the paddle down on the board and then held her hands palms up and stared down at them, an odd, nightmarish-dreamy look on her face.

It grew so still, no one moved.

Blood, bright, red, and watery, dripped onto Anna Kay Wingfield's best quilt. Great scarlet drops fell, and the quiet was so complete that they could clearly hear the plop-plop-plop. Both of Lina's hands were bleeding from blisters that had formed and now burst, deep wounds in her palms.

She took one faltering, searching step backwards and fell to the ground, hard, in a sitting position with her legs turned to the side. Still she held her hands out, now over her apron. Her head down, her face invisible, Lina started to cry, great tearing sobs of defeat and discouragement.

Afton must have moved, for Kyle made an imperative chopping gesture with his hand. Peregrine stood up and took a step forward. "No! She's acting. Leave her alone!" Kyle commanded in a grating whisper.

"No," Peregrine said loudly and clearly, crashing into the silence. "That's real blood, Patton. You're so lost in your little fake world that you don't know the difference between real hurt and blood and playacting." With furious steps Peregrine stalked to the huddled form of the actress, went down on one knee, put a comforting arm around her shaking shoulders, and gently lifted up her hands closer to see, talking softly and soothingly to her.

"Cut," Kyle yelled with disgust.

He wheeled around, crashing into Afton, who was standing and watching Peregrine and Lina with a strange expression, forming and reforming itself every few seconds as it alternated between compassion and strain and worry and suspicion and anger.

"She was acting, Afton," Kyle said in a low tone. "Believe me, I know. Did you see that fall? Expert choreography. How graceful her position, legs tucked neatly to the side, hands artistically posed, helpless, bleeding. She's superb, you must admit, because it was just an act." He walked away.

But Afton wasn't so sure.

Peregrine, his arm securely around Lina's trim waist, walked her back down to the camp. No one stopped them, and Lina didn't speak to anyone, keeping her head down and holding her hands in a painful way. They weren't dripping blood now, but they were smeared. Peregrine took her to his cabin, Afton saw with a distressing wrench of real jealousy. She'd never been inside Peregrine's cabin, and as far as she knew, no one else had either. The rest of them ran in and out of each other's cabins at will, considering the unusual circumstances of the camp; it was in effect one big movie set.

With determination Afton retrieved her constant companions—her legal pad, her pen, her cell phone, and her pager—and concentrated on helping her father. It was necessary for them to break down all the equipment and haul it back to the trailers because none of it could be left outside in the elements and there wasn't enough room in the little cabin to stow anything.

Afton was mindful of her solemn promise to Molly Frame. Quickly she straightened the cabin, then got a prop boy to empty the sloshing kettles and stow them under the wooden slab that served as a kitchen counter. Afton carefully checked to make certain the boy had dried them properly. They couldn't be left outside either because they were made of rude iron and would rust overnight. Then she brought in the paddle and bucket, and the prop boy, a shy boy of seventeen named Sig, helped her bring in the battling board. Afton refused even to leave the weathered wood-and-log construct outside. After that she locked up the cabin.

The crew was filtering back down to the camp, heading for the trailers with various pieces of equipment and supplies. Dave, along with six assistants, was still breaking down the boom, which had to be dismantled into three bulky and heavy pieces before it could be moved. Afton gamely grabbed a coiled and secured roll of electrical cord, slung it over her shoulder, and headed toward the camp. Sig, however, ran up and took it from her, saying bashfully, "You don't have to haul stuff, Miss Afton. Plenty of grunts like me to do that."

She surrendered it to him gratefully. "You're not a grunt, you're Prop Boy Number 16, Kentucky Location, and that's more of a title than I have, Sig."

He grinned, ducking his head, and mumbled, "Can't believe you remember all our names and even our jobs. That's real nice,

Miss Afton. Makes a nobody like me feel pretty good." Awkwardly he trundled off with his electrical cord and two microphones.

Afton reflected on this and thought with satisfaction that it was a good thing, a kind thing, an admirable thing, to pay attention to people and remember them. It was a gesture of simple respect, perhaps the only respect they would ever receive in their whole lifetime. She'd always been able to remember people from the Salvation Army, even the worst and most hopeless of those nameless ones who shrank away from the world. She could remember their names, their circumstances, the streets they haunted, even their peculiarities—sometimes their private insanities.

Suddenly she thought of Colin, and it was a jolt to realize that she hadn't thought of him in days. But now, thinking about the hard but rewarding work at the Army, she could see him clearly, ministering to the hopeless, giving them simple kindness and understanding, listening to them, sometimes in delirious ravings, for hours, even washing them and hand-feeding them. And always he maintained a great dignity, an aura of strength and purpose that made the people realize he was not doing this because of some private demon he must exorcise; he was not helping them because he felt guilty; he was not a bleary-eyed dreamer who believed in serving Man but not this filthy man or that insane woman or that orphaned child. He did it because he wanted to, because he had great joy in doing it, because it was his ministry from the Lord. It was his yoke, and it was light, and his burden was easy. Afton admired Colin McDaniel almost as much as she did her Grandfather Malcolm.

Everyone was outside, doing odd tasks, some bringing equipment down from the cabin, some going in and out of the makeup trailer with their carry-around satchels, some going in and out of the Wardrobe trailer with costumes they'd been working on. Peregrine and Messalina came out of his cabin, Messalina looking pale but calm, Peregrine still grim. He left Lina, however, and hurried to talk to Kyle. At that moment everyone stopped, for they heard a loud command.

"Look! Look, everyone! I'm doing it! I've got it!"

Tru Kirk was yelling like a wild schoolboy. He was walking along about five feet behind Tango and Cha-Cha, who were yoked and clomping along so patiently, with such long-suffering on their great bovine faces that Afton thought with delight that they too were glad to indulge the kindly and gentle Truman Kirk.

The stately procession made its way right through the camp, and everyone began clapping and cheering wildly. Every person, without exception, liked Truman Kirk. Tru treated everyone the same, from the last prop boy to Miss Messalina Dancy, and even the most cynical and hardened of them responded to his solid honesty and truly kind heart.

Afton, too, clapped and called raucously, lapsing into British exhortation. "Carry on, Tru! Jolly good, jolly good!"

"Jolly," Kyle said sourly, though he was grinning and clapping himself. "He's trooping them right down through the middle of my woodland clearing. Scene One Hundred Fourteen, Lina and Tru argue and kiss."

"Aw, a few ox prints won't matter, Mr. Patton," Peregrine said. "Genuine, you know. True-to-life. Bound to be tracking all over the place, especially if you have a whole herd of them." He kept a straight face, and Kyle gamely grinned.

The oxen and Tru plodded on, Tru, with high color and a reckless grin, waving to the crowds like a triumphant gladiator. They came right down the middle of the camp. "Uh—Tru! Tru!" Peregrine called with rising urgency.

"Huh? Yeah?" Tru heard, craning his neck.

"Don't you think you might—"

"Oh! Hey! Uh—uh . . . Haw! Haw! Tango, Cha-Cha, please, haw!"

The rowdy crew responded by laughing, "Haw-haw-haw, Tru! Haw-haw!"

"Tap 'em, Tru!" Peregrine called, straining to keep from laughing.

The oxen were slowly and determinedly headed straight for a cabin, which turned out to be Tru's own. They would, unless they were commanded to turn, walk right up to it, their noses almost touching it. And turning a pair of yoked oxen when they were nose-up to a wall was no easy job.

Tru skittered closer to the oxen's behinds and tapped them so easily a gnat wouldn't have flinched. "Haw, please! Haw!"

They turned, keeping their slow but relentless pace.

"Peregrine, why don't you have reins or something on them?" Kyle said with a hint of irritation.

Peregrine laughed. "Mr. Patton, you really think Tru could make them go someplace—anyplace—with reins? No man can control a brace of oxen with brute strength. They respond to voice commands only."

"Oh," Kyle said. "Well, then, maybe you'd better check your training manual. 'Cause it looks like Tru and his buddies are gonna march to Atlanta."

At that moment Tru, who was steadily heading out of camp

behind Tango and Cha-Cha into the wild blue yonder, was passing right by Kyle, Afton, and Peregrine. Uncertainly he said, "Uh—Peregrine?"

"Yeah?" Peregrine was grinning.

"How do you get 'em to stop?"

"Simple, Tru. Try 'whoa.'"

"Okay. Now?"

"You where you want to go?"

"Guess so. Sure." Tru was getting farther and farther away.

"Then give it a shout."

"Whoa!"

The great journey ended.

◊ ◊ ◊

It was a good week, that first week of October. The blazing colors, the bracing chill, the breath of excitement stirring constantly throughout the camp at each new scene and each new shot completed.

Kyle had decreed that no one could leave the camp until the film was completed. This was harsh, but it was justified. It took a good two hours just to get to Ajax, and another two to get to Lexington, and many members of the crew weren't responsible enough to go out somewhere for dinner or a night on the town without disappearing for perhaps days.

Tru and Messalina and the key people like Dave Steiner and Charlie Terrill and Harlan Freeman were so tired by the end of each day that they didn't care. If Kyle found out something was needed in camp, he would ask Joel Frame, who would make arrangements in his quick way for someone to fetch and carry, and whatever they'd needed would appear, usually by the same afternoon.

Joel appeared before dawn each morning, and Molly usually came with him. They rarely stayed past early afternoon, but the couple was faithful to report in every morning. Often Joel's "advice" as Chief Technical Advisor, Kentucky Location, took the form of getting in the way and taking up too much time telling stories of the old days, but Kyle patiently indulged the man. As often as not, he not only had truly valuable input and insight into the props and sets but also occasionally envisioned a slight change in a scene or in the wording of the scripted dialogue that enhanced the integrity of the film.

Afton agreed with her father's decree to stay at the camp, understanding the reality of his concerns, and she knew that he—rightly—didn't expect her to ask for an exception for herself. But she was regretful that she couldn't go to church.

She'd always attended church every Sunday morning all her life. Not only could she not go, but she saw that Kyle intended to work on Sundays, just as if it were any other day. She spoke to him about it, but he just shrugged. "Afton, I appreciate your sentiments, but it's only you that has this personal—um, constraint. No one else minds working on Sunday. After all, we are in extreme circumstances here, and everyone is working unselfishly to get this film done. I'm not certain we could accomplish that if I give everyone Sundays off. Besides, it would be meaningless to them; it would just be a day off, not a day of—um—"

"Consecration?" Afton suggested with heavy meaning. "Dedication?"

Kyle merely shrugged, but he averted his gaze from hers. "Well, you have my permission to have a service in the chapel if you'd like. And anyone can attend. But it's got to be early, really early, before dawn. And only for an hour."

"Thank you, Father," she said with delight. "So, will you come?"

"No, can't swing it, love," he said with mounting embarrassment and hurried away.

Afton didn't ask anyone to come or make any announcements. She simply walked to the chapel just before sunrise on Sunday morning, dressed in a long pleated wool skirt, soft black leather boots, and a thigh-length burnished gold turtleneck sweater. She wore a pendant, a waist-length gold chain that held an antique magnifying glass, set in an elaborate golden circlet. It had been Malcolm's glass, which he had used the last two years of his life, when he had been losing his sight along with his strength. Afton would never forget the poignant sight of her strong, blustery grandfather, thick shoulders bent over his huge, giant-print Bible, struggling to see the words with his magnifying glass. She carried that same Bible, as bulky and aged and careworn as it was. It was one of her most valued possessions.

As she walked, at least a dozen people greeted her, then asked curiously, "Where you going, Afton?"

Lightly she would reply, tailoring her answer to whomever she spoke and their temperament. "I'm goin' to church, you heathen pup! It be Sunday morn, and the Good Lord's day!"

"I'm going to go into the chapel and pray for a while. I'll pray for you, Linda, for that bit of a runny nose you've got, and for you, Drew, for that burned finger."

"To the church, young lads. It's spelled c-h-u-r-c-h, for your future reference. Know you haven't ever heard of it, much less seen the inside of one! That's all right, I'll say a special prayer for you!"

She went. She prayed. No one came.

Afton didn't mind. Maybe no one came today, this first Sunday in this exciting place, amid such exhilaration. But she knew that one Sunday some of them would come, some sidling in shame-facedly, some coming in almost fearfully, some—generally the ones who were the most sarcastic to her—defiant, even angry. But some of them would come. She'd already seen the need and the wistful longing and the curiosity in some of them. It was always the same, no matter what kind of people. In a crowd of a dozen people, at least half of them were conscious, on some level, of the call of the Lord in their hearts.

When she came out of the chapel, the sun was majestically ris-ing. The cabins looked toward the east, and despite the hurly-burly activity in the camp that was already at full gallop by sunrise, most mornings the people couldn't help but stop and watch the sun coming up. Every morning was different; every one was breathtak-ing; every day that the sun rose to rule the day was a solemn moment of recognition in every heart.

Kyle was standing out in the middle of the grounds with about a dozen people, including Messalina, who was holding a cup of cof-fee in her bandaged hands, Tru, and Dave Steiner, who was fiddling with a mounted camera. As Afton headed for the group, she heard Kyle say, " . . . can be fixed, can't it? C'mon, Dave, you don't fool me. I know you eat with your cameras and pet them and tuck them in at night. You can do it."

"Just a minute." Dave sounded irritated. "Look, it's just that ratchet. What's in there—a colony of rats?"

Messalina peeped over his shoulder and said, "Oh, Dave, it's just some lint! You'd think you were doing brain surgery!"

"Kentucky lint," Dave growled. "More like sticks and stones. Hello, Afton. This be a hard and cruel country, it do be," he finished in a fair imitation of a Highland accent.

"Aye, my lad, that it be," Afton solemnly agreed. "Kentucky lint's famous for its viciousness."

"Shut up!" Kyle gasped. "I mean, look!" He pointed frantically with his finger toward the north.

A figure, outlined in a glorious crimson dawn, stood on the tip of the rise. Black against the scarlets and pinks and oranges creeping northward and intensifying was the figure of a man, standing triumphant, his fist raised to the sky. Afton automatically searched the dim skies high above and saw a soaring black speck barely outlined against the soft gray. "There she is," she whispered to herself.

"She?" Kyle asked without turning around.

"Boadicea of the Iceni," Afton breathed. "Peregrine's falcon. She's coming to him."

"What?" Kyle searched the sky above Peregrine and saw the bird. "Oh my—Dave, quick, you gotta get this. Quick now."

Dave was aggravated, and stubborn for the first time Afton had ever seen. "Camera's broken, Kyle. That's why I've got it vivisected like this," he said with irritated injury.

"We're gonna lose it," Kyle muttered, searching frantically around. "Dave, hand me that camera. Or give it to somebody. Get over there on number three, right now. Jo-Jo's got it almost set up."

"Not set," Dave grumbled. "Don't have time."

"Just do it!" Kyle almost screamed. A quarter-sun had seeped inexorably up, and the hue of dawn's palette was getting to be at its most intense. Afton knew, as did everyone from watching the sunrises, that the dazzling spectacle would be cruelly short-lived, no more than two or three minutes. Then the sun would turn to its normal innocent yellow, and the spectacular garish brush strokes of dawn would fade.

With irritation, Dave dumped the camera into Tru's hands, who barely seemed to notice. He too was mesmerized by the dramatic sight. Now the hawk could be clearly seen, and as if she were determined to stun the watchers, she cried, long and sad, over and over. She was still high above the small dark figure, but she was circling him as surely as if he were her prey.

Dave finally trudged over to Jo-Jo, who had upon seeing the scene and hearing Kyle's frantic orders frantically set up the big heavy camera on a teetering tripod. As Dave had argued, Jo-Jo, with an air of desperation, had peered through the viewer and fumbled with controls and levers, the camera jerking about erratically. But just as Dave reached him, he stepped back. Dave peered through the viewer and said with real pleasure, "I can't believe it. It's perfect, Jo-Jo! Why have you been pretending like you're an idiot, fooling me all this time?"

"I haven't," he said indignantly.

Then everyone grew quiet and watched.

It was magnificent.

As the sun rose, the hawk grew nearer and nearer to Peregrine, who stood perfectly motionless, an ancient statue of the eternal falconer, longing for his prize.

Afton, standing by Messalina, heard her whisper in a deep

whiskey-throaty voice, "I caught this morning morning's minion, kingdom of daylight's dauphin, dapple-dawn-drawn Falcon . . ."

Kyle snapped his fingers. "You! Yes, you with the mike! Turn it on and bring it here, right now. Messalina, do that again."

"Sorry, Kyle, I've forgotten the rest," she said with true regret, her eyes never leaving Peregrine's still figure and the bird's sweeping flight. "Except for . . . um . . . My heart in hiding / Stirred for a bird, the achieve of, the mastery of the thing!"

"That's good, Lina," Kyle said happily. "We'll find that poem— Gerard Manley Hopkins, isn't it?—and I'll get it on audio for a voice-over later. You're a genius, you know that?"

"Sure, Kyle," she said shortly. Obviously she didn't want to talk anymore.

They all watched, enchanted, bewitched, enraptured until Peregrine snared his lady hawk on his hand.

SEVENTEEN

◇

INDIAN SUMMER," Joel Frame asserted with an ominous air. "Indian summer," Afton repeated happily. "It's marvelous! We don't have surprises like this in Scotland. The weather stubbornly conforms to the season."

"Enjoy it," Frame responded dourly. "We'll pay for it."

"Frame, you're a joy to be with this fine morning," Molly commented. "It's nice, warm, sunny, not a cloud in the sky. If you don't quit grumping I'm not going to make your Saturday pancakes. I'll feed you curds and whey, like Miss Muffet. She was scared of a spider, and you're scared of a little spell of warm weather."

"But I don't understand," Afton said, interrupting Joel Frame's response. She and Joel and Molly were enjoying a cup of coffee in their canvas chairs, just outside the cabin, while the crew was setting up. "Why should one be so gloomy about this Indian summer?"

"Always signals a bad winter," Frame answered, though in a less dire tone, with a guilty glance at Molly. "You know it, too, Moll. Never fails."

She shrugged, then said sturdily, "Doesn't matter. No sense in darkening the days fretting about something you can't help. And *you* know *that*."

"That I do," Frame meekly agreed, and he smiled repentantly at Afton. "Don't pay any attention to me, Miss Afton. I'm just a grouchy old man."

"Nonsense, that's just not true," Afton said, her eyes sparkling. "You're not at all old."

All three of them chuckled at Afton's sly joke, and then she asked, "But how long will this last? Is it just one blessed jewel of a day or what?"

Frame shrugged. "Week, maybe two. Never longer than that, usually no shorter."

"A week of this weather," Afton sighed. "I'll be glad to pay for it. And so will the crew, and my father, I think. We still have two scenes to shoot that were supposed to be in early spring, and I know Miss Dancy will be glad not to be out shivering in a thin cotton dress."

"Heard she hurt her hands something awful, doing the washing," Molly said with sympathy. "I remember my grandmother doing that, in a little cabin not far from here, much like that one. It was always terrible toil, even for those who knew nothing better."

"Peregrine put something on her hands, some secret ointment he conjured up," Afton told them with a careful lack of inflection. "Messalina called it 'balm of Gilead.' It did make her hands visibly better overnight. It softened the chafed parts but helped the sores to scab up. It is quite a miracle medicine."

Joel Frame and Molly looked at each other, then laughed. "Horse liniment?" Joel guessed.

"Of course," Molly said with delight. "But maybe we better not tell Miss Dancy that."

"Peregrine certainly didn't," Afton said with a hint of disgust. "He was acting like Sir Galahad defending Guinevere."

"Think you mean that Lancelot fellow, don't you?" Frame idly mused. "I was of the mind that Sir Galahad didn't take much to—"

Molly gave Afton a quick, cunning look and blithely interrupted her husband's mutterings. "Maybe I will tell Miss Dancy about that 'balm of Gilead' being horse liniment after all."

The week began, like the weather, with a sunny outlook. On Monday they shot one scene of Messalina quilting with two friends. Kyle, who had initially planned to fly in two minor actresses for this and three other scenes, decided to cast two of the wardrobe girls. Both quiet little seamstresses, they were close friends and, astoundingly, were not aspiring actresses. They were thrilled by a chance to appear in the film, and neither of them ever evidenced delusions of grandeur, which Afton suspected was exactly why Kyle chose them. They had such a skeleton crew, and each person had to shoulder such an array of responsibilities that if some prop girl or camera assistant got too starstruck to actually work it would leave a serious gap in the workload.

They also managed to get some footage of cabin-building scenes, including some great shots of Tru confidently working the oxen as they hauled the big, freshly cut logs. Peregrine showed Tru how to hand-strip the logs, square them off, and dovetail them so that the cabin he was building would match the cabin they were filming. Unlike Lina, Tru readily did the grueling manual labor but paced himself. "I don't fool myself," Tru told Afton. "I'm in pretty good shape, I guess, but after about half an hour of stripping that log, I knew if I overdid it I'd be down for a couple of days. So Peregrine coaches me. He's great."

"Great," Afton echoed hollowly. She'd barely seen Peregrine in passing for two days, while it seemed that Messalina required his presence for a great number of things, both business and personal. She asked him for more "balm of Gilead" and declared that only he could bandage her hands properly. She needed him to help make a good pulley to lower and lift her quilting frame. She required his expert advice on the correct cooking pot to use for this stew and that porridge. And on and on.

Afton was never able to keep the sequence of the movie straight, as they filmed in what seemed to her to be an indecipher-able tangle that had nothing whatsoever to do with chronology. But Kyle assured her that sticking the stuff together was part of his job, and that he and Stella working as a team were particularly good at sequencing.

"She's coming home tomorrow, early," Kyle told Afton happily. He truly did depend on Stella, and he missed her when she was gone, Afton reluctantly admitted to herself. Her personal feelings were that the work was much more fun without Stella Sheridan, and the crew was much more relaxed and affable. Stella, while obviously intelligent and knowledgeable about the moviemaking business, was quite an intense and driven person on the set. That affected everyone, it seemed, especially Kyle.

He was so much more . . . morose and bad-tempered when Stella was here . . . but maybe that's just because things were so bad. Perhaps this time he won't be so unhappy, so worried . . . The film is going so much better now, so many good things have happened . . . Afton anx-iously hoped and prayed that the difficult operation would con-tinue to go so smoothly.

Unfortunately, Afton's prayers seemed to be unheeded by the Lord of creation. It seemed that Indian summer wrought other woes besides heralding a bad winter.

But Indian summer couldn't be blamed for everything, Afton reflected morosely at the end of the week. It seemed that what started it all was when Stella Sheridan arrived at the camp.

Kyle went to pick her up at the airport in Lexington, impatiently refusing to send someone else. They didn't get back until about two o'clock that Monday afternoon, and as soon as they got out of the Cherokee everyone in camp knew they were fighting, for the simple reason that they were both yelling at the top of their lungs. Even Stella, in jarring contradiction to her normally reserved, sophisticated manner, was shrieking like a fishwife.

Slamming her passenger door with a vengeance, she shouted, "I did the best I could, Kyle! How dare you accuse me of short-shrifting this! I had to get the best money I could in a short time! What possible good would it do to make an extra 50,000 if the deadline's past and Rini owns us lock, stock, and barrel?"

"But you lost me almost 50,000 dollars, Stella!" Kyle retorted angrily, slamming his door and stalking around to where she stood, angrily propped against the Jeep with her back to Kyle. "That's ridiculous! Peregrine's dog could have made a better deal than that!"

Stella pulled herself perilously straight and pointedly looked around at the two dozen or so people milling around within earshot, trying to do their work while appearing to be deaf and blind. "Let's discuss it later, Kyle," she said in a low, strained tone. "The peasants will revolt."

She took off at a reckless stride, then turned and demanded of a group that included Afton, "Which of these dismal shacks is ours?"

"Hello, Stella. I'm glad you made it back safely," Afton said with calm and deliberate politeness. She knew that her lack of temper would shame Stella Sheridan, who took great pains to be poised at all times.

"Thank you, Afton," she said after a hesitation for a quick adjustment. She showed no shame, but she was a little stiff with discomfort. Still, she resumed her usual cool demeanor quickly and asked, "Would you mind showing me where to go? This is the first time I've been here, you know."

"Yes, I know," Afton said, moving to walk at her side. "This way. You have a nice cabin, and I'm sure you'll find it comfortable enough to rest. I know how wearying traveling is."

"Perhaps I will take a nap," Stella said, tension creeping into her voice. "It's been a very difficult week. And of course, I don't do well when I'm not with Kyle." She gave Afton a quick, judging look to see if her loyalty declaration had worked, but Afton's expression of neutral politeness remained exactly the same.

"Of course," she replied. "Here we are. And I'll see that someone brings your luggage."

"Thank you." Stella hurried inside the cabin.

Work resumed, and more footage was shot with no hitches. Then, at about five o'clock that afternoon, Stella and Kyle were at it again.

They had gone into the sound trailer, which wasn't just for the audio portion of the movie but also had monitors and projectors so footage could be viewed. Kyle had been excited about his scenes of Messalina's washing and Tru's oxen and Peregrine and Boadicea.

Stella had what one prop girl called, unaware that Afton was standing behind her, a blue-faced hissy-fit. Jo-Jo remarked to one of his buddies that Stella had gone postal for sure.

"Do you mean to tell me that this pile of trash is your crowning achievement, Kyle?" she clamored, coming down the steps of the trailer like a freight train. Stopping, she looked back over her shoulder at Kyle, who, with a stunned, white-faced look, was feeling his way along behind her. "It's garbage, Kyle," Stella said in a bloodless voice that was much, much worse than her shriek. "It's a pitiful waste of film. Don't you have any idea what the date is?"

"Of course—"

"Don't you know that the cabin burned over a week ago? And that we lost a week's worth of work then?"

"Yes, but—"

"Don't you have any clue that none of that worthless footage has anything to do with this movie? Do you by chance remember which movie you are supposed to be filming?"

Kyle pulled himself erect, then said in a voice that was weary beyond endurance, "That's enough, Stella. Enough."

She shrugged, then turned and went to their cabin. She didn't appear again until the next morning, when she and Kyle seemed to have worked out their differences and were back on their normal footing. But Afton thought that somehow much of the fire and excitement had left her father.

That stick insect is sucking him dry, Afton thought maliciously. She was having a very difficult time forgiving Stella Sheridan but was trying not to hate her. In fact, Afton was having an impossible time doing either. She couldn't forgive her or forget her father's stricken face at her cruelty. She nursed a growing bitterness against Stella that entire day. As usual, Afton couldn't go to bed in anger; the Lord simply wouldn't let her sleep. She had to stay up and pray for a long, long time before she could freely confess her feelings and ask for forgiveness. But eventually, inevitably she did.

The next morning, Tuesday, October 10, started what the crew came to call "Days of Plague and Pestilence."

It began with the wasps.

Deliriously happy with the warm weather, the insects buzzed and swarmed and dive-bombed anyone who came within twenty feet of nests that were evidently hidden in every single building on the place. Even Peregrine's cabin had wasps, and he had thought he'd cleared his place of every nest that summer.

Afton had a swarm of them fogging out from a chink in the logs just above and to the right of the front door of her cabin. Coming in and out was a running, white-faced, gulping ordeal.

"What can we do?" Kyle demanded of Peregrine. "What kills them? Nuclear weapons?"

"Yeah, that'd do it," Peregrine answered dryly. "But not much short of that. Spectracide is the only thing I've ever found that kills 'em quick. If you get some other stuff, it might kill 'em, but it makes them real, real mad first. They have a few minutes before they drop, and that can seem like a long, long few minutes."

"Okay, well, someone's got to—" Kyle looked up and said with concern, "Tru, what's the matter?"

Truman Kirk came hurrying up, casting fearful looks behind his shoulder, jerking this way or that, hiding from invisible wasps. "Listen, Kyle, I'm allergic to bee stings."

"Huh? Oh, well, Tru, these are—"

Afton stepped up and said in alarm, "You've never been stung by a wasp?"

"No. Might not react to them, but still—" He looked around, haunted.

Kyle said with forced cheerfulness, "Well, I sure don't want you or anyone else to get stung, Tru, but come on, they're—"

Afton laid her hand on Kyle's arm and spoke with quiet intensity. "No, Father, you don't understand. If Tru is allergic to wasp venom too—and most people who are allergic to bee stings are also allergic to wasps—then he could go into anaphylactic shock if he got stung."

"Been there, done that," Tru said with forced cheer. "No fun at all."

"That . . . doesn't sound too good," Kyle said warily.

"It's not good," Afton said vehemently. "And out here, so far from a hospital . . ." She glanced cautiously at Truman Kirk.

"I could buy it, Kyle." Tru said what Afton had been reluctant to say. "No kidding."

"Oh, man!" Now Kyle looked around with a truly frightened expression. "Oh, man! Peregrine, take Tru to the Holiday Inn right now. Then go buy gallons of that stuff you were talking about."

Without speaking, Peregrine grabbed Tru's arm and hustled him to one of the Jeeps. All of them had the keys left in them, so, carefully watching to guard Tru, he headed directly for the nearest one. Then he made Tru wait while he checked the inside because the wasps had even gotten into the vehicles. Finally they piled in and took off in a whirl of dust.

"There goes at least two days' scenes with Tru," Kyle said regretfully. "Poor guy. No wonder he looked scared."

Behind him, Stella took a long drag on her cigarette and muttered, "You should be the one who's scared."

The next crisis was early the next morning. Harlan Freeman went into the sound trailer and came flying back out again as if his clothes were afire. "Oh, man, it's like *Swamp Thing* or somethin'! There's things growin' in there! I ain't shuckin' you, man. Go eye-ball it yourself! But this black fool ain't goin' back in there!"

Alarmed, Peregrine ran into the sound trailer and instantly came back out. "Don't worry, it's just dirt dobbers, Harlan. They won't hurt you; they don't even sting."

"Man, I ain't talkin' 'bout no bugs! I'm talkin' about them woodworm things crawlin' all over the place!" Harlan was walking up and down, making outrageous gestures, and Afton was having a hard time not laughing.

"That's just their nests, Harlan, made out of hardened dirt. Don't worry, I'll take care of it. But, Mr. Patton—" He signaled for Kyle, and Kyle went up the steps of the trailer, not looking too eager himself. He'd never heard of dirt dobbers and wasn't too interested in woodworms either.

"They're harmless," Peregrine said as they went into the trailer, but those outside could hear him say, "But I don't know about all this equipment. If they got inside anything—"

This got a truly horrified shriek from Harlan, and he forgot his fear of the woodworms. Leaping back inside the trailer, he yelled with outrage and injury, "You mean them devils might be eatin' my stuff? Wait, don't touch anything! Whatcha think you're . . . Don't do that! You can't be bangin' around on this stuff, man. It ain't a lead box and you ain't Superman! I'll kill them things if I have to gas this place!"

Laughing, Kyle and Peregrine exited the horror-film trailer.

But later that same day they weren't laughing at the pestilence.

It was all because of the wind chimes.

The previous night the "treasure hunt" crew had found some wind chimes in their nightly exploration of one of Mammy

Murdock's boxes. The contraption was obviously homemade and old. It consisted of rough bits of tin, probably scrap pieces from someone's woodshed, Peregrine had said. They'd been beaten thin and were odd shapes and sizes, strung unceremoniously on thin copper wire threaded onto a roughly rectangular piece at the top.

The crew had taken the chimes outside and hung them, so they could hear how they sounded in the evening breeze. Afton, Peregrine, Lina, and Kyle had followed them, amused at their childish delight at their discovery. Afton thought the crude chimes would sound jangling, jarring, unpleasant.

Instead, they heard a gentle, tuneless singing, muted notes that sounded solitary but not lonely.

Lina liked them and asked Kyle if she could have them up at "Anna Kay's cabin." This began a quite serious and quite technical discussion of how the chimes might be interwoven into the story, as Kyle agreed that they were unique and evocative.

Ultimately it was decided that they would substitute the wind chimes for a carved bird that John Allen Wingfield gives Anna Kay for her birthday. They had, in fact, planned to shoot that scene the next day, but since Tru was still off-site because not all of the wasps had been exterminated, they decided to shoot another scene that would come chronologically later and therefore include the wind chimes in it.

With that charming lead-in, they set up at the cabin the next day.

Lina was going to do a short scene. Tru was supposed to be in it, but the scene called for a few moments of her piddling around, cooking, while Tru came out of the woods and entered the cabin. Lina was to run to the window and look out as Tru arrived, and the chimes were supposed to tinkle faintly.

For some reason she regretted later, Lina had taken away the chimes from the prop girl and decided to hang them herself, having spotted a nail half-hidden on the eaves of the porch. She was playing with the chimes, idly shaking them, going up the steps, when she froze. Even her back, which was to the entire crew, looked paralyzed with horror.

The playful wind blew, the chimes softly clanged, but Lina didn't move.

"What's going on, Lina?" Kyle called from Dave's boom. "What's wrong?"

Lina didn't move or answer.

Suddenly Peregrine, who was standing back with Afton and the crew, called out in a thickly urgent tone, "Lina, don't move!"

"I—I can't anyway," she replied in a shaky whisper.

The silence was profound as everyone was mystified and frozen in bewilderment.

The chimes sang their tuneless song.

Underneath the melody, they heard something else, a rhythm, a rough percussion, a sly castanet . . . a dry rasp of rattles . . .

An enormous rattlesnake was coiled around one of the poles in the crawl space beneath the porch. His head, weaving drunkenly, was only inches from Lina's foot. His forked tongue shot out, licking the air, tasting it.

Peregrine looked around despairingly, not moving yet for fear of startling the snake into a strike. "Just be still, Lina, I'm coming," he said in a calm voice.

The unnaturally warm Indian summer ruffled their hair and caressed their hot faces and stirred the chimes. Suddenly the snake reared, rattling loudly and frantically. They could see the tail, a blur behind the snake's triangular head. The snake made a halfhearted strike, and Lina made a horrible, helpless little sound, quickly choked back.

"Drop the chimes, Lina!" Peregrine ordered, his voice hoarse with dread. "Just drop them!"

They banged, jangled, crashed down. The snake jerked, unloosed, then coiled tightly again. His head wove back and forth faster, jerkier now, his tongue flashing in and out.

"Aw, man," Peregrine said hoarsely and then recklessly ran to one of the sound men, who was frozen in mid-stride, holding a mike boom. There was simply no weapon in sight, not anything, not a stick, not a rock, not a shovel or pick or even a hammer.

Only the mike stand.

Peregrine grabbed it out of the stunned man's hand, wrenched the mike out of the double-pronged grip, and threw it down. Then he raced to the cabin. With desperately fast jabs, he snapped at the snake's head, and the snake began making lightning-fast head strikes. He couldn't close down on the thin prongs to fasten his fangs, however, so it turned into a horrible back-and-forth fencing match between Peregrine and the rattler. "Run, Lina! Now!" he said between gritted teeth.

Lina picked up her skirts and ran faster than she'd ever run in her life.

Everyone was still, frozen, helpless, frightened, bewildered.

Peregrine, the air whistling between his teeth, jabbed the mike stand up, then yanked it back, over and over. His thrusts began getting longer and longer. The snake was retreating, and at first Afton was relieved. But then she realized that this was not, definitely not, a good thing.

Because now the snake was under the cabin.

Peregrine, still searching the ominous shadows under the porch warily, muttered, "Now all we can do is wait."

"How long might he stay under there?" Kyle asked in a shaky voice, holding Lina and patting her ineffectually.

"It's a she," Peregrine said grimly, "and probably 'til next spring if she's smart. One thing she sure is, and that's pregnant. She'll probably have 'em right under there, snug and dry."

"Oh, no, no, no!" Kyle groaned. "What . . . how many babies do snakes have?"

Peregrine shrugged. "Ten to twenty, my friend. Ten to twenty."

Lina jerked up and stared at Peregrine with white-lipped horror. Then she took a deep breath, pulled herself upright, and told Kyle, "Today, Kyle, you can take this job and keep it—I don't want it right now it. I need a drink."

She stalked off down the hill.

Kyle looked around helplessly for a moment, then called, "Hey, Lina, wait up! I'm buying!" They disappeared into Lina's cabin and didn't come out for several hours. By then both of them were profoundly drunk.

Work was over for the day anyway. Without Lina and Tru, there was no one to film. The crew began breaking down, but not before Dave called out, "Hey, Peregrine, would you mind just kinda patrolling here for a while? Just so we don't see a snake behind every blade of grass?"

"Sure," he said, seating himself comfortably on the porch. Then he got up and hurried to the man whose mike stand he'd stolen. "Oh, here, sorry."

The black man, one of Harlan's assistants, threw his hands up as if Peregrine had thrust a burning firebrand at him. "Hey, no, man, you keep it. It's—I don't need it."

Peregrine grinned. "It doesn't have anything on it, you know. I never touched that snake."

"I don't care, man. It might have some snake juice or germs on it," the man said, backing off a long way. "Just throw it out or burn it or something. Hey, you can bill me."

Peregrine shrugged and carried his snake wand back to the steps, watching the ground in front of the cabin for the snake's encore.

Afton, staunchly putting aside her fear and revulsion, walked over to seat herself by Peregrine. *At least this way I know I'll get to be alone with him for a little while,* she thought with grim humor. *Nobody else is fool enough to sit in the snake's lair or whatever it is that snakes have . . .*

"Hello," she said, trying to sound breezy.

"Hello."

"That was a very brave thing you did."

Peregrine shrugged. "You're pretty brave too, coming to sit here, aren't you?"

She gauged his face shrewdly. "Not really, I don't think. I think there must not be much danger now."

"Why should you think that?" he asked her curiously.

"Because," she replied with a superior air, "if there were, you would have said, 'Get away from here, woman! Don't you know they's a hongry snake here!'" She did a pretty fair imitation of his inflection, if not of his deep voice.

He laughed, pleased. "Do I talk like that to you?"

"Yes, much of the time."

He leaned back, resting his elbows on the porch step behind him, crossing his legs at the ankles. "How irritating."

"Yes."

"Remind me not to do that anymore."

"Gladly."

"Know what?"

"What?"

"That snake . . . she shouldn't have been here."

He had spoken in the same light, careless tone, so Afton didn't immediately comprehend the meaning of his words. When she finally did, she merely asked, "Why not?"

He shook his head, whether with doubt or dread, Afton didn't know. "Snakes hibernate in early fall. Just a couple of days of Indian summer shouldn't thaw 'em out, get 'em stirring. She was sluggish, confused."

"Sluggish!" Afton repeated the word in a too-high, shocked voice. "You mean, that—that—was when she was moving *slowly*?"

"'Fraid so," he said, but went on impatiently. "Anyway, she was disoriented and scared before Lina ever started up those steps. And as far as her being pregnant . . . well, maybe I was wrong. She had a lump, but maybe it was just a couple of field mice or a little rabbit or—" He caught a glimpse of Afton's face and hastily said, "But I think she's pregnant. It's unusual for this time of year, but maybe not impossible. I'll have to talk to Mr. Frame . . ."

"But—but—" Afton's tone was ridiculously high and tremulous, so she cleared her throat and began again. "Peregrine, just say what you're thinking, please. I—I need to know."

His smooth brow furrowed, and he looked away. "I could be wrong. Real wrong."

"All right, I won't take you to court," Afton said with a small attempt at a smile. "Please."

He still hesitated, but finally he said in a quiet voice, "I don't think she was here. I think that if she had been under that porch, she wouldn't have come out until spring. No reason to. I think someone found her in a nice snug hidey-hole somewhere and brought her here. Probably just before dawn this morning."

Afton swallowed, a hard painful gulp. "Where . . . where in the world would one go to find a rattlesnake?"

"Easy. In the woods. In a hollow log."

"Peregrine, do you ever have any doubts?"

"About what?"

"Anything."

"Sure, lots of times." He studied her for a long moment, then asked quietly, "You getting the willies?"

"I don't know what willies are, but I have a faith problem from time to time." Afton's shoulders drooped, and she said wearily, "I have such awful doubts about things, and what makes it worse is that I know God can do anything."

"You're right about that."

Quickly Afton turned to him, noting the strong sweep of his jaw and the steady gaze of his eyes. "God has a lot of trouble with me," she said finally. "I want to have great faith, but sometimes it's like waters are closing over my head. As long as things are going well, it's easy to have faith—you don't really *need* it. But when things are dark—well, that's different."

Peregrine nodded slowly. "The dark night of the soul?"

"Yes! You know about that?"

"I know a little, Afton."

Without another word, Peregrine turned and walked away. His shoulders were stiff, and Afton knew he was hurt. *God, give me faith! I've hurt someone with my doubts, and I need to throw my whole weight on You!*

And then she was aware that God was giving her some sort of comfort, and she could only say, *Oh, Father, let my faith in You be greater than any other thing in me!*

EIGHTEEN

◇

"YOU HAD A RATTLER, a six-footer, out in the open, mad as a wet tomcat?" Percy Glass repeated in disbelief.

Peregrine eyed the giant with dark humor. Percy Glass was the crew chief of the loggers, a great bear of a man with thick black hair all over every bit of skin that showed, except for his eyes and palms. Every single working day of his life he'd worn Big Smith overalls, and they must have been size XXX-Large. He was as gentle as a doe with everyone but his loggers. To them he was a nightmare. No one ever called him "Percy." They didn't even call him "Mr. Glass." Mostly they just called him "Sir." "Mad as a wet mama cat maybe," Peregrine replied. "Female snake. Looked pregnant to me."

Percy Glass glowered, and he looked like he might open his mouth wide and growl deafeningly at any moment. "That ain't right, Peregrine. Ain't none of that right. Takes a real determined man to roust out a female this time of year. And that's all that'll do it, 'specially a pregnant one. Has to be on purpose. They'd swim the Cumberland to get away from you."

"Thought so," Peregrine said evenly. "But it's done, and there she is. Got any suggestions?"

"Hm. Don't guess you want to burn down that cabin."

Peregrine's eyes flared, but he saw that the logger was joking while he was considering. So Peregrine waited, and after a few moments Percy said thoughtfully, "Can't hose 'er out neither, huh? Nothing but that hand pump up there, is there?"

"That's it."

Percy shrugged. "Then we'll have to do it the old-fashioned way. Surround the cabin and prod her out with poles. You gonna take her when we get her rousted out?"

"Nope. I'm no lover of rattlesnakes, but this poor girl, I think, was just caught in the wrong place at the wrong time," Peregrine said casually. "I'm going to take her to the Animal Medical Research Center in Lexington. They'll make a celebrity of her and her brood. Milk 'em for anti-venom, you know."

"Uh-huh. Molly Frame's idea, is it?" Percy asked, his black eyes sparkling as brightly as a spaniel's.

"You know it."

Percy eyed him with much more astuteness than his appearance and demeanor would indicate. "Wonder how and why that girly-snake decided to take on fifty people in a crowded and noisy camp?" he speculated idly.

Peregrine said nothing.

Percy went on, "Must've taken something to get her in that there predicament."

Still Peregrine said nothing. He merely frowned, staring off into space.

But Percy Glass could be as stubborn as he wanted to be. "Don't guess there's no way to find out who might've thought that was a funny joke on them high-falutin' movie folks," he grunted.

"Guess not," Peregrine said flatly. "Unless you'd like to finger-print her."

"No, thanks," Percy said hastily, grinning. "Me and my boys will chase her out from under your cabin, Peregrine. But after that she's yours."

Peregrine sighed theatrically. "'S okay. I understand. And lately here, I'm gettin' used to dealin' with mad ladies. Me and Miss—I mean Miz—Rattler'll do just fine."

By that evening Mrs. Rattler was safely ensconced in a warm, roomy cage in her new home.

◊ ◊ ◊

After the "Days of Plague and Pestilence," and particularly what the crew dubbed "Evil Day of the Serpent," much of the enthusi-asm and "rah-rah, team" attitude of the crew slowly spiraled down-hill. Tru came back and was as strong and immovable as a rock; he was cheerful and worked like a field hand, never complaining, often trying, in his awkward, gentle way, to buoy up everyone else.

Stella and Kyle seemed to have made their peace. Stella smiled warmly and often at Kyle, and he seemed relieved and even content, though he was noticeably not as energetic and fiery about the film. Still, Afton was glad for the truce; she even saw her father and Stella occasionally holding hands or walking with their arms entwined about each other's waists. Deep down Afton knew that no possible good could come of their relationship, which was not only adulter-ous but seemed to be more of a business arrangement than anything else; but still, she was glad of the respite for her father. After he and Messalina had gotten so drunk on the night after the snake incident,

Afton was afraid he would allow himself to fall right into that pit and stay there. But he showed no signs of beginning his heavy drinking again after that.

But Messalina Dancy was another story. On Monday night the next week Afton was watching Lina as she retired to her cabin for the night. It was early, even for this crew, who were usually so tired that they considered 10:00 a late night. Lina had barely touched her dinner, sipping a bourbon-and-Coke and smoking incessantly. Her color had been sickly, and her hands were trembling—almost imperceptibly, but she was definitely shaky. This had become her nightly habit and demeanor. When she excused herself from the table, where they were seated in their makeshift cafeteria with about a dozen people, Afton had slipped out to watch her go to her cabin. She was so eager and walked so quickly that she was almost running.

Peregrine appeared out of the shadows and muttered, looking after the actress, "She's in trouble, you know."

"I know," Afton said sadly. "I'm just wondering if my father realizes it."

Peregrine grimly replied, "He knows it all right, because I told him. She's on dope. Cocaine, I think, from the way she's acting and the way she looks. That and who knows what else."

Afton jerked painfully. "How do you know? You can't know that for sure!"

"I don't. Stonewall does. Or did." At Afton's baffled look Peregrine grimaced and said, "He's trained. He's a drug-sniffer, and he can't stand the stuff. That's why I asked Joel and Molly to take him for a while. Drives him crazy. He can't understand why I don't—" He stopped abruptly and then went on in a dismal voice,

"I told your father, and he refused to do anything about it. So I told Miss Dancy that I didn't want the stuff on my place, and if I caught her with it or could find it, I'd call the police and have her arrested."

"You—you did?" Afton asked, amazed. It seemed, from all appearances, that Peregrine and Messalina Dancy were very good friends. Without appearing to do so, the actress demanded that Peregrine be near while she was filming, most often under the pretext that she needed his advice on a myriad of things.

"Yes, I did," he said with a hint of sadness. "And she promised me she'd get rid of it and not bring any more here. But I think she lied. Anyway, I know she's been partying pretty hard with a couple of the crew members and some of those loggers—Roy Dale Puckett and his brother and that other young 'un named Andrew Dayne—"

"But doesn't that—um, upset you? Make you angry?" Afton asked him.

He gave her a sharp look. "Jealous, you mean, Miss Afton?" he responded in his crafty-dumb Peregrine voice. "Naw, huh-uh. My heart belongs to . . ." He baited her, and in spite of herself Afton leaned closer, her eyes wide, and he finished mischievously, ". . . Boo. And Greta and Billie Jean."

Afton, drawing back and making a face at him, responded smartly, "All that competition makes a girl feel hopeless. Who, may I ask, are Greta and Billie Jean? Are you breaking the hearts of not one but two poor Ajax girls?"

"Not 'zactly," he replied, teasing her. "I'll introduce you to them sometime." Then, sobering, he shook his head decisively. "No, I'm not jealous of Miss Dancy's party buddies. To tell the truth, I understand her all too well, and that makes me feel sorry for her and want to try to help her. Messalina Dancy is a woman who gets more than her share of attention and adoration and not enough support and friendship."

Afton could hardly keep from questioning Peregrine further about his past, but she knew all too well that he stubbornly refused to respond to direct questioning and simply ignored subtle hints. It seemed all she would ever find out about the man was in snippets and bits, and she resignedly decided to make do with that. As she mulled over his sympathy for Messalina Dancy, she decided with some shame that she too would try to be more friendly with the actress and stop being so petty about Peregrine's friendship with her. Earnestly she prayed for the actress and asked the Lord to give her an opportunity to help Messalina.

Later that week Afton had cause to recall this prayer with some ruefulness and reminded herself again to be careful what she asked for.

Indian summer was in full bloom on Sunday, beginning the third week of filming at the camp. But then, as if the dark night of the new moon were an ominous sign, on Monday night a stiff wind blew up and grew steadily colder as it gusted first north, then east, then north again. Within an hour the temperature had dropped ten degrees. By the morning it was in the low forties and raining dismally.

"So what!" Lina demanded recklessly. "Life went on even in the rain. Come on, Kyle, we can do the last scene! Just think, in the rain it'll be even better!"

Kyle, after thinking on it a while, agreed with Messalina. She was, as she had been for several days, bursting with energy and recklessly enthusiastic in the mornings. Her face was drawn and pale, but streaks of crimson colored her fine cheekbones. Fine lines seemed more pronounced at the corners of her eyes, and her eyes were puffy and red. But by the time Charlie Terrill finished his magic, she looked wonderful, just as Anna Kay Wingfield would—seasoned like a fine, rich wine, strong and healthy.

"Okay, Messalina," Kyle instructed her after they got set up in the rain. It took all morning, for they had to scrape up whatever they could—tarps and quilts and blankets—to cover the sensitive equipment. But finally they did, and Messalina and Tru appeared ready to do the crucial last scene.

"Just keep it simple and direct," Kyle instructed them. "The scene speaks for itself. Tone down, Messalina. You're still a little keyed up. Anna Kay is determined and passionate, but not frantic."

"I will, I will, I will," Messalina almost chanted to herself, touching her hair and smoothing her white apron. The scene required that she and Tru burst out of the cabin during the argument about leaving and going back to the city to live. Again Afton was slightly confused because Tru and Lina had shot the scene inside the cabin the week before, and she was amazed that they could just pick up out of nowhere, re-create the personae, and start in the middle. But they were skilled professionals, and they did.

Tru came out frowning, but his face clearly also showed grief and worry. "Anna Kay, it's no use. It's wearing you down, it's wearing me down, and it's just not worth it." He spoke clearly, but with just the right weary timbre to his voice. Leaning against the porch pole, watching the sodden rain, he was a poignant and saddened man.

Lina stayed inside the cabin for long moments, which made Kyle frown a bit, but then his face cleared. The effect was good, and

Tru was relaxed with it, recognizing that she was giving the camera time to absorb his conflicted state of mind.

Finally she came out, stood behind him, and spoke in a calm
voice that was still diffused with strength and warmth. "You're
wrong, John. It's not wearing us down—it's polishing us, it's brightening us, it's refining us. And not worth it?" Her voice dropped, low
and compelling, like a dignified old church bell on a bright Sunday
morning. "Not worth it? It's everything, John, it's all we are and all
we'll ever be. And it's good. It's good now, and it can be good all
our lives. Please, listen. That sky, that water, this place . . ." She
raised her arms in a grand epic gesture, then ran down the stairs
into the rain. Kyle almost fell off the boom but let the actress work.
Tru, surprised, ran down himself and took her by the arms. Lina
wrenched away from him, bent down, and grabbed two handfuls of
dripping black mud. "It's good, John. Smell it, look at it, feel it! It's
rich and it's alive! And it's our life, ours!"

Tru stood still, staring at her with wonder, and Lina grabbed
both of his hands with her dripping, black ones. They stood
motionless, quiet, tense in the rain. Then slowly Tru smiled. Kyle
knew he'd forgotten his line, but it didn't matter.

Lina smiled.

Then they laughed.

And then Lina, mischievous and quick, rubbed Tru's face with
her muddy hands, and he threw back his head and roared. He
grabbed at her, but she picked up her sodden skirts and skittered
away. They played a merry game of chase that would have put four-
year-olds to shame, with Lina hiding behind trees and Tru grabbing
for her on each side. Lina fell, sliding a glorious six feet, and Tru
threw himself down by her.

"Keep filming," Kyle whispered.

They threw mud on each other until they were covered from the tops of their heads to the soles of their old boots, and finally they collapsed, laughing helplessly. Lina laughed so hard that the tears running down her face made pitiful little clean tracks on her face.

Kyle yelled "Cut!" and beamed. Stella, sitting in a chair with an ankle-length London Fog raincoat pulled tightly about her, her hair covered by a scarf and an enormous umbrella, glowered but said nothing.

The assistants hurried over to help the stars. With a giggle, Lina threw mud all over her assistant Linda's boots, and then Tru, with great seriousness and deliberation, wiped his hands on his assistant's jeans.

The scene eventually turned into a free-for-all, and eleven people—including Afton, who could never recall exactly how she got involved—not only had to wash their clothes twice but had to use Joel Frame's grandmother's battling board to battle them clean.

◊ ◊ ◊

The mud fight was fun, and it lifted the spirits of the cast and crew immensely. But Messalina paid for her inspiration, as the most intelligent and sensitive artists so often seem fated to do. She got terribly ill.

At about 10:30 that night a surreptitious knock sounded on Afton's door. She hadn't gone to bed yet, though she was just about to. Hurrying to the door, she whispered, "Who is it?"

"It's—it's me, Miss Afton," a voice answered, but Afton

didn't know who "me" was. Impatiently she pulled open the door and saw that it was Jo-Jo. He was shivering and sopping wet from the rain.

"Come in, for heaven's sake, and dry out by the fire—"

Shaking his head, he looked down and said, "Miss Dancy's real sick, Miss Afton. Some of us were at her cabin, and she—she's been—she was—well, anyway, she just got real sick, scary sick a little bit ago. She told all of us to leave her alone and not to worry anyone about it, but . . ." He looked back up at her, shamefaced. "I went back to my cabin with the others, but I'm scared. And I remembered that you're a nurse, and you're also a real sweet lady." His voice held a plea.

"You mean—is she in a coma or passed out?" Afton demanded harshly.

"No, no, it's not 'cause of . . . no," he stammered, his face reddening. "It's like flu or something."

"All right, Jo-Jo. I won't say anything to anyone," Afton assured him with only a hint of impatience. "I'll go over as soon as I change. You go on back to your cabin and get into some dry clothes and get warm," she said severely. "I don't need two patients. I would imagine Miss Dancy will be enough."

"Boy, ain't that the truth," Jo-Jo muttered as he sped away.

Afton changed into thermal underwear, jeans, a turtleneck, and a warm wool sweater. The night was not only cold but damp and clammy. She imagined that she'd have to keep a good fire for Messalina all night, and that would mean going in and out of the cabin several times. The firewood that the loggers provided was dry and easily set ablaze, but it burned hot and quick. It was almost impossible to bring enough in for an entire night, as the cabins were small and the hearths weren't large enough to stack any number of great logs.

Throwing on her macintosh—*raincoat*, she reminded herself of the American word—she hurried to Messalina's cabin, on the other side of Peregrine's. She noted that firelight flickered in his windows, but no lamps were lit. She sloshed in thick deep mud, the grass as slippery as a sheet of cold glass, and she almost fell. A black figure loomed up beside her, and Afton gave a little scream, skidded to a stop, and almost fell again.

Peregrine grabbed her and held her tight. He bent down close to her, and for a heart-squeezing moment Afton thought—hoped—he was going to kiss her. But he merely growled, "What are you doing out on this cruel night, woman? People running around like it's Times Square or something!"

"Messalina's sick," Afton answered, slightly breathless. "I've got to go to her."

"Oh . . . how sick?" To Afton's dismay, Peregrine let go of her to adjust the hood of his black raincoat. He looked like the Grim Reaper.

"Um . . . I don't know yet. Someone—someone just came and told me."

"You're no tattletale, huh?" Peregrine mused. "Okay, let's go."

"I'll take care of it, Peregrine. You don't have to—"

He shook his head, a firm negative. "I saw her this afternoon. Heard that funny bugling sound to her voice, saw pain in her eyes. You're going to need a good fire, lots of cool water, some hot broth, lots of fruit juice, and probably a vaporizer. I'll do all that while you do the nursin'."

"I am a nurse," Afton said glumly as they hurried to Lina's cabin, "but you saw she was getting sick, and I didn't even notice."

Peregrine shrugged. "I take care of sick animals all the time," he said quietly. "And for all her star-bright and starlight, she's just like a little, lost, sick creature to me. Here you go, I'll wait 'til you get in, and then I'll go to the meeting hall kitchen." They could see a low fire flickering through the thin curtains of her windows.

Afton went and knocked lightly on the door, calling, "Miss Dancy? Miss Dancy, it's Afton. May I come in?"

There was no answer and no sound.

Afton, with a grim look at Peregrine, pushed open the door and marched in.

◇ ◇ ◇

For two days and two horrible nights Afton rarely left Messalina's side. Everyone came at one time or another and wanted to see her. The first day Afton let in her two assistants, Linda and Drew, thinking that Lina might prefer their ministrations to hers. But Lina grew restless and upset when anyone else, including her two assistants, was in the room, and as if she could do it at will, her fever rose. After that Afton claimed supreme authority and refused to let anyone into the cabin.

Except for Peregrine. After coming in and out at least a dozen times that first night—bringing firewood, scrounging up kettles and pots to use for heating water and broth in Lina's fireplace, bringing tempting juices and cold drinks from the kitchen refrigerator—he impatiently stopped the rather silly process of knocking and Afton being obliged to either call out to him or come to the door if Lina was sleeping.

Lina's sunken, fever-glittered eyes followed him every moment that he was in the great room, but she didn't grow agitated at his presence. Afton thought she even seemed to rest a little easier when he was there and asked him to come stay with them and just sit by the fire as much as he could. Without asking for a reason, he agreed. He came several times a day and stayed late at night, reading a book. He barely spoke to Afton and paid even less attention to Lina. But she almost always slept soundly after he'd been there awhile, and when he left she'd wake up. The ease with which Afton accepted this bond between Messalina and Peregrine amazed her; she actually was glad that Messalina had anything to make her feel better, for she was without doubt gravely ill. It was not a life-threatening disease of serious import; it was just a cold and fever. But she was so weak, and her body had been so ill-used for the last few weeks, that she was exhausted and unable to cope with, much less fight against, even a slight illness.

Afton washed her, cajoled and threatened her to drink fluids, cleaned it up when she promptly vomited them, covered her when she was cold, and sponged her when she was fevered. On the third day Messalina insisted that she take a shower, and with Afton's help she did.

By that night Lina was visibly better.

"I thank you for taking such good care of me, Afton," she said with great dignity. "I am in your debt, and I always honor my obligations. One day I will repay you for your kindness."

"Nonsense," Afton said sincerely. "I was happy to do it."

Lina nodded. "Thank Peregrine for me too. I'd like to be alone and rest tonight. I think in the morning I'll be fine."

Afton thought that might be premature, but she knew well the kind of patient who truly did better without someone fussing over them and fiddling with them all the time. Messalina Dancy was that sort of woman.

"Like a wild creature," Peregrine mused when Afton conveyed Lina's gratitude and wishes to him. "You can help them up to a point, but after that they just want to be left alone, to heal themselves—or die."

"Thank the Lord it's not that serious," Afton said, dismayed.

Peregrine shrugged. "Not this time."

The next morning was Friday, October 27th. Kyle had been worried to death, as Messalina still had three important scenes to do, and midnight of November 2, Rini's deadline, was looming ominously close. But Messalina, though obviously subdued, appeared to be in good spirits and determined to work. Although Charlie had to work on her for two hours, his makeup toned down her starkly pale face, gave her some color, and brightened her eyes. Even her hair looked shinier and healthier after he'd shampooed and fixed it. With a strong will she managed to film one of the scenes, though it took several takes, as she tired easily. But by the end of the day she was still in good spirits and actually did look a little better, a bit more enlivened.

Then that night she disappeared.

NINETEEN

◇

GROGGILY AFTON PEERED at her tiny travel clock. The luminous dial read 2:10. *What—where—why am I awake?* she wondered foggily. Then, because it happened again, she knew. Noise, voices had awakened her. *Something's wrong . . . Lina sick again?*

She was so tired. Like the rest of the crew, she felt that she never got enough sleep. Snuggling back under her pile of quilts, she assured herself, *All that noise . . . Peregrine's surely awake . . . He'll come get me if someone needs me . . .*

But though she lay with her eyes tightly squeezed shut, determined to go back to sleep, her mind woke up completely and began chattering along. *Peregrine's gone, remember? Stella insisted he take her to the airport . . . Red-eye was all she could get . . . Supposedly on a last try on an "old fool" who just might come up with backing for Kyle . . . She told Kyle that Peregrine was expendable, but no one else was! She didn't know I heard her . . . I don't think she did anyway . . . Anyway, Peregrine's gone; he was going to visit the Frames and see Stonewall and spend the night . . .*

Aggravated at this ceaseless inner chatter, Afton popped up in bed and listened to the noise outside begrudgingly.

"It's nothing," she grumbled. "Just some people talking, probably saying good night."

But it wasn't nothing. It was people talking in muted voices at 2:00 in the morning. And Afton heard footsteps—heavy, hard footsteps. But they sounded odd somehow, muted but crunchy. As if a big man were walking on packing peanuts. And thumps and thuds, and a woman's giggle, stifled suddenly.

Resignedly, telling herself she was a nosey parker—a busybody as they would say in America, Afton got out of bed, shivering, and went to the bedroom window. Unmistakably, the noise was in back of the cabins, not out front on the grounds.

Pulling open the curtains, she gasped with pleasure. It was snowing.

Fat, sassy flakes swirled and flirted in merry clusters. The snowfall was so thick that looking out the window was like trying to see through a thickly embroidered curtain. Afton could see movement but no detail.

But she heard a voice, and she knew it instantly. Messalina's distinctive low-pitched laughter sounded again, and then she said something in that odd kind of strained whisper when you are talking to someone who is a distance away from you but you can't yell. "Wait! Wait a minute! I've—I dropped it!" She burst into another fit of giggles. "Did you hear me? Dropped the snow into the snow!"

Afton paid no attention to what Messalina was saying, and she didn't notice the peculiar high pitch of her voice. Afton was furious. With no thought but anger at Messalina for her selfishness and carelessness, she pulled on a thick pair of woolen socks, and then another, her warmest thermals, jeans, a cotton shirt, a wool crewneck sweater, and an oversized turtleneck over that. Afton was accustomed to dressing for cold, wet weather, and she dressed quickly and efficiently for the bitter night without even thinking about it. Smartly, she also pulled on waterproof rubber boots—Britishers called them "Wellingtons" or "Wellies" and everyone had them—and her fur-lined canvas jacket with a hood. Running out the door, she pulled up the hood and struggled to adjust it as she ran behind the cabin.

"Messalina!" she hissed. No need to wake up the entire camp. "Miss Dancy!"

No one was behind the cabins.

But to her left Afton heard one of the Jeeps start up. Without thinking, she ran to the line of vehicles. One of the Cherokees' lights came on, highlighting the frolicking snow.

Afton ran to the passenger side in her anger and confusion, thinking it was the driver's side. She intended to stop Lina who, knowing her tendency to dominate every situation, she was certain was driving.

She wrenched open the door—empty. She jumped inside, protesting, "Miss Dancy, I can't believe—"

As it turned out, Afton had just made several serious errors.

For one thing she had eagerly jumped into the passenger seat, not the driver's seat, and she had securely slammed the door behind her.

For another, Messalina wasn't in the driver's seat. Roy Dale Puckett was.

And there was more. In the back, between Jo-Jo and the other logger that Peregrine had mentioned, Andrew Dayne, sat Messalina. She held a rolled-up hundred dollar bill and a mirror with fine powder, looking just like snow, sprinkled all over it.

Afton was so shocked and so stunned that she couldn't move or speak.

"Well, well, Miss Afton," Roy Dale said with the overdone jol-lity of inebriation, "welcome to the party!"

With that, he revved the Cherokee's powerful motor twice and took off across the grounds, spraying fallen snow high into the air to join with the new.

◊ ◊ ◊

Kyle had fallen asleep in an overstuffed leather armchair beside his fireplace. He stirred, thinking something was wrong, something wasn't right . . . For a moment he opened his eyes and looked blearily around. He'd left a cigarette burning in the ashtray, right next to his fifth now watered-down drink, he noted stupidly, and the ash was still whole, a long, limp, gray cylinder right down to the filter.

It reminded him of Stella, and he told himself with the pathetic self-pity of so many drunks, "Stella lef' me again . . . But mebbe when this film is finished . . ." He left the thought unformed and unsaid, and it was just as well. It would be of no consequence anyway.

He forgot that an odd noise, something disturbing, had roused him and instead welcomed the feel-nothing stupor's return.

◊ ◊ ◊

Linda and Drew, Messalina's assistants, both woke up when the Jeep trundled across the grounds. They sat up in the twin beds, looking at each other blankly.

"She's out again," Linda said grimly, though she still looked like a pouty little cherub. "We're going to pay through the nose tomorrow."

"The nose is right," Drew, a stern and severe, plain girl said. "I hate it when she's snorting that stuff. It's a lot worse than when she's just drinking and popping Valiums."

"Sounds like the whole arsenal tonight," Linda said, yawning and burrowing back underneath her warm covers. She could see her breath frosting in the air. "Go back to sleep, Drew. You know there's nothing anyone can do about it. All of Peregrine's oxen couldn't drag that woman back when she's out partying."

Flouncing indignantly, Drew remarked, "Maybe not, but I bet Peregrine could. I bet she'd let him boss her. He's the only man that hasn't tried to get next to her, and she can't stand it. She'd do anything for him."

Linda said speculatively, "You sound jealous."

"So?" Drew belligerently replied. "At least I don't chase him all over the camp when I burn my finger."

"No. You did it when you got wasp-stung though," Linda argued.

"Yes, I did. It was worth it too," Drew said sleepily, lying back down and pulling the covers up to her chin. "He put some stuff on my arm . . . He's some kind of man. Like Jeremiah Johnson or something."

"Nope. Wrong."

"What do you mean?" Drew demanded indignantly.

"Peregrine," Linda said dreamily, "is much, much better than Robert Redford."

◇ ◇ ◇

"Mr. Puckett, please stop," Afton said, trying to remain calm. "I assure you I had no intention of joining your party. I want to go back to my cabin."

He gave her a sidelong glance that he appeared to think was cunning, but as he was making the overly cautious movements of a very careful drunk, he merely looked as if he were squinting at Afton. "Okay," he said, nodding repetitiously for emphasis. "I'll take you back in minute. We're jus' goin' for a l'il ride. Snow ride. Slow ride. Take it easy . . ."

The three in back joined in the song, which Afton had never heard and hoped never to hear again. They had forgotten all of the words except those two phrases, and they sang them over and over like idiots, laughing and pinching each other.

With disgust Afton studied the three in the back. Jo-Jo wouldn't meet her gaze, but Afton wasn't certain he was actually capable of focusing that well. He was drunk, though not as out of control as Roy Dale. But he was obviously determined to party recklessly with Messalina Dancy. Afton then watched the logger, Andrew Dayne, hoping to find an ally. But the handsome, young, Nordic-looking man was indecipherable to her, merely another tiresome drunk spouting nonsense in slurred words.

Then Afton glared at Messalina. The cocaine was out of sight, and Lina returned Afton's severe gaze with the height of defiance. She stopped singing, which made everyone else stop so abruptly it would have been comical if it weren't for the horrible circumstances.

"You owe me, Miss Dancy," Afton said calmly. "Tell him to take me back. Please."

For a forlorn moment Lina's sculpted features flashed shame and regret, and Afton's heart rose. But then Lina glowered with temper. "Lighten up, Afton, it's a party! Don't be such a stuffing!"

Her face was ghostly white, her eyes preternaturally brilliant. "We just wanted to see the snow. Isn't it gorgeous?"

"No, it's a furious, blinding sheet o' white," retorted the tight-lipped and infuriated Scotswoman. "And this drunk you've let drive canna possibly see a thing. At least—" With sudden quick-ness Afton pulled on her seat belt, fumbling because American ones were shoulder harnesses, and her little old car had only lap belts. "At least put on your seat belts. Please."

Roy Dale laughed hilariously. "You're such a little bit of a cute, little, helpless thing. You're so cute when you're mad."

"And you're a dangerous fool," Afton replied. She tried to see where they were going, but she couldn't see anything. They were heading for the hills directly across from the camp, she supposed, but outside the Jeep's windows were only malevolent barrages of white flakes. Afton noticed with dismay that the flakes were smaller, more crystallized, and it wasn't only because the speed they were going made them fly so viciously. The wind was rising, begin-ning to moan and hum, and the pastoral snowfall was rapidly turn-ing into a dangerously thick snowstorm.

Afton looked at Roy Dale, who had, she saw for the first time, a bottle between his legs. He unscrewed the top, turned it up, and made a hateful glugging sound as he drank. Afton almost gagged from the sickening, bitter-sweet smell and saw with hopelessness that the bottle was still about half-full. Turning, she tried to speak to the three in the back, but they were giggling and wrestling like stupid children, making fools of themselves as they tried to sort out the seat belts Afton had asked them to put on.

The Cherokee jolted wrenchingly, then seemed to take flight. Afton steeled herself automatically, but she saw Roy Dale come at least six inches off the seat when they crash-landed. "Whoo-oo-oo!" he shouted maniacally, and the crazed laughter in the back-seat got even higher. The three had banged their heads on the ceiling and then been thrown back down to the seat in a heap, which somehow they thought was terrifically funny.

Afton was beginning to get truly, heart-stoppingly frightened.

Roy Dale had driven into the tree line, and the vehicle was spinning, sliding, rolling, heaving around, careening around trees that seemed to jump into the blazing headlights. He managed to straighten the Jeep somewhat, then slammed on the brakes. After turning in a wild circle, the Jeep came to a shuddering stop. Afton frantically tried to loosen her seat belt, fully intending to jump out of the ship of fools and take off running back to the camp. But she couldn't; she was too scared to be able to figure out how to get the belt's lock undone.

Either unaware or uncaring of Afton's desperation, Roy Dale reached up to the overhead control panel and flicked a switch, then reached down and yanked on a gearshift on the floor. "Here we go! Four-W-D, and we can drive to Africa if we want to!"

Again he took off.

Afton was now so frightened, and the ride so jarring, that she didn't try to speak anymore. Roy Dale and the other three sang some more, something about the rains down in Africa. Afton paid no attention to them. She was watching where they were going, desperately trying to keep her sense of direction.

But it was useless. Roy Dale careened this way, then that, cir-cled trees, turned doughnuts in clearings, went back the other way. Once he found a dry creek bed, and they thumped and jumped down it for what seemed like miles. Afton's teeth felt as if they were

cracking, and her neck ached. But the other four appeared unaf-
fected, and she thought bitterly, *Well, I'd always heard you can't hurt
a drunk . . . No wonder—they'd roll up into a doughy little ball and
laugh their way through a cyclone . . .*

They had been steadily climbing, and Roy Dale had driven in
a sort of sideways crab motion, going forward but conquering the
ascents by driving broadside to them. He discovered the joys of
going straight up, however, and began to push the Jeep to roar
upwards, the nose of the vehicle far above the rear. "Whoa, whoa,
whoa! She's a little feisty one, ain't she? Love Jeeps, jus' love Jeeps,"
he declared.

Jo-Jo declared with vigor, "Me too! Me too! Love Jeeps!" He
turned to Messalina and said with great intensity, "That's your middle name, right? Jeep?"

The four thought this, and all of Jo-Jo's rather cloudy sallies,
very funny. But Afton was almost in tears from fright and disgust.

They rumbled up hills, then circled around them. Whenever
Roy Dale got a whim, they would go down a ways, then back up
again. Afton was lost, hopelessly confused, and gave up trying to
remember their route. It wasn't a route—it was a maze chosen by
a demented man.

"Listen!" she said, almost shrieking. "Listen to me! That's not
snow, that's ice! Hear it?"

"Well, I'll be dipped in choc'lit," Roy Dale whooped. "Iss ice.
Ice is nice."

They burst into laughter again, and Afton frantically tried to
speak to Roy Dale. "Listen to me! That is *ice*! Four-wheel drive
won't be a bit of good on ice! In just a minute or two you're not
going to be able—"

But yelling like an attacking Comanche, Roy Dale turned the nose of the Jeep up the hill. The ascent on this hill had not been steep, but Afton thought they had been going up on this particular hill for a long time.

That means we're in the mountains!

The thought struck her with the force of a blow, and she couldn't finish railing at Roy Dale. It was useless anyway. He had begun a wild ride up the mountain, steering around trees, thumping over rocks that had grown to boulder-size, shouting and whooping. In the back the three were cheering, "You can do it, Roy Dale! Less go to the top! All the way!"

The Jeep shuddered, roared, groaned, rocked.

Then it slid, wetly and fussily, and in nightmarish slow motion spun around, nose-down. They were suspended in time, in space, in a white purgatory.

The little Cherokee started sliding downhill and within seconds was like a bullet speeding and whistling through the air.

The last thing Afton saw was Roy Dale leaning backwards impossibly far, his face in a trance, standing on the brake.

Then came an explosion of noise, a piercing metal scream.

A mind-numbing jolt.

A bright blaze of red.

The dead white of snow.

◊ ◊ ◊

Afton never did pass out, for the simple reason that she wasn't injured. But, she supposed upon later reflection, she did go into a sort of dreamy catatonic state that must have been shock. She saw everything, heard everything. She sat, for a long time it seemed, replaying everything in her head, visualizing it, her inner voice speaking to her, explaining to her what had happened, but in a thick-tongued, painfully slow manner.

Finally she comprehended everything fully.

We had a wreck.

We hit a tree.

I'm not hurt.

Fire.

"Fire," she repeated helplessly.

Suddenly coming alive, she wrenched desperately on the seat belt, pulling at it, crying, praying. "Oh, God, please no, not to burn . . . no, please no . . . help me, help me . . ."

The seat belt fell away from her hands. She stared stupidly at it for a second, then wrenched on the door.

It wouldn't open. Afton wailed, a hysterical note that rose quickly to a frantic scream.

It was cut off as neatly as a butcher knife when she heard a dry, weak cough from the backseat. "Locked."

Her eyes wild, Afton stared, then pulled at the lever. She heard an obedient *snick* and almost cried with relief. Then she yanked on the door handle and banged against the door with her side, futilely. After hearing that pitiful voice in the backseat—she dared not look at the others yet, not until the fire flickering and sparking from the crumpled hood of the Jeep was out—Afton was calm. She was desperate with fear, but she was thinking clearly.

"Jammed. Have to—roll—" She tried, but the window was electric, and the switch had that rubbery feeling when it wasn't connected to an answering spark.

"Oh, no—no!" Valiantly she fought down the panic and looked around the cab with wild eyes.

"T-t-tire tool." Afton looked back with frantic hope and saw it was Jo-Jo speaking to her. His face was covered with blood, and his arm and shoulder were funny-looking, deformed-looking. He couldn't raise his head, but his eyes were alive—and terrified. "T-tire tool in the back," he whispered in a painful groan. "Have to smash . . . window . . . hurry . . . please . . ."

The fire was hissing and sizzling, and foul-smelling smoke was seeping into the cab.

Afton shut her eyes, knowing that she couldn't do what she had to do while she could see. She climbed over the seat back, put one foot down on something soft—human-soft—and vaulted into the small storage space behind the backseat. Someone cried out in horrible pain, but Afton steeled her mind and fumbled, feeling frantically for the needed implement. Her fingers closed on freezing metal, a slender iron bar with an L-shaped end. Picking it up, she began banging on the back window with more strength than she'd ever had in her entire life.

Then, as if it burned her, she dropped it and began to feel around for a blanket, some rags, anything, but found nothing. Wrenching off her coat, she laid it over the three mute white faces behind her. No sense in showering them with glass, maybe putting out someone's eye . . .

Dead, doesn't matter, all dead—dead eyes, dead . . .

"No!" Savagely Afton picked up the tire iron and beat the window until it burst, almost in a whole piece, out into the storm.

She leaped out the window as if she'd been catapulted.

Running around to the front of the Jeep, she was almost paralyzed mid-stride at the horror of it all. They'd hit a tree, a relatively small tree, head-on. The front of the Jeep was wrapped around it in a circle. It was like a vision of a cruelly insane person. The lights were still on but pitifully crossed like deformed eyes. It almost looked as if the Jeep had tried to devour the tree.

Afton shook herself, trying to keep her mind intact. It would happen to her over and over again that night.

The fire wasn't so much a roaring blaze as a sizzling electrical burn. But it was still dangerous, and not only because of the occasional flicks of blue blaze that popped up first here, then there. Afton had no idea where the gas tank was, but she did know that no one should be trapped in a car with any part of it on fire. Also, she was certain the smoke that was leaking into the cab was toxic. Helplessly she looked around, confused, for now that she had accomplished her major goal—getting out of the Jeep—she didn't quite know what to do. Certainly she couldn't open the hood—nothing would ever do that again. Finally she started piling fresh snow on the mangled hood, making certain that it was sifting down to the tortured engine. She packed the crystallized, hard snow into hard little balls and shoved them frantically in holes that had formed from the hood crumpling upward from the impact. She packed and cried and shoved, and the Jeep hissed and sizzled. Finally she saw no more sparks and heard no more ominous crackles.

She stood numbly and stupidly, listening and watching the Jeep as if it were a cunning mortal enemy. Finally she was satisfied that the electrical fire was out.

She noted, as if clinically noting a stranger's symptoms, that she couldn't feel her hands. Then she became aware that her teeth were chattering, and she was making little moaning sounds. Again she collected herself, steeled herself, and said a frantic little prayer. *Help me. Whatever I have to do, just . . . be with me, don't leave me,* she begged.

She heard her Grandfather Malcolm's voice so clearly that without thinking she looked around for him.

Lass, I don't hear ye beggin' like a puir slave, do I! No, no, girl! Ye're a child of the King, and the apple of His eye too, I shouldna wonder! Pleadin' for Him not to leave? He was here, right here, where you and I are, for aeons and ages afore you landed here, cryin' and scairt . . . No need, child . . . He's there . . . He's here . . . He is . . . He is . . .

Afton's helpless shivering stopped, and she hurried to the back of the wrecked Jeep and crawled back in.

TWENTY

◇

Go WAKE UP that fool Patton," Peregrine growled. "Tell him to help you get everybody into one of the four-bedroom cabins— they've got the biggest great rooms. On second thought, maybe you can just leave Patton to freeze to death. Serve him right." Viciously he pulled on leather boot strings, looping around a half-eye, and the slim leather string broke, popping like a cap pistol shot. Peregrine scowled at the short piece of string in his hand.

Quietly Joel Frame said, "Calm down, John. You're not going to do anybody any good if you're out there flailing around like a madman."

"You have extra bootlaces?" Molly asked.

"Yes, over in the cupboard. Second drawer." While Molly went to fetch them, Peregrine started lacing up his other sturdy hiking boot. They were made for hard going, with supports that came up about six inches to support his ankles. But they were made of leather—tough, strong leather, yes, but not waterproof.

Joel Frame frowned. "Them boots ain't made for running around in snow."

"I know. But they're the best I've got." Grimly Peregrine tied the lace and took the long leather thong from Molly. "Afton kept telling me I needed some of those knee-high waders. Calls them 'Wellies.'" He almost smiled.

"Well, mebbe she had sense enough to put them on," Joel sighed. "What I can't figger is why all the good sense flew outen her head to go joyridin' with them fools in the first place."

"Doesn't matter now," Molly said crisply. "I'll bet you've got some lard around here somewhere, don't you, John? I know I sent some in the supplies for the camp."

"Some right there in my kitchen," Peregrine said, obviously mystified.

"Good. If we rub down those boots and the tops of your socks with it," Molly advised him, "I'll guarantee you that you won't have wet feet. Sticky boots, yes. But no wet feet."

"Thanks, Molly, you're a genius," Peregrine said. Molly agreed, then went into the kitchen Peregrine had fashioned from his second bedroom. They could hear her rummaging through cabinets.

"Help me," Peregrine said gravely. "Help me decide what to take, Joel. I just don't know, and it's going to be mighty limited, what Stonewall and I can carry." Stonewall, resting by the fire, close to Joel Frame's rocking chair, alertly pricked up his ears at his name.

"Lemme think on it a minute," Joel responded, already deep in meditation. Absently he caressed the dog's ears.

Though every nerve in Peregrine's body screamed for him to jump up and run out the door shouting Afton's name, he made himself stay still and quiet. Giving Joel Frame a few minutes to make a life-and-death decision was a wise thing to do.

Molly returned with an unmarked silver can and knelt down at Peregrine's feet. Unprotesting, he smiled and said, "You're a good woman, Molly. A strong woman, full of courage and fight. Will you marry me?"

"Get rid of old Frame, and I'll do it," she answered, rubbing Peregrine's boots vigorously. "Prop up. Good." She even rubbed the bottoms of the boots and slathered the white goo thickly onto the seams and wherever the soles were attached to the boots. She put great globs of it along the upper surfaces, where the opening for the tongue was. "Now this stuff ain't very pretty, but it's the best seal we got right now. Here—let me get right along the top—"

Peregrine, scarcely paying attention now, muttered, "Good thing you woke up, Molly, and saw that snowstorm. We probably couldn't have gotten here if we'd waited much longer."

"Probably not," she replied calmly. "But I didn't just wake up. The Lord woke me up, sure as I'm talking to you, and told me to gather up my scattered wits. I knew then that something bad had happened, and I knew it was here at the camp."

Peregrine said nothing, and Molly, still rubbing his boots briskly, gave him a shrewd look. "Don't you give me that doubting Thomas eye, John. You of all people know the truth of what I'm saying."

"It wasn't doubt, Molly," he said softly. "It was regret. I wish it had been me."

"Oh, it will be again, John," she said with certainty. "It's not that He doesn't speak to you, you know. It's that you quit speaking to Him."

"Be sure and pray for me—and for all of them," Peregrine pleaded.

She smiled up at him beatifically. "Pray for yourself. You've got just as much pull as I do."

"All right, I will," he answered with a ghost of a smile. "I believe I will."

Joel Frame, as if he had just walked into the room and begun a conversation, announced, "I think you better put them chains on the pickup and take her as far as she'll go. We'll load her up with food and blankets and tools and medicines and some good firewood. The extry weight in the back'll help the traction."

Peregrine looked doubtful. "But I don't think I'll be able to track them in the pickup. I'm almost sure I'll end up on foot."

Joel nodded sagely. "If'n you do, take two sleeping bags, a coupla them cheater fire-logs—them little ones—a hatchet, a good knife, a rope, that Marlin thirty-thirty, and some meat. Don't worry about water; this here air's clean and good, and that snow'll melt up just fine."

"All right," Peregrine agreed. "Everything but the rifle. No gun."

Joel shrugged. "Reckon you better pray extra hard then, boy. Snowfall makes bear come down to the valleys to hunt."

Stubbornly Peregrine said, "No gun. If I'm bear meat, then more power to him." He stood up, and Molly and Joel came together and clasped him close. Without asking, Joel bowed his head and prayed, and he prayed the same way he believed and lived—simple and straight to the point.

"Father, keep those people up there alive, I ask You in Jesus' name and for His sake. For we know they're not in Your fold, Lord, except for Miss Afton, and we come together now, we three, to ask Your mercy on them this night. Give John strength. Give him warmth. Give him wisdom and cunning. Give him a straight and narrow path to the lost. We three ask this in His Name, the Most Blessed Name of Jesus. Amen."

"Amen," Peregrine echoed. But he didn't sound nearly as strong and sure as Joel Frame.

Outside, the sweet silence of snowfall turned to ominous rattles and crackles. The snow had turned to ice.

◇ ◇ ◇

"But I—I'd like to go," Tru said, watching Peregrine's ancient yellow pickup disappear into the grayness.

"Not a good idea, Mr. Kirk," Joel Frame said kindly. "You're not cut out for such. Most men ain't."

"But I feel like—like—useless, like a coward," he said with a hint of shame.

"No call for all that." Frame's brow wrinkled, and he spoke with great deliberation. "They could just be out of sight, over the first rise, you know."

Tru shot him a knowing glance. "You don't think that, not really, Mr. Frame. Because you would have gone with him if you did."

This man sure ain't as dirt-dumb as people try to make out, Frame thought dryly. Reverting to his natural honesty, he shook his head. "No, I don't think so. I think if they was close, they'd be here."

"Yes, sir, me too." Tru knew exactly what Joel meant. Rubbing his hands together, he told Joel unhappily, "Did you know the water pipes are frozen? In *my* cabin anyway. And the electricity's out."

"Figures. Temperature's dropped about twenty degrees, I reckon. Still dropping too." He searched Tru's drawn face. "Mr. Kirk, you up to some hard work?"

"Yes, sure, anything," Tru said eagerly.

"Well, we got to tend to these folks, that's for sure," Frame said, and Tru's troubled face cleared at Frame's show of respect by including him. "But first," he went on, satisfied at Tru's attitude, "I feel like we orter take care o' them beasts. They feel cold too. And they ain't got no way to warm themselves up."

Tru snapped his fingers. "That old potbellied stove in the barn!"

Frame looked pleased. "That's right. Now, you'll have to chop some wood short, only about a foot long, to fit in there good. You start a good hot fire with some pine knots, then pile on all the oak you can shove in there. Then shut that door up tight, and that thing'll put out enough heat all day to give them oxen a tan."

"Good, I'll do it. But what do we need to do about the crew?" Tru said anxiously.

Frame replied, "Molly's going about waking everyone up and herding them over to that four-bedroom cabin . . . Think it's got about a dozen girls in it?"

"Yes, the girls on the camera and sound crew," Tru said.

"Well, we're gonna need to build the biggest fire you ever saw in that cabin," Joel asserted. "And we're gonna need to keep it going for a long time. That means hauling a whole bunch of wood. We could try it in one of them Jeeps, but unless some chains are lurkin' around here I don't know about, I don't think they'll get far, 'cept maybe in circles. 'Specially with this nice layer of ice on top of that hard snow." The icefall, so far, measured about two inches, on top of four inches of snow.

"I'll do it. I can haul it by hand," Tru said, already heading

down the steps. Frame surreptitiously grinned. The man was likely
to work himself half to death, but Joel knew that for a man like
Truman Kirk, that was a lot better than huddling up and crying.

Tru turned and looked up at Joel, his eyes filled with dread.
"You—you think this storm's going to last a while then?"

"'Fraid so. Coupla days maybe."

"And—and they're somewhere up there in a Jeep? Without
chains?"

Frame looked at him with a touch of pity. "I ain't even got no
chains, Mr. Kirk, so I'm pretty sure nobody on this crew thought to
get 'em. Only reason Peregrine has 'em is that they been stuck back
behind the seat of that pickup since it was born in 'bout 1940, I cal-
culate. Peregrine just never had taken 'em out. Thank the Lord,"
he added fervently.

Tru nodded, squared his shoulders, and said, "I'll get the
wood from two cabins over from the number twelve cabin first.
Then I'll rest, then go get the wood from the cabins on either
side."

"That's the smart thing, Mr. Kirk," Joel told him in a kindly
manner. "Take the longest, hardest road while you're fresh. Save
the easiest 'til last."

Nodding, Tru hurried away. As he headed through the pelting
ice, he wondered exactly what Joel Frame was doing standing on
Peregrine's porch and staring out into the vicious storm.

Tru didn't realize it, but on that day everyone would have their
tasks, all assigned to them by Molly and Joel Frame. And Joel
Frame's task was to pray. He would pray constantly, without ceas-
ing, until Molly took a turn. They wouldn't stop until John Dunne
came home.

◇ ◇ ◇

Afton dozed uneasily, wandering in a frightening world of night-mares. But there were no monsters, no fearsome creatures, no threats of any kind. It was just white, a flat, dead, white land . . .

"Afton . . ."

Jerking, she came awake instantly. "Yes?"

"Afton, would you do me a favor?" Jo-Jo's eyes were dark and tragic. His voice was weak and breathy from pain.

"Of course, if I can," she said.

"Would you please let me have a sip of that whiskey? I'm so cold, and it hurts . . . just a sip?"

Afton considered this and finally said, "Yes, all right, Jo-Jo. But just a couple of sips."

"Thanks. Oh, one more thing . . ."

"Yes?"

"On the rocks, with a splash of soda?"

"Funny little man," she grunted, taking the precious bottle of whiskey and pouring just a teaspoonful into the cap. Then, lean-ing over the back of her seat, she held it steadily to Jo-Jo's lips. He finished it in one slurp. "Ahh, man, that's the best drink I ever had," he said. "And I don't even like sour mash. Can I—"

"No. Any more and you'll just get sick," Afton said clinically, screwing the top back on firmly. It was miraculous that the whiskey didn't get broken in the wreck. Jo-Jo had even made a comment about how many bones were broken, but thank heavens the whiskey wasn't.

There were plenty of bones broken, Afton thought darkly. Jo-Jo's shoulder and right arm, and probably his left wrist. Both of

Messalina's legs. Andrew Dayne's ribs, at least two, maybe more. And Roy Dale's skull. He had a goose-egg-sized bump on his forehead, and he hadn't awakened even once. Afton didn't think he would. The steering wheel had crumpled up and was pressing into his midsection, and she thought that he likely had a flayed chest and internal injuries, though she couldn't tell by feel. It was a miracle that he was still breathing, and that he hadn't frozen to death. Afton had covered him with her coat, hoping that at least would keep the blood from literally freezing in his veins.

Messalina was watching Afton and Jo-Jo as well as she could. Her lovely face was swollen beyond recognition. Her eyes were just two slits in purple mounds. Her nose was broken, and several of her teeth. She was the most pitiful thing Afton had ever seen; she almost cried every time she looked at Lina. The other two in the backseat had escaped with what seemed to be minor injuries—relatively speaking. But Messalina Dancy was in bad shape.

Afton transferred her gaze away from Messalina's pitiful, crumpled figure. The three in the backseat were crushed together in awful nightmare positions. The front bucket seats were jammed all the way back and had left them only about four inches of legroom. But Afton had sternly told them not to move and that staying close together would help them keep warm. She'd ripped out the carpet from the back of the Jeep and covered the broken back window with it. That had helped some, but it was cold, a dead, numbing, sapping cold.

Staring out the window, Afton noticed for the first time that the grayness outside had turned from charcoal gray to gunmetal gray. "Daylight," she murmured. "I have to go."

"No," Lina whispered, her voice distorted and thick. "Don't leave me . . . Afton . . . don't . . . ."

Afton resolutely refused to look around. "I have to, Lina. You know I do. It's the only way."

Uncertainly her gaze fell on Roy Dale Puckett's still figure. He seemed smaller, more childlike, a pitiful, lost thing. She didn't know if she could take the coat away from him. It was almost certainly a sentence of death.

"Take the coat," Jo-Jo said hoarsely. "You have to, Afton. You have to live."

"I know," she said, and a bitter tear coursed down her cheek. It was hot, and she fiercely thought that it felt good. Gently she picked up her coat from Roy Dale's slumped figure. He still breathed, but shallowly, very slowly.

"I'll be back," she said in a thick voice. "Soon."

"Afton . . . wait . . ." Lina pleaded.

Afton turned and leaned over close to her, though she didn't touch her. "I have to go, Lina. I'm sorry, I'm so sorry!" She was steadily crying now.

"No—no—don't cry," Lina said, and a pitiful tear squeezed out from between the almost-shut lids. "Pray. Pray for me, please. I . . . I'm afraid . . . I'm going to die, and I'm afraid . . ."

Afton was taken aback. Lina had never shown any fear, any weakness, and certainly not any interest in the Lord. In her ear Malcolm whispered, *There's no lost men in foxholes, lassie . . .*

Lina might die. They all might. But the four injured people in the Jeep would almost certainly freeze to death, by nightfall likely, if the temperature didn't go up. Afton swallowed hard. Messalina Dancy was watching her closely.

"Will . . . is it too late for me . . . too late . . . ?" the actress asked, her voice thick with terror.

"Never," Afton said, suddenly firm and sure of her ground. "Never, not while you breathe, Lina. But listen to me . . . I can't pray and ask the Lord to save you. It doesn't work that way. You have to do it yourself."

"Can't . . . don't know . . . how . . ."

"All right then, you listen to me, and you'll know how to pray in your own heart," Afton told her softly. Bowing her head and clasping her hands, Afton prayed, "Oh, my Father, I pray for Messalina. She's a sinner, Lord, as we all are. She doesn't know You, and doesn't know how to talk to You, and she doesn't know what You've done for her. In faith I ask You, Lord, to teach her about Your blessed son Jesus and how He died for her sins, all of them, and how You only see His precious blood and not our filthiness. Cleanse her, make her whole, give her peace. I ask Your mercy and pity for these men too, Lord. I hand them over to Your care and Your love. Amen."

She looked up and said, "I'll be back soon, Lina. But while I'm gone there's something I need you to do."

"Wh—what . . . can I do?"

"You pray for me."

◇ ◇ ◇

"Wonder if it's noon?" Afton asked herself idly. The light was so unlight, only a pervasive sort of lesser gloom, that she honestly had no idea what time it was. It was still snowing, a light, feathery snow of big individual flakes. The snow was about a foot deep now. It was perilously close to the tops of Afton's boots, and when she stepped in low places it showered down into them. Her feet were wet and cold and numb, and she thought she would likely get frostbite. But at least her hands were relatively warm. She always kept gloves in the pockets of her coats, and now she had her wool-gloved fists pushed tightly into the pockets of her coat.

Several times she'd fallen, sliding on the perilous ice still lurking beneath the layer of crisp snow. She was wet, thoroughly wet, from the hips down. Her canvas jacket had kept her upper body dry, but her legs felt icy except when the cruel wind engulfed her, and then they burned.

"Actually, Lord, I'd rather be out here walking than in that Jeep," she said conversationally. "So again I thank You that I wasn't harmed, that I can walk, that I have my hands and my eyes and my strength." Shuddering, she mentally shoved away the remembrance of the hours in the death-car, waiting for the first glimmer of daylight. The inside of the Jeep had stunk of sour whiskey and vomit and blood and death. She might be able to forget the sight of it, but she'd never forget the smell.

"I wonder if I'm still in Kentucky," she mused. "What's next to Kentucky? Doesn't matter, I suppose. But it would be nice if I had the first clue where I am . . . and where I'm going . . . and where the camp is . . ."

Afton knew that she was light-headed and a little silly. But it wasn't delirium, and it wasn't a mask to chase away her fears.

I'm not really afraid . . . that's not the right word. I'm concerned for the others, and horrified at the tragedy, and I hope—hope—hope!— that I can find help . . . But afraid to die? No, not really . . . I've heard when you freeze to death you just go to sleep . . . But Lina was so afraid, and I suppose I've never known that kind of fear . . . coming face to face with hell . . . and thank God, thank You, God, I'll never have to!

She was in an alien world, a world that deafened her by its

silence, that blunted her vision with its formless humps and bumps of white, that dulled her mind with its unfamiliarity. Though she felt hurried and urgent and wary in such a hostile territory, Afton Burns definitely was not afraid. And she was not alone. Her God was watching over her, her Jesus was speaking continually to her, and her Holy Spirit was guiding her. This, to Afton, was more real than the snow-ghosts and silence.

And without warning faith came. Her mind had been filled with uncertainties that fluttered like frightened birds in a cage. But suddenly the confusion and doubt were gone!

Afton stood stock-still, amazed at the peace that flooded her. Then she remembered a Scripture from the book of Hebrews, just a fragment—". . . there remaineth a rest for the people of God."

Tears came to her eyes, and she whispered, "Thank You, Father! You have taught me to have faith—and now You are giving me your blessed peace. I *know* that all will be well—and I give You thanks!"

◊ ◊ ◊

"Okay, boy. This is it." With deliberation, Peregrine switched off the truck. The soothing thrum of its engine stopped, and it creaked regretfully in the sudden onslaught of silence. "Half a tank. Won't do any good to run it past there. Couldn't get back."

Stonewall cocked his head, listening, and appeared to be agreeable. Peregrine looked at the dog indecisively. German shepherds really weren't made to slog through snow for long periods of time. Their paws were sensitive and could chafe, then crack and bleed within short periods of time.

"Tell you what, we'll try it for an hour at a time," Peregrine promised. "Then we'll stop and I'll warm up your paws and rub them with some good ointment. Okay, boy?"

Stonewall, sensing action, stood up on the cracked bench seat of the truck and wagged his tail, then barked once. It was deafening in the enclosed small space of the truck.

Peregrine dreaded leaving the warmth of the cab, for he knew it would be hard to get this warm again. He and Stonewall had been jumping in and out of the truck all morning as they picked their way first through the foothills, then deep into the first range of the Cumberlands in Daniel Boone National Forest. But Peregrine had left the truck running when they were out scanning around, and so they had always returned to a cozy cocoon.

"Let's do it," he said and jumped out of the truck. Stonewall bounded out behind him.

With quick, efficient movements Peregrine shouldered the big backpack that Joel Frame had packed for him. Tightening the chest straps, he adjusted it until the aluminum frame was comfortably settled on his shoulders and back and started walking. The backpack weighed close to sixty pounds, but Peregrine knew he could carry it all day, as long as he took frequent rests and watched his breathing.

"Go on, boy, don't wait for me," Peregrine urged the dog. "Where are they, boy? Where'd they go? C'mon, let's go!"

Stonewall nosed around the area in circles, stopping here, running there, skidding to a stop to double-check a scent. Peregrine actually had no idea if the dog was tracking the Jeep or not. He didn't know if the dog was tracking the right Jeep or not. He didn't know if the dog was tracking at all or merely having a good time playing this odd game out in the snow with his master. After a few moments he bounded up the slope at full speed and disappeared. Peregrine followed him.

"Okay, Lord," he said experimentally. It sounded like a mild threat. "Okay, Lord," he tried again. It still sounded awkward. Clearing his throat, he stubbornly began again. "Hello . . . hello, Lord. It's—me. Pere—I mean, John Dunne." He made an awful face. "You remember me. The blithering idiot."

He took a few dogged steps, his face dark. He felt silly. He felt presumptuous. And he felt like he was talking to himself.

But after a few moments he lifted his face and looked up through the whirl of soft flakes that barely brushed against his skin before melting. "Doesn't matter," he whispered. "Doesn't matter how I feel. I know You're there, and I know You're listening. You promised, and You don't lie. So, Lord, here am I, and I'm asking for Your forgiveness for a multitude. . . for *years* of sin. I'm asking for You to put it under Jesus' blood, so You won't see it anymore. I'm asking for a new start, right here, right now." He stopped walking and stood motionless, his eyes wide-open, staring up at the color-less sky, oblivious to the playful flakes that dusted him.

After a while he nodded with certainty and murmured, "Thanks, Lord. It's really, really good to be back." He started walking again.

◇ ◇ ◇

Afton was sleepy. She kept stumbling along and sometimes thought she had actually fallen asleep, but she kept walking.

Something wrong.

Wrong.

Something wrong.

Her mind prodded at her, picked at her, fretted within her. Afton tried to dull the nagging little voice so she could have some peace and quiet, but it just wouldn't shut up.

Too cold. Too cold. Don't go to sleep. Don't go to sleep.

She looked up, startled. She found herself sitting on a big, snow-covered, fallen log, her hands limp at her sides, her chin pressed against her chest. Afton had no recollection of sitting down.

With alarm she jumped up. "Well, a' the clans be blasted!" she shouted at the top of her lungs, just to show herself she was still alive. "If I'm to die, at least I'll lay me down a' do it wi' some dignity! Aye! That I will!" She shook her fist at a mute sky in fierce rhythm to her speech.

She felt immeasurably better and stalked down the mountain. *Endless mountain. Slogging to China. That's what the other end of the world is, isn't it? Keep going down, down far enough, and you'll be going up, up to China . . .*

She stopped so abruptly that she fell to her knees in the deep snow. She was trying to say something, but no words, not even a sound, would come from her constricted throat. Putting out her shaking hand, she reached for the dog, praying feverishly that it wasn't a dream.

It wasn't. It was Stonewall, the big, ugly gargoyle himself, and he bounded happily to her, oblivious of blood and death and tragedy and suffocating fear. He licked her face happily and knocked her down with his roughhousing. Weakly Afton laid in the snow, the big dog frolicking like a little puppy all around her and barking like mad, and she cried. The tears, she thought, rolled down the side of her face and melted the snow beneath her cheek.

Stonewall, still barking deafeningly, ran off. "No . . . no," Afton sobbed. She stood up and blinked.

But then, with a surge of strength, she jumped up, threw her arms open wide, ran as fast as the stormy wind had blown that awful night, and jumped into John Dunne's arms.

TWENTY-ONE

◇

A S PEREGRINE CAUGHT the flying Scotswoman, they both crashed to the ground, rolling and laughing in the snow. Then he tried to get up and fell back down, and she tried to get up, and he pulled her back down, and they laughed some more. Stonewall thought it was a great game and joined in boisterously.

Finally the two stood close. Afton took off her gloves to lay her hands flat against his chest, inside his heavy sheepskin-lined leather jacket. She stood for a moment, marveling at his warmth, at his strong heartbeat. Finally she whispered, "Oh, Peregrine, Peregrine—"

"Don't call me that ever again," he said harshly. She looked up at him. His wild amber eyes softened to a fine burnished gold. "My name is John—John Dunne."

"Such a pleasure to meet you, John Dunne," she whispered.

"Pleasure's all mine."

"You're named after a poet too?" she asked, her mind in a hazy neutral.

"No, Sweet Afton, it just sounds that way. Never mind all that for right now." He bent and kissed her, softly, for a long time, as if he were reassuring himself that she was real, a warm woman with blood in her veins, and not a snow sprite. He lifted his head and pulled her even closer. "I've been looking for you."

"I know," Afton sighed. "I prayed you'd come."

"No, Afton," he said hoarsely. "I've been looking for you . . . all my life."

"I know," she said again with gentle insistence, "because I prayed you'd come."

She raised her eyes just to search his face, his so familiar, so beloved face, with its disheveled growth of beard and too-sharp cheekbones and peculiar wolf eyes. She loved his face. She loved John Dunne. She loved John-John. She even loved Peregrine.

With a last light kiss, he pulled away from her to shuffle off the heavy backpack. "You're half-frozen. Your jeans are icy. I'll bet your feet are close to frostbite."

With an effort Afton pulled herself together and tried to clear the confusion and overstimulation her mind had suffered the last twelve hours. "No—don't—or maybe do take that off," she faltered. "But, Pere—John, the others are right up there, and we have to go—help them. Go get them."

"Where? Where are they?" he demanded, stopping halfway to pull off his backpack.

"Just—right up there. Straight up, I think. I—I might have wandered some coming down, but I was trying to just come—straight down," she said, unable to recall exactly if she had made a beeline straight down the mountain.

Peregrine stared up into the heights, but the crests of the mountains were shrouded in a fluffy, snow-thickened fog. "How are they? Are they hurt or something?"

Afton nodded, suddenly having difficulty swallowing a burning lump of dread in her throat. John waited patiently, and finally in a raspy whisper Afton went on, "We had a wreck. Everyone got hurt but me. So I had to go find help."

He held her again. Tears flowed again, hot and fast, and she allowed herself to dissolve in them and in John's arms for a few minutes. But only a few. With a great effort she stepped back, scrubbed at her cheeks, and continued, "They're hurt badly, John. All four of them."

"Four?" Peregrine repeated, shocked. "We thought only Jo-Jo and Miss Dancy and you were missing."

"No. Roy Dale Puckett and Andrew Dayne are in the Jeep. Roy Dale—" She stopped, unable to go on, her face working painfully.

"Is he dead?" John demanded harshly.

"Not . . . not when I left . . . but . . ."

"What were you doing with them?" John said, his eyes flaring like night beacons.

"I—it—I didn't—can we discuss this later?" Afton said, a whit of her spirit returning. "We have to get to them, John. We have to do something. Right now."

He relented and frowned with concentration. "Four . . . I could maybe have made two trips, carried one at a time . . . but not four."

"You couldn't have carried someone all the way back to camp!" Afton cried. "Not even once!"

"No, but I could have maybe gotten them to the pickup," he absently replied, staring around as if the answer might be in the air or the snow that flirted around them. "It's about a mile from here."

"Pickup? Can you get it up the mountain?" Afton pleaded.

John shook his head firmly. "No way. It's too wooded and has some bad ravines crisscrossing the ascent. I don't know how your Jeep got all the way up there. Just stupid dumb luck."

"No, it wasn't," Afton corrected him dully. "It was a bad wreck."

He gave her a look of sympathy, but she determined not to weakly dissolve again. "Think, think! John, they are going to freeze to death, even without their injuries, which are terrible! Oh, God, what can we do?"

She meant it as a prayer, and he knew it. To her amazement, he said quietly, "Well, I suppose there is that. We can ask God."

Recovering, she nodded. "Yes, yes, I must pray. Right now."

Without asking, he stepped forward and took her hands, and the two bowed their heads. They prayed silently, but they were together in spirit, and in the Spirit. Both of them looked up at the same time. John had made a decision, and Afton had too.

"We have to bring up the truck," John said.

"Yes," she said happily. "I'll stay in front and direct."

"Yes," he said. He watched her, brooding, holding tightly to her hands. Then he asked with a hint of embarrassment, "Did you see it?"

"Oh, yes," she replied readily, "and so did you. So that means, John, that it's already done in His will. We have nothing to fear. We'll get the truck up here, and we'll get all of them in it, and we'll be back at camp before nightfall. It's done."

Thoughtfully he nodded. "Okay. Let's do it. And, uh, thanks, Lord."

"Amen!" Afton added.

◇ ◇ ◇

Bowie County Hospital was small, old, and built of concrete blocks in the 1940s that had been painted white about forty times but always faded back to their original dingy gray. Behind it the

steel framework of a new hospital rose four stories, like a brooding giant skeleton.

John cleared his throat painfully. "That's our new hospital.
Going to be named after the family who financed it. Frame
Memorial Hospital."

"My Frame only financed half of it," Molly replied. "Got three
private donors for the other half."

A short chuckle, like a growl, came from John's throat. "Yes.
Joel, Jr. and Rudy Ray and Angela's husband."

Molly shrugged, then explained to Afton, "Our kids."

But Afton obviously hadn't heard a word. She sat in the middle of the bench seat of Peregrine's old pickup, slumped with
weariness. Occasionally, as if startled out of a nightmare, she would
jerk and turn to search out the back window at the man, dressed
in so many layers that he looked much like an enormous troll,
crouching protectively over four vague lumps laid out in the bed
of the truck. It was difficult to see anything more than six inches
away. The snow was still falling, so thickly that it seemed to be solid
curtains of white with only a few lacy airholes poked in it.

None of the three of them were able to keep their minds on a
conversation for long. All three of them—particularly Afton—
were so tense, so wrought up, that they were almost hyperventi-
lating. The last hours—a day and a night for Afton—had taken
them to the extremities of human endurance.

It had taken John and Afton hours to get the truck up to the
Jeep. It had taken two hours for the two of them to get the four
injured people out of the wrecked car. Afton had been shocked
anew when she saw it again. It was unthinkable that she had

walked away literally without a scratch. It had taken them nearly an hour more to get the four loaded into the pickup truck.

Then it had taken hours of slow, agonizing, stop-and-go driving to get back to camp. John lost count of the times he had to stop the pickup, walk ahead to plan a route, measure between trees, gauge the height of boulders. Still, even with the chains, the truck had slipped, lurched, slid, and jerked with heart-stopping drama the entire horrific journey.

And on top of that, John had Jo-Jo and Andrew Dayne in the cab with him, and both of them looked like ghastly, pitiful ghouls. Even worse, Afton was in the back with Roy Dale and Lina. Afton had finally made the difficult decision of who would ride in the warm cab and who must lie down in the back on top of one sleeping bag with the other covering them. She had thought Roy Dale was past caring for and, truth to tell, couldn't understand why he was still breathing. Lina had fainted dead away when they'd moved her, and Afton insisted she must lie perfectly flat. One of her legs had an open compound fracture. Afton had hoped—prayed—that she wouldn't wake up again until she was safe and warm in a hospital.

When they had arrived at camp after their unending nightmare, it was almost dark. And they found that the nightmare had not yet ended; they had to keep driving. Molly jumped into the back of the truck, then into the cab, and looked at the four injured people. She succinctly announced, "John, no ambulance is going to get out here. Even if they could, it'd take them longer than it'll take us to drive them in."

Kyle, who was so pale and broken that he appeared ill, was holding Afton wordlessly in a crushing hug. But she turned when

Molly spoke and was wrenched by the renewal of fear and strain on John's face. But John merely said quietly, "Okay. But this time Afton rides in the cab."

"No! I'm not even hurt!" she protested. In spite of herself, it came out a pathetic whimper.

"Oh, yes, little girl," Kyle said in an unrecognizable, hoarse voice, "oh, yes, you are."

"Afton, you're probably frostbit," John said reasonably. "You're going—in the cab. We can make them warm and comfortable—"

"No!" Afton tried to recall the reasons, the valid and compelling reasons, why she couldn't go, but the logic was entirely too fuzzy and faraway.

So Molly Frame did what she did best—she took charge and told people what to do. And they did it, and quick. "You're going, Afton. You people over there—get all of those heavy-duty sleeping bags and all of the wool blankets! Somebody go get me some boards, four of them, about a foot wide and two feet long! And somebody go find some duct tape, lots of it!"

People scattered.

Kyle held Afton again and started murmuring, "I'm sorry, I'm so sorry, it's all my fault . . . I wasn't watching out for you . . ."

"No, no, that's not true, Father," she argued weakly. But then she began to cry, and Kyle was so repentant that he stopped reproaching himself and spoke to her in soothing half-sentences, as one does with a frightened child. He stroked her hair over and over.

Within twenty minutes the four injured people were secured to back boards, loaded onto two unfolded sleeping bags in the truck, and covered with two more sleeping bags, which were pulled tightly to the sides of the truck and then expertly tied down to keep the injured parties as immobile as possible. Then four wool blankets were piled on top of them, even over their faces, and lightly weighted down the sides. Truman Kirk volunteered to ride in the back, and nothing and no one could dissuade him. Kyle tried to shove him aside, but Molly Frame put a quick end to that nonsense. "Mr. Patton, you're half-sick yourself. Tru's strong. Stay here, and help all these people. They depend on you."

Kyle looked rebellious for a moment, but then his face cleared and he accepted the wisdom of her words. He gave Afton one last kiss, and she got into the truck.

Molly jumped in the cab of the truck, merely giving Joel a quick kiss good-bye, and the truck inched its painfully slow way along.

It took them five agonizing hours to get to the hospital. John had to drive no more than ten miles an hour. It was still endlessly snowing. The roads were invisible. The chains bumped and clanged monotonously, causing a jangling headache that crept inside one's head and gritted one's teeth and hurt behind the eyes. Afton couldn't imagine what the injured ones were going through. She hoped that, mercifully, they were all unconscious.

They finally pulled up in front of double doors that had a small neon sign that said *Emergency*. His hands knotted so fiercely they looked deformed, John shakily switched off the pickup's engine and rested his forehead on the steering wheel for long moments. It was 11 P.M.

Molly jumped out and ran inside. In only seconds lots of people in green scrubs came flying out with wheeled stretchers. Afton watched, dazed and uncomprehending, then laid her head back on the seat. Immediately she went to sleep.

◇ ◇ ◇

"Afton miraculously has mild frostbite but no tissue damage," the harried young doctor told a calm Molly, an anxious Tru, and an almost demented John Dunne. "The other lady—you did say it was Messalina Dancy, right? The movie star? Would never have known it. She's got two fractured legs, a concussion, and hairline facial fractures. Andrew Dayne has two broken ribs, four broken fingers, and a broken ankle. That Jo-Jo, he's got a fractured clavicle and broken arm, fractured wrist, facial contusions and bruising, but no concussion. Roy Dale—" He frowned darkly. "He's got a skull fracture and probably a cerebral hemorrhage. Also, eight broken ribs and internal injuries, most seriously to his spleen and small intestine.

"Funny thing about it is, the four of them are suffering from hypothermia, and Roy Dale's is the worst, but that helped him in a way. The reduced blood pressure actually kept him from hemorrhaging quite as badly. Anyway, we've got him stabilized, but it—well, it doesn't look good. He's waiting for surgery, but Dr. Allbright's not here right now. He's trying, but it's going to be a while before he can make it in. And Dr. Allbright's a good man, but he's a general surgeon. Miss Dancy needs a skilled orthopedic surgeon, and Roy Dale really needs a good neurosurgeon, and he could use a thoracic, although I think Dr. Allbright is going to handle those internal injuries just fine. When he gets here," he said cautiously, "I must warn you that it could be . . . too late."

"I suppose the medical choppers can't move in this weather," John said shortly.

Molly stoutly replied, "Frame already tried to get a chopper. Nothing in the state is in the air right now. As soon as it is, though, he'll either be flying these people out or flying some fancy doctors in, you can bet. But for right now—" She turned back to the doctor and asked clearly, "I need to see if I can get Roy Dale's brother here, right? That's all the family that boy's got, except for one sister who moved somewhere years ago. Don't know her married name."

"Yes, Mrs. Frame, somebody needs to get in touch with the brother," the doctor agreed gravely. "As soon as possible." Down the hall behind him, a nurse leaned out and called, "Dr. Kildare! We need you, please!"

The doctor walked away briskly, his white coat billowing out behind him, his straw-colored hair mussed and cowlicked. The chief resident was young, passionate, dedicated, and very busy.

Tru looked at John with innocent blue eyes and asked, "Did she say 'Dr. Kildare'?"

"Sure did," John answered with weary humor. "Dr. Joshua Kildare III."

Tru looked back down the hall and smiled. "Kildare—like in the old movies and TV series. That's gonna make Lina real happy."

◇ ◇ ◇

"You were a policeman," Afton said thoughtfully. "A—a—what do you call it? A canine unit. In New Orleans, I think."

John's eyes narrowed. With deliberation he pulled his chair up closer to Afton's hospital bed. She looked like a small, ill child. The lamp above cast a ghostly white glow on her face and made her eyes look dark and otherworldly. "You've been talking to Molly. You must have."

"But there was a fire," Afton continued dreamily. "A terrible fire. Someone . . . died. You were sure it was your fault. You still are. But it wasn't. I know it wasn't. God knows it wasn't. But you still think it was."

John took the slim, bloodless hand that lay limply outside the covers. It was cold, so cold. He pressed his lips to it for a moment. "Don't, don't, Afton. We can talk later. You need to sleep, you have to sleep."

"I'm thirsty," she said quietly. "Please, would you give me some water?"

He fixed her a cup of cold water, then stuck a straw in it and held it to her lips, supporting her head so she could sit up a little. "How wonderful," she sighed. "I was so thirsty, I wanted a drink so badly . . . but I knew if I ate the snow I'd freeze."

"That's right," he said softly. "You were wonderful. You're brave and smart and strong, Afton."

Afton smiled, then closed her eyes. "Did you know I've loved you from the first moment I saw you? I tried not to . . . I was afraid . . . but I fell in love with you, Peregrine . . ." Her voice faded away to a whisper, and then her breathing became soft and even, and for the first time in a long, hard time she truly slept.

◇ ◇ ◇

Two nights and a day passed before Life Flights from Lexington General resumed. The snowstorm, with its treacherous winds and occasional fits of ice, died down early on the morning of November 1. So finally a volunteer surgical team, including a neurosurgeon and a thoracic surgeon, could helicopter in and land right on the grounds of Bowie County Hospital. Mr. Joel Frame, who felt responsible for the accident because Roy Dale Puckett and Andrew Dayne were his loggers, offered to assume the entire liability for all of their medical treatment. This Kyle refused, insisting that Summit Decipher's insurance would pay 100 percent of all costs for Messalina Dancy's and Joe Randall's medical care. Mr. Frame did assume all expenses for Roy Dale and Andrew Dayne, vowing darkly that if they lived they'd sure belong to him for the rest of their lives.

The thoracic surgeon announced that Dr. Allbright's surgery for internal injuries on Roy Dale Puckett had been more than adequate, and he couldn't see any reason for the patient to go through the trauma of another surgery. Dr. Allbright, a sixty-two year-old general surgeon who'd been the only surgeon in Bowie County for thirty years, seemed surprised, and flattered, by the specialist's analysis of his emergency surgery. "It was the fastest, and the messiest, sop-and-sew job I ever did," he grunted. "You coulda knocked me over with a hankie when Roy Dale didn't depart this earth while I was fumblin' around in there. Never done a surgery like that in my life."

The thoracic surgeon, a brilliant thirty-year-old German man named Lichtenstein, eyed the aw-shucks old country doctor with a jaundiced eye. "So. You're one of those."

Dr. Allbright shrugged. "Prob'ly am. Depends on which of those you're talkin' about."

"One of those," Dr. Lichtenstein replied somberly, "who just knows how to heal. Even when it makes no sense, when you only have the basic grasp of anatomy and the rudiments of surgical technique."

"I got that," Dr. Allbright replied, his eyes twinkling. "And not only of humans, but of sheep and cows and horses and pigs . . . I help out the vets sometimes." He was trying to shock the aristocratic young doctor, but it didn't work.

Dr. Lichtenstein nodded. "This is not unusual at all. Not for men like you, with an instinct."

"Well, I had an instinct about that cerebral hemorrhage," Dr. Allbright told him, suddenly somber. "My instincts told me that if I touched a hair of that man's head he'd die for sure."

"And you were right," Lichtenstein replied. "He probably wouldn't have made it another day. No one should ever try neurosurgery unless the patient is already dying."

Dr. Allbright pronounced laconically, "I don't think I would have tried it even if he were dead."

Dr. Langford, the neurosurgeon, then worked on Roy Dale for six hours. He lived, but he was in a coma. Roy Dale's brother Bobby, who was slightly retarded, couldn't understand anything that had happened or what might happen to his brother. Molly and Joel Frame pitied him, and they provided for him and cared for him during this time.

Dr. Allbright, who had set maybe 5,000 broken bones, animal and human, in the last thirty years, took no time at all repairing the simple, clean fractures that Jo-Jo and Andrew Dayne had sustained. Messalina Dancy's required a skilled orthopedic surgeon, however, and so Dr. Allbright simply stabilized her legs until she could be flown to a private hospital in Los Angeles. There she would receive the best of care from both an orthopedic surgeon and a team of cosmetic surgeons. She was Life-Flighted back to Lexington General to wait until a flight to L.A. could take off. Rini had sent his Lear, along with two experienced surgical nurses, to St. Louis to wait out the weather. Later that afternoon the Lear flew in, and Messalina was flown with first priorities back to L.A.

When Afton woke up early the next morning, she saw John Dunne asleep in the chair by her bed. She was thirsty, she was hungry, and she was weak. But she left the hospital that afternoon. John was anxious to get back to his camp, and Afton was anxious to get back to her father. As she left, she prayed somberly for the others.

TWENTY-TWO

◇

I CAN'T BELIEVE it's actually finished," Afton declared. Her face was aglow with the warm wind that had come that morning to begin the great task of melting the four feet of snow that had fallen constantly for five days. "And a day early at that. Father said Mr. Santangeli didn't sound too happy, but he's on his way. Showing tomorrow night at nine o'clock, John. At the Holiday Inn. You'll be there, won't you?"

John Dunne actually got a schoolboyish pleasure at her anxiousness to be with him. Reverting to Peregrine-speech but not the Peregrine mask, he nodded. "Yes, Miss Afton. I'll go, just for you."

Afton nodded, somber in spite of John's lightness. "Father said he doesn't really think he'll get away with it. The scenes for the movie are all shot, but he didn't have time to send them to the editors. It's a very rough cut, he said, although he and Harlan and Dave have worked on it night and day for the last two days. He thinks Mr. Santangeli is going to call in the paper and take him to court if necessary. And Father says it's going to be necessary. But who can afford to fight Monarch Cinema's legal team?"

"It's going to be fine, Afton. I just know it is. Everything," he said with emphasis, standing up and squinting at the sky, "is just so fine! Look, there's Boo . . . want to go see her?"

"Oh, yes, please," Afton replied quickly. She rose from the rocking chair that Peregrine had put on her front porch. Though she'd only stayed the one night in the hospital and had sustained no permanent tissue damage from the frostbite and had only suffered from mild hypothermia, she still felt weak. Also, she was still very sore from the wreck. The soreness in her right side, her ribs, and her legs hadn't really begun until two days after the wreck, but it had been a deep, wearying ache that seemed to begin in her bones and seep up to her muscles. Dr. Kildare had said this was common and could take anywhere from a couple of days to two weeks to completely heal. Afton fervently hoped that she'd heal from this deep pain quickly.

Stretching reluctantly, pressing her hands against the small of her back, she chastised herself again for being ungrateful. Considering the injuries of the other four people in the wreck, Afton was a walking miracle. *I should thank God every moment for my health . . . and all the other blessings I have! My father, for one . . . and of course, John . . . my John . . . .*

Her John came out of his cabin, whistling and holding the gauntlet for Boadicea. When he came back to her, he saw how she was looking at him, stopped, and said uncertainly, "What?"

She took his arm, and they started walking toward the rise. "Oh, nothing. It's too bad Boo won't come down to the perch." Boadicea wouldn't land in the camp while all the people and cars and equipment were there. Not even for Peregrine. She would condescend to come down to him if he was standing on the rise close to the cabin, however.

He said thoughtfully, "She has her own place, I know. Somewhere high, way above all of us, all of this. It's always a wonder to me that she'll come down for even a few minutes."

"As I told you once before, she loves you," Afton said mildly. "You're the one who is bearing the needless burden of guilt, John."

He gave her a quick glance. "You aren't talking about Boo, are you?"

Steadily she replied, "Only if you want to."

They walked for a while, and Afton waited, trying to be patient. She had known for a long time that John Dunne was not a man who spoke of himself easily, good or bad, past or present. She was determined to always give him time, give him breathing room, and most of all give him a choice.

John said nothing until they topped the little would-be hill, and he pulled the gauntlet on, then searched the sky. "How did you know all about me? I asked Molly. She didn't tell you, and I know Joel didn't."

"You told me mostly," Afton replied, her eyes darting this way and that, looking for the hawk. "When we first started talking about your longbow, you told me that you used to carry a gun, and you never would again. You said that you'd rather use a bow and arrow or a slingshot or throw rocks at danger."

He grinned. "True. I still feel that way. I can throw a mean rock, too, I'm here to tell you."

Afton giggled, then went on, "So I figured you were either a policeman or a soldier. But you didn't seem like a soldier; it just didn't seem to . . . fit. And then there was Stonewall. I knew he was a highly trained dog, and I knew that you'd been his trainer because of the uncanny bond between you. And that one night you told me Stonewall was a drug-sniffing dog. So I was certain that you had been a police canine unit."

"And the fire," John said, refusing to meet her eyes. He searched the sky longingly. "It's not hard to guess that, seeing Stonewall. It was a bad fire, and a bad situation." He grew silent again.

Afton carefully considered her words. Then in a measured tone that held the ring of certain truth, she said, "John, I'd like to know because I do love you, and I want to know everything about you. Especially this—bad thing, this defining thing that shaped you, that affected you so strongly that you played a sly joke upon the world by inventing Peregrine, so you could laugh all alone. But I also want you to know that I'm not wise enough, always, to sense when people should talk about their past. Sometimes it's good for them, a catharsis, if you will. But sometimes it is not good, it's harmful. They need to forgive themselves, ask God's forgiveness, put it aside, and move on without it. So you choose. Either way, I love you, and I respect you as an honorable and honest man."

A sudden flutter and the sound of two-inch talons scraping leather announced the arrival of Boadicea of the Iceni. John spoke quietly to her, and she fussed and shied and finally settled down. He brought her close, began to stroke her, and then began to talk.

"It was two years ago, and it was hot. New Orleans in August is hot, steaming, scorching, like you've never felt before in your life, Afton," he said. He spoke in a distant voice, an impersonal voice, as if he were relating events seen on a screen to a blind person. "Patrol got a call, a domestic disturbance. That could mean anything from a half-hearted shouting match to a lead-in to an ax mur-

der. Then the call came for me and Stonewall because the address
was where the Vice Squad had been watching for a long time,
thinking they were a PCP pipeline. Do you know what PCP is?" he
asked with polite interest.

"It's the drug that makes you a little mad, isn't it?"

John sighed. "Psychotic, demented, completely out of touch
with reality. And it also pumps the system full of gushes of adren-
aline. Users feel no fear, and they feel no pain. Bad stuff. Anyway,
Vice was wrong. It wasn't a PCP pipeline—it was a PCP
laboratory."

He stopped to study her for a moment. Afton carefully kept her
expression neutral, nodding politely. She knew she didn't need to
show any kind of strong reaction, whether revulsion or fear or horror, to John's story. If he thought she was strong enough to hear it
and help him with it, then she would be, always.

He appeared to be satisfied with what he saw and continued
stroking his hawk and talking in the same conversational tone. "It
went bad, quick. Regular patrol was there, Vice was there,
Stonewall and I were there. Shooting, screaming, a couple of people running out of the house . . . Then there was an explosion. It
was pandemonium. No one knew anything; no one knew what to
do. We were trying to rush the house, running low for cover . . .
and then this fire. Do we go in and get shot? Do we let—whoever—
burn up? Would they rush us, shooting? We—we were confused,
and lost . . ." He paused for a moment, gathering strength and consciously toning down the urgent pitch that had crept into his voice.

"Anyway, Stonewall broke loose from me and ran around to
the side of the house. I followed, but I was slow, ducking and running and wasting my breath hollering at him. He sailed right

through a window that had burst from heat. I—I—after a minute, I think, I went in after him. It was a little girl tied to a bed. The room and the bed—and the little girl—and Stonewall, they were all burning . . ." He choked.

Afton didn't know what to do or say. She sat cross-legged on the ground near him, looking up at him, and tears rolled down her cheeks. She wasn't sorry for crying, and she wasn't ashamed. What John Dunne had been through was a tragedy, a great sorrow. Weeping, to Afton, was a clean thing, a right thing to do sometimes.

After a long time he lifted his head, and his face was wet. Boadicea, sensitive as most loyal animals are, moved closer to him. Afton watched with wonder, for John had told her that hawks always insist upon being at the highest point they can, which is why one must hold the gauntlet upright or the hawk will start climbing up your arm. But now Boadicea moved lower voluntarily, until she was perched on his forearm and leaning slightly against him. He started petting her again, talking to her quietly, soothing her. Afton could see that his actions soothed himself as well. After a few moments the bird walked sideways, picking her way back up the height of his gauntlet.

"I quit the next day," John continued, now in a weary and sad voice. "I couldn't even put in notice. The little girl was dead by the time we got her outside. Stonewall almost died . . . I still don't know how that dog got through it. Just—heart. Courage."

"So did you," Afton said softly. "Get through it."

"I ran and hid behind an idiotic half-wit," John argued.

"I know. Peregrine. I'm crazy about him," Afton said sweetly.

Amazingly, John grinned. "I think you're telling the truth."

"I am. I don't lie. I can't. Terrible at it."

"Good. Then I have a question."

"Go ahead."

"If I were to ask you to marry me, would you say yes?"

"Yes," she said instantly. "If you were to ask me."

He studied her face with great seriousness. "Okay. Just wanted to know. I'll get back to you on that."

Afton nodded complacently. "All right. When?"

"Later. After all this movie business is over, and I can think straight again. And—hey, there's one more thing. How did you know I was in New Orleans?"

"I heard some of the girls talking about it for hours on end," Afton replied with disgust. "Someone had taken one of your letters up to the mailbox, addressed to Twyla Dunne. The girls kept fretting that it was your girlfriend, but I knew it was your mother." She lifted her chin with a superior air.

"And how did you know that?" John gamely asked.

"You said your last name was Doe. Close to Dunne, isn't it? Besides, I knew you were in love with me all the time."

"Ah," he said gravely. "By the way, these girls, who were they again?"

"Their names have quite slipped my mind," Afton said with a dismissive wave of her hand. "I do seem to recall that they were uncommonly ugly girls. All those warts and such excessive facial hair. Of course, with the crossed eyes and the bowed legs, one hardly noticed the lack of teeth—"

"Enough!" John laughed. "I thought you never lied!"

"Perhaps," she said thoughtfully, "I was lying." She winked.

"Wicked girl. You've had me going in dizzy circles since the first time I saw you!" he replied, shaking his head. "My mother is going to approve of you. It's kind of frightening, really, to think of the conversations you two are going to have about me. Maybe I'd better not leave you alone with her. And my father's going to love you dearly. He's a good man, and he's been good to me. But I know he always wished he could have had a daughter. Most men do." He sounded a little wistful.

"Yes, it seems so. I'm so glad for my father. He truly does seem to love me . . ." she said, ducking her head and speaking so quietly John could barely hear her. Before he could answer, she brightened and asked, "So you're from New Orleans? I thought you had been long-time friends with Mr. and Mrs. Frame. You certainly are close."

"Oh, yes, my family has been friends with them all my life," John answered. "In fact, besides the Coopers—that's Molly's family—the Frames and the Dunnes are the oldest families around here. My father's family has lived here for almost 200 years. But he joined the navy when he was eighteen and made a career of it. He met my mother in New Orleans. He retired when I turned eighteen, and she has an extended family there. So they've been living there since then. I wasn't really brought up here—" He looked around with appreciation at the pastoral scene. ". . . but it always seemed like a touchstone, a base, a part of me, during all the years we were moving all over the world. My dad never sold this place, though he sold his parents' house as soon as they were gone. And we used to come back here whenever we could, and we'd spend most of the time with Joel and Molly. They've got two sons, one older and one younger. They called me their 'middle one' until I grew up. I spent four summers with them, and they sort of got to be my second parents."

"So you were in a military family? Oh, you must have been to some exciting places!" Afton exclaimed. "Where all have you been? Have you been to Scotland?"

"Sweet Afton, we have plenty of time for me to tell you my life's story," he protested. "I've already talked more in the last ten minutes than I have in the last two years. My mouth is tired."

She smiled briefly but then sobered somewhat. "I do have one question, John. Indulge me, please."

"All right, my love. But I warn you, I've already told you my deepest and darkest."

"What about Messalina Dancy?" Afton asked in a muffled voice.

Without hesitation John answered sadly, "She's a sensitive, tortured soul, and she has her own private hurts. I don't know what they are, but I recognize the symptoms all too well. And my feelings for her are and have always been exactly as I told you, Afton. I pitied her, and I sympathized with her. But she did do me one great service, and I'll be in her debt all my life for it."

"And what was that?" Afton had to ask.

He met her gaze directly now. "I saw myself in her. But I didn't want to be like her, not in spirit, not in my private thoughts, not in my soul. I'm not, well, crazy, Afton. I didn't have a nervous breakdown or a fashionable phobia or the latest disorder. I don't think—I certainly hope—I'm not that weak-minded. I just made a conscious decision to withdraw from the human race, and from God. But when I saw how pathetic Lina Dancy is, with all of her hundreds of faces and her only emotions those of fictitious people, her very facial expressions belonging to someone else, I felt disgusted—not with her, because at least she's honest enough to know she's an actress. I was angry with myself. I think that's when Peregrine truly began to fade."

"And God?" Afton asked with some concern.

"My parents are Christians, and I've been a Christian since I was seven years old. But I put it away from me, shoved God away, along with everyone and everything else. But now I'm groping my way back—you know, you've seen," John answered as honestly as he could. "Will you help me come back to Him? I want to be . . . alongside you, even with you, with the Lord. Does that make sense?"

Afton scrambled to her feet to hug him but stopped herself as Boadicea cast an unfriendly dark eye at her. "Sorry, Boo. Yes, my love, it makes wonderful, perfect sense. And I know that we'll be together, one, in the Lord Jesus one day. And that reminds me . . . could you elaborate a bit on that marriage topic again?"

◇ ◇ ◇

"I thought this was supposed to be a private showing," Afton commented. "There must be 200 people here."

"Joel invited the county to come see his credits," John told her with amusement. "And this county generally responds to his invitations." Molly and Joel sat at a four-seater, and though they were surrounded by people coming and going, they waved Afton and John over to sit with them.

The premiere was taking place in the dining room of the Holiday Inn, which Kyle had paid generously to reserve for a pri-

vate party. But as it turned out, more people were there than generally came to the Inn in an entire week, and most everyone came
early to eat. It was a merry bunch who waited, watching with anticipation as Dave Steiner prepared the projector and Harlan
Freeman set up an enormous screen.

Merry, yes, except for a couple of tables down front. At one
Stella, Kyle, and Santorini Santangeli were seated. Rini's twin thugs
glowered behind him, standing against the wall, sunglasses intact.
His three lawyers slinked at the other front table, briefcases in hand.

Dave made a signal to Kyle, and he stood and held up his hand
for silence. Standing in front of the screen, he made a short,
poignant speech. "Making this film has been one of the most difficult, most challenging, and most sorrowful tasks I've ever done.
You all know about the wreck, and about the latest news on Joe
Randall, and of course Roy Dale Puckett and Andrew Dayne. But
right now I'd like to tell you the latest on our friend, Miss Messalina
Dancy. She is doing very well in a private hospital in Los Angeles.
It will take her several months to recover fully.

"She sent me a message, however, to give all of you on this
night. Some of it was private, some for others, but for the first showing of this movie, *Hearth and Home*, she wished me to tell you for
her that she will always be grateful for the opportunity to do this
film. Lina said it changed her life, and she believes with all her
heart that it can change yours—and mine. She asks especially that
you remember her in your prayers. I don't think I can add to that,"
Kyle said quietly. "Thank you for attending, and I hope you'll enjoy
Hearth and Home."

The lights went out, and Dave started the projector, and
Harlan played with the sound board.

The first screen was black except for simple white lettering that said: "This film is dedicated by the cast and crew of *Hearth and Home* to Alastair Cowan's honorable memory. You made all of us proud."

With a sigh Afton thought, *I'm going to cry—and the movie hasn't even started yet!*

It was, to put it mildly, marvelous. It was a simple film, really, though Kyle had added some touches to it that were of a dreamy, poetic quality—a hazy, slow-motion shot of Boadicea, circling, circling, crying . . . fading to a close-up of Lina's face, upturned toward the afternoon sun, watching the hawk. A voice-over of her fine alto voice softly quoting Gerard Manley Hopkins's *The Windhover.* As Afton had suspected, and had told Kyle it would, it affected people, even though the poem was difficult to understand. The poem painted a word-picture, a delicate and detailed word-picture, of a hawk in flight. Afton, who was surreptitiously wiping tears, heard other sniffles.

Tru, in a bittersweet and unscripted scene, tiredly leaning against Tango, resting his head wearily on the beast's massive, powerful back. With one hand he petted the great animal as gently as if he were an old, favorite dog.

The cabin being built by an entire community of men who worked just as hard for their neighbor and his family as they did for their own.

A young couple had their troubles, their joys. They had their love, which was hard work of the spirit, and their living, which was hard work of the hands. But always their dedication was followed by triumph. They had their home, their land. Keen temptations, to give up, to lessen the sacrifice, to stop the honorable fight, rippled through their lives.

But they survived.

Not only that, but they loved and laughed. The last scene was magnificent. Lina looked luminous, glowing with triumph and an inner joy, even in the rain, hugging her precious mud. Tru looked surprised by joy—in his wife, in his work, in the view of his future. They laughed and played and kissed in the rain . . .

The view softened, running around the edges as if the picture were indeed out in the rain. Slowly the gloomy day faded out to a soft dove gray, then brightened to white.

Messalina Dancy's lovely voice filled the room as she sang "Amazing Grace" a cappella. The credits began running, a small list on the right side of the screen.

The transformation of the scene was complete; the gray day had turned into a bright one. The two young figures, running and laughing in the rain, had aged gloriously, grown wise, their faces lined and creased by understanding, by the sun they owned, by the wind they had captured. They were in the snow, a pretty clean snow with a benevolent yellow sun warming them, and their grandchildren all around them. Behind them was their home, their own, a grand and gracious house of white stone and stately pillars.

Molly Frame, looking as lovely as the wise woman of Proverbs, threw a snowball at her husband. Laughing, Joel Frame moved to her and kissed her lightly on the lips. And then they smiled at each other, perhaps for the ten thousandth time, as Lina sang the last line of the old song.

The screen went blank. The film clapped in the reel. Dave hurriedly stopped it. The silence was long.

Then a large man dressed in Big Smith overalls stood up and

began clapping. His wife, crying, stumbled to her feet. The entire room exploded into thunderous applause, deafening whistles, and cries of "Whoo-ee!"

Kyle, with tears in his eyes, stood and lifted both fists, clenched tightly. He looked around and made eye contact with just about every member of his crew as the applause and shouts went on and on. Finally he sang out triumphantly, "For you!"

◇ ◇ ◇

"Have you seen Father?" Afton asked John. "He's just disappeared."

Looking up at once from the book he was reading, John nodded. "He took a walk—down to the creek, I guess."

Afton hesitated, then said, "I think I'll join him." She took the path that led down to the small stream behind the motel, and as she rounded a clump of undersized pines she saw her father sitting on a rock beside the stream.

As she approached, Afton started to speak—and then saw with a sense of shock that her father's shoulders were shaking.

Why—he's weeping! Afton had never seen her father cry, and now she could not decide what to do. But suddenly he turned and came to his feet. His face was wet with tears, and he looked like a lost soul.

"What is it, Father?"

"Afton—!" Kyle's face contorted, and he dropped his head, unable to say another word.

Afton ran to him and put her arms around him. He clung to her almost fiercely, and the sobs racked his body. Afton could only hold him, for he clung to her like a hurt child.

Finally the weeping stopped, and Kyle released her. "Afton, the film came out so wonderful, but that doesn't change who or what I am. I've failed."

"No—!"

"Yes, I have! I failed your mother—and you." The words were little more than a tortured whisper, and then he said, "And worst of all—I've failed God!"

Afton suddenly realized that her father had come to the end of himself. Softly but firmly she said, "Sit down, Father—it's time for you to find out about forgiveness."

"Me? How could God forgive me? I've broken every law He ever made. I'm nothing but a sinner—a rotten sinner."

"Well, praise God!"

Kyle stared at his daughter, pain and confusion etched on his face. "You're thanking God that I'm a rotten sinner?"

"Yes—but only because the Bible says that Christ Jesus came to save *sinners*! Come now, sit down and we'll seek the Lord together. It's your time, Father . . ."

The two of them sat down under a walnut tree. Kyle wept much, and Afton prayed much, and finally Kyle bowed his head and accepted the mercy of a God who will not ever despise a broken heart or an afflicted spirit.

TWENTY-THREE

◇

IT WAS ALMOST two o'clock in the morning before the dining room of the Holiday Inn cleared out. Most of the townspeople, unaccustomed to the outrageous hours of outlanders, left long before midnight. But the crew talked and laughed and broke up into other groups and talked some more. Kyle Patton mingled with everyone present for hours. Afton anxiously watched Santangeli for signs of temper, but he seemed relaxed and unconcerned at Kyle's lack of attention to him. *He probably is laughing, thinking Father might as well have these last fleeting moments of glory,* she thought warily.

Finally the only people still roaming around the dining room were crew members except for Rini and his party, Molly and Joel, and Afton and John. Kyle raised his hands and waved them over his head. "Listen up, people! Cast and crew party in the lounge! Go on, there's eats and drink awaiting you—but don't start having fun 'til I get there!"

That effected a very quick exit.

Afton, John, Joel, and Molly stayed where they were, two tables over from Rini and Stella. Santangeli hadn't given them a single look the entire evening, and he didn't deign to notice them now. Kyle went back to Rini's table, stood looking down at him, crossed his arms, and waited.

Rini stayed seated, toying with a half-empty drink, his eyes narrowed to dark, impenetrable slits. But his air was one of long-suffering and patience, and when he spoke, his well-modulated voice was touched with just the right hint of regret. "Kyle, you are a gifted director, and you have a particular genius for producing, for bringing together a team that works in beautiful unison. But unfortunately you are not a shrewd businessman. This film is pathetic. Aside from the obvious defects in its premise, it views like an old, very bad home movie. This film is hopelessly amateurish and is of such shabby quality that it will never be finished. Because you were under-budgeted and under-scheduled, your movie is ruined, and you have no one to blame but yourself. And since you made the mistake of refusing Monarch Cinema's offer for more money and more time—which they could well afford, but I personally cannot—I find that I have some distressing news for you."

Kyle had stayed perfectly motionless, studying Rini with an odd expression, almost one of pity, the entire time the man was lecturing him. When Rini had said the film was "pathetic," Afton had jerked, a prelude to her rising from the chair. But Molly Frame sternly laid a hand on her arm, frowned, and shook her head firmly. Afton settled into her seat, but her gentle features were set with a rebellious expression.

Kyle commented, "I don't think you could call that 'news,' Rini. After all, we all know exactly what you've done here. There's no need to camouflage it with pitiful justifications and self-righteous explanations."

Santorini Santangeli showed no hint of unease; in fact, he

looked slightly bored. "Very well, Kyle. First thing in the morning
I'm beginning proceedings to take over Summit Decipher. That's
the end of it."

Kyle said quietly, "No, Rini, it's not the end of it. But before
we get to the real end of it, I want to say something to you." He
paused, studying Rini with such a penetrating stare that the man
actually showed the first signs of discomfort—he blinked, then
actually sipped the drink he'd been holding for hours.

"Well?" he finally said with only a tinge of bluster. "Let's get it
over with, Kyle. Just be warned, I'm not going to listen to you crying or begging—"

"No," Kyle interrupted sharply. "You're sure not going to have
to listen to that, Rini. All I want you to do is answer some questions. First, about the cabin burning. I—we—" He made a sweeping gesture, including everyone in the room. ". . . know that you
arranged it."

Rini bounded up, the goons stepped up, and Kyle lifted his chin
defiantly. Rini snarled, "I did no such thing! You can't prove that!"

"No, I can't," Kyle admitted. "But you're a powerful man, Rini.
Why don't you stand tall and admit it? Aren't you proud of your
actions, your decisions? Or do you really have a sneaking suspicion
that they're sleazy, criminal, so that deep down you feel ashamed?
That's how I think you feel. If I'm wrong, why don't you stand up to
me, face me like a man? I've already admitted I can't prove a thing."

"Patton, I'm ten times smarter than you. You're so stupid you
didn't even know—" Rini snarled, his eyes now wide and blazing.

But for the first time the little rumpled lawyer made a sound.
"Er—um—hrum! Mr. Santangeli!" He sounded like a twelve-year-
old with a high, tinny voice.

Rini turned on him, and the little man flinched, but he didn't back away. "Er—um, Mr. Santangeli, it would appear to me that Mr. Patton is attempting to trick you into incriminating yourself. I fear I must intervene."

"'I fear'?" John repeated with disbelief. "Did he really say that?" Molly shushed him, and he quieted, though he mutinously grunted every once in a while.

At first it appeared that Rini was going to lash out at his lawyer, but the little man stood his ground, albeit shakily. Then Rini's smooth, elegant features broke into a badger's snarl that passed as a smile. "It won't work, Patton," he taunted, turning back to Kyle. "You won't bait me into making a fool of myself. I've done nothing to delay the production of your silly little movie. I didn't need to. It's pathetic enough without anyone having to sabotage it."

"Sabotage," Kyle mused. "Now there's a word for you. Like someone burning that cabin down. That was sabotage, pure and simple. But the rest of it—" Kyle shook his head slowly and deliberately, his gaze never leaving Santangeli's dark and angry face. "The rest of it was something else altogether, Rini. That snake— attempted assault, reckless endangerment. Cocaine all over that camp as deep as the snow—control and distribution of an illegal drug. And finally, Rini, your crowning glory." The loathing on Kyle's face was so pronounced that Santangeli's face flushed a deep, alarming crimson. "Manslaughter. If that boy dies—and don't you dare give me any pious outrage, you little weasel! I know you paid those boys to bring dope to Lina and to take her out joyriding. But then they had the wreck. So instead of kidnapping, it's aggravated battery, four counts for sure. And if I ever find one iota of evidence,

I'll have you slapped in jail so fast you won't leave anything behind but a greasy skid mark!"

"You're crazy!" Rini screamed, banging his hands on the table. "You can't prove a thing! Especially against me! You couldn't get a cop to give me a parking ticket!"

"Aw, give it a rest, Rini," Kyle scoffed. "I know that. I know all of it. It's just that I want you to understand, and to remember that I and all of the rest of these people know the truth about you. We know exactly what you are. I'm not saying I'm any better, understand, but I've finally found the forgiveness I needed—a forgiveness I hope you find too."

Rini hesitated, almost panting with the pressure of his vicious anger. "Come on," he finally grunted. "Let's get out of this stinking place. But you just remember, Kyle, I'm taking Summit Decipher with me," he added nastily.

"I've about had it with this," Joel Frame said loudly, rising from the table, his old, lined face distorted with disgust. "Mr. Patton, I'm pleased to notify you that I ain't a-gonna let this—this *person* take your company. After our talk I got to studyin', and I figgered something like this might happen," he grumbled, shuffling over to the table where Rini and Kyle still confronted one another with deadly enmity. Stella still sat at the table, rigid and pale, smoking constantly with jerky movements, her eyes flat and empty as she stared into the far distance. Frame went on forcefully, "I decided I wasn't gonna wait 'til this poor excuse for a man took us to court. I'm gonna put a cork in his dirty little bottle right now!"

"Who—who is this senile old fool?" Rini snapped, his thin veneer of elegance and sophistication completely shattered. "Never mind, forget it. I'm leaving!"

"You don't want to leave without this, Mr. Santa Angie," Joel
Frame said, mispronouncing the name with gusto and disdain.
Afton, John, and Molly had all stood up and followed Frame, standing close behind him. Frame was searching through a wallet that
looked as if it might date back to the Dead Sea scrolls. Afton
thought he'd never looked so determined and in control of the situation, a sorry contrast with Santorini Santangeli. Joel Frame's face
was burned to the texture of leather, thanks to the sun and wind and
snows of over sixty years. There were lines etched by trouble too, for
he'd had his share of the hardships that all men shoulder on this
earth. Time had stooped his once proud back, and although he carried his years better than most, he looked quite inadequate as he
stood in front of the man who was as sleek and elegant as a shark.

"Now, just how much money is on that paper you got, Mr.
Santi Indi?" Frame grumbled, looking up at Rini.

Santangeli looked at Kyle, at Stella, and finally at Joel Frame
and his humble companions with an air of stunned disbelief. Then,
crossing his arms and assuming a superior air, he said, "All right,
I'll indulge your little grandpa here, Kyle, just out of curiosity. Mr.
Piedmont?"

The little lawyer busily took a paper from his breast pocket and
recited, "Three million, eight hundred sixty-six thousand, two
hundred twenty-four dollars, and fifty-five cents."

Joel chuckled dryly. "You folks carrying on such! Act like
you're talking some big money!"

Rini had lost interest in this nonsense and made as if to leave
again. "Kyle, tomorrow—" Kyle reached out and grabbed Rini's
arm, none too lightly. Rini froze.

Afton turned toward the big bodyguards, afraid they might

take out Uzis and strafe the place or something. They hurried over to Rini, but Kyle didn't look at them. "You'd better listen, Rini," he said quietly. "You'd really better pay attention to this man." Only then did Kyle let go of Rini's arm.

"Him?" Rini sneered. "He wouldn't know a fifty dollar bill from wallpaper."

Joel Frame, too, had lost his taste for the scene. "Here, Kyle. You give it to him. And that'll conclude our business, so we can all go get some fresh air." When he looked at Rini, his nostrils distended as if he smelled something foul.

"Frame, quit showing off," Molly ordered him. "You're ten times the man—no, he sure ain't a man, and I can't think of no animal I'd insult by calling him that either. Anyway, you don't need to be bullying him."

Now Rini looked as if he positively might explode. But Kyle thrust the small slip of paper Joel had given him right under Rini's nose, and Rini's eyes widened to round black glass. Slowly he took the paper. "What's this? Some childish joke? I'm not going to accept this!"

"You'd better," Kyle said conversationally. "Or you'll lose it all, Rini, because of the forfeiture clause. You know that."

"But—but—" he blustered desperately. Then his strained face grew crafty. "What about the interest? This check's for four million dollars, and with the interest, you owe me almost six million!" Rini's voice had risen to a hysterical whine.

Joel Frame shook his head slowly and spoke with great deliberation. "That there clause is illegal, Mr. Santangeli. I done had some mighty fine attorneys—not like Larry, Moe, and Curly over there—check up on that there little provision. That ain't interest, and it ain't legal. It's a little offense by the name of 'usury.' So I think you better take the check."

Rini's eyes honed in on his little lawyer's face like two torpedoes. The man, busily wiping his glasses with an enormous white handkerchief, sighed and nodded an emphatic yes.

"I'm not taking your check for legal tender!" Rini snapped arrogantly to Joel Frame. "Who *are* you anyway?"

"Beggin' your pardon, Mister Fancy Britches, but we been properly introduced. If you ain't smart enough to remember people's names, that's your problem. And that there's a cashier's check and is legal tender," Frame snapped back. "Now look who don't know the backside of wallpaper!"

Mr. Santorini Santangeli's sculpted features drained of all color. He looked down at the check, the room laden with silence, each person perfectly motionless. The only movement was the smoke from Stella's cigarette, which meandered up in a thin blue stream and then dissipated to a nebulous fog near the ceiling.

Finally Rini muttered in a strangled voice, "Let's go. Kyle, you're going to pay for this."

"Just hold up there, Mr. Sandaninny," Joel ordered. But now his face was alight with amusement. "I b'lieve you owe me—" Pursing his lips, he stared at the ceiling and counted on his fingers. ". . . one hundred thirty-three thousand, seven hundred seventy-five dollars. And forty-five cents. In change. Got it in your pocket? 'Cause I ain't too sure you're good for it, if you latch onto my meanin'."

"Big show-off," Molly muttered. But she said it real low and was trying, unsuccessfully, to hide her amusement. Joel Frame's chest puffed out just a bit more.

But now Santorini Santangeli wasn't aware of anyone else in

the room except Joel, and he was far from amused. "Of course not, you—no, I don't have that kind of cash on me! No one carries that kind of money around!" Rini stammered.

"I do," Joel replied mildly. He was thoroughly enjoying himself now. "Can't see what all the fuss is about, just over pocket change. Anyways, I know you run a little behind everybody else, so I'm gonna give you a hint. That check's marked 'Principal and Interest.' So if you take it, you ain't gonna have much of a basis to try and snaggle me and Mr. Patton up in court over your loan-sharkin' clause that you try and call 'interest.' But if you do, you're gonna find out that my Atlanta lawyers can make your peepin' little chickens over there run in circles 'til the sky falls in."

Santorini Santangeli, though he did appear to be slightly ill, left the Holiday Inn with his advisers without saying another word.

Kyle now turned his attention to Stella. She looked like a harsh modernist painting. She was bone-thin, her hands holding the cigarette, having long crimson nails that looked like claws. Her face was a stark white, her lips a slash of crimson. She didn't look at Kyle or anyone else. She just stared into space, her face set in bleak and bitter lines.

"He's waiting for you, Stella," Kyle said. "I think you'd better go on." His voice was gentle and sad.

With great deliberation Stella ground out her cigarette in the overflowing ashtray. Still she didn't look up. Neither did she bother to deny it. She nodded faintly, then swallowed very hard. "I want you to know, Kyle, that when I started, I—I never thought . . . I didn't want . . . ."

Kyle sighed. "Just go. There aren't any excuses, Stella. You know that."

In a voice so low and choked they could barely hear it, Stella whispered, "Yes, I do."

Without giving any of them, including Kyle, a single glance, Stella gathered up her purse and coat, leaving her briefcase behind. She walked out of the dining room, her head bowed, her walk a portrait of shame and defeat.

A long silence reigned in the room for a moment.

Then Molly Frame, earthy and sensible as always, said, "Well, Kyle, you're better off without that one. I do swear, I half expected her to slither outa here on her belly, fangs drippin' and forked tongue flickin' in and out!"

The shout of laughter in the dining room was merry and lasted long. Even Kyle finally joined them. Turning to John and Afton, he said a little wistfully, "Anyway, maybe you two will live happily ever after. If this movie does as well as it deserves, then you, Mr. John Dunne, will have done very well for yourself." As part of the crew, John was included in the contingency percentage split.

He grinned at Kyle wickedly. "You worried about looking at an unemployed son-in-law, Mr. Patton?"

Recovering his good spirits, Kyle shot back, "Not if you're not worried about your unemployed father-in-law moving in with you!"

Afton said, her face and eyes positively glowing, "All of that would be just fine with me!"

◇ ◇ ◇

The movie *Hearth and Home* had a successful twelve-week run in theaters all over America. It grossed over eighty million dollars.

John Dunne's percentage was over $145,000. He wanted to spend it all taking Afton to Scotland for their honeymoon. Afton wanted to spend her honeymoon at the camp.

So Afton Burns and John Dunne made a compromise.

They honeymooned in Scotland.

They lived at a place, a wonderful, magical place where people had lived and loved and worked and toiled and cried and laughed for over 200 years. The resort was called *Falcon's Draw*. The peregrine falcons, who soared and circled endlessly around it, never left.

THE WINDHOVER
TO CHRIST OUR LORD

◇

I caught this morning morning's minion, kingdom of

daylight's dauphin, dapple-dawn-drawn Falcon, in his riding

Of the rolling level underneath him steady air, and striding

High there, how he rung upon the rein of a wimpling wing

In his ecstasy! then off, off forth on swing,

As a skate's heel sweeps smooth on a bow-bend: the hurl and gliding

Rebuffed the big wind. My heart in hiding

Stirred for a bird—the achieve of, the mastery of the thing!

Brute beauty and valour and act, oh, air, pride, plume, here

Buckle! And the fire that breaks from thee then, a billion

Times told lovelier, more dangerous, O my chevalier!

No wonder of it: sheer plod makes plough down sillion

Shine, and blue-bleak embers, ah my dear,

Fall, gall themselves, and gash gold-vermilion.

GERARD MANLEY HOPKINS